SUNKEN TREASURE
LOST WORLDS

**THE RISKY BUSINESS CHRONICLES
BOOK 1**

A COLTEN X. BURNETT NOVEL

HEP ALDRIDGE

Copyright © 2019 by Hep Aldridge

Published by BUOY MEDIA LLC
All rights reserved.
https://www.buoy-media.com

No part of this book may be reproduced, scanned, or distributed in any printed or electronic form without permission from the author.

This is a work of fiction. Any resemblance of characters to actual persons, living or dead is purely coincidental. The Author holds exclusive rights to this work. Unauthorized duplication is prohibited.

Cover design by Juan Villar Padron,
https://www.juanjpadron.com

Special thanks to my editor Janell Parque
http://janellparque.blogspot.com/

———

To be the first to hear about news, new book releases and bargains from Hep Aldridge.

- GO HERE TO SIGN UP TO BE ON THE VIP LIST:
https://mailchi.mp/b0c291dd854f/hep-aldridge

Learn more about Hep and his background on his webpage:
https://hepaldridge.com

You can write directly to Hep and connect with him online.
EMAIL: cxburnett@gmail.com
FACEBOOK: https://www.facebook.com/hep.aldridge.7
TWITTER: https://twitter.com/AldridgeHep

PREFACE

My name is Dr. Colten Burnett, and I'm retired. I'm not rich; I don't live in a big house or drive a fancy new car, but I'm comfortable. I have hobbies to keep me busy. Working on and restoring old cars, riding my motorcycle, a long-running interest in Archaeology, music-both listening and playing guitar. Taking my 21-foot fishing boat out and... well, fishing. I'm happy, more or less, and that brings me to the "wrinkle." Many years ago, I was bitten by what I'll call the treasure bug; as a junior in high school, I lived in New Mexico and heard the stories of buried stolen gold and silver throughout the region. The one story that caught my interest was of Montezuma's treasure. As the story went, the treasure was taken out of Mexico by the Aztecs before the Spanish conquistadores could get their hands on it. It was moved north up through New Mexico to the Four Corners region of the Southwest. Along the way, so it's said, the Aztecs hid smaller caches of the treasure. Local stories and newspaper articles confirmed gold and silver treasure had been found in or near the Organ Mountains, right in my backyard.

As a high school kid, that was all I needed to spark my on-

PREFACE

going interest, not only in the treasure but in the culture known as the Aztecs. I read all I could find in the library on both subjects. Unfortunately, from my readings, I came away with more questions than answers. Years passed, and the questions remained. While in the Air Force, stationed in South Florida, I received my scuba certification. There, I heard the stories about the Spanish treasure fleets that sailed from the port of Havana. They Sailed up the coast along the Florida peninsula before turning east and heading for Spain, and many of them sank along the coast. From Vero Beach to Sebastian.

During that time, I was lucky enough to meet Art McKee, an old Navy hardhat diver who had become one of the first to dive for treasure in the Keys in 1948. He was about five foot six, had an infectious smile, a barrel chest, and a shock of dwindling gray hair. His rolling gait was a true sign of someone who had spent many years on the sea. He had a roadside museum on Plantation Key that I visited often. I spent hours listening to the stories of his exploits while searching for the gold of the 1733 fleet. On one of my last visits, being the only visitor there, and him having seen my enthusiastic interest in his stories, I got invited into the back room. There, he pushed aside a curtain covering one section of the wall. To my surprise, behind it was a bank vault door. After dialing the combination, he pulled it open to reveal a room six feet wide by ten or twelve feet long and seven feet high. In the back two corners and along the back wall were waist-high stacks of silver ingots and a small bronze cannon. On the floor were sacks of coins. Along the side walls were shelves stacked with silver and gold coins, gold jewelry encrusted with emeralds, and assorted other delicate gold and silver artifacts. My eyes must have been the size of saucers.

He grinned and said, "This is only a small portion of what one ship in the 1733 Plate Fleet was carrying. There is a lot more out there still to be found."

PREFACE

That did it; the treasure bug took a bigger bite!

Five years later, I found myself living on Central Florida's Space Coast, and as fate would have it, I met Kip Wagner, founder of the Real Eight Company. He and his partners had been finding treasure from the 1715 Plate Fleet along Florida's coast for several years and had established a beautiful treasure museum in Cape Canaveral. They had been searching the waters and beaches from Ft. Pierce to Sebastian and done extremely well for themselves. I had an offer to dive for them one summer. Unfortunately, it came immediately following my acceptance of a "real" full-time job working at a local college. I had to turn Kip's offer down, and it became a missed opportunity I regretted for many years.

Time flew by and with my retirement date fast approaching, I was being asked on an almost daily basis, what are you going to do when you retire? Teach? Do some consulting?" My stock answer became, "Oh, I have plenty to keep me busy." In reality, that was true, but I gave the question increasingly more thought. When asked the same question sometime later, on a whim, I replied, "I'm going to start a treasure hunting Company!" (Remember the "wrinkle" I mentioned earlier.)

The response was, "You're going to do what, really?"

"Sure, I said, "Why not? I'll be retired and have the time to dedicate to it." That created a stir amongst my colleagues and really got me thinking, why the hell not…if not now, when? During my time at the college, I had been reading about or seeing on the news, things like individuals finding gold coins in six feet of water on Florida's East Coast. Spanish cannons had been found in 12 feet of water. Gold pie-shaped wedges were found north of Ft. Pierce. An individual found a gold snuffbox in a sand dune near Sebastian. A person found a basketball-sized lump of silver coins in the surf. All from the 1715 Plate Fleet, and all within an hour's driving distance of my home. Why

PREFACE

shouldn't I take a crack at it? As I pondered that question, I thought, lost treasure has been following me all my life, from New Mexico to Florida, coincidence? I think not! My new retirement course had been set… well, sort of.

This is my story…

PROLOGUE
July 30, 1715

Somewhere off the east coast of Florida

The sun was setting, and a stiff wind blew from the east. Gomez loved this time of day and did not mind that the captain had assigned him evening watch. Most of the crew were below decks, having their evening meal or tending to personal needs. The deck was mostly deserted and, from his perch in the rigging he had an unobstructed view of the surrounding sea in all its blue-green glory. As the waves rocked the ship and the wind kept the sails billowing and blew across his face, he felt as though he were the only person on board, this was his ship, his domain, and he felt in charge of its every move as she powerfully surged through the waves.

This was a far cry from reality… however, but for the moment, he was lost in his fantasy, and he reveled in it. As he scanned the horizon to the south, he spotted the ship that he had observed following the fleet since they had left Havana. The vessel never came close enough to get a clear view of her, but he was sure it was the galleon he had seen taking on cargo at the wharf in Havana harbor. He had noticed her because of the large number of soldiers posted at her mooring and the fact that she was painted completely black. Rather unusual for a ship of the day. The wagons that had approached the galleon had all been heavily guarded and he could only guess that her cargo was extremely valuable and demanded the utmost protection. Of course, the entire Plata fleet (that his ship was part of) was carrying riches beyond his wildest dreams back to Spain, but none of the ships had the number of guards around them that he had seen around the black galleon. Gomez guessed it was a wealthy merchant sailing privately and was following the fleet for guidance or safety, although he remembered the full complement of gun ports on the vessel and the number of soldiers aboard hardly made her defenseless. Oh, well, the black galleon posed no threat to his ship or the fleet, so he continued his scan of the horizon and went back to his world of daydreams.

As the evening light began to dim, Gomez noted that the wind had picked up and the waves were steadily growing in height. He looked down from his perch and noticed the helmsman, Fernando, was working harder at the wheel to keep the ship on course than he had been earlier and was shouting something to one of the few crewmen on deck. He could not hear what was said but saw the crewman disappear below decks as a large wave rocked the vessel, and he had to tighten his grip in order not to be thrown from the rigging. As he repositioned himself, he noticed that the black ship had gained on them dramatically and was moving further out to sea. He was able to get a better look at her and noticed that her sail configuration was different than that of most galleons and her speed was much greater than that of the fully loaded vessels of the fleet. In fact, he estimated she would be passing them on their starboard side within the hour as she was continuing to move further east-north-east, out to sea.

The wind was picking up dramatically, and the crewman who had gone below at Fernando's orders had returned with the captain. The waves were increasing in size as the wind grew stronger. The Captain and Fernando were engaged in an animated discussion while scanning the darkening skies. Gomez noted the oncoming darkness not just from nightfall, but also from the ominous thunderheads that were building in the east. As he had predicted, the black vessel passed them in less than an hour and was moving at an incredible pace, even under these extreme conditions. He estimated she would pass the lead ship of the Floata by morning at her current speed. He had to use his glass to get a closer look at the galleon as she was passing and noticed, in what remained of the twilight, the flag she was flying. He had only seen it once before, in the harbor of Cadiz, Spain. It was the king's personal crest, one that was used by only a few vessels operating directly under king's orders.

Now, Gomez understood the large number of soldiers; they must be under special orders from the king himself and what they were carrying in cargo must be very important and valuable. However, he couldn't imagine anything more valuable than the gold, silver, and other precious goods that his fleet was carrying. He didn't have time to ponder the question further as the captain shouted the order for him to come down from his perch just as a large wave broke over the bow. His last glimpse of the mysterious black ship was as a dot on the darkening horizon as he descended the rigging to the deck.

At two a.m. the next morning, the hurricane struck...

CHAPTER ONE

The Beginning

Thunk, thunk, thunk... there it was again... that damn irritating noise. How the hell could I get any rest with that continuous hammering going on? All I wanted was a little sleep, just a little more; I was tired... Thunk, thunk, thunk. Again, that noise but this time it was accompanied by a shooting pain in my left leg. As I opened my eyes, I realized this was not the scene my mind had painted for me. It was more like something out of a B-rated action movie. The sun was blazing down. I was hot, and rivulets of sweat were running down my face, as I found myself lying behind large coils of rope and hawser lines. I was facing some beautiful blue-green water, and my leg hurt like hell. As I looked down at the bloody rag tied around it, some of the fog cleared in my head. I remembered I had been shot. Who the hell did that? My question became more urgent as rounds being fired from automatic weapons hit the pile of rope I was leaning against and the barrels next to it. Thunk, thunk, thunk... there it was — the source of the sound that had awakened me. Son of a bitch, I was being shot at by parties yet unknown for reasons my foggy mind was still trying to sort out. What the hell!?

I carefully peered over the ropes to assess my situation and also clear the fog that continued to swirl in my head. I was at the end of a dock. At the other end, I saw a large group of barrels and crates effectively hiding my assailants from view. Some small fishing boats with their nets hung out to dry were tied to the dock.

Where the dock reached land, two pickup trucks and a Land Rover were sitting with their doors open. I surmised these were the vehicles that had brought my new friends to visit. I had no idea how I had gotten here, but right now that was unimportant. Another volley of automatic weapons fire opened up, and I ducked for better cover. From the sounds of it, they were AK-47's, some serious firepower. At that moment, my brain made an attempt at coming back online, and a flood of information poured in, pushed along by the pain in my leg. I held my Glock 21 in one hand and the handle of a metal briefcase in the other. I felt the empty shoulder holster under my left arm and equally empty extra mag holder under my right. I could hear voices coming from the direction of what I guessed were bad guys. For the moment, I was thinking of myself as a good guy. Funny, how your mind works under stressful situations.

I heard running footsteps on the dock. I figured I had better let them know I was still alive and kicking. I rose up enough to see three men running in my direction, carrying assault rifles. I brought the Glock to bear and saw one man fall. That sent the other two ducking for safety behind some barrels stacked along the dock. I wish I could say I hit the one guy due to my stellar marksmanship, but my vision was still blurry, and my hand was shaking a wee bit. So, I'll just go with what my granddaddy used to always say: "Colt, I'd rather be lucky than good." Trying to think beyond my current predicament was still difficult. Things like what did I do to piss these guys off and what the hell was in this metal briefcase I held so tightly, still escaped me.

The staccato chatter of the AK's brought me back to my

current plight and the need to come up with a plan; some kind of plan, hell any kind of plan to get myself out of this mess. Once again looking around, I saw the makeshift bandage on my leg continuing to turn bright crimson. Shit, how long have I been here? There was one empty 13-round magazine lying next to me, and when I dropped the clip out of the Glock, I had just four rounds left. As I felt my vest pockets, I found another full clip in one and, in another, a small electronic device with a blinking red light. Interesting, but the brain fog kept its function hidden from me. Since it was in my pocket, I guessed it must be important, just not sure why. Sporadic gunfire drew my attention back to my immediate imperative, how to stay alive…

As my mind took another of its leaps out of the fog, I ticked off a few of the facts as I saw them. One, these guys were really pissed; for some reason, I felt the briefcase had something to do with it. Two, they were willing to kill me for it. Three, number two was a real possibility. Not an outcome that I relished. A thought pushed its way through the haze… maybe, if I gave them the briefcase they would be so happy they would just let me go! No, no, no… a little voice in my head said, Colt, that's not an option. The heat and blood loss were taking their toll. Not enough to stop that little voice from saying that "giving up the briefcase would be very, very bad. Destroying it would be a better alternative than giving it up." Aw, shit, now what do I do? Got to stay focused and hopefully stay alive, but that damn brain fog kept trying to return.

As I hunkered down-with the sun now relentlessly searing my body and brain, I pondered the 64-thousand-dollar question. What the hell was in the briefcase? If I could only remember… Whatever it is, it seems to be worth killing for! The gunfire erupted again, and more voices shouted back and forth. I'm thinking these guys are getting hot and impatient. They want to finish this thing and get back to wherever for a cold cerveza. Huh… Why am I thinking of beer in Spanish? Were the voices I heard shouting back and forth in Spanish?... Where the hell am I? As I took in my surroundings a little more clearly, I thought it's tropical. I saw palm trees on the beach beyond the dock. It's hot, salty air, there are sea birds all around and the sun is sinking towards the watery horizon, so that must be west. If that's true, then that means I'm looking out across the Pacific. Well, that sort of answers the question of where I am. Ha! I'm on the west coast of somewhere where they speak Spanish. "Great," I sarcastically thought, that narrows my location down to a few thousand miles of coastline. Sure as hell doesn't help the current situation, Crap! Okay, file it away, Colt, and move on.

As I peeked over the top of my rope fort, rope fort...that's funny... Focus, damn it, Colt, your mind is wandering again, and you don't have time for that. I took a deep breath and let it out slowly as I looked over the pile of ropes protecting me. There was something I hadn't noticed earlier. Another guy was lying further down the dock. Guess I had done more damage than I thought. Jesus, I was tired, thirsty as hell, and my whole left leg was going numb. Salty sweat burned my eyes, making it even harder to focus. It's obvious I'm outnumbered and out-gunned, so I wonder why these guys haven't rushed my position. No doubt, looking directly into the sun made it difficult for them to see me as I hid behind my "rope fort." That would make them more cautious. Hmm... if they have those cool mirrored Reflecto sunglasses that all the Spanish speaking bad guys wear in the movies... That little voice in my head said to stop with the bullshit, Colt, and focus! I now realized my mind was wandering all over the place, and my situation was on the verge of becoming deadly.

I take another peek and see two or three of my attackers moving toward me. They were using barrels on the dock, crates, draped fishing nets, whatever they could for cover. Two more came out to follow the others firing in my direction. Well, if this is going to turn into the OK Corral, I had better start with a full clip! As I fired my last four rounds and reloaded, I thought, last clip, Son of a bitch! Looking over my rope barrier again I saw more armed guys running on the dock heading my way, double damn! Sure didn't look good for the visiting team as gunfire erupted. Accuracy suddenly became very important and I knew I had to make all my shots count. Hiding behind barrels full of something is not necessarily a bad idea in a gunfight; however, hiding behind empty barrels from a guy with a .45 caliber Glock 21, not so much. Two more of the attackers found that out the hard way as my slugs blew right through the barrels and find their target. That slowed the rest of them a little, but they still looked like ants swarming on the dock.

A new voice, someone with real authority, shouted orders, and all these guys moved forward at once, firing as they ran now with little regard for cover. Two more went down, and that slowed their forward progress. I was still outnumbered and losing real estate fast as the bad guys approached. They were maybe 20 yards away when I saw them slow and point in my direction. That's when I heard the noise, a kind of hum, strange in a familiar way. It kept getting louder, and I realized it was coming from behind me. I quickly turned and, for a minute, was blinded by the sun low in the sky before I saw a black blob silhouetted by its orange glow growing larger and larger, moving in my direction. The voices became more animated and the gunfire started up again. I turned and returned fire and realized that not all these guys were firing at me. Some were firing over my head, in the direction of the black blob I had seen. The hum was loud now, and I turned to see the black silhouette had turned into a black and grey helicopter that looked to be something like a Huey UH 1 that could have been in *Star Wars*. It was crabbing sideways toward the dock, its side doors open. There was something strange about its shape and sound, but I didn't have time to ponder the question as more gunfire erupted. As it got closer, I saw two people in the open doorway, and then the unmistakable drone of a six-barreled mini gun assaulted my ears. It ripped the dock to shreds just beyond me, right in the middle of my assailants. It's a fact that 3,000 to 5,000 rounds per minute of 7.62mm ammo can ruin your day in a heartbeat… that is if you're on the receiving end. The guys who were charging me soon that found out the hard way. When the Huey got to the end of the dock, it went into a hover 20 feet from my position and one foot off the dock's deck. The big guy who jumped out and came running my way looked vaguely familiar, and by the time he got to me, the mini gun had done its work. Some of the barrels behind me must have held fuel as they exploded with their black smoke billowing skyward. All hostile gunfire had stopped.

As the new arrival stood over me, he said in his best Boris Badenov, from the *Rocky and Bullwinkle* cartoon show, Russian accent, "You call for taxi, Da?" I could only grin as I recognized Dimitri and his damn sense of humor.

"You took long enough," I said. "I hope the meter hasn't been running this whole time." He dropped to one knee and checked the bandage on my leg, tying it tighter, much to my annoyance. "Dimitri your bedside manner sucks." He only grinned and grabbed my arm and pulled me to my feet. I felt the world around me swirl and started to fall as he quickly changed his grip. The next thing I knew, he had me in a fireman's carry and we were headed for the open doors of the chopper. That was impressive. At 6'5" and 300 lbs. I'm no ten-pound sack of potatoes you toss in a grocery cart, but I might as well have been, as easily as Dimitri threw me over his shoulder.

It was then I realized I had dropped both my gun and the briefcase, and I exclaimed, "Stop, we have to go back."

He said, "Don't worry. Sparky will get your gun and the briefcase," and continued to the bird. He lowered me into the door, and I was pulled inside by a third person I had not seen earlier and propped against a seat.

    I looked up and recognized the concerned face of Dr. Ryan Greene. Dimitri followed me in with Sparky right behind him, briefcase and my gun in hand, his MP 90 slung across his chest. A face suddenly appeared looking back at us from the pilot's seat.

    "You boys about ready to get the hell out of Dodge? Don't think we want to be around here if these guys have friends and they decide to join the party." The black Stetson with officer's gold braid and 7th Cavalry emblems, aviator sunglasses, and a cigar butt sticking out from under a bushy mustache made for a rather interesting image. With a thumb's up from Dimitri, the hum increased, and I could feel us gaining altitude and moving out to sea. The almost non-existent turbine and rotor noise added to the surreal nature of the vista unfolding below. The dock receded in the distance; through the black smoke of the burning fuel barrels I could see that it had been cut in half by the massive firepower of the mini-gun. Barrels and bodies were floating in the surrounding water. My God… it looked like a scene from *"Apocalypse Now,"* and all I could think was, "There's no replacement for superior firepower."

    As we moved further out to sea, the mini-gun in the doorway turned barrels up and slid smoothly into a compartment in the fuselage. When the door closed, you would never know the compartment was there, let alone the destructive power hiding behind it. It was just another one of Col. Duncan Fitzsimmons', (U.S. Army ret.), many modifications to his favorite bird, the *Raven*.

    Dimitri looked at me and shook his head. Even though he had been born and raised in the U.S. and spoke perfect English, the "Boris" accent spoke again. He thought that Boris thing was funny… "Good thing you trigger Arc Angel, or we would never have found you."

"Arc Angel?" I questioned.

"Da," he said as he tapped the pocket of my vest that held the electronic device with the blinking red light. "Our handy-dandy, super-duper, worldwide personal GPS locators that Sparky make for us. What... you don't remember that? Green light... Come pick me up, I need ride; Red light... Come pick me up, bring Cavalry; you had red light, see? So, we come, make big boom, and pull your ass out of jam again."

My answer was an unintelligible mumble, and he grinned.

In his normal voice, he said, "You are one lucky SOB, Colt," and as he turned away grinning, he said, "You can thank Sparky later."

Joe Sebastiani, or Sparks as we affectionately called him... he hated being called Sparky, which only egged Dimitri on, was our electronics wizard. After stowing his MP 90, he sat down next to me and pulled out our med kit. He helped Doc Greene cut off the make-shift bandage on my leg and the pant leg covering the wound.

"Hey," I said, "don't cut that pant leg; this is a perfectly good, almost brand-new pair of jeans." As if that were his cue, Doc Greene jabbed me in the arm with a needle and told me to shut up, go to sleep, and let them work. Within a few seconds, Doc's commands sounded like the best idea I had heard all day. As his magical elixir coursed through my body, I felt the pain in my leg receding and my mind, drifting into a relaxed state of nothingness. My last thought was, "I'll bet that shit's illegal," and then nothing.

I awakened with a start to a cool breeze blowing across my face and the chirping of birds in the distance. I was in a bed with clean, crisp sheets in a room with a large open window that that gave me a view of lush green jungle trees. The tall trees with vines and other plants diffused the sunlight coming in, and the rich smell of flowers and other growing things assailed my senses. The room was Spartan but clean and the slight antiseptic smell gave it that rural hospital feel. A far cry from my last memories of being hauled into the chopper and whisked out of a shit storm by my comrades in arms, I thought. I turned toward the door as I heard a voice say, "Hey, he's awake." At that, a grinning Dr. Ryan Greene, Joe Sebastiani and Dimitri Sokolov entered the room and came over to the bed.

Dimitri, in his offhanded jovial way, back in "Boris" mode, was first to speak, "So, you back with us, Sleeping Beauty?"

I only grinned and said, "Yeah, thanks to you guys I'm back. How long have I been out?" I asked.

Doc Greene filled me in, "Thirty-six hours, the doctor here said you needed to rest after they got that slug out of your leg and stitched you up. Plus, you were dehydrated and had lost a lot of blood. So, until they got you stabilized and some fluids back in you, he kicked us out." My memories flooded back as my head cleared, and I realized it was because of them that I was still alive and in one piece.

"Where are we?" I asked.

"It's a small clinic outside of town. Fitz set it up; he said it was safe and discreet," Doc Greene replied. My next concern was if we had gotten involved with local authorities. Doc said no, we had gotten out of there before any arrived and, according to the news reports, the incident was being attributed to rival drug cartels involved in a nasty turf war. There was no mention of a helicopter being in the area.

"We got lucky," I replied.

"No shit," Joe said with a smile.

So much for the accuracy of the local media… and another bullet dodged (literally) I thought with a small grin. As I relaxed a little more, I realized we definitely had lady luck on our side. Despite the pain in my leg, an ironic grin locked itself in place. If it hadn't already been done many times in the past, the last 72 hours were confirmation I had chosen my team and the name of my company well when I dubbed it Risky Business… Ltd.!

"Where's Fitz?" I asked. Joe told me he was at the airfield, putting the *Raven* back in its nest and getting *Tweety Bird* ready for our imminent departure. *Tweety Bird* was Fitz's pet name for his highly modified C-130 J Hercules. We used it to transport the *Raven*, ourselves, and other equipment on long hauls.

As my memory continued to come back, I immediately asked about the briefcase, and Joe assured me it was fine and already stowed on board the aircraft, unopened, along with my Glock. I felt another layer of tension peel away, and with a sigh, relaxed a little more. I started remembering the details behind my concern for its safety. We had flown to Salinas, Ecuador in the 130, and landed at a small, little used airport on the outskirts of the city. Fitz knew about it and its operational capabilities. When I asked where he got the info, he said buddies of his had used it before and vouched for its security and anonymity. Friends from one of the many "Alphabet Soup" organizations he had been doing contract work for, I guessed.

It was run by an American ex-pat. Passport control, customs, and refueling were taken care of with a stack of hundred-dollar bills, no papers needed, or questions asked. They provided us with a secure hangar large enough for the 130 and the *Raven*. Damn, one stop shopping at its finest!

After *Tweety* was tucked away, I had been taken to the outskirts of a little coastal village south of Punta Carnero Beach in the *Raven*. We had armed ourselves before we left the 130, not knowing what to expect. The guys dropped me off to meet with Fr. Eduardo Gonzalez, a Jesuit priest that had contacted us concerning our search for the Golden Library. He said he had information and, according to him, it was tied directly to our current investigation. This could be a major clue in the unbelievable mystery we found ourselves involved in… I hoped!

Friar Gonzales had semi-retired to a small parish on the coast after spending over 45 years in the mountains of Ecuador on the eastern slopes of the Andes. He had been working and living amongst the Shuar Indians, the indigenous tribe that has inhabited that area for many hundreds of years. That's where the briefcase came in. The priest had given it to me when we met at his home, telling me its contents were of the utmost importance and may help us in our search. He also stated that others had found out about its existence and would do anything to get their hands on it. Emphasizing the word, "anything," Friar Gonzalez said I should be very careful leaving the village because he was sure he and his house were being watched. I assured him I would. I thanked him as I extended an envelope filled with hundred-dollar bills, five-thousand dollars in total.

He pushed my hand away, saying, "This is not for sale and was never mine to take payment for. I do not own this," he said, tapping the case. "I have only been its caretaker as have the others before me. It is now in your hands, the new caretaker, may it serve you well."

I took the case and as I turned to leave, I laid the envelope on a small table by the door,

"A contribution for your parish then."

I opened the door and heard him say,

"You know you are about to change the world as we know it."

I turned and said, "Yeah, I kinda figured that," and walked out the door. As it was closing, I heard his last words to me.

"Via con Dios, my son."

"But this is not the place our story begins. I guess, for your sake, I need to start at the real beginning some three and a half years earlier. It all began in a bar, in a marina on Central Florida's Space Coast. I mean what better place for an adventure to begin…?"

CHAPTER TWO
The real beginning

Okay, so I'm going to become a treasure hunter, but I know I'm going to need help and advice. For a second opinion, I chose my good friend Dimitri to be the first person to bounce this whole idea off of and see what he had to say. I had decided to call the company "Risky Business." Hey, diving was risky, and treasure hunting was risky, pretty appropriate name, I thought. Anyway, Dimitri was a logical choice; he loved the water and had lived on a trawler for several years. He was an experienced boat operator, a certified diver, and just a little crazy. Plus, he was one of my best friends. We had worked together for over a dozen years and had been on a couple of sketchy underwater adventures together in Mexico. I knew I could trust him with my life. These were attributes I found highly desirable for members of my new company.

After a few beers at one of our favorite bars, "Nautical Spirits," I explained my idea to him and asked if he was interested. He didn't hesitate, "Hell, yes," he replied! Now, there were two of us.

In the following days, much discussion ensued regarding how to move forward with this endeavor. A week later, we held our next "official" meeting at the bar. We came up with a list of other individuals we would want to have involved. Knowing full well it would take at least four or five more people besides us to take this treasure hunting idea from just an idea to reality; we decided our recruits should be people we knew/had worked with, liked, and trusted. They needed to have skill sets and/or resources that would benefit the Company. So, basically, they should love being on the water, it would be nice if they were divers, liked hanging out in bars, and should be as crazy as we were. No problem!

After more discussion, we came up with The List: Joe Sebastiani lived on a 40' sailboat in the marina where our "official" bar was located. He was a certified diver and had a double E Master's degree. He was an electronics wizard with a specialization in acoustic research. He had done contract work for the DOD's Acoustic Weapons division, decided he had had enough of that world, bailed, and wound up here. Dr. Ryan Greene, a former paramedic, attended the Coast Guard Academy. He had gone through rescue swimmer and SAR (search and rescue) school and later earned a doctorate in linguistics. His area of specialization was ancient languages and dialects. He was multilingual, Spanish, Italian, French, German, Chinese, Russian, and a bunch of other esoteric and forgotten languages. He was still working at a university but could make himself available when needed. Nils Sorensen was a retired NASA engineer who started a Marine Surplus business prior to his retirement. That business had grown dramatically and kept him Comfortably in the black. He holds a captain's license, master's degree, and was a certified diver. Our list also included Tony Donaldson, self-employed computer hacker/genius, and certified diver. Bachelor's degree in Math, started a master's program but got bored and dropped out. However, not before hacking the university's computer system and awarding himself an honorary doctorate in Computer Science. Tony and his wife lived on a deep-water canal

100 yards from the Banana River and a 15-minute boat ride from the locks at Port Canaveral. Finally, Dr. Lawrence Goodson, retired professor, advanced degrees in biology, microbiology, JD, a certified diver, and self-proclaimed ladies' man.

So, there you have it, the initial draft line-up for "Risky Business." Now, all we had to do was extend the invitation to be part of this hair-brained scheme. I contacted our draftees and invited them to a meeting at what Dimitri and I now called "The Corporate Bar." After some scheduling adjustments, they all accepted… like we could keep these guys out of a bar. There was much discussion that night and lots of beer and tequila. I explained my idea and emphasized we would basically be looking for needles in a very large haystack. There were no guarantees of finding anything, and there would be risks involved, both physical and financial. The room was quiet for a couple of minutes and then a chorus of, "I'm in," broke out! They had all accepted the offer to join the quest.

I was the last one to leave that night and stood on the bar's back porch with my Scotch in hand, staring at the moonlight reflecting off the ripples in the water of the marina. What had I done? With nothing but a tantalizing prospect, I had enlisted a computer hacker, an ex-lawyer microbiologist ladies' man, a real rocket scientist, a guy who could read and speak languages I had never even heard of, the creator of some kind of sonic death ray for the military, and a crazy Russian-American Cossack! As I tossed down the last of my Scotch and headed for the door, I thought, "What a great bunch of guys!"

Risky Business is our name, and treasure hunting is our game!

First order of business, we needed a boat, or I should say vessel. I'd had my eye on a 46 ft. single diesel engine trawler for sale for a couple of months now. She was older, wooden-hulled with a moderate-sized wheelhouse, good storage below decks, and a sturdy looking trawling net A-frame on her deck. I thought we could modify it to lift cannons and chests filled with gold fairly easily. Yes, I was dreaming already; reality had not yet reared its ugly head. I negotiated a good deal on her, and, by month's end, the *Lisa B* was mine. I moved her to the canal behind Tony the IT genius' house, and that became our initial base of operations. All the guys chipped in time, effort, and some money. A month and a half later, we had gone over her from stem to stern. New paint, refurbished the wheelhouse, new steering controls, gauges, and the six-cylinder Ford Lehman 120 diesel was purring like a kitten.

It was time for another company meeting at the corporate bar. This time, we got access to a nice little private dining area off to the side of the main room. The order of business that evening: how do we go about finding all this treasure lying around on the ocean floor? We came up with our first list of necessary items: a good GPS unit, a high-end sonar/depth finder, VHF radio, a winch, lines, cable, and underwater metal detectors for starters. Not only that, but I had been doing a lot of research on the subject and determined that if we were serious, we also needed a Proton Magnetometer. This was a device towed behind the boat that measured slight variations in the magnetic field of the earth caused by ferrous metals on the bottom. These would be like cannons, anchors, cannon balls, and metal fastener's and might show a wreck's debris field. Unfortunately, it also registered any other modern ferrous metal junk down there. Expensive, but just something we would have to work through. All total, my cost estimate was around twelve to fifteen thousand dollars at discount prices! (This was the reality rearing its ugly head part!). Before everyone choked on their beers and headed for the door, I assured them I was confident we could get the equipment for less than that. We had to get creative, very creative. Thank goodness, Nils piped up about then, saying he had a decent GPS unit in stock. He knew where we could get a good sonar/depth finder fairly cheap. He also had a contact for line, a winch, and a source for cable. We decided we would get one handheld underwater metal detector and Dimitri volunteered to make that purchase on his own. Phew… that only left us with the VHF radio and mag to worry about. Nils said he would track down the radio, and I volunteered to bird-dog the mag. I asked all the divers in the group to go through their gear and make sure it was in good working order and ready to use. All agreed, and I was thrilled that nobody had bailed on me so far.

Over the next couple of months, we gathered and installed our gear. I started a serious hunt for a magnetometer. During this time, we took the *Lisa B* out for a couple of shakedown cruises, which went well. We had come up with the VHF radio we needed and other bits and pieces. Dimitri and Joe installed the gear while Tony set us up with an onboard Wi-Fi hotspot and other neat computer gadgets. Six months after our initial meeting, we had a working salvage vessel and crew, just no mag. Treasure hunting season didn't really begin until the winter seas calmed down, beginning in March or April, so we still had time to get things ready. Doc Greene received an invitation to present a paper in November at Oxford University in England. It was on some of his esoteric language research, which he accepted. I never pretended to understand everything he studied, but on this trip, he had volunteered to make a side trip to the national maritime archives in Seville, Spain. He and some colleagues would research the 1715 fleet. We accepted his offer wholeheartedly, chipping in to cover costs for the side trip from our very limited resources.

It was early January, windy and cool. I had just poured myself a steaming cup of coffee and sat down at my computer to perform the ritual I had been performing for the last three months. As I started my search, I had no expectation I would get anything other than my usual "no matches found" message. So, you can imagine my surprise when I received, "one match found." Looking further, there was a mag for sale, new, in Georgia for $3000. I almost spilled my coffee reaching for the phone. My call was answered on the second ring. The gentleman on the other end said yes, the mag was still available; he had just posted it last night. It was brand new, never been in the water. He had moved to Georgia from Daytona Beach and was prospecting for gold in a stream that ran through his property there. Another treasure hunter, I thought. Great! He had bought the mag to do exactly what we were planning on doing but wound up moving to Georgia before he could get it wet and now had no use for it. After some skillful negotiations, I got him down to $2,000 and made the purchase. Within seven days, I had the unit in my possession, and Risky Business was now ready for business!

The mag we purchased was an entry level unit. To purchase it from a dealer would have cost $6,000. The reviews I had read about it gave it high marks in almost every category: durability, sensitivity, reliability, ease of use, and great value for the price.

By the end of March, Doc Greene had returned from his trip, bearing reams of papers copied from the archives. The end of March now became a time of intensive research for the Risky Business team. Lawrence Goodson was totally immersed in the underwater lease process and other legal maritime documents pertaining to treasure hunting off the coast of Florida. He had spent three weeks in Tallahassee doing some of his research. When we next met as a group, we all noticed he came in with a rather long face and a folder full of papers; he was not happy. Oh, boy, I thought, he must be the bearer of ill tidings, so we started our discussion with him. His report was rather disheartening. Most of the eastern coastline waters had already been leased to one or two individual's years ago. Okay, so what did that mean for us? Well, everything from Melbourne, Florida to the Ft. Pierce/ Stuart area, from the low tide mark out to the three-mile limit was under lease.

This was the exact area where the ships from the 1715 fleet would have sunk. If we wanted to work any of the area, we had to receive approval from the lease owners, and a percentage of everything found would go to them. Talk about getting your hackles up; I thought Dimitri would go through the ceiling.

"Why the hell should we have to pay someone who is not even working an area a percentage of anything we find?" he shouted, "When all the costs for salvage are incurred by us!"

Time, personnel, equipment, fuel, research… No freaking way was he going to give away a portion of anything he found just because a guy had a piece of paper saying he owned what was on the sea floor. "How the hell could you own that anyway?" he fumed after a series of what I can only guess were Russian expletives.

Lawrence let out a long sigh and said, "Money and politics." The state would get the first choice of anything found up to 20%; the lease holder and salvors would split what was left 50/50. So, for the people who had done all the work, we would wind up with 40% of what we found, while those other guys sat on their fat asses in Tallahassee or wherever and did nothing but hold their hands out!

And that's how it began. I could see by the look on Tony's face he was siding with Dimitri, as was Joe. Hell, I was even siding with the crazy Russian. In our minds, this was tantamount to highway robbery! Doc Ryan had his poker face on, Nil's was just shaking his head, and Lawrence was trying to explain the legal ramifications of not playing by the rules to everyone. Nobody was listening! I knew we needed to get things back under control and stood up. It was time for "the voice of reason!"

"What I think we need to do," I said, "Is take some time here, put our options on the table, and think them through." Most all agreed, and much of the fuming and bitching quieted down as Lawrence pulled out a blank sheet of paper and started writing. After 45 minutes of heated discussion, we had our options laid out. Either play by the rules and go to work, giving away over 50% of what we find; don't play by the rules and go to work, taking our chances of being arrested, fined, losing the boat and all of our equipment and going to jail; or, hang it all up dissolve Risky Business, liquidate our few assets, divvy up our investment money, call it a day and all go our separate ways. I felt like someone had just kicked me in the gut.

    None of the options were sitting well with any of us. We had two large charts spread out on the table, showing the coast from Stuart/Ft. Pierce to Cape Canaveral. We had marked the approximate locations of the known wrecks or areas where treasure and cannons had been found with a red grease pencil. Through this whole discussion, I had noticed Doc Greene had been staring at the charts intently, more so than anyone else. Now, he spoke, "You know Gentlemen, we may have another option to consider."

CHAPTER THREE

Doc Greene stood and pushed back his chair, leaning over the maps on the table. With his finger, he drew an oval around the marked wreck sites. "So, these are the wrecks that have been identified and are being worked."

I said, "Yes."

He paused and then said, "There were 11 ships in the fleet, and only one survived?"

Again, I said, "Yes."

He continued, "There have been six or seven ships identified, so that leaves either three or four ships unaccounted for." There was not a sound in the room; where was he going with this?

Lawrence spoke up, "Yes, but the area where they are suspected to have sunk, is all under lease as I pointed out earlier."

Doc Greene paused and, looking at us sitting around the table like a professor about to announce final grades, said, "What about the twelfth ship?"

You could have heard a pin drop as we gawked at him in astonishment.

"The what?" I blurted out. What the hell was he talking about? When I gathered my wits about me, I said, "What do you mean the twelfth ship? There were only eleven in the fleet; we have copies of the records documenting that." That's when the Cheshire cat grin spread across his face.

"That's what your records say, but that's NOT what my records say."

Again, stunned silence... after a few moments, Dimitri spoke, "Please, Doc, do go on!"

Still smiling, he said, "As you wish, but we'll need much more to drink for this story."

Mitch, our server and bar manager, who was also the daughter of the owners, delivered a new round of beverages as we all pondered Doc's revelation in brooding silence. Doc returned to his seat, settled back with a cold beer in his hand, and said, "I do believe my visit to Seville will prove to be worth its weight in gold if you'll pardon the pun." We were all still so stunned nobody caught his joke, so he continued. "I reviewed the volumes of documents concerning the 1715 fleet, and they confirmed what we already knew. However, going over them again, I found an obscure log entry from the commandant of the fort at St. Augustine. It was about a sailor on the last ship in the fleet. It was a page that had gotten folded over and a notation in the official commandant's log, almost as an afterthought. Hardly legible, however, I scrutinized it closely and came up with this bit of information. He stated a black ship had passed them on their starboard side heading north-northeast at dusk the evening before the hurricane hit. It had a rather strange sail configuration and was traveling much faster than his vessel." He paused. "That would have been the twelfth ship. I looked back over the documents thoroughly, and there was no mention of this vessel anywhere in the official 1715 fleet records."

We were engrossed in Doc's story now, leaning forward in

our chairs, eyes glued on him with our drinks practically untouched. He continued, "I reviewed the records from the Port of Havana to see if I could find any reference to this mystery ship. After more digging, there it was: a notation of a special vessel sailing under direct orders from King Philip V himself, that had docked in the harbor. It was loaded with an unspecified cargo and had no passengers other than guards. A portion of the cargo, however, had come from South America. No more information was given. There was a side notation that additional cargo from the mint in Mexico City was included. Her departure date was listed as the same date as the Plate Fleet, but it was not registered as part of it."

Breaking our spellbound silence, Mitch stuck her head in the room and said that "the bar was closing in ten minutes," and she needed to cash us out. She saw the consternation on everybody's face and hesitated. We pulled money from our pockets and began putting it on the table. She must have sensed the level of tension in the room; she took our money and said, "I've got a couple of hours of book work to do in the office, so if you guys aren't done and want to hang around a little longer, I'll lock the outside door. Just let me know when you're ready to leave." A huge sigh of relief was expelled by one and all. As she was leaving the room, she turned back and said, "You know where the taps are. Don't get thirsty just because we're closed," smiled and left.

It's good to be a regular! We were like kids at a Saturday adventure matinee and immediately turned back to Doc and said, "Go on, man; go on!"

He took another swallow of his beer and began again. "As I read through every document I could find, there was nothing about this ship and not a word about it reaching Spain. I reviewed the documents from the Spanish settlement at St. Augustine, where a number of the survivors of the 1715 fleet's shipwrecks made their way afterward. There, I found an entry concerning a sailor that was brought to the garrison. He told the following story. Let me read it so you can get an accurate feel for what was said; we will really need to discuss this later!"

"It was reported that on August 9, 1715, a sailor was brought into the garrison at St. Augustine nearly dead. He was dehydrated, sunburned, and delirious. After two days in the infirmary, he could finally recount his story. He had been on a vessel under orders from the king himself when it got caught in a tremendous storm, the hurricane. As the captain realized his ship was lost, he sent this sailor and nine others out in a longboat with ten crates. He told them they had to get to St. Augustine and then to Spain and deliver the crates directly to the king. They pushed away from the ship and turned landward. Only a short distance from the ship, looking back as lightning lit the night sky, they saw the mighty galleon rise and then get inundated by a huge wave.

"To their horror, she never returned to the surface. Fearing for their own lives, they manned the four sets of oars and pulled with all their might toward what they hoped was shore. After what seemed like hours, they found themselves in breaking waves. At first, they thought they had made it to the shore break; too late, they realized it was a shoal. The waves tossed their boat into the air and then smashed it upon the jagged coral just below the surface. As their boat was broken to pieces, the impact threw the sailor through the air and into the frothing cauldron, never to see his comrades again.

He found a piece of floating debris and clung to it for dear life. He must have passed out, for when he regained consciousness, he was lying face down on a sandy beach. The sun was shining, and his crewmates were nowhere in sight." Doc paused and finished what was left of his beer as he surveyed the rapt faces staring at him across the table.

I rocked back in my chair, staring into space, trying to

process the bombshell that had just been dropped by our dear friend, Doc Greene.

"Holy shit!" I exclaimed under my breath, "Doc, do you know what this means?"

As he looked at me, he grinned and said, "Colt, of course, I know what this means. It means there is indeed a treasure ship out there to be found, and very probably in a place no one else has thought to look!"

The enormity of his revelation started to sink in as everyone began to speak at once. "What was the ship's location? What did she carry? What was in the crates loaded on the longboat?"

"Hold on, guys," he said. "There's more," and he began again. "The story about the sailor ends here. He was in such bad shape he died that same day without revealing the approximate location of the ship or small boat's sinking. I dug further and looked into the Seville archives and found a reference to the *Nuestra Senora de Conception*, a personal ship of the king, leaving the port bound for Havana on September 10, 1714. That would have put her in Havana by around the middle of February 1715. That could easily accommodate a departure from Havana in July 1715, the same time as the treasure fleet. Also in the Seville records, it noted that half of her 126 cannons, cannon balls, and powder had been left behind. I thought that highly unusual for a galleon heading into an area notorious for pirates with only half its normal armament."

By now, we had burned up our two-hour window provided by Mitch and decided we had best adjourn for the night. Getting everyone to leave and agree to wait for the rest of Doc's story till later was like pulling teeth from an alligator. It could be done but would be damn difficult! Eventually, all agreed, and after leaving another pile of money on the table, decided that we would continue the discussion the next evening on the *Lisa B*.

By the time we left, it was almost two a.m., and I don't even remember my drive home. My head was literally a whirling maelstrom of information, questions, suppositions, and excitement. I had gone from the pits of despair at the thought of all our work being for naught earlier in the evening to the unbelievable heights of Doc's revelation; it was almost too much to comprehend. The Z monster was kept at bay that night as sleep eluded me.

Our gathering the next evening on the boat was a spirited one. The beer fridge and the grog locker in the wheelhouse were hit immediately. Deck chairs and a folding table were set up under the tarp hung over the rear deck. As we settled in to the sound of waves lapping on the sides of the boat, ice crackling in glasses, and beers being opened, the air was electric. We were all trying to be cool about everything but, following the first sip of beverage, we could contain ourselves no longer, and questions came out in a flood tide. Doc, amused by it, only laughed and calmed us all down, saying we would get to the questions soon enough, but first, there were a few very pressing points he wanted us to discuss.

"One, why did the ship leave behind half its armament, two, what was this unrecorded mission for the king all about? And three, foremost in our minds, where did she sink?"

Joe spoke up first, "Well, leaving that many cannons behind would have made her lighter and therefore faster. She could probably out-run most privateers under normal conditions."

"Good point," I agreed.

Tony asked, "How much did a cannon weigh?"

We thought for a bit, and Doc said, "Probably around 2,000 to 3,000 pounds. Include cannon balls and powder, and you could add about another 500 to 700 pounds." I could see the wheels turning in Tony's head.

"And the top speed for a galleon?"

Again, Doc answered, "About six to eight knots or between seven to a little over nine miles per hour."

Tony nodded as his mental calculator shifted into high gear.

"That would mean if my calculations are correct, that a lightly loaded galleon could potentially travel about 11 or possibly 12+ miles per hour and make the crossing from Seville to Havana in less than the normal six months."

"Possibly," Doc agreed.

Dimitri spoke up then and asked, "But what would be the reason for wanting to make a faster crossing?"

"Another good point," I interjected as I looked at the faces around the table.

It was Joe's turn to jump in and he said, "What if it wasn't to make a faster crossing but to carry more cargo on the return trip?"

Tony added, "It would give them somewhere around an extra 110.25-ton cargo capacity and not be overloaded".

It was Doc's turn to chime in, "That's exactly what I was thinking."

Lawrence, who had been quiet through most of the discussion, looked over the rim of his rum and tonic and said to Doc, "That report on the cargo from the Havana records stated that they received stuff from South America, but nothing specific was listed and a load from the Mexico mint. We also know most of the silver would come from South America, most likely Potosi in Bolivia, but there was no mention of silver."

"True," Doc agreed. "There would be no reason that I can think of to hide the fact that silver was part of the cargo when they make a note of the cargo from the Mexican mint, which would obviously be gold."

I jumped in then, "So, your reasoning trail leads us to what? We have a mystery cargo from South America which may or may not contain silver and a load coming from the Mexican mint of gold."

"Holy crap," Tony said, "That means there could be an extra 110 tons of gold added to the ship's normal cargo of 600 to 2,000 tons of cargo, depending on her actual construction. On today's market, that means, let's see…" After mentally calculating for a minute or two, he said, "an additional five billion 292 million dollars' worth of gold if my figures are correct! That's in addition to their normal tonnage." Tony's figures are always correct, I thought with a huge grin on my face. Now, our heads were really spinning. Could it be possible that that much treasure could be out there somewhere? We were talking tens of billions of dollars!

Doc's next Comment brought us back to reality. He said, "Now, all we have to do is figure out where the *Conception* sank…"

Tony had gotten up and hit the beer fridge, bringing back a round for the table. As he sat down, he had a thoughtful expression on his face, and after a few minutes said, "You know, Doc, if you could provide me with the information you have and I could identify the variables involved, I could build a Computer model of the *Conception's* probable course."

Nils, who had been quiet for most of the evening said, "Then from that, we might determine where she could have gone down. We know she didn't break up on a reef from the sailor's account, so there's a chance she may still be mostly intact on the bottom!"

Doc replied, "I'll send you all the details I have by email tomorrow."

"It will take me a few days to a week or so to get it together," Tony replied. "No problem," I said. "Take your time; just be as accurate as possible."

Tony looked at me with an exasperated expression, "Really, Colt?" Sheepishly, I realized I had stepped on my you know what! Tony's work was always accurate!

"Sorry," I said. "Heat of the moment…"

He laughed, "No worries, Big Guy."

As our meeting drew to a close, we set the tentative date and location of our next gathering. We said our goodbyes, and I told

Tony that I would stow the chairs and table and make sure the boat was secure before leaving. He said thanks and headed inside to his family. Dimitri stayed to help as I folded chairs and put them below. In a few minutes, only two chairs and the table were left. Dimitri headed into the wheelhouse and shut down the deck lights, leaving the only illumination the battery-operated naked bulb over the helm. It cast its faint yellowish light through the window, adding an ethereal glow to the deck. I plopped down in one chair as I heard the fridge open. A minute later, Dimitri came out with a frosty bottle of Russian potato vodka in one hand and two frosty shot glasses in the other. I knew this was his private stash, kept in the freezer of the beer fridge. He sat down, put the glasses on the table, and poured two shots of the frosty liquid. I was staring intently eastward across the Banana River to the lights of Cape Canaveral.

He handed me a glass, "Prost."

"Prost," I replied.

After a short pause he said, "You seem troubled, my friend; what's the matter?"

I thought for a moment and then replied, "I'm not sure, just revisiting tonight and the last few days and weeks." I let my voice trail off.

"And so?" he asked.

"And so, Dimitri, I'm not sure what's going to happen."

"What do you mean?"

I said, "I guess that whole voice of reason thing got me to reconsider the reality of all this. What if all this is for nothing? What if we don't find a thing and are just wasting our time and money?"

He poured our glasses full and followed my stare east before speaking again. "So, you are having your doubts about your hair-brained idea? No offense, Colt."

"None taken," I replied, "but, yeah, I guess that's it. Think of all the people who search their entire lives for lost or sunken treasure and find nothing, losing their life savings, family members, and friends, for what... nothing!" I tossed down the clear liquid in one swallow, its heat sliding down my throat, sending a wave of warmth through my body.

As Dimitri refilled our glasses and set the bottle on the table, he turned to face me. "Colt, how long have we known each other?"

I said, "Close to 20 years, I guess."

"And how long have you known the others?"

I thought for a minute and said, "From around 10 or 12 years to over 40."

"And," he said, "we have all been going our own separate ways, making lives for ourselves, becoming successful in our own right, and then you called us together. You presented your hair-brained idea, no offense."

I could only laugh, "None taken, Dimitri."

"And what happened? Every one of us agreed immediately to join you! No matter what else we had going on in our lives, without so much as a minute's hesitation, we agreed to join you in your..."

"I know, Dimitri," I said.

"Okay, see what I'm saying?"

I paused. I wasn't sure I did and said so.

He shook his head and said, "Colt, for a really smart guy, sometimes you're dumb as a stump."

"Hey," I said, "Offense taken."

"No, what I mean is you didn't have to twist our arms or convince us to join you; we did it willingly and immediately. Doesn't that tell you something? You pulled this unbelievably diverse group of individuals together with one phone call, and next thing you know, we have all agreed to be part of this "thing" you have created! Did you ever think it may not be about the treasure? We're not a bunch of youngsters going out for a joyride with a buddy. We've all been around the block, some of us more times than we would like to count. None of us really need the money; I mean it would be good and all, but our lives could have gone on comfortably without your call. Colt, I'm speaking as your friend. I feel we are all here, not because of the promises of riches at the end of the rainbow, but because of what you have created, a new raison d'être for us! You're right; we may not find a thing, but we will search for it together, sharing whatever trials and tribulations that may come along. It won't be easy; in fact, it will probably be hard as hell, but that doesn't matter."

"Dimitri, you're getting all philosophical on me, man."

"No, listen to me, Colt; this is important. The path you have set us on is a path we have agreed to travel together, and I think from it we will all go away with riches beyond measure, whether or not we find treasure! Remember, it's not the destination, but rather the journey that will fulfill and define us."

Sweet Jesus, I thought, as Dimitri got up, washed the glasses, and replaced them and the bottle in the freezer. As he crossed the deck, he clasped my shoulder and looked at me, "Get some rest, my friend, you look like shit!" He stepped off the boat and disappeared into the darkness.

I shouted after him "Hey, for a Socialist Rooskie Cossack… You're not such a bad guy."

From out of the dark, I heard, "Coming from an American Capitalist Pig like you, I'll take that as a compliment," followed by a hearty chuckle.

Maybe Dimitri was right; maybe we had all reached a time in our lives where we needed something else. Not something material but something more important than silver or gold. Maybe it was more personal for each of us than I could have imagined. Some of us had families or significant others to consider when making this decision, but in my gut, I knew this wasn't some quixotic adventure. It was much more than that. Maybe we would each find our own treasure, not necessarily at the end, but along the way. I stowed my chair and turned out the light in the wheelhouse. As I came out, I looked to the east once again, the lights of Cape Canaveral reflecting off the Banana River and beyond that, the blue-green waters of the Atlantic... "Dimitri," I thought, "If you are right, then let the journey begin."

CHAPTER FOUR

My phone rang five days later at about 10 a.m. Doc Greene called and said Tony had contacted him and had something for us to see. I let the rest of the crew know, and later that evening, we met at the boat. Tony invited us into the house. They had put his two young daughters to bed and his lovely wife, Susan, with one of those motherly smiles, asked us to keep it down since she didn't want anyone to awaken them. She knew us all too well and knew how rowdy we could get. With a straight face, I held up my hand and said, "Scout's honor, we will be on our best behavior." She only laughed and shook her head.

As she turned away, she admonished me with, "Colten, it will be your ass if you're not." With that, we retired to Tony's office/work room. Tony pressed a button on the wall and what looked like a 70" diagonal piece of acrylic lowered out of its nest in the ceiling. It turned out to be an HD computer/video touch screen.

We all grabbed seats; as he talked, he touched the screen and a chart of the Florida coastline from Stuart/Ft. Pierce to Amelia Island came up. On it were several lines, arrows and notations, and the locations of all the 1715 ships that had been found so far. He walked us through the logic behind his approach to the problem. Taking the information that Doc sent him and the research he had done on the tides, wind speed, and currents for July 30, 1715, he built his model. Using the speed estimates for the ship he and Doc had come up with and taking into account the hurricane-force winds and sea state, he created an algorithm that would manipulate all the variables, crunched the numbers, and plotted a projected course for our mystery ship.

As he spoke, he touched the huge screen again, and a line appeared from the Ft. Pierce area north following the coast but veering to the east on its northward plot. As we studied the image before us, he explained he had used the information from the commandant's report to get started. It had said the mystery ship passed the last ship in the Plate fleet before dark on the 30th of July and was moving at an unusually high rate of speed for a galleon. Also, it stated that it passed on the seaward side, looking to be moving further out to sea as it was heading north. All the ships of the fleet had orders to sail in sight of land, but the only ship to survive the hurricane, the *Griffin*, disobeyed orders and went further out into deeper water. It seemed safe to assume the *Conception* had a seasoned captain, and he was smart enough to know one hell of a storm was coming.Knowing this, he would have realized that his best chance for survival was also in deeper water. Taking a course heading further out to sea before the hurricane hit, he probably tried running in front of the storm. The captain had every inch of sail he could use, deployed. He would have been in the big rollers but from what little description we had of this ship, it was an unusual configuration both hull-wise and sail-wise for a galleon. The consensus of the group was that they built this ship for speed and survivability.

Now, the real mystery story began. Tony continued, "As close as we can figure, he passed the last ship somewhere just north of Ft. Pierce, as the sun was going down. This is where it gets a little speculative. Sunset on that date was about eight something. He was about 90 miles from the tip of Cape Canaveral, and the full force of the hurricane hit the fleet around two am. That would have given him six maybe seven hours of hard sailing before the main storm hit. If he could run with the wind, in the 10 to 13 mph range, in our estimation, he could have covered 90 miles in about seven hours, which would put him somewhere in this circle, before he got hit with the full force of the storm." The large circle was east of the Cape with its center about six miles offshore. We all sat there in silence as we digested this huge chunk of information.

I was the first to speak, "There's a lot of guess work in there, Tony."

Tony said, "I agree, but it's guesswork based on the facts we have at hand. There are a hell of a lot of variables in the model that are unverifiable. If anyone has a better idea, I'm all ears. Truth be told, this is just a SWAG done with a computer. I've played with changing the wind and speed variables and the program still comes out with center points that are only three miles from this center.

"Actually, Colt," Joe said, "I think Tony has given us a good idea of where to look. Now, all we need to do is work on refining the model and maybe, just maybe we can come up with a starting point for a search.

Nils chimed in, "He's right, Colt; this is based on the facts we have so until we get more or different information, I think we should take a serious look at what Tony is suggesting."

"Oh, I'm not saying no to any of it; I'm just saying there are quite a few variables we can't narrow down and confirm."

Dimitri spoke up, laughing, "That's why they call it treasure hunting, Colt, NOT treasure finding!"

As the laughter died down, "Very funny Dimitri!" Nils said. "Let's look at that circled area a little closer." Tony did some screen touching again, and we zoomed into the circle now displaying all the attributes of a full nautical chart. The depth in the area ran from 30 to 60 ft., not impossible working depths, but no walk in the park either. Getting down to the two-atmosphere range with scuba would require mixed gas diving if we wanted to spend any significant time on the bottom. Dimitri, Joe, Doc, and Tony were all Nitrox certified, which was a big plus.

We pulled out Doc's notes and looked at the area before us based on the sailor's account. The water was deep enough to swallow a galleon whole. A mile to the east of the center point, there was a small shoal that rose to less than ten feet below the surface. After that, there was no shallow water till you hit the southeast shoal and the water got shallower, 20 feet, the closer you got to shore four and a half miles away. I had been thinking if the sailor said they hit shallow water and then deep water again, the small shoal was the only place within miles that might fit the location in his story. It was within Tony's circle and worth a look for the longboat.

In storm surf, waves would top at least 15 to 20 feet and the troughs of them could easily uncover a shoal that was only eight to ten feet under the surface to start with and make a nasty place for a longboat to land. I told the guys what I was thinking, and they agreed with me. If, and it was a big if, the longboat hit that shoal, where would that put the galleon? It was clear finding the answer to that question would require an on-site search. That meant dragging the mag across the area in a linear grid search pattern or, "mowing the lawn," as it was called in treasure-hunter speak.

I thought out loud, "I wonder if we could see anything from the air?" That started a lively discussion with feelings on both sides, maybe yes, maybe no.

Lawrence spoke up, "Could we afford to hire a plane and pilot to take us up to do the searching?" Did we want anyone to know what we were up to? From the size of the area, the consensus was no, we couldn't. Besides, a plane may not give you enough time to study an area or anomaly if you spotted one.

Not to be dissuaded, I said, "I may know someone who would help us out."

Nils said, "If you can get it for free, then, by all means, let's do it."

I replied, "It might mean adding another person to our group." When quizzed about the person, I said, "Oh, don't worry, guys; he'll fit right in!"

And that's how Col. Duncan Fitzsimmons (U.S. Army ret.) became part of our merry band of adventurers. I had known Fitz for about thirty years and I could guarantee he was one crazy MOFO! He joined the Army, went through helicopter flight school at Ft. Rucker, finished top in his class and was shipped to Nam, flying slicks doing insertions, evacs, and Medevac. He did two tours; the second tour he flew Huey gunships. Said he liked that better because instead of just getting shot at, he could shoot back.

Got out, but stayed in the guard and retired full bird colonel, which is amazing in and of its self. This is the guy that flew a bunch of Alabama National Guard medics in his UH 1, Huey when they were down here doing weekend warrior maneuvers, nose down attack mode through Main Street Disney, around Cinderella's castle and back down Main Street, having to pull up to clear the monorail!

He had declared engine problems to the ATC before dropping below the radar. He thought he had it made until he got back to Herndon Field, where the flight had originated, and a full colonel and a major were waiting for him. Said his ass was about 25 pounds lighter after they got done chewing it. Someone in the castle had gotten his aircraft numbers and called it in. Sons of bitches, no sense of humor! He was the unit's top pilot with awards and commendations and shit, so he walked away with only a wrist slap and the ass chewing.

Just knowing this one story, and trust me, there were many others, it was obvious he had a great resume and was going to fit right in if he agreed to join us.

The next day and a phone call later, Dimitri, Joe, and I had an appointment with Fitz at his office in Bithlo, Florida on Thursday afternoon. We arrived at what looked like a small well-used, if not run down, airfield just outside of town. There were half a dozen rusty hangars in sight and a tower that looked like it had seen better days. What got my attention was the 12-foot chain-link fence with rolls of razor wire on top surrounding the whole place and the guarded entrance gate.

As we pulled up to the gate, a guard came out, and I gave him my name. After checking my driver's license, he said, "Yes, Sir, Colonel Fitzsimmons is expecting you." When he turned towards the guard shack, I saw the sidearm in a shoulder holster under his lightweight windbreaker. The electronic gate opened as I thought, armed guards, 12-foot fences, razor wire, what the hell has Fitz been up to since we last talked? I followed the arrowed signs that said headquarters building to an old, not in the best of shape three-story building. The parking lot was nearly empty in front and a big Acme Corporation sign was affixed to the exterior.

Another armed guard opened the door for us as we walked up to the entrance. Inside was a nicely appointed atrium with a reception desk in the middle. This was a stark difference from the building's outside appearance. Sitting at the desk was one of the most beautiful women I had ever laid eyes on. As we approached, she greeted us with a picture-perfect smile, her red hair and crystalline green eyes sparkling. She said, "You must be Dr. Burnett." All I could do was nod; speech eluded me. She pressed a button and said, "Colonel, Dr. Burnett has arrived." There was a response, which we could not hear, and she answered with a, "Yes, Sir," handed us three security badges, and told us to make sure we displayed them at all times. She smiled and said, "We wouldn't want any of our distinguished guests getting shot, now would we?" It was then I noticed the slight bulge under her fitted suit jacket that showed she was also armed. Holy shit, I thought, she's not kidding. This is better than in the movies. She pointed us toward an elevator and said with that beautiful smile, "Third floor."

As we turned toward the elevator, Dimitri leaned over and whispered, "I like this guy already, beautiful women with guns. Wow."

I shook my head and didn't bother to respond. We were quietly whisked upward, and when the door opened on the third floor, it was into a modern and spacious office, at the far side of which was a large desk in front of a glass wall that gave a panoramic view of the airport's tower and flight line. Behind the desk, in a cloud of cigar smoke, sat Col. Duncan Fitzsimmons. As he stood, kicking the chair out from under him and placing his cigar in an ashtray, he came around his desk with a huge grin and grabbed me in one of his signature bear hugs. "Colt, you old son of a bitch, good to see you again!" This was no "girly man" Bro' hug! This was a genuine crush your chest hug! Fitz and I went way back!

"Good to see you again, Fitz," I managed to get out while gasping for air. As he stepped back and my lungs refilled, I introduced Dimitri and Joe. Handshakes all around, and then with a slap on my back that I'm sure loosened several vertebrae, we moved toward a large conference table. Fitz was about my height, 6' 4" or 5" about 265 lbs., strong as a bull and solid as the Rock of Gibraltar. Not the kind of guy you would want to piss off in a bar.

"Come on in and grab a chair." As we sat down, he looked at me and said, "Now, what's this about sunken treasure?"

That's Fitz, no bullshit, cut to the chase and get right to the point! I filled him in on our endeavor and progress to date. "Risky Business," he said, "you and your silly ass names."

"Me?" I countered, "As I recall, wasn't Acme Corporation the Company that Wiley Coyote bought all his 'stuff' from in the Road Runner cartoons?"

His grin got bigger, "Touché, nice catch. So, tell me, what can I do for…Risky Business?"

I paused and then said, "We were wondering if you would be interested in joining us?"

His smile faded a little as he pondered the question.

Before he could speak, Dimitri spoke up, "Or… you could just stay here in your nice cushy air-conditioned office and smoke your expensive cigars and answer your telephones, and we could send you pictures and texts filling you in on our exploits!" Feeling pleased with his sarcastic remark, he rocked back in his chair with the typical Dimitri sardonic grin on his face.

I said, "Knock it off, wise-ass!"

Fitz looked at him for a couple of minutes, his grin returning slightly, then looked at me. "He doesn't know."

I shook my head, "No," I replied, "they haven't had the 'full' briefing yet, but he is housebroken." Now Dimitri, red-faced, and Joe both looked at me with questioning looks. "I'll explain later," I said as Fitz got up, went to his desk, and retrieved his cigar. Re-lighting it, he returned to his seat, and once a nice cloud of smoke had been established, spoke.

"I don't know, Colt. I'm not sure I can spare the time to go off on some wild goose treasure hunt. I've got a serious business going on here, a large serious business. I have several contracts in the works that must be fulfilled within their specified time frames, or it will cost me a ton of money." He paused for a minute and said, "I'll have to think about your offer and get back to you."

"I understand," I said. "That shouldn't be a problem, but just be aware, if you accept, there may be times we need you for a few days in a row or maybe even a week or so."

"Got it," he said, "we'll cross that bridge if we come to it. So, what else should I know about this treasure hunt of yours?"

We all rocked back in our chairs; the die had been cast, and we began our conversation. I filled him in on the details to date and told him we needed to do some aerial surveying over our potential search area as soon as we could.

He said, "I can help with that." He would make the arrangements and get back with us in a few days once they were complete. As we wrapped things up, I said we needed to get on the road.

Fitz said, "Sure thing, but first, let me give you a quick tour of my little enterprise." We accepted and headed for the elevator. Fitz said, "Whoa, not so fast; this way." We turned as he was walking toward one of the floor-to-ceiling wood panels that covered the walls of the conference table alcove. There were pictures and commendation certificates, medals and awards hung in that area, but what drew your attention was the wide-brimmed black Stetson Cavalry officer's hat hanging on a hat rack, gold braid and all. When we got closer, we could see the 7th Cavalry insignia on it. Behind it on the wall was a black-and-white photograph of a bunch of guys standing in front of an old UH-1, and in the middle was a young Fitz, wearing the same hat. The caption at the bottom read "7th Air Cavalry, Viet Nam 1969." As Fitz approached the wall, a panel slid open, and the interior of another elevator presented itself.

Dimitri leaned over and said, "This just keeps getting better and better."

Fitz heard him and turned and said, "Just wait; you ain't seen nothing yet!" He punched in a code on the keypad in the elevator; the door slid shut, and we started down. Three, two, one showed up on the display, but we didn't stop and continued down until an X appeared on the display and the door slid open to a soft electronic chime.

We exited into a sterile looking corridor with a large impressive looking steel door at the far end. Surveillance cameras were strategically placed to cover the entire corridor. Fitz led the way down the corridor and slid a card into a slot on the wall next to the imposing door. A panel opened, and he leaned forward and placed his eye against an eyepiece that had appeared. The door unlocked with a heavy thunk, and Fitz pushed it open. It looked to be about four inches thick and, as we entered the new area, he said, "Bomb proof." I could only gawk at the door and the space we entered. You couldn't call it a room because it was huge, I mean freaking huge! Probably 15-foot ceilings, no side or end walls in sight. Technicians in white lab coats, electronic gear, computers and all kinds of stuff I had no name for filled my view and created a subdued hum in the surrounding air. "Since my Company is working on several sensitive DOD projects a high level of security is necessary, hence my underground lab area" Fitz said. "We wouldn't want prying eyes to get hold of our research."

As we moved further into the room and got a good look at our surroundings, I heard Joe speak for the first time since our meeting had started. With a huge grin on his face, he said, "Now this is more like it!"

CHAPTER FIVE

The tour lasted the better part of an hour and a half, and it was amazing. I now found out what Fitz had been doing since we last spoke. In a nutshell, he had purchased this old airfield before he finished up his time in the guard, and while he was working on his master's degree in Aeronautical Engineering. During his time in school, he took some theoretical physics classes beyond what was required for his degree and became friends with some guys who were actual physics majors. After graduating, he started a small Aeronautical R and D company in the hangars on the airfield. He had an idea for a new rotor shape for helicopters that would increase efficiency, was lighter weight, stronger and could produce more lift. He got a patent on it and then sold it to the DOD for a shit-house full of money, well into the seven figures. The thing was, during the time of development he had come up with an even better design, solving the same problems, with even more efficiency, but kept that design to himself.

With the money he made from the DOD, he invested into expanding his company and bringing on board some of the brightest hot shots he had met in college from both the aeronautical and physics programs. The company had grown exponentially and now was doing all kinds of R and D work for the military and the private sector. That further explained the big fence and security guards. Fitz had always been a big fan of Kelly Johnson and his Skunk Works at Lockheed Martin, of U2 and SR 71 fame, so he started his own right here in Bithlo. He called it the "Skunk Works II" and by his account had some cool projects going on. Hell, he even had his own skunk logo. That part was still off-limits to us for now. We found out that the big research facility we had gone through was built underneath two of the hangars at the field.

In the hangars above, he kept the company helicopters, machine shop, airframe and avionics shops, and his Steerman Bi-Plane. He had restored it himself and flew as often as he had time to. We took another elevator up and came out into the second hangar above and he said, "I've got one more thing you need to see before you leave." We all jumped in one of those multi-person golf carts he had parked in the hangar. Fitz grabbed a handheld radio from its charger attached to the wall and called the tower. "This is Fitzsimmons requesting permission to cross taxiway L-1 and runway 2- 9'er."

"Roger that *Raven* 1, taxiway is clear and there are no aircraft in the pattern. You are cleared to cross, Colonel."

"Affirmative, *Raven* 1 clear."

I looked at him and said, "*Raven* 1?"

He smiled and said, "You'll see." We crossed the taxiway and runway, pulled up to a large rundown looking hangar, and stopped at the small door going in. Fitz did his card swipe, eyeball thing again and the door unlocked. Walking into the dark hangar from the bright sunlight outside blinded us all until the big overhead lights came on. Before me sat what I thought at first was a beautifully restored black and grey Bell Huey UH-1 copter, Viet Nam era. But on closer inspection, something was wrong; no, not wrong, but different about it. For one, it had two sets of three rotors stacked, instead of the normal two or three rotor blade systems, and I swore there were two turbine engine pods on top, smaller but distinctive.

Then I noticed the absence of a tail rotor. The new configuration was a shorter tail than the old UH-1's, and it had a pair of stubby wings just in front of what looked to be a pusher prop attached to the rear. There were other fuselage changes. Some looked like the angled exterior panels of an F-117 Stealth Fighter. This was not your everyday Bell UH-1.

Fitz walked over to us and said, "Gentlemen, I'd like you to meet the *Raven*."

I said, "Fitz, I thought at first you had restored a bird like the one you flew in Nam."

He chuckled, "I only wish I had had this baby there. No, she's a one of a kind prototype built by me and the boys at the Skunk Works."

Upon looking closer, several things jumped out at me, but I said, "Two turbines?"

"Yep, 1,800 shaft horsepower each, thanks to some major proprietary modifications by my engine guys. Running through a special transmission designed and built by the Skunk Works boys for the counter-rotating rotors. She's faster than an Apache or Gazelle, has a faster climb rate fully loaded, and a 27,000-foot operational ceiling."

"No shit… how fast?" I asked disbelievingly.

"I've had her to about 305 mph but didn't have the hammer all the way down. I figure she's good to 350 or so." Now, I gaped. "Yeah and we're not done yet! She's still got a few bugs to be worked out. I need to quiet her down some more. Turbine and rotor noise is still a little more than I want."

"So, you're building a stealth helicopter."

"Not exactly, but I want it quieter."

Joe piped up, "Fuselage mounted transducers, sending out a 180 degree out-of-phase return signal?"

Fitz looked at him quizzically. "You know something about acoustics?"

I answered for Joe, "Yeah, Joe's kind of an acoustic savant. Did some work for the DOD in their acoustic weapons research division."

"Really?" Fitz said. "My guys have been talking about a system like that but haven't been able to come up with a transducer design that could handle the job."

Joe said, "Maybe I could look at what they've done and offer them some suggestions."

"I think I could arrange that, thanks," Fitz said.

Before anyone could speak again, Fitz's radio squawked, "*Raven* 1, you have an urgent call on line 3."

Fitz keyed his radio, "Roger that; I'll be back in the office in 5."

"Affirmative *Raven* 1; just so you know Sir, it's the Pentagon."

"Roger that." Fitz headed for the door. "Sorry, boys, duty calls. We'll continue the tour another time."

Dimitri said, "You mean there's more?"

As the door closed and Fitz got into the golf cart, he smiled and said, "Oh, yeah… There's more!" He dropped us off out in front of the main building, collected our badges, and with a wave said he would be in touch in a few days as he disappeared inside. We stood there dazed, from what we had just seen and what we had accomplished.

As we walked to the vehicle, no one spoke. We were ten miles down the road before Dimitri said, somewhat in awe, "Who was that guy?"

I grinned and began the story. "Fitz is a character I've known for over 30 years, a retired Army pilot, Ranger, now an entrepreneur. Before he retired, they assigned him to SOCOM at MacDill. He flew for the Delta boys and with the Nighthawks.

After he retired he did contract flying for them and others, the dicey off the books stuff. So, trust me when I say he's been there and done that… and they don't make a T-shirt for it! I guarantee you can trust him with your life, and you don't want him as an enemy!" The rest of the ride home was done in contemplative silence. We were all bursting with excitement at the prospect of our aerial search, but more than that, the potential addition to Risky Business had our minds swirling with possibilities and questions.

When we got back, we let the rest of the guys know we had been successful and, in a few days, we could do our aerial search. The excitement level ratcheted up a notch or two, and we agreed to meet in two days at the boat. It had been an exhausting day. By the time I got home, all I wanted to do was crash, but my mind had other ideas, so I lay on my bed fully clothed and let the information in my head run its course. This was a roller coaster ride, and right now we were on the big downhill, accelerating faster and faster. Things were happening so quickly I was having trouble trying to get a handle on them all and put them in some kind of order, which I felt desperately I needed to do. I had a boat; I had a team; we had a target; our resources had just gotten a major shot in the arm with Fitz's aerial support, and by God, we were going treasure hunting! With that final thought, I dozed off and didn't wake till the next morning, still fully dressed.

The next few days were filled with mundane chores at home and on the boat in anticipation of Fitz's call. In the meantime, Doc Greene had left for Washington D.C. to attend a meeting at the National Archives; Nils and his wife had headed up to North Carolina to deliver a load of boat props to a client, and Tony was neck deep in following up on a Cyber-attack on one of his Fortune 500 client's computing systems. Since Dimitri was still working, more or less, that left Joe, Lawrence, and me with some free time, some of which we spent together at the Corporate Bar.

One hot Florida afternoon, we met for a cool beverage and to catch up on research that Lawrence had been doing on salvage beyond the three-mile limit since our search area would be between five and six and a half miles offshore to start. We ordered our drinks from Mitch and jumped into discussion. Lawrence informed us he had some good news and some not so good news... "Okay, what's the good news?" I asked.

"First off," he said, "we don't have to give the state of Florida shit! We're in Federal waters so the state statute on treasure recovery does not apply." We agreed that was good news; now what about the not so good? He continued, "Because we are in Federal waters, we have to go by Admiralty Law to place a claim on our search area. That means we would have to go through Federal court to get our claim legalized. If we didn't and found something and then left the site for whatever reason, someone else could move in and work it. We would have no legal recourse in the claim jumping. Going through the Federal legal claim system could take two to three months."

"Crap," I said, "that is bad news."

He continued, "We can't legally look for anything till we file the paperwork."

"That complicates things," I said. "Even if we started our search illegally and found something there's no way we could spend 24 hours, seven days a week on site till the red tape was taken care of."

Lawrence said, "Well, that's the only way you can protect and maintain a claim on what you've found; stay anchored to the site until you can file Federal papers and get salvage rights approved."

Damn, if we found something, and that's a big if, we would have to come up with a way to protect it when we had to leave until all the paperwork got final approval. Now there was a problem that would require a creative solution. Our drinks arrived, and we spent more time in our own worlds, pondering this new dilemma.

I said, "We'll just have to cross that bridge when, and if we come to it." We agreed, and I asked Lawrence to let the rest of the guys know what he had found out as soon as he could. We spent the rest of the afternoon looking at the boats tied up in the marina slips and sipping frosty cold beverages. Two days later, I got the phone call from Fitz.

We were to meet him at Merritt Island Airport at 0900 hrs. the next day. Dimitri took off work, and Joe, Lawrence, and I all met at the airport at 0800. At 0900 hours sharp, a nice-looking Bell Jet Ranger with the Acme Corporation logo emblazoned on its side landed. As the rotors spun down, we walked out on the tarmac to meet Fitz. He was talking to the guy that had pulled up in the refueling truck.

When he finished, he came over to us and said, "Top o' the morning to you, gentlemen." We all greeted Fitz, and I introduced Lawrence. Greetings completed, we headed to the chopper, just as the co-pilot's door swung open and the woman from the reception desk climbed out. Dimitri stumbled when he saw her, and Lawrence's jaw dropped a couple of inches.

I said, "Fitz… the receptionist?"

He laughed and said, "She doesn't spend all her time behind the desk; that's Shannon O'Reilly, one of my best operatives and one hell of a pilot."

I looked at him and said, "Really?"

"Yep, stole her away from one of those alphabet soup organizations as you call them, about three years ago. She'll be flying co-pilot today. I would give you the honor, but she's a lot better looking than you. Besides, she can actually fly this bird if she has to."

"No argument from me," I said. Fitz and I watched as Dimitri and Lawrence made a beeline for her.

He chuckled. "Those boys had better watch themselves, or she'll eat them up and spit them out before they know what's happened."

"That tough, huh?"

"You better believe it; she's as tough as nails and can be as ornery as a rattlesnake that's just had its tail stepped on, and just as deadly." I heard Joe chuckle behind me. Damn, first impressions can be deceiving! O'Reilly had just given me a whole new level of respect for receptionists! As we got to the bird, I herded Dimitri and Lawrence away from our co-pilot and into the passenger's compartment as Fitz settled up with the guy in the fuel truck. Within ten minutes, we were in a low hover over the runway and cleared for take-off. Fitz came on over the headsets, "Okay Colt, where we headed?"

I leaned forward and handed O'Reilly a piece of paper with the GPS coordinates on it. She took it and entered it into the navigation system as we rose and headed eastward down the runway. Once we broke out over the Banana River, we started a serious climb and turned north. Within minutes, we cleared the beaches, and I heard the turbine winding up as we gained altitude and speed. We had the doors open on both sides, and the view was impressive. The blue- green Atlantic rushing by below, sun glinting off its surface, salt air filling the cabin; it was a very smooth and enjoyable ride, if short.

In about fifteen minutes, Shannon came over the Coms, "Dr. Burnett, we're approaching the coordinates."

"Great, when we get there, can we go into a hover so we can get our visual bearings?"

"Roger that," she replied. In another couple of minutes, we were hovering about 500 feet over our destination. There was minimal chop, so bottom visibility, even from this altitude, wasn't too bad. Binoculars and video cameras came out of our bags as we positioned two people in each door, Joe and I on the port side and Dimitri and Lawrence, the starboard. We did a quick orientation scan and then asked Fitz to take it down to 250 feet. We maintained the hover but slowly descended.

He came back saying, "I'm in a due north hover, port side is facing due west."

"Roger that," I said. "Can you crab to the west and let's see if we can find the shoals?"

He said, "Love to." The chopper started a westward crab at 150 feet. We scanned the waters for the next five minutes to no avail.

"Take us north about a mile and then back west." Again, we made the maneuver, and as we started our westward course, we spotted the shoal. "Okay, hold it here for a minute." We stopped and hung motionless. "Take us to the southernmost end of the shoal and then run parallel to it for its entire length and can you get us down to about 100 feet?" Again, the chopper moved in a smooth arc and when we got to the end of the shoal, turned again descended and made its run northward. We had been video-taping the whole run, but nothing jumped out at us. I moved forward to talk to Fitz, and when I leaned into the cockpit, he was sitting there with his arms crossed and head laid back, resting peacefully. I looked at Shannon and realized she was the one doing the flying.

Fitz sat up and looked at me and said, "Told you."

"No shit!" Then I spoke to them both, "Take us back to our starting point and do a straight line north to a mile beyond the shoal, come about, and do a run to the southern end of the shoal about 100 yards west of our first track. Keep the back and forth up till we get about six miles west of the shoal."

Fitz looked at me, and then at Shannon, who replied, "Roger that," and banked to our new heading. I moved back and told the guys what the plan was, so keep their eyes open and video cams running. In two minutes, Shannon came across the Com channel, "Starting our run now." And so, for the next hour, we covered most of the identified search area, spotting several dark spots on the bottom and marking them with the camera's built-in GPS and our handheld units for later investigation. Shannon called the search area covered; we had been in the air for almost two hours.

I said that should do for our first outing and we could head back anytime. The whine from the turbine increased as we gained altitude and speed heading back to the airfield. After landing, I invited Fitz and Shannon to join us for a beverage and a little debriefing. They accepted, and we adjourned to the Corporate Bar.

When we got there, I asked Mitch if we could use the small dining room (our conference room). She said sure and led the way. As Dimitri and Lawrence jockeyed to see who would get the seat next to Shannon, Mitch took our drink orders. When she got to Fitz, he ordered, "A double Dewar's on the rocks and for Ms. O'Reilly, a sweet tea with lemon."

She looked at him and said, "You know I hate sweet tea."

He laughed and said, "You're in the South now, O'Reilly, so when in the South do as the Southerners."

She snorted, "Bullshit," and then to Mitch said, "Unsweetened tea, no lemon."

"He laughed and said, "Ugghhh, undrinkable."

She replied, "Well, I am driving!" That got a chuckle from all of us.

In the next hour and a half, we discussed the day's search. While not extensive, we did at least cover the area within the circle of Tony's computer model and were able to shoot video of the shoal. I felt pretty good. Having Fitz and his crew on board with us would make a hell of a difference.

On our drive back to the airport, Fitz said, "Give your computer guy my number and tell him to call me in a day or two. We will send him our data as soon as we get it downloaded from the bird."

I said, "What data?"

"Oh, didn't I tell you? While we flew the search patterns, we were recording the sea bottom with a neat little gizmo the boys in the lab came up with last year. It's kind of like LiDAR for water."

"What?" I said.

"Yeah, you know LiDAR, right?"

"Yes," I replied. "Light detection and ranging, uses a laser and stuff. I'm familiar with LiDAR, but for land, not water?"

He nodded "My boys have come up with something new. This is cutting-edge stuff. NOAA is sniffing around, and the military has recently taken an interest. It takes the LiDAR concept to a whole new level by making the water invisible. Good to about 70 feet for now. It then gives us a high-definition image of the bottom and whatever is lying around. I won't bother to try to explain the science behind it. It's proprietary and classified. Just be ready for some nice 3D images of the bottom and what's lying around down there. It will be better than any side scan sonar image we could have gotten."

I said, "Wait a minute, you tell us this now…! After we sat back there shooting hand-held digital video, you come up with this space-age imaging. That makes what we did look like stone axes and flint knives! Why didn't you tell us about this earlier and we could have just flown the pattern using your stuff?"

"Well, I didn't want you to feel useless; after all, it's your company."

"Damn it, Fitz, from now on could you be a little more forthcoming with your toys, their capabilities, and availability? I have a feeling it will save us a lot of time and effort!" I could see his grinning face reflected off the windshield of the bird.

Without turning, he said, "Sure thing, Bucko, whatever you say."

We dropped them off and watched the Jet Ranger fade into the distance. Joe broke the silence, "That guy is one hell of a trip."

"Yeah," Dimitri replied, "and he's got one hell of a co-pilot." I shook my head as we headed to the vehicles, these guys. I held my excitement in check on the drive home, but all I could think of was that with what we already had in place, and now Fitz's resources, we might have a real chance of finding this mystery ship and unlocking its secrets after all! Hot Damn!

CHAPTER SIX

I contacted Tony with Fitz's information, and true to his word, got a call from him two days later saying they had sent the data. Within thirty minutes, an excited Tony called me, saying he had gotten the data and holy crap, I had to get over there to see it. It was "way cool." As I drove to his house, I came up with a plan, sort of. Over the past few months, when weather permitted, we had been towing the mag behind the *Lisa B* in the Banana River, getting a feel for operational handling. The controller that came with the mag was a series of LEDs that lit up when it detected an anomaly. The more-LEDs lit, the stronger the signal; it was okay but not optimal. Its box had a USB port, so it could connect to a computer.

Software was available, but Tony didn't care for it, so he wrote his own program that took the data coming from the fish and plotted it in a three-dimensional grid with depth, signal strength in a numerical readout from one to ten and exact GPS location of the hit. It saved all the data it received from the fish to the hard drive of a laptop for later retrieval and analysis. Then we could print everything out and compare it to chart information. That made it much easier for us to return to the precise location of the anomaly after completing a full sweep of an area.

We had gotten good at working with it, thanks to all the pieces of pipe and metal junk Nils had provided us for bottom targets. We tied a line and float to the objects, both large and small, and made passes over them, and from the computed data, learned how to figure approximate physical size, location, and depth. This was when Nils got the nickname, "Junkyard." He had an unending supply of "stuff" that we could use for targets. We burned a fair amount of fuel but were happy with the results. We now felt confident we could take her out to sea and be productive. School was dismissed; it was time to get serious!

I thought now with Fitz's data and our video footage, once we reviewed it, we were ready to move to the hunting phase of this operation... at last! When I got to Tony's place, he was as excited as a kid on Christmas morning. "Colt, this is great," he said. "It's so cool; check this out." He had the big 70-inch screen in place and displayed on it was a view of the shoal in such detail it was breathtaking. I couldn't believe what I was seeing; it was as if someone had drained the ocean, revealing the bottom and its contours in high definition.

"Damn," I said, "that will beat anything our video gives us."

Tony said, "Well, yeah!"

Stone axes and flint knives, I thought. I asked Tony if we could manipulate the image.

"Heck, yeah, watch this," and he touched the screen and zoomed in on a specific section of the shoal. It was amazing. I could see individual outcroppings and rocks laying on the bottom all in fantastic detail. Tony went on, "And we can watch the entire thing like a video or stop it at any place and zoom in for a closer look and shift the perspective, so we are almost looking at it from the side." As he was speaking, he went through everything he was describing on the screen. He said, "But wait, there's more!" He had downloaded our video footage into his computer and now pulled it up on the screen, above Fitz's data. I could sync both images based on the GPS data so we could run them together and have a view from the surface and below."

"Now that was slick," I said. I had him run the data and video for the shoal. Beautiful pictures, but except for some junk scattered around, there wasn't anything that resembled the wreck of a Spanish galleon. Well, I thought, it was over 300 years ago. I said, "Let's call a meeting for tonight, and we can go over all the footage." Tony agreed and said he'd contact Nils AKA "Junkyard" and Lawrence.

"I'll contact the rest, and we'll meet here at 7."

If our level of enthusiasm and excitement was high before, this meeting pegged the excitement meter! When we gathered that evening, we went straight into the data; no one hit the beer fridge or the grog locker first. That was unheard of in the annals of "Risky Business." However, what we saw kept our minds off drinking for a while. Tony explained that Fitz had set us up with a secure data link, encrypted. There was no way our data or communications could be monitored. He had said he felt better having it that way. We were all impressed. I guess we will have to call him Santa with all the presents he was providing.

As we went over the shoal data and video, it impressed the guys as much as Tony and I had been when we first saw it. From there we moved to the search footage from our search pattern. Unbelievable is the only word I could think to describe it. We could identify what remained of at least four small boats on the bottom along with more "space junk," probably old booster parts from the early days of the Cape launches and one larger vessel that looked to be a trawler around 75 feet long lying on its side. There were a few more anomalies we couldn't identify that will require closer investigation.

After an hour and a half of viewing we took a break. It was time for a round of cold beverages. As we sat and talked about what we had just viewed, Dimitri spoke up, "I'm thinking we need to dive on those things we saw on the bottom. If they look promising, we can run the mag across the area and see what we get. I'm ready to get wet!"

Doc agreed. "We've done a lot of research over these past months. I think it's time to see if any of it will pay off. I'm with you, Dimitri; time to blow bubbles!" A chorus of assents sealed the deal.

I spoke up then and said, "Agree, but I would like to start with the shoal and see if that gives us any clues. We should either confirm or eliminate it as the place where the longboat sank, if possible. If it was, it would help us in determining which of the targets we have seen on the bottom would be a good starting place to look for the ship. Besides, it's shallower diving for starters, and we could use the handheld detector instead of having to drag the mag." There was a lot of discussion on this topic; I knew the guys were itching to get in the water, but I felt that we needed to clear up the question about the shoal first. Was it where the boat sank or not? If we found nothing, then we may have to rethink our whole search area, despite what our computer model was telling us. I convinced the guys to think on it for a day or two, and we would meet again and come up with a decision. All agreed, and in the meantime, we needed to keep close tabs on the weather for planning because, one way or another, we were hitting the water.

The next day I called Fitz and let him in on our plan.

"I'm glad you're happy with the data. I was pleased when I reviewed it here." I asked if his new gizmo had a name and he replied, "For now, we're just calling it Neptune. I'm sure that will change."

I said, "Well, it will revolutionize underwater research."

"Yep, that's what we do," he said with a laugh. "So, you're going to hit the water?"

I said, "Yeah the guys are chomping at the bit to get in

and start working. We'll take our underwater metal detector, and I hope to work the shoal region first."

"That's a big area to scope out with one detector," Fitz said.

"I know, but that's all we have for now."

There was a pause, and Fitz asked, "You going to be home tomorrow around 3:00?"

I said, "Yes."

"Good, I'm going to send you a present."

"A present," I queried?

"Yeah, consider it part of my investment in Risky Business," he said with a laugh.

"What are you talking about?" I asked.

"You'll see tomorrow; gotta run. Talk with you later." And that was it. Damn Fitz, he had turned into the most enigmatic SOB that I knew, but then I thought, maybe he was Santa after all.

At 2:59 the next day, there was a knock at my door. When I answered, three guys were standing there in Acme Corp. windbreakers, carrying two large and one medium-sized duffel bags. The lead guy spoke, "Dr. Burnett?"

"Yes," I said.

"May we come in?" I stepped back to let them in, and they deposited the bags on the floor. "These are compliments of Colonel Fitzsimmons; he wished you good luck." As I was about to ask some questions, they turned and walked back out the door with a, "Have a good day Sir."

I watched them walk to the dark blue Suburban with dark tinted windows. There was another guy standing next to the vehicle with what looked like a compact assault rifle hanging under his windbreaker; all were wearing dark sunglasses. I thought, what the hell…? They got in their vehicle and pulled out of the driveway as I stood in the open doorway. Damn, this is getting more interesting by the day! I closed the door and turned my attention to the bags on the floor. In the two larger ones, there were three-LAR V Draeger re-breathers with full face masks and Com-links built in. Holy Shit...in the last bag there was a compact Com control unit that was the shipboard station to communicate with the divers while underwater. Son of a bitch, I thought; this is incredible. I then noticed the folded piece of paper lying on top of a brown paper bag. I opened the paper and recognized Fitz's handwriting.

"Colt thought these might come in handy for your shallow water work. They are courtesy of my buddies at SOCOM...don't break them; I may have to give them back! Good Luck, Fitz." Then a P.S., "Oh, by the way, buy yourselves a couple more underwater detectors. I hate to see people wasting their time just because they don't have enough equipment. I guess I'll accept your offer to join your quest, so just consider this part of my investment in Risky Business." I reached into the duffel and pulled out the brown paper bag. Inside, all neatly wrapped, were ten stacks of 100-dollar bills, 5,000 dollars each! I dropped to my couch in disbelief. That was 50 thousand dollars... Shit, there is a Santa!

I called the guys and gave them the news. They were as dumbfounded as I had been at first, but it didn't take long for them to figure out ways to spend the money. We had been working on a limited budget for a while now. We weren't broke; we just didn't have a significant quantity of cash to throw into the business, so we had been monitoring our purchases closely. As of today, all that changed, and Dimitri was first to head out to buy three more underwater detectors at around a thousand dollars apiece. Tony spent money on computer/satellite up and down-link stuff for the boat. Junkyard suggested a good radar system and went shopping. I played First National Bank, handing out cash like it was candy, but it felt good.

We had to be careful about spending the money. We didn't want to draw attention to our newfound wealth. We spread our purchases around between us and made a few on-line. At one meeting we decided that since we would be working in international waters, we should have some means of self-defense. The addition of firearms had become a priority for us. We had each been researching them based on personal taste. A shark gun was mandatory since we would have divers in the water. So, for starters, a 12-gauge Mossberg Mariner pump shotgun was put on the list. 2 CAR 15's were added, a 30.06 with scope, and Dimitri said we must have a Barrett model 82 A1 50 caliber sniper rifle with a scope.

I said, "A what? What in the freaking hell do we need a sniper rifle for?" He looked at me, straight-faced and said, "Zombies."

I stared at him... How can you argue with that...?

The night before our first venture out, we met to go over final details. The weather looked good, boat was fueled, all electronics were working, and we had all been checked out on the new re-breathers in Dimitri's pool. The military instruction manuals that came with them were straightforward. They even had pictures! Once we were done, we felt we were ready to go. The Coms worked great and spirits were running high. It was agreed that the shoals would be our first dive. It would be a shallow dive around 20 to 25 feet max, shallower on the shoal itself. We could continue to familiarize ourselves with all the new gear and get comfortable with it before going to deeper water. I decided we would put three divers in the water, Dimitri, Tony, and Doc. Lawrence, Joe, and I would stay on board.

It took about an hour and a half to clear the locks at the port and get to the shoals. We made our way to the GPS coordinates we had recorded at the southernmost end of the shoal and prepared to put divers over the side. The atmosphere was electric with excitement and anticipation. The sun was brilliant, the sky crystalline blue, and the salt air invigorating, so with a thumbs up, all three divers hit the water and disappeared below the surface. It had begun.

At ten feet, we did a Com check; everyone was loud and clear. As they descended, a running commentary began. When they reached the bottom, they had about 8 to 12-foot visibility and a slight northerly current. This worked to our benefit since we were starting at the southern end of the shoal and working north. Two detectors were sent down with the team; the third person would be on the watch for any gray-finned surprises.

We listened intently as the divers worked their way north. They reported sandy bottom, some odds and ends of junk lying around, a few hits with the detectors but nothing of any real interest. After an hour, I called the dive. We had moved the *Lisa B* north, following the divers' progress. They had covered about a quarter of the shoal's length when they surfaced. Ugly clouds were building, and it looked like bad weather was moving our way. We packed it in for the day and headed back to port. We made it through the locks when the storm hit. Perfect timing; 20 minutes later, we were pulling up behind Tony's house in the pouring rain.

We secured the boat and had already stowed the Coms and computer we had out. The dive gear had been on deck, and the rain had rinsed the salt-water off, so there was nothing much to do but get out of the weather in Tony's place and do a quick debrief. It only lasted fifteen minutes, and then a time was set for the next day to meet and cover things more in depth. Not a bad trip, I thought on the way home. No major discoveries, but I had expected none. What I liked was there were no real problems with the dive equipment or vessel. We had passed our first test with flying colors, something to celebrate.

When I got home, it was still storming, wind blowing and raining hard. I got into the house and pulled off my wet T-shirt and shorts and hit the shower. The rain had chilled me, but the warm water soon took care of that. Getting out and throwing on a pair of shorts, I padded into the kitchen, grabbed a glass, filled it with ice, and poured myself a nice stiff Beam and Ginger. I moved into the living room and flopped down on the couch. I have to admit; I was pleased with myself. The plan was coming together; the guys did great, and we had made our first dive with no problems. I laid my head back and relaxed as the drink did its job. Not bad, Colt, not bad at all.

Tomorrow, we would meet, go over the details of today's dive, and plan our next trip to the shoals. Who knows? We may even find treasure. Ha, I thought, I'll show you Dimitri, treasure hunting my ass! About ten minutes later, the phone rang, and Fitz was on the other line.

"Well, how did it go?" he asked.

"Pretty good," I replied. "No problems at all and thanks for the presents, all of them."

"Good to hear and glad to help out," he replied. "So, you got all the stuff and my note?"

"Yes, I did; that really helps us out, much appreciated."

"Excellent, yeah, I gave your offer some serious thought and realized I haven't had anything close to a vacation in over five years, so spending time helping out in your endeavor might be a nice break from time to time. And that's my only caveat. I'll gladly help out on the resource end of things and get away when I can, but my main focus has to be my business, at least for now. I hope that's not a problem."

"Not at all," I said, "any support or help you can give us will be appreciated, and you're welcome to drop by anytime."

"Great, then I guess we're treasure hunting partners!"

"That we are," I said, and with that, we hung up.

The next few dives on the shoal went about like the first, good dives but nothing of any significance was found. We were over halfway along the length of the shoal on this our tenth dive. We had picked up visitors on our last dive, five six- to seven-foot nurse sharks and two black tips, just something for us to keep our eye on. It had been three weeks since we began, and we were getting into a real routine. Divers had been in the water for about ten minutes when Joe called me into the wheelhouse. I turned the Coms set-up on deck behind the wheelhouse over to Lawrence and went inside. "What's up?" I said.

"Probably nothing, but check this out," Joe said as he pointed to the radar screen. A small blip appeared about a mile and a half away and to our west.

I said "So?"

Joe said, on our last trip, he had spotted a vessel in the same area, and when we fired up to leave, it had left. "Could be a fisherman," I said.

"Yeah," Joe responded. "I thought so too until I went back on the computer and checked the stored radar data from our previous runs out here. The bogie appeared on our third trip out, same location and same pattern; we leave, and he leaves."

Now that got my interest. "Hmm," I said, "you think he's following us?"

"Could be," Joe said.

It was a clear day, so I grabbed the large pair of Bushnell's we had hanging in the wheelhouse and stepped outside for a look. Sure enough, after a few minutes of scanning, I spotted our bogie. It looked like a fishing boat from where I was. I went back inside and reported to Joe. "Are you sure it's the same boat?"

He nodded. "I would bet money on it"! We hadn't disguised our actions except for putting our divers over the side with the wheelhouse between them and shore. If someone was watching us, they wouldn't have seen them enter or exit the water. Plus, they geared up and took off their gear in the cover of the wheelhouse. Their wetsuits were taken off before roaming around the deck. This is strange, I thought.

I was rolling this new development around in my head as I looked at the radar screen when Lawrence hollered for me to come there. I said to Joe, "Keep an eye on them."

"You got it, boss."

When I got to the table where the Coms had been set up,

Lawrence keyed the mike and said, "Dimitri, repeat your message. Colt is here."

I heard Dimitri's voice, "I may have found something."

I grabbed the mike and keyed it, "Say again."

Dimitri said, "I'm on my way up." Within a few minutes, Dimitri broke the surface on the seaward side of the boat. As he swam to the dive ladder, I saw he had something in his hand. We helped him aboard, and he handed me an encrusted piece of rusty metal.

"This looks like an oar-lock and a good-sized one at that."

He agreed and said his detector picked it up right at the edge of the base of the shoal about ten inches deep in the sand. The whole crew had gathered around me as we examined the find when the radio came to life with Tony's voice.

"Holy Shit, Holy Shit, Holy Shit."

We all made a dash for the table. Joe, getting there first, grabbed the mike and said, "Tony, are you all right? Is everybody all right?"

There was a pause and then another extended, "Holy Shit."

Doc's voice came on next. "We're coming up." Something in his voice sent chills up my spine. We all rushed to the dive ladder and waited. They broke the surface about ten yards from the boat and with BC's inflated made their way to the ladder. As they got there, I could see the huge grins on their faces through their masks. My first thought was, thank God they are okay. As they got to the dive ladder, in unison, they raised one hand, palm up, and in each were small bars about four inches long and a couple of inches wide with the unmistakable glint of gold!

CHAPTER SEVEN

It was my turn then. "Holy Shit," I said.

Doc said, looking up at me, "We found it, Colt; we found it!" As the four of us stood there in stunned silence, eyes wide and mouths agape, Doc said, "You should see your faces; if only I had a camera."

"How about a little help here, guys?" That was enough to break the spell, and we quickly helped Doc and Tony aboard. There was so much adrenaline pumping, we practically yanked them and their gear out of the water and onto the deck. Before removing their re-breathers, they deflated their BCs and then reached into the pockets. They normally contained the bags of lead BBs that helped compensate for the buoyancy of their bodies and gear in the water. Instead, they pulled out more gold bars. We were all speechless as we looked on. They laid the bars on the deck and then removed the rest of their gear.

After they had stripped out of their wetsuits, we handed them towels and after staring at the pile of gold bars again walked around to the rear deck where we had chairs and the table for the Coms. We passed around bottles of water, and then I said, "Okay, tell us everything."

Doc looked at Tony and said, "Go ahead, kid; you're the one that found them," and Tony began his story.

They were working their way along the base of the shoal using the detectors and heard Dimitri's message to us. He had shown them the oar-lock before heading up. After he left, they continued their search with Tony right next to the base of the shoal and Doc a few feet further out. Tony had gotten a hit, not very strong, but he wanted to check it out. He fanned the sand next to the wall away with his hand and uncovered an indentation in the rock.

As he continued, the indentation got larger and went further back under the rock of the shoal base. He had cleared enough to stick his detector in and got a strong reading. He dug with his hands and opened the depression even more. Doc had seen what was happening and came over to help. In a few minutes they had cleared about a foot and a half of sand from under the rock and uncovered a rock overhang. As the sand settled, Tony stuck his detector under the ledge and into the hole they had cleared. It went nuts and almost pegged the needle on the gold scale. Doc saw that, and they began digging vigorously. In a few minutes their gloved hands uncovered broken pieces of wood, and as they pulled them out, they could tell they had been part of a box. As they kept digging, they finally uncovered one last large piece, and pulling it out of the way, they saw row upon row of gold bars.

I burst out laughing and said, "I'll bet that was the Holy Shit moment." Tony just grinned.

Doc said, "We were so excited. We pulled the bars out and stacked them next to the hole. We realized as we removed them there was another layer of bars underneath the first, so this is only part of one layer. There's a hell of a lot more."

Our minds were racing now, and everyone tried to talk at once. I let them go. After a few minutes the discussions died down, and I said, "We came out here on a search mission that has now turned into a recovery mission, and we're not prepared for that today."

"Yeah," Joe said, "but we can't leave the gold down there. What about that boat?"

Dimitri immediately said, "What boat?"

Joe filled the rest of the guys in on what he had found out and told me. Dimitri got up and grabbed the Bushnell's and scanned the horizon.

"Sit down," I said. "If we are being watched, the last thing we want is whoever it is to know we know."

He complied, and then more covertly scanned again. "Got 'em," he said, "about a mile away, maybe a 30-to-40 foot fishing boat, looks like."

"Yep," we said, "that's them."

"Can't tell much from this distance, so they're just anchored and have been there the last three times we've come out?" Dimitri asked.

Joe replied, "Yep as far as I can tell, it's been them."

Lawrence and Junkyard chimed in, "Who the hell do you think they are?"

I shook my head. "Don't know. That's what we need to find out, but first, let's get back to the gold." It became clear to all of us we had major problems on our hands. The kind that needed to be dealt with right away.

I said "Okay, Tony, Doc, feel like hitting the water again?"

Doc said, "Hell, yeah."

Tony replied, "How about I stay on board and let one of the other divers take my place? I've got an idea how to identify the mystery boat."

I agreed and said, "Dimitri, you're up." As he and Doc suited up behind the wheelhouse, I said, "Junkyard, Lawrence, which one of you wants to be the floater and man the recovery lifts?" Junkyard volunteered, and Lawrence said he would man the

Coms. I turned to Joe, "We still have those small recovery lifts on board?"

He said, "Yep, we have three."

"Great, grab a scuba tank and regulator. Dimitri, take it down with you and use it to fill the lifts. Junkyard, when they hit the surface, bring them to the side of the boat, and Joe and I will lift them aboard and you can re-deploy them if necessary." While I had everyone's attention, I said, "Remember, they may be watching us. So, everyone slow and easy, no running around, relaxed slow movements. There is no reason for excitement on this boat; take it nice and slow… business as usual." Then I added, "Just because we've all just become millionaires, there's no reason to get excited." That got a healthy laugh from everyone, and then it was down to business.

Things worked like a well-oiled machine. Dimitri informed us there were two more layers of bars to come up, 12 bars to a layer. Jesus Christ, I thought, this just keeps getting better and better. They rated the little lift bags for a 50 lb. lift, so four or five of the gold bars were the absolute limit. The bars must weigh 12 to 13 pounds each, I thought. We were all working on pure adrenaline now, no wasted motion and a nice slow pace on deck. I even had the guys bring out some beers from the "beer fridge" and place them on the table. Nobody consumed any, but it looked good.

Joe and Tony had ducked inside the air-conditioned wheel house and Tony was peering at a computer terminal in the corner. Joe came in and out, and we all walked around the deck, sitting down, getting up now and then and moving to other chairs. We hoped that our watchers, if that's what they were, were far enough away not to be able to tell we were two guys shy on the deck. After about 45 minutes I heard Dimitri calling on Coms, "Colt, you copy?"

"Got you, Dimitri; what's up?"

"We loaded the last of the bars, and guess what?"

"What?" I asked.

"There's another crate under what's left of the empty one, still sealed."

"Oh, shit." We had already recovered 36 bars. I said, "We'll have to leave it; can you cover it up, so no one will know where we've been working?"

Doc replied, "Yeah, I think we can. We'll bring up the bottom part of the empty crate and try to fill in the hole." Twenty minutes later, they both surfaced, carrying the remains of the crate with them. Luckily, it was fairly small and easily handled by one person. Once it was all aboard and the guys were unsuited, I had them come on deck one at a time every few minutes from different sides of the boat. I hoped my little deception worked.

Tony hailed me from the wheelhouse, "Got'em." I looked at the video screen in front of him. I was looking at a satellite image and asked, "Real-time?"

"Yep."

"Can we zoom in and get a closer look?" Tony got us a closer view, at an angle, and I could easily see the "mailbox" hanging on the stern and three or four people on deck. "Man, this is cool; how the hell did you do it?"

"Yeah," Tony said, this is one of the older Keyhole spy satellites, pretty much outdated technology with all the new stuff floating around up there, but still transmitting. Not sure whose signal I'm piggybacking on, but I can assure you they don't know I'm there."

As I looked at the screen, I remembered seeing that vessel in the marina we passed on our way out of the port. I said, "Okay, that's good enough for now. We can track her down in the marina later. Joe, weigh anchor and take us along the shoal about a mile and shut her down. We'll sit there for an hour and then move north again for a mile or two and repeat."

He replied, "Aye, aye, Captain," and I heard the windlass being engaged as the anchor line got reeled in.

I looked around at the guys standing on deck, and said "I think it's time we put those warm beers on the table back in the fridge and replace them with cold ones that we drink this time, what say you?" A round of laughter and, "Hell, yeahs," answered my question. We had covered the gold bars with a small tarp and then thrown rope and a boat fender on top. Perfect disguise, I thought, looked right in place with the rest of the stuff on deck. We continued our milling around the deck as we got underway, but this time with a vigor that couldn't be contained.

Tony walked out with a beer in hand and said, "You know, I've been doing a little calculating and if those bars are around 11 or 12 pounds that means we have around 390+ pounds of gold or over 6,000 ounces. On today's market, we're carrying almost 9 million dollars over there, more or less." That stunned me. I hadn't even thought about it, and from the looks on the other guys' faces, neither had they. We had been so busy retrieving it and then playing cat and mouse with our friends in the other boat, the enormity of our discovery hadn't really sunk in.

With a huge grin on his face, Dimitri said, "And there's more down there." Now, we all took a minute and caught our breath. Doc looked at me and with a raised beer said, "Colt, you've done it. You've found your treasure."

I smiled and said, "Doc, not just me. We have found OUR treasure."

He returned my smile and said, "I stand corrected: Hear, hear!" and with that took a huge swallow of beer as we all responded, "Hear, hear!" and followed his beer example.

We got to our new location and dropped anchor. Now, it was just a matter of killing time and looking busy until our next move. Joe let us know our friends had followed suit and moved with us. That confirmed it; they were tailing us, and I didn't care for that one bit. After an hour, we made our last move a mile and a half north, dropped anchor again, and had more beer. By now, it was getting later in the afternoon and clouds were forming, so we weighed anchor and turned toward home. On radar, we saw the other vessel turn and head to port at a good clip, so as not to be seen by us, we figured. We were in no big hurry, so we gave them plenty of time to "get away."

When we went through the port, we spotted our mystery vessel at the fuel dock of the marina. I got her name, the *"Carrie Ann,"* as we passed and made a mental note to do some homework on her as soon as I got the chance. When we docked, it was still daylight, so we waited and unloaded our "booty" under cover of darkness. We sat out under the tarp over the rear deck and continued our discussion of next steps. First, we had to decide where to store the gold.

Dimitri volunteered, "I have a large gun safe at home; we could store it there for now."

"How secure would it be?"

"Pretty secure," he told us. It was steel two-and-a-half inches thick and was rated at being able to withstand a house fire for an hour and a half before any damage would occur to its contents. We agreed that sounded like a good idea. One problem solved.

Next was the *Carrie Ann*. Obviously, they were treasure hunters and very interested in what we were doing. Were they guessing we were on-to something or did they know something was up? Lawrence said he couldn't believe they had any idea what was going on. He thought they probably were just fishing for leads. I had to agree with him. We had been very careful in our discussions and closed- mouthed around everyone except our immediate group. Silence reigned as everyone processed their own thoughts on the problem.

After grabbing a new beer, I asked Tony, "That thing you did with the satellite, can you do it from here as well?"

He said yes, he could.

"So," I continued, "we could keep an eye on the site when we weren't there?"

"As long as there is a bird overhead, I can probably grab a signal." It would all depend on the flyover schedules of the various satellites. But he said there were a lot of them, so odds were good we could keep an eye on it most of the time. Next problem, what to do if these guys tried to grab our spot and start working it?

Dimitri said, "Since we have no legal claim to protect us, we just have to make sure they don't do that."

"Okay, how?"

He said, "Don't worry; I'll think of something." I cringed at the thought.

Next order of business was back to the gold. How did we go about turning it into cash without drawing attention to ourselves and letting our secret out, causing who knows how much chaos in our lives? I suggested we update Fitz and see if he could help.

All agreed, and Tony jumped on the encrypted Com-link Fitz had set up for us. In two minutes, we were "virtually" sitting face to face with the colonel in his office. "Hey, Colt, what's going on?"

"Well, Fitz, I've got good news."

"Yeah?" he said…

"We found it," I replied.

"No shit," he said, "you found the ship already?"

"No, not the ship, but we found the longboat wreck site."

"And…?" he asked.

"Gold," I replied.

He let out a low whistle, "How much?"

I grinned and said, "A lot!"

"Well, hot damn, boy! You guys done good!"

"Yeah, but we've got issues we need your input on."

He said, "Shoot; I'll do what I can."

We told him of the guys who were following us, and then we talked about the gold. "Well," he said after a few minutes thought, "your claim jumper problem could get nasty. Legally you don't have much of a leg to stand on. About the only thing I could suggest is to convince them it would be in their best interest to go away and stay away. Now, how you do that is up to you. The other thing might be easier to deal with. How much gold did you say you had?" We told him, and he said, "Can't handle that much at one time, but I can help you if we take our time and break it into smaller chunks, say, about two million at a time."

"What's it going to cost us?" I asked.

He said "Probably about a buck, buck and a half. I could probably have something set up by the end of next week if you can get me the bars by tomorrow."

I said, "Give me a few minutes. We need to talk this over." He said to call him back as soon as we decided; in the meantime, he would start making his contacts and tentatively put the wheels in motion. We said we would be back in touch within the hour.

"Great, and congrats to you and the guys; nicely done!"

"Thanks, Fitz. We'll talk in a few." The link went dead. I turned to the guys and said, "Well, you heard the man, what do you think?"

Joe said, "Not sure we have much choice."

Junkyard agreed, "Right now, we have no other viable options I can think of, and one hundred and fifty thousand dollars to turn two million in gold into spendable cash. I think we should do it."

I looked around, "All in favor?" Everyone agreed. I said, "So be it. Let's get him back on the line." Within the hour, we set the plan in motion, and Dimitri, Joe, and Lawrence would deliver the bars the next day. I looked at all the guys and said with a smirk, "I guess its official; we're millionaires!" And the serious celebrating began!

The next few days were a frenzy of activity, Tony setting up the satellite surveillance of the shoal, Dimitri, Joe and Lawrence making the delivery to Fitz, and Junkyard and I discussing the problem of securing our claim. He had said we would need a larger boat if we were going to spend days at a time on site. I agreed. I wasn't too crazy about buying another boat, but not sure what other option we had.

Junkyard sat thinking. "I know a guy at the port who has an old 65-foot boat that had been a long liner back in the '70's. Her captain and his family and crew would spend days at sea fishing for swordfish before the fishing ran out. The boat and captain are still at the port. He lost his wife to cancer about eight years ago, and last I heard, he was thinking of selling the boat to help pay some medical bills."

I considered it for a minute or two and asked if he could arrange for a meeting with the captain and me.

"Sure, I've known him for quite a while, sold him a lot of stuff over the years. He's a good guy. I'll get in touch with him and set something up."

"Great; call me when it's done."

"Will do," and with that Junkyard left.

Two days later I had a meeting with Captain Augustus Falconetti.

CHAPTER EIGHT

In the early afternoon, two days later, I drove to the port for my meeting with Captain Augustus Falconetti and my first look at the *Falcon*. As I walked down the dock toward his slip, I had already formed a mental picture of what to expect. What I saw was not what I had envisioned. I stopped two slips away from the *Falcon* and took a few minutes to look her over before approaching. She was nothing like I had expected. I had expected an old fishing boat that had been sitting at the port unused for years and in a state of disrepair. Not at all; she was clean and her paint, while not new, was in great shape. Her brass and stainless were shiny, and the lines were stowed. The windows in the wheelhouse and the exterior of the cabin area gleamed brightly in the afternoon sun. In fact, she was beautiful.

As I walked down to her, a man came on deck from the cabin and moved to a table and chairs set up behind the wheelhouse. It was protected from the afternoon sun by a canvas tarp suspended by cables. He was a little older than me with a tuft of gray hair visible under the Greek fisherman's cap he wore. About six feet tall, his skin was the color of burnished leather.

The muscles in his arms and expansive chest let me know right away that this was a man used to hard work. As I walked up the dock, the man on deck turned towards me.

"Captain Falconetti?" I said.

"Who's asking?" he replied, rather gruffly.

"My name is Colten Burnett. I'm a friend of Nils Sorensen."

His demeanor changed. "Nils, huh? He called and said you might come by." "Permission to come aboard?" I asked.

A slight smile crossed his face. "Permission granted," he said. No sense in ignoring maritime protocol, I thought as I stepped aboard. He motioned toward the table and chairs. "Have a seat, Mr. Burnett."

I said, "Please, call me Colt," as I extended my hand to him.

He took it and replied, "Gus."

His grip was a solid one, and his hand was rough, only confirming my previous notion. On the table was a piece of paper with a hand-scrawled message on it. Boat for sale, contact Gus, Slip 23.

I asked, "Selling the boat?"

Gus picked up the paper, looked at me, then back at the paper. He wadded it up in a ball and threw it back on the table.

"Not sure yet," he said. I could tell it upset him, either my question or maybe just the idea of selling his boat. I changed the subject.

"She's a beauty; that's for sure."

He nodded, "She may have a little age on her, but she's still as seaworthy as the day they made her."

"How old is she," I asked?

"They laid her keel in '58."

"Man," I said, "she's not showing her age at all. I would have guessed much newer."

Now he smiled a look of pride showing on his face, "She only gets better with age," he said. It was my turn to smile. We sat there for a few minutes neither of us speaking.

I asked, "Did Nils tell you why I wanted to meet with you?"

"He said you might be looking for a boat."

"Well," I said, "maybe… if I were, the *Falcon* would fit my needs."

He looked around the deck fondly and said, "I wouldn't even consider selling her if I didn't need the money." He paused and looked at me, and his story came out as if he were glad to have someone to share it with. Why he chose me, I don't know, but he did. "It's my daughter; she's not well, and I'm all she has left for family. The medical bills keep coming in, and I'm damn out of options; the *Falcon's* all I have."

I leaned back in my chair and paused for a minute. "So, that's the only reason you're considering selling her?"

"Yeah," he said, "there's no more fishing around here or shrimping, and this ain't no cruise ship. I can't leave my daughter, Catherine, by herself, so that's it." I paused again; I could tell Gus was upset, his blue-grey eyes filled with sadness and love. So, I chose my next words carefully.

"Gus," I said, "I may have a business proposition that would interest you." "What?" he said, "You here to buy my boat or not?"

"No, I want you to keep your boat; I would like to hire you and it." He looked at me quizzically, and, I went on. "I'm involved in a business venture that requires a sea-going vessel; one that can stay at sea for a few days up to two weeks, if not longer. You wouldn't have to leave the area. If something came up with your daughter, one radio call, and you could be back in your slip within two hours."

Now, it was his turn to sit back in his chair and stare at me. When he spoke again, he was frowning and very animated.

"I don't run drugs or anything like that."

I grinned and stopped him before he could continue.

"It's nothing like that; I promise you, but it pays just as well, if not better." Now he looked puzzled, I knew I had his undivided attention.

You know how sometimes you meet a person and you can tell a lot about them in the first few minutes of conversation? Well, this was how it was with Gus. I knew in my gut he was honest, trustworthy, and a man of his word. I can't explain how; I just knew. So, I continued and hoped that my intuition was correct.

I asked him, "Can I trust you, Gus?" He looked at me, stunned.

"What do you mean?" he said.

"Can I REALLY trust you? I think I can, but I need to hear it from you. What I am about to tell you can change both our lives forever." He looked me square in the eye for what seemed like a long time.

A few seconds passed and then he said, "Mr. Burnett you're a strange sort of character, but I think you're an honest one, and Nils said he trusted you and that I could too. I've known him for over 20 years, and he's a straight shooter, even if he rattles on at times. If what you want to tell me will help me keep my boat and be able to take care of my daughter, then you can trust me. Till hell freezes over, and the devil goes ice skating!"

I laughed out loud. "Good, Gus, that's what I wanted to know." He stopped me there and said just a minute as he disappeared into the wheelhouse of the boat. When he came back, he had two ice cold beers and a bottle of whiskey.

He set them down on the table, pulled his chair up, and said, "Mr. Burnett, from the look on your face, I think we're going to need this," and opened both beers.

"You may be right, Gus," I said.

After taking a long pull on the beer and chasing it with a swig of whiskey from the bottle, he said, "Now… what have you got on your mind?"

I felt obliged to follow suit, and as the whiskey burned its way down my throat, I said, "Treasure, Gus, sunken treasure."

He almost choked on his second swallow of beer. "What?" he said, "You want me to hunt for sunken treasure with you; are you crazy?" He broke out laughing, shaking his head.

"No," I said, "Gus, I'm not hunting for treasure; I already found it and want you to help me recover it!" Now, he did choke on his beer!

After the coughing and hacking, he looked at me and said, "Are you kidding?" I took a wrapped stack of hundred-dollar bills out of the small gym bag I was carrying and placed them on the table.

"No, I'm not kidding," and sat looking at him as I reached for the whiskey bottle, took another pull on it, and thought, damn, this is starting to taste good. Another minute or two later, I said, "So, Gus, are you interested?"

He reached for the bottle and said, "Okay, Mr. Burnett, tell me more."

"It's Colt," I said...

"Okay, Colt... tell me more."

I recounted a general version of the past ten months and our discovery. I told him of our need to have a vessel anchored over our find 24/7. "As you can see, Gus, I need someone that is a Competent seaman and trustworthy." I gave him a general idea of where we would be working. I wasn't about to give away all the details yet. He stared at me with those steel blue-grey eyes.

"So, you're afraid of someone moving in and jumping your claim when you're gone?" he said.

"Yep" I replied, "in fact, we think our activities are under surveillance by that someone already."

"That could mean trouble," Gus said.

"Yes," I answered, "there could be physical risks involved, both to you and your boat."

Gus paused, took a drink of beer, then a hit off the bottle.

"Well," he said, "that would make things a mite more interesting, now wouldn't it!"

"It would," I agreed, "that's' why I'm willing to pay you one thousand dollars a day for your boat and your services. There's ten thousand dollars on the table and another ten in my bag if you agree to accept my offer. I would consider that a retainer and payment for your first seventeen days on the job." His eyes stared straight at me and got a little wider. I could see him running the possibilities through his head. After a few minutes, he got up, entered the wheelhouse and came back out with two fresh beers. He sat down and passed one my way.

He spoke, "Is all this shit legal?"

I smiled and said, "Well, not yet, but we're working on it!"

"So, will it be legal by the time I start?"

"Um, don't think so," I replied.

After a couple of minute's consideration, a smile spread across his face, "A kind of pirate thing," he said with the slightest gleam in his eye.

"I guess you could say that," I replied.

"You know I could lose my boat and everything else I have."

"Yes I know," I replied.

"I'm going to have to think on it a bit," he said, "can I have a couple of days?"

"Sure, but time is of the essence; we need to move quickly." I gave him my cell phone number, picked up five thousand dollars off the table, and left five. If you decide not to accept my offer, consider that five thousand payment for your time and hospitality." I left him sitting on the deck staring out to sea. Three days later, I got the call and headed back out to the marina.

Gus was sitting on the back deck as I walked up to the *Falcon*. "come aboard, Colt," he said as I approached. I sat down at the table as he slid a cold beer my way and said, "You're really serious about all this treasure stuff?"

"Yes, I am," I said, "very serious."

"And you think it's worth the risk?"

"I am positive it is worth it."

Another pause, "Well, then, hope you don't mind drinking with the hired help, Captain, I'm in!" he said with a big grin as he opened his beer.

"Not at all," I replied and did the same. After we talked and he gave my offer more thought, he said, "I might need a crew to handle the job the way it needs to be handled."

"We need to keep this quiet as possible, for obvious reasons."

"I understand," Gus said. "That wouldn't be a problem; two of my old crew are still in the area, and I don't think they're working. If that's the case, I would like to bring them on board. You can trust them; they both were shipmates of mine. We go way back, and I would trust them with my life, and you could too."

I pondered his statement for a minute, then said, "They would need to know the risks involved."

At that, he laughed. He pulled up his sleeve, revealing the tattoo of a striding muscular frog in a sailor's cap, carrying a lit stick of dynamite and smoking a cigar.

It was my turn to laugh, "Freddy the Frog, UDT Gus?"

"Yep," he said, "we've weathered many a shit storm together, last one was Nam. All of us got out in '65; things were changing, and we'd done our time." It was my turn to pause, damn, not only did I find the perfect boat for our job; a Naval Underwater Demolition Team comes with it! I pulled the other stack of hundreds out of the bag and put it on the table.

"Well Gus, I guess we have a deal."

Gus smiled and lifted his beer in one hand and the whiskey bottle in the other and said, "Yes, Sir, Captain, that we do."

Over the next hour, we hammered out the details of our agreement, two to three additional crew members for the *Falcon*, to be decided by Gus and some new tech/electronics to be provided by Risky Business. Gus assured me he could be ready to move to the site in four to five days. I said that would be fine. I gave Joe a call with the list of what we needed to update the *Falcon* and he assured me he could have it purchased and installed within the allotted timeframe.

I called Tony and told him we would need secure computer up-and down link capabilities for the boat. He let me know that would take a little longer to make happen, but it could be done on-site at the shoal. He also let me know he had the satellite surveillance of our site set up and working. That was great news. I shook hands with Gus and said, "Welcome to the team."

He smiled and told me he wouldn't let me down and looked forward to meeting and working with the rest of my crew. I swear; he looked 10 years younger when I left.

As I walked down the dock toward the parking lot, I felt good about the deal Gus and I had struck. Talk about a beneficial arrangement, and besides, I liked Gus and knew the rest of the guys would too. He was a seasoned sailor and a good fit for Risky Business.

The next day, about ten in the morning, I got a somewhat panicked call from Tony. "They're at the shoal and diving," he said.

"Crap." I asked him if he had called Dimitri. He said yes, he had called him first. He said for you to meet him at Blue Skies Marina at the port, dock C.

"What slip?" I asked as I was throwing on my shorts and T-shirt.

"He said, don't worry; when you're near it, you'll hear it."

"What?" I said, "I don't have time for his games; what slip?"

Tony said, "That's it; that was all he said."

I told him to get back in touch with Dimitri and get more info, then call me. "I'm on the way; be there in 15 to 20 minutes." Dimitri had stepped up when we discussed this potential problem and said he would take care of it; I had said fine and turned my attention to other issues. That's just the way Dimitri and I operate, but this was, well, it was downright silly. What was that crazy Cossack up to? I slid into the parking lot of the marina with no new information. I jumped out of my vehicle and headed to C dock. As I ran down the dock, I was doing the full scan for Dimitri, nowhere in sight, Shit, not good.

As I was nearing the last of the slips at the end of the dock, there was an outrageous growl coming from the other side of a 45-foot Sea Ray tied there. I passed it and, in the slip next to it sat a 38-foot Fountain go-fast, idling with a sound like some caged beast trying to get out. As I stopped on the dock, there was Dimitri, in a pastel salmon-colored muscle T-shirt with white linen pants, Huarache sandals, and aviator sunglasses!

When he saw me, a huge grin split his face, and as he pulled the sunglasses off with a flourish, he said in his "Boris" speak, "Hey, Colt, Sonny Crockett from *Miami Vice*, Da?" "What you think?"

As I undid the lines and jumped on board, I said, "You're out of your freaking mind!"

He replied, "Da, but how do I look?" With that, he pulled the boat out of the slip and into the waterway, easing into the throttles. I detected the high-pitched whine of superchargers; the boat was beautiful, and from what I could tell, I guessed extremely fast. As we cleared the last slow speed markers, he turned and said, "Hold on; we go now!" I had grabbed the hand rail on the passenger's side as he slammed the throttles forward.

"Holy shit," I exclaimed as the boat leaped forward and my grip tightened. The seas were calm, and, in seconds we were literally flying across its surface. Dimitri still had a huge grin on his face as I glanced over at him, then down to the digital speed readout on the dash. Ninety mph and still climbing. I was thinking, damn this is cool, but I would never tell Dimitri! Within 20 minutes, we were two or three miles beyond and parallel to the shoal as Dimitri started a slow turn to port. I figured his plan was to go past the shoal and come up on the other vessel from the seaward side; I was right. He had slowed, and the engines were just putting out a low growl as we nosed back to the west. He pulled a pair of binoculars out of a large duffel bag on the floor and handed them to me.

"Let me know when you spot them," he said in his normal voice. I took the glasses and scanned the horizon to the west. It took about another 15 minutes before I spotted the boat. It was identifiable by the mail box hanging on her stern. It was a large device that was lowered over the prop to direct prop wash downward. It was shaped like a ninety-degree PVC fitting and was used by treasure hunters to blow holes in the sand. The vessel was at anchor and lying parallel to the shoal; we were about a mile away from them. We continued moving in their direction at a slow-speed, engines softly growling in the background. At about 700 yards, Dimitri shut off the engines and let our momentum keep us moving slowly toward them. The sun at our backs, the low profile of the go-fast hull and the blue color of the boat did a lot to camouflage our approach.

Dimitri leaned down and opened the duffel bag and pulled out his Barrett .50 caliber sniper rifle. Now, I grew concerned.

As he was attaching a noise suppressor to the barrel, I said, "Hold on, Dimitri, we're not here to shoot people. I don't care what they're doing!"

He looked at me and said, "Don't worry, Colt; it will be all right," and handed me a spotter's scope. He pulled a small sandbag from the duffle and laid it on the top of the mini windshield of the Fountain.

We had drifted another 75 yards closer when he laid the barrel of the Barrett on the sandbag and said, "Give me a reading." I took the spotter's scope, supported it on the small dash, and put my eye to the eyepiece. It took me a few seconds to get used to the digital display, but when I did, I could see the boat and the three men on deck. They had their backs to us, looking over the port side; they had not spotted us.

Dimitri said, "Range?"

I pressed the button on the scope and the laser hit the boat's hull. "six-hundred-twenty-four yards," I said. There was no wind, and the sea had a gentle ten second swell to it. I watched as Dimitri settled into a comfortable crouch, eye to his scope.

As he was getting his breathing established, he said, "I'm zeroed in at 500 yards." That meant that, at this distance, he would have to make adjustments to hit his target.

I said, "Dimitri, what's the plan?"

He said, "You'll see. Range?"

"Six-hundred-fifteen yards," I said. Momentum was still carrying us west.

"Let me know when we get to 605 and then count me down to 600."

"Roger that," I said. I could tell he was now in his zone; his breathing had settled into a slow regular pattern as he made two scope adjustments. Nothing mattered but what he saw in his scope. I put my eye to mine and hit the laser again, 612, 611, 610; I took a deep breath, myself and steadied one hand on the dash of the boat. 607, 606, at 605 I counted down," "602, 601, 600." I immediately heard the pop from the rifle and saw a splash about eight to ten feet from the boat's hull and told Dimitri. He made another change to his scope. None of the men turned; at 598 yards, the rifle spoke again. "Splash about three feet from the hull," I reported. Within the next 30 seconds six more rounds hit the water at about the two-foot mark from the hull, tracing a line towards the transom with their small splashes. One man turned and looked around at the deck of the boat. He must have heard something that got his attention. As I watched, he grabbed one of the other's shoulders and pointed at the deck. Dimitri had already stowed the weapon and sandbag and started our engines; we made a quiet but abrupt 180-degree turn, our low-profile stern towards the boat. The last thing I noted before we turned was a small wisp of smoke rising from the deck of our interloper's vessel. Dimitri slid the throttles forward slowly, and we made a quick but stealthy retreat seaward. I had traded the scope for binoculars, and as the boat grew smaller, I could see no one was looking our way; they focused all their attention on the deck.

Once we had gotten beyond a mile out to sea, Dimitri pushed the throttles once again to their stops, and they stayed there for the next fifteen minutes. It was then he made a slow, gentle turn to the south and brought us around in a maneuver that put us about ten miles offshore and 18 miles south of the shoal. A slight chop had developed as the heat from the sun warmed things up and got the breezes blowing.

Dimitri stepped back and said, "Take the helm; I need to stow the gear." As I took the controls, we spoke for the first time in 20 minutes.

I said, "Not bad, Dimitri, not bad."

He gave me one of his grins and said, "Zombies." He stowed the rifle and gear in what I would call a "secret" Compartment, which brought a few questions to mind.

"Dimitri, whose boat is this anyway?"

He replied, "A friend's."

"Really?" I asked.

"Yeah, he owes me big time, so I have use of it anytime I need it. I felt it prudent not to ask any further questions as I slowed the boat from the 85 mph we had been running down to 50. A more sedate speed I hoped would draw less attention. As we got back into the sight of land, I saw we were south of the inlet by about five or six miles, so I turned to a northerly heading and sat back and enjoyed the ride. As we passed the jetty and turned into the channel, we saw a Coast Guard rigid-hull heading out full speed. We had heard the chatter on the VHF radio about a vessel in distress north of the port. A second

Coast Guard vessel passed us with lights flashing and moving at a rapid pace.

"Gee," Dimitri said as he gave them a wave as they went by, "Hope it's nothing serious." He let out a laugh and said, "Freakin Zombies."

After a minute or two, I said, "Damn that was close; I guess timing is everything."

Dimitri had put his sunglasses back on, slapped me on the back, and in his best "Boris" voice said, "No problem for Sonny Crockett, *Miami Vice*... Da?"

I just shook my head and thought, "Jesus this guy is crazy.... glad he's on my side!"

CHAPTER NINE

The next three days were what I would call organized chaos. I sent Junkyard to the port to nose around and see what he could find out about the encounter. There were no incidents reported. They attributed the emergency call from the *Carrie Ann* to a burst water line that flooded the bilge and shorted out some electrical equipment, starting a small fire on board. The engine had suffered damage as a result, and the Coast Guard towed the vessel to port. They reported nothing out of the ordinary. The vessel was laid up at the port for repairs.

Dimitri speculated that one or more of his rounds hit their engine and caused enough damage to disable it. Not our intent, however, if true, then just a lucky side benefit. Guess these guys didn't want to get involved in something they may have a harder time explaining than a broken hose. I hoped they realized now we were not someone to be screwed around with and best stay away from us and our site. We took the lack of any formal Coast Guard report as message received and continued with our planning. With any luck they were smart enough not to try and retaliate, but you never know the depth of stupid.

We needed to be on our guard from now on. Gus was about ready to go on station at the shoal. Fitz had come through, and three large duffel bags were delivered to my house by the same crew that had brought our other presents earlier. All armed to the teeth and with the message that he would be ready for another package in five days. I will be the first to admit that having 1.85 million dollars in cash lying around the house in duffel bags is a little unnerving. I mean, where the hell do you hide that much money? You don't just stick it in the dirty laundry hamper... on second thought...!

Two days after our boat assault, we all met on the *Lisa B* for a planning and funds distribution session. Each member received one hundred thousand dollars, and everyone agreed they would leave the rest in my keeping for the time being. Now came the hard part; we all understood we had to keep a low profile and no spending binges! In the big picture, we knew we were breaking several laws, some blatant...others more obscure, but no one volunteered to research the details! We shut Lawrence up twice as he brought up legal points we didn't want to hear. Everyone understood the ramifications of screwing this up and agreed to be cool. I think by now we all had adopted a pirate's mentality.

Finders' keepers!

Hell, next thing you know, we'll all be wearing eye patches and have parrots on our shoulders. After more discussion, we decided we would play the recovery of the longboat treasure loose. There was nothing on the bottom to show any wreck, so, yes, that means finders keepers; damn the legalities to hell! Once we finished with the longboat, we would apply for the appropriate "legal" Federal permits in our search for the ship itself and abide by the rules from then on... well, mostly, anyway.

That out of the way, the next order of business was coming up with a working plan for our salvage operation. We needed a means to move the sand that had accumulated at the base of the shoal covering the next crate. We also needed larger lifting bags to bring their contents to the surface. We didn't want to be observed using a deck-mounted hoist bringing up items from the bottom. That could draw too much unwanted attention to our activities. Even if we weren't harassed, we were sure we would be watched.

Based on Doc's research, the longboat had ten crates on board. We had uncovered two… that meant there were eight more crates waiting to be found. Maybe close to the two we had uncovered, maybe not. We decided to return to the location of the first two crates and continue to remove sand from the undercut of the shoal. We needed to see how far it ran; it was highly possible that some of the other crates may have fallen into the area along the undercut and gotten buried close to the others.

We would slowly move north along the base of the shoal, using the metal detectors, and see what we could find. I also wanted to have two of the guy's start a longitudinal grid search about 10 to 15 feet away from the base of the shoal and search that area following the line of the base until we had covered at least twenty feet eastward from the shoal. When the longboat hit the shoal, as heavy as the crates were, they would have probably dropped straight to the bottom. But Mother Nature, being a finicky Old Girl, it's possible some of them got thrown around in the currents as they fell or even broke up and scattered their contents on the bottom. I wanted to make sure we conducted a thorough search of the entire area.

We sat around the table discussing this rather matter-of-factly, and I couldn't help but get the sense that the enormity of our situation hadn't really sunk in on the crew. I was viewing the whole thing as a surreal experience. Here we had found enough treasure to make us all millionaires, and we hadn't even found the ship yet, only part of the cargo on the longboat. It was crazy how many millions still waited to be recovered from the ocean floor.

Whoa, boy, pull back the reins, Colt; you're getting a little ahead of yourself here, and that could be dangerous. I mentally reeled myself back in and got into the conversation at the table. Junkyard said he could make us an air-lift with bits and pieces he had lying around, some six-inch PVC pipe, air hose, and a scuba tank. We all understood that, whatever we did, it couldn't look like we were excavating or looking for treasure; it had to be covert. If we were detected we would have the Feds on us in a heartbeat. Coming up with a plan for our search and recovery was becoming problematic. It's easy in the movies, but in real life it's a bitch! We needed a cover!

The recent contact with our new "friends" and the delivery of our "message" left me feeling we no longer needed to station a vessel on the shoal immediately as previously planned. I figured it would be safe for the time being, and I would let Gus know in the morning that he could stand down for a while. In fact, I felt it a good idea to stay away from the shoal and just let Tony's birds keep an eye on it for us till we were sure things had cooled down. I also thought Dimitri and I should keep a low profile at the port for the time being.

I told the guys we needed to be concerned about our meetings and conversations. In the beginning, it was all fun and games, but now, we were up to our asses in a situation that could prove disastrous for all of us. I said I think we need to change our meeting places and be more cautious in our daily activities. Call it paranoia or whatever you like, but the safety of this team and our discovery had become paramount in my mind. I call it Common sense.

There was a murmur of agreement and I said I also think we need to bring Fitz into any future discussions. He had been the man behind the curtain mostly, but an indispensable member of our group and unbelievably resourceful. All agreed. I also told everyone I thought we should move our main base of operations to the mainland away from the *Lisa B* and Tony's place. Again agreement, Joe asked if I had any ideas and I told him I did. A spot in an industrial area near my place, but I needed to check it out further. I could do that tomorrow, I said.

Lawrence said why not put further discussions about the project on hold till we could set up the new secure meeting place and get word to Fitz. In the meantime, he said, let's let Junkyard work on his lift idea so that when we moved forward with the salvage operation, we could have it ready to go. Joe volunteered to follow up on the new lift bags, and I said I would let them all know what I found out about the potential facility as soon as I had more information. We all agreed and cold beers were distributed to end the formal part of the meeting.

Dimitri regaled the group with his story of the offshore "Zombie hunt" and details of the 38-foot Fountain and its capabilities with its two 502 Supercharged Chevy Big blocks. I interjected a few of my observations concerning our 90 to 100 mph white knuckle run off-shore and my meeting with Sonny Crockett of *Miami Vice* fame to rounds of laughter by the group. The evening drew to a close to more stories and beer till finally the group started saying their good byes and headed out with smiles on their faces, their new-found financial stability in the brown paper bags they carried. Excitement filled the air as they departed with the expectation of a grand adventure in our futures. We were all oblivious to the magnitude of what this adventure was about to throw in our laps!

The next day, I took a drive into the industrial park on the mainland after a call to Gus, giving him an update on the situation. He said the delay was good. It would give him and his crew more time to prepare and Tony time to finish the Computer systems installation at the dock as opposed to at sea. Dimitri was contacting Fitz, and Lawrence was doing more research into

Admiralty Law concerning the process of placing a claim in Federal waters, so things were moving along at a good pace.

I had remembered a small gun manufacturing Company that had started up in our area some time ago. Over the years, they had outgrown their original facility and a couple of years ago had moved to a larger facility in a new location. Their old place had been empty and for lease for all this time. It was a secure area with some unique features that made it hard to lease. It was not your normal industrial space, which for most purposes was bad, but for our needs, I thought was perfect.

I had contacted the realtor and met them at the facility at 1:00 that afternoon. The building was about 12,000 sq. ft. surrounded by a ten-foot chain-link fence with barbed wire leaning outward across the top, for a total height of 12 feet. Inside, the building had a loading dock and a roll-up cargo entrance door, large enough for a cargo van and medium sized truck to pull into the building. The previous tenant had left the security system behind, which was good, punch code on a key pad with thumb print recognition. When we got inside, the building was fully air-conditioned with a large cargo/work area, and offices on the ground floor, plus more offices and a conference room in a loft arrangement overlooking the cargo/work area below. In a corner on the ground floor in what I guessed was a security office was a large steel bar door behind which was a large bank-vault Combination-lock type door.

I asked about that, and the realtor said it had been a prototype storage area for the previous Company. They had it specially installed, and she had been told it was as well constructed and as secure as any bank vault in the area. I smiled inwardly and said the Company I represent wouldn't have much use for something like that. Her smile dropped, but I added it wouldn't really be a problem. The smile came back. As we walked around the outside, I saw ample parking in front and on the side. The rear parking lot was large enough to hold several tractor-trailer trucks, which meant it was large enough for a helicopter to land. Since there was a 50-foot cleared security area around the outside perimeter, and all power and teleCom cables were underground, there would be no obstructions or dangers for a chopper coming in.

As we walked back around the front, I asked, "How much to lease the property?"

The agent almost apologetically said, "The owner wants $3,500 dollars a month," trying to maintain her smile.

Although this was an older facility, it was in great shape, so I played my next card, "How long has it been empty?" I asked.

She replied rather slowly, "A little over two years."

I then said "The environmental research Company I represent is grant funded and really can't afford that level of rent," and waited.

The silence grew as her smile faded, then she spoke again and said, "There might be a little flexibility in the price." She also said she would need to consult with the owner as she pulled her phone from her pocket.

I said, "Please do. I am interested in the property but not at that price."

She excused herself and stepped away as she dialed a number. There was an animated discussion for a few minutes; then she walked back to me. She had the phone in her hand with the owner obviously still on the line. They could probably rent it for $3,000 per month if I were really interested. I hesitated as if thinking about the offer when, in reality, I was thinking this was chump change Compared to the assets we already had on hand, but I was playing a game here and did not want to show my hand as a big spender. People may talk, and that might provoke more interest in our activities than we would want. After a minute, I said, "I will make one offer and, if that is not acceptable, I will look elsewhere." I said it loud enough so the person on the other end of the line could hear me. "I will pay $2000 per month for a one-year lease, not rent, with an agreement for a second year at the same price. Further, I will pay the full one year's lease of 24 thousand dollars in advance upon our signing of the contract, providing we can close the deal within the week, and we can move in on the weekend." I was banking on the fact that the reduced price would be better than the owner continuing to have an empty Commercial building just sitting there and having cash up front would sweeten the deal.

The agent put the phone to her ear and took a step away as she relayed what I said to the owner. After only a minute or two, the agent came back, smiling and said, "Dr. Burnett, you have a deal. Can you meet in my office day after tomorrow, Thursday, say 1:00?" I said I could and shook hands with a thrilled real estate agent.

As I pulled out of the parking lot I put a call in to Fitz, was put on hold, and a moment later he came on the line, "Hey Colt, what's up?"

I quickly filled him in on the latest happenings and he burst out laughing. "Jesus Christ boy, you're having more fun than I am, and that's saying something!"

I replied, "I'm not sure it's what I would call fun, but it hasn't been boring." I told him of the rental property and the phony environmental Company cover.

He said to hold on a minute, and when he came back on the line, he said, "Use Consolidated Environmental Services."

I said, "What?"

He said, "Yeah, that's one of mine; they have been known to do contract work for NOAA, the Navy, and a few others. It will stand up to the closest scrutiny. You are now a subsidiary of Acme Corp. I'll send official documents to Tony electronically in case you need them, then you'll be all nice and legal; you should be set."

Damn, Fitz comes through again. "Thanks," I said and asked

when he could get over here for a meeting. He said he would have some time on Monday of next week. I said that would be fine and, "By the way you wouldn't happen to have a spare chopper with the environmental Companies logo on it, would you?"

"Damn Colt, anything else you need, corporate jet, limo...?"

I laughed and said, "No, not yet, but I'll let you know."

He laughed again and said, "Seriously, everything good over there?" I assured him it was, and we would bring him up to speed on Monday. We said our goodbyes, and I hit Tony on speed dial. He picked up on the second ring, "Hey, Colieutenant"

I told him to expect the electronic documents from Fitz and about the new corporate office.

"Cool," he said and reported no new activity in the shoal area since our altercation. That was good news. He said he would let me know as soon as the documents came in and print out a couple of copies for us.

We hung up, and I immediately called Joe and told him to buy us a white cargo van, not new, but a couple of years old, no clunker. He said he would get right on it and let me know when he had it. I headed for the port to meet with Gus and give him an update. When I got to the *Falcon,* a new face greeted me, "You must be Dr. Burnett," he said as I stepped up to the small gangplank.

I stuck out my hand and said, "Colieutenant"

"Petty Officer First Class Bill Simpson," he replied, standing at attention, "my friends call me Wild Bill, Sir."

"Great to meet you," I replied "You're one of Gus's old crew?"

"Yes, Sir, we served together our last eight years in the Navy, and then I crewed for him while he was fishing here, me and Smitty both."

"Where's Gus?" I asked.

"The Master Chief is below with Smitty."

"Smitty?" I questioned.

"Yes Sir, Chief Boatswains mate Reginald Smith, Sir, he don't like to be called Reginald or Reggie, so we just call him Smitty." I thanked him and headed into the cabin. Master Chief I thought, I'd never known Gus's Naval rating before this. That was the highest enlisted rating you could get in the Navy, and they didn't just give those away. Another bit of information about Gus to file away, I thought as I made my way below decks.

I found them both in the engine Compartment having a heated discussion about something to do with the large diesel generator that sat next to the engine. As I approached, Gus saw me, and his demeanor changed with a big grin spreading across his face. He said, "Captain Burnett, welcome aboard again." I nodded and took his extended hand. He turned to Smitty and said, "Chief, this is Captain Burnett, our employer."

"Pleased to meet you, Sir."

"Likewise, Smitty," I said. "Problems?" I asked.

"Nothing we can't handle, Sir," Smitty replied.

Gus nodded at him and said "Let me know when you're finished."

"Aye, Master Chief," Smitty replied as Gus and I turned and left the engine room.

I asked, "Gus, got a few minutes?"

"Yes, Sir," he replied as he led the way to the galley and the small table there. He opened the fridge and pulled out two cold bottles of beer as we sat at the table. He passed one my way and said, "I'm all ears, Sir."

"Please, Gus, it's Colt; enough with this Sir stuff."

He took a swig from his bottle and said, "I understand but, the man in charge has always been a Sir to us, and that's the way we like it. We're comfortable with it, and anything different would be real hard to get used to. I'll try, Colt, but no guarantees."

I said, "Fine," and decided not to push the issue any further. I went over the last couple of days' events with Gus to bring him up to speed. When I got to Dimitri's part, he got kind of wide-eyed and said, "Now that's a man I'm looking forward to meeting."

"You'll get your chance soon enough, but be careful what you wish for," I said with a smile. "Considering recent events, as I told you on the phone, we have bought ourselves a little more time to prepare for your departure, so that takes the pressure off us all. Continue with your preparations and let me know if you need anything. Has Tony finished with the Computer installations?" I asked.

"Yes, Sir," Gus replied, "not sure what I'll do with all that stuff, but Tony said he could teach me and the boys what we need to know in short order. Guess I know how some of our extra time will be spent."

"Not to worry Gus, you'll pick it up in no time, and if you have questions, give Tony a shout." He said he would as I finished my beer and stood up. "Anything else we need to go over while I'm here?" I asked. He said he couldn't think of anything and that they would be ready to haul anchor whenever I gave the word. "Great," I said.

As I turned to leave, Gus said, "Colt," and I turned back. "I just wanted to say thank you for what you're doing for me and my little girl." Those blue-grey eyes were misting up. "I can't tell you how much it means to me."

I clasped him on the shoulder and said, "Gus, you being part of this team and doing your job is all the thanks I need."

He looked at me and said, "Till Hell freezes over, Sir… and the devil goes ice skating!"

I looked him in the eye and said, "Roger that, Master Chief, roger that" and walked out.

CHAPTER TEN

The deal went through on the building lease without a hitch. Consolidated Environmental Services now operated an office in Cocoa. Joe got the van purchased a 2015 Ford E-350, a nice one ton heavy hauler. They made our signs on Friday for the van and exterior of the building and on Saturday we moved into our new digs. The security system guys and a locksmith showed up on Saturday. They re-activated the security system and changed the combination on the vault The power hadn't been disconnected; that meant we had power and A/C for all our systems, no issues there. The previous tenants left furniture, two desks and some chairs, a conference table and its chairs, and some cabinets. They also left metal storage racks in the bay area which we knew we could use. Tony came in to set up a new Computer system. Joe checked out the outside for additional surveillance camera placement. By the time Sunday evening arrived we were pretty well moved in. We stocked the new fridge with our favorite beverages. Joe got the outside electronic locking gate and security system activated. We tied in the existing surveillance cameras to our Computer system. We weren't Fort Knox, but we were damn close. I decided when we met with Fitz at our new office, we would move our "resources" to the vault That would sure make me sleep better; besides, my dirty laundry hamper was overflowing.

Risky Business had turned the page on a new chapter in its story and, so far in our minds, it was a barn burner. We met at 1:00 the next afternoon; Fitz showed up at 1:05 with Ms. Shannon O'Reilly in tow, much to the delight of Dimitri and Lawrence.

As he surveyed the new space with an approving look, he said, "Ms. O'Reilly is the official pilot of record for CES. And yes, there is a chopper available with the CES logo on it. We'll keep it at my place, but it will be available when you need it. Give us as much notice as you can. We can be here in less than 20 minutes if we push it."

"That's great" I said.

"I see you have a nice large parking lot out back we can use as a pad for the bird."

"Yes," I replied, "I think it will be perfect."

Ms. O'Reilly smiled and looked at Fitz, then me, and said, "Fifteen minutes tops, from the time we get your call to touchdown."

Fitz shook his head. "Lead-foot".... She smiled and gave me a wink as we headed toward the conference room.

Once we all had beverages and got settled around the big table, I slid a brown paper bag to Fitz containing one hundred thousand dollars. He opened it and looked at me questioningly.

"Your first installment from Risky Business," I said.

He laughed and said, "You know I don't need this, don't you?"

I said, "Fine, then just consider it a repayment of your investment, with interest."

He nodded. "If that's what you want, then it's fine by me," he said as he closed the bag and passed it to Ms. O'Reilly, saying, "Have this put into the CES account as a donation from an environmentally concerned anonymous source."

She said, "Will do Colonel." We had moved the ten gold bars from Dimitri's gun safe along with the cash from my dirty laundry hamper, how à propos, I thought with a chuckle, to the new safe. I had held out the one hundred thousand dollars and two more gold bars also in a brown paper bag and slid it to Fitz.

"I believe you stated you could help us with this sometime later in the week?"

As he took the bag without looking into it, he said "Should be able to have something for you by Friday."

"Excellent," I replied, "but I need to ask you a question."

"Shoot," he said.

"I know what we're doing is… questionable," I said. "I don't want to know any more details concerning your transactions than you feel comfortable letting us in on. But I am slightly concerned where the gold is winding up and what it's being used for."

Now, he laughed out loud with one of his deep from the belly roars. "Colt, you are the master of understatements. Questionable? Hell, man, we're so far beyond that, the light from questionable doesn't even reach us!" We all laughed. "But to set your mind at ease, it never leaves these good old United States, if that's what you're worried about."

Actually, it was exactly what worried me, I thought.

"Since we will be involved in more questionable activities" he said with a laugh, "the people I am dealing with are longtime associates of mine. Suffice to say, they are American patriots who are fed up with the corruption within our political system and many of its so-called agencies. They are doing what they can to mitigate the negative impact it is having on our nation. They're not radicals or nut jobs, no taking over the government or anything. They have their own substantial resources.

They just happen to be willing to help people who have the balls to put their asses on the line."

"Really?" I said, "Did you tell them about us, who we were?"

"Some," he said "only what I thought they needed to know, but they are very smart people. They know how to fill in the blanks." He paused and then said, "They sent you a message which I didn't think I would deliver."

Now, I was really interested, "What was it?"

He paused again and with a laugh said, "They said to tell you they thought you guys had some pretty big balls to be doing what you're doing and to keep up the good work! The world could use a few good pirates." Now, it was my turn to laugh; I had no idea who these people were. With any luck, I would never know.

But to have earned that level of, I guess you would call it respect from them was very much a surprise.

As everyone was having a good laugh over this, I mumbled a "thank you and said that we planned on keeping up the good work."

"Oh," he said "there'll be no charge for any additional conversions we do. It will be at whatever the going market rate is for gold from now on. These people must like you guy's," he said with another chuckle.

After our interlude of laughter, I got down to business again. I told the group I would like to have Gus brought in as often as he could make himself available to these meetings, at least once a month. No one objected; in fact, all agreed that would be a good idea. The next order of business was Fitz presenting us with copies of contracts and approval documents from NOAA, EPA, and other Federal offices approving our work on determining the impact of past rocket launches from the cape on sea life offshore. Including but not limited to the retrieval of debris or any objects we deemed unsafe to the aquatic environment. They described our physical area of investigation in the paperwork and included the area identified by Tony's algorithm.

I looked at him in amazement. "Are these legit?" I asked.

"Mostly" he replied, "they will stand up to scrutiny by any local and state agencies. Should it get to the Federal level, they are buried in so much red tape it would take years of digging for anyone to find out the particulars behind their validity, like I said, my people are very good at what they do."

We talked over a few more details and decided that we should wait four or five days before moving the *Falcon* to the shoal site. Lawrence would handle getting our papers to the proper port authorities and the Coast Guard and we would have additional CES signs made for both the *Falcon* and *Lisa B*. Something to the effect this vessel is under contract to CES, etc. to add to our cover. Junkyard said we should probably have some "official" shirts printed up with the CES logo and that he had a source for those. So, by 3:45, having accomplished quite a lot, we concluded our business and Fitz and O'Reilly headed west. The rest of us grabbed another beverage and sat around the CES van parked in the open bay area taking in our new facility.

After a bit Dimitri spoke up, "I think this should be the Risky Business Lair."

"What?" I said. "Where the hell did that come from? This isn't a lair."

"Yes, it is." he responded defensively, "it is definitely a lair."

Joe asked why he would want to call it a lair. Dimitri stood and, in what I can only call a theatrical oratory, said, "Batman had the Bat Cave, his lair; Superman had the Fortress of Solitude, that was his lair; and it's where they kept all their secrets hidden and cool stuff. So, I think we should have our own lair. For short, we can call it the RBL."

"So now you're equating us with fictional super heroes?" Lawrence asked.

"Why not?" Dimitri said, "Those guys called us good pirates, didn't they? So, we deserve our own lair; pirates always had hiding places for their treasure."

Doc spoke up then, "Dimitri, do you even know what a lair is?"

Dimitri looked a little puzzled and said "Yeah, I told you a place to keep all our cool stuff hidden."

"No," Doc said "a lair by definition is the habitation of wild animals."

Dimitri frowned slightly as he digested Docs information and then with one of his grins said, "Well, hell Doc, that works too."

I turned and headed to the fridge for another beer, shaking my head and mumbled "Whatever."

Dimitri jumped at the opening I had unknowingly given him and said, "See, Colt agrees, so I hereby declare this place the official Risky Business Lair! A toast." As he raised his drink, we all just looked at one another and finally raised our drinks.

Joe said, "Sure what the hell?" and in that instant, it was sealed; we had our own "Lair."

As I sat back down, I said, "Dimitri, your mind must be one interesting place to live."

He replied, "Yeah, pretty cool... Huh?" Once again, we all broke into laughter, not sure at what exactly, but a healthy round of laughter none-the-less. Dimitri and his damned theatrics... Crazy Cossack!

The next few days were rather uneventful, considering the past couple of weeks. We purchased a small rigid-hull inflatable Zodiac and suspended it from davits on the stern of the *Falcon*. Gus got things wrapped up on board. Joe had the additional surveillance cameras up and running at our new facility. Tony got the secure up/down link set up with the "Lair's" Computer system. All our security measures were in place and operating optimally. We picked up the signs for the boats and got them installed, and Lawrence got all the official paperwork on file with the officials at the port. Now, we could make departure plans for the *Falcon*. We got together on the back deck of the *Lisa B* on Friday afternoon after receiving our package from Fitz, as promised and securing it in our new vault. This was more of a social gathering than anything official, but our discussions soon turned to the upcoming project at the shoal.

After some general discussion I said to the group, "Something has been bouncing around in the back of my head ever since Doc gave us the information on the longboat and I think it's worth mentioning."

Junkyard said, "What's on your mind Colt?"

"Consider this," I said, "You're the captain of a sinking ship that probably has quite a few tons of gold on board. You realize your ship is in peril, so you send out one longboat, in the middle of a hurricane with ten crates of something. You give orders to the men on board that it must get to the king. Now from where I stand that just doesn't make sense. Ten crates of gold are not going to help the King of Spain that much and a small boat would have very little chance of surviving, so why send it out in the middle of a hurricane?" Everyone sat staring at me. "I'm just saying, it doesn't add up."

Joe finally asked "Could there have been something else in the crates? I mean we know there's gold but what else could there be that would be that valuable or important?"

"Hell if I know," I replied. "Doc, do you have any ideas?"

"Actually, no, but that's a good question. If the captain was as experienced as we think he was he must have had a good reason to do what he did."

"You see what I'm getting at," I said. "Why would he do that? If he were just trying to save the treasure, he would have put more boats in the water with more of the gold on board." It wasn't making sense. Now the discussion buzzed, all kinds of ideas were being thrown around but none of them really answered the question. We all finally fell into thoughtful silence with puzzled looks on our faces… time for more beer! We left that evening no closer to an answer than when I brought it up. It was confounding and gave us food for thought for days to come.

We decided that weather permitting, Monday would be the day we would send out the *Falcon*. It had been almost two weeks since our encounter with the *Carrie Ann*. Junkyard reported no interesting chatter coming from his contacts at the port. Although he mentioned that they had hauled the *Carrie Ann*, and it was in the boatyard for hull and engine repairs. Nice, I thought, one less bother to contend with.

I met with Gus over the weekend and he and his crew were set to spend at least two weeks on site for starters; I planned on sending Joe out with them. I thought it best if they dropped anchor away from the shoal and slowly, over a few days, worked their way towards our site. Joe and Wild Bill could make some preliminary dives and record anything of interest that might be in the area. That would also help us with our cover should it come into question. Gus had volunteered Wild Bill. He had said, "He is a first-class underwater operator and would be perfect as Joe's dive buddy." During the previous week, we had purchased four diver propulsion units to help us cover more area while on the bottom. Battery operated, they pulled the diver along saving on physical exertion and air while allowing the diver to cover a large search zone visually. Since we were still looking for the actual location of the ship, they could use their dive time to scan the area for any possible clues. Dimitri, Tony, and Junkyard had work or other Commitments they had been putting off attending to and wouldn't be available till the weekend. So, Lawrence and I would join the *Falcon* in the *Lisa B* on Thursday and continue moving slowly toward our treasure site, the shoal. The weather was looking good, our gear was stowed on both boats, and the team was eager to get started.

The *Falcon* anchored south of the shoal by a couple of miles with no incidents. By the time Lawrence and I got to them in the *Lisa B*, they had worked their way to within a half mile of the shoal and had covered the bottom pretty thoroughly in that area. They had even identified and marked old cape rocket debris on the bottom and plotted it on the chart on board the *Falcon*. "Nice touch," I told them; our cover was coming together. Lucky for us they had done that because the next day we had an unexpected visit from the Coast Guard. It was nothing special, just a cursory visit and general vessel safety inspection, which we passed easily.

They checked our papers and looked over the chart with the notations on it and seemed pleased with what they saw. As they left, they said if we needed anything, just give them a call. We said we would and with that our first "official" inspection was passed. We all breathed a little easier after they had left, and got back to work.

We spent the night on anchor near the *Falcon*. The next morning, Joe and Wild Bill continued with their diving as we went over the equipment that Junkyard had put together for sand removal. It wasn't pretty, but he guaranteed it would do the job. The plan was to get back to our site the next day, Saturday, and do our first excavation that afternoon. We would follow the same drill on the *Falcon* that we did on our first dives. She would anchor parallel to the shoal, and they would put the sand removal rig over the seaward side hidden from view from the west by the cabin and mostly from the east by the *Lisa B* anchored there. We would head back to port that afternoon and pick up the rest of the guys and bring them out Saturday morning to help with diving, and with luck, the recovery of the two crates we had left hidden in the sand.

By Saturday morning, as we gathered, the air was electric; we were all wired to the max. As the *Lisa B* left the port and turned north for her rendezvous with the *Falcon*, the guys were checking and re-checking gear, looking over the radar and sonar screens, and generally pacing around the whole deck of the boat. If I weren't as wrought up as they were, I would have been laughing my ass off at them, but I was having trouble staying at the helm and not joining them in their nervously excited antics. We got to the *Falcon* by 8 a.m., staying clear of the large orange buoys with the dive flags attached to them that they had set out, denoting the current search area and divers down. We dropped anchor and Dimitri, followed by Tony and Doc, immediately went over the side and swam to the *Falcon*. I figured they had planned this little swim on our way out. Junkyard, Lawrence, and I waited for the dingy to arrive and shuttle us over. Gus and Smitty greeted us as we arrived and said Joe and Wild Bill had gone down about 15 minutes ago. The three mad swimmers were already getting into wet suits and pulling out scuba tanks and gear we had stowed on the *Falcon* as we came aboard. The seas were calm with a very mild swell and what looked like good visibility. As had been planned, the guys went over the side to meet up with the other two divers on the bottom and get to the location of our hidden crates. They had already dropped a small buoy marking the location based on our GPS numbers.

Once they definitely located the site, they would move the marker, return to the surface for the rest of the gear, and get busy with the recovery. The rest of us would stand by on board to launch the inflatable and man the Coms. It took about 15 minutes to find the exact location and uncover the undercut in the shoal by hand. We listened to the conversation going on below between the divers and could tell by their voices when they had uncovered the open crate. I heard Wild Bill's awed voice over the Coms as he saw the gold bars lying in the crate for the first time. "Holy Shit, Master Chief!"

CHAPTER ELEVEN

The moment got a little chaotic as Wild Bill and Joe viewed the treasure for the first time. Everyone wanted to speak at once. I finally got their attention and instructed Joe and Bill to return to the surface for the excavation gear. Since they were using two of the re-breathers, they didn't have to worry about limited air supply as the others did using Scuba tanks. They surfaced a few minutes later, and we offloaded the device for clearing sand and three of the new 1,000-pound lift bags. Once they were all on the bottom, the excavation began in earnest. The lift was 20 feet of lightweight PVC pipe with an air nozzle inserted in it about 12 inches from the suction end.

The nozzle was pointed toward the far end of the pipe and had an airline from one of our scuba tanks hooked to it. The exhaust end of the pipe had a small bit of floatation material hooked to it and a weight so when the air was turned on the pipe floated at about a 30 to 40-degree angle. As the Compressed air entered and rose up the pipe it expanded and pushed the water inside out the end thus creating a vacuum at the mouth of the pipe which sucked sand and more water in, then spit it out at the exhaust end. We had rigged a catch net for the exhaust of the pipe to retrieve any small artifacts that might get picked up by the suction.

All in all, it was a very clever, efficient, and cheap way to remove the bottom sand. Although it was a little clumsy to handle, it got the job done. I could see the brown cloud forming in the water below us as the sand was lifted from the bottom of the shoal and deposited about 20 feet away by the lift. The larger the cloud, the more material being moved; luckily, the cloudy water could only be seen close-up or from the air. I wasn't too worried about anyone seeing our operation. If spotted, it would be easy to identify as a dredge in use, and that wouldn't be a good thing. In a few minutes, we got word from the divers that they had uncovered the second crate about four feet deep in the sand and were turning off the lift to start loading the lift bags. If I thought they sounded excited before, this was like kids on Christmas morning. With our cover in place, we didn't have to worry about using the deck-mounted hoist anymore. Once the lift bags reached the surface, Smitty, who was in the water waiting, floated them over to the winches' hook/net and we lifted the bags out of the water, rotated the hoist, and placed them on the deck. The first bag contained the remainder of gold from the first crate, 24 bars. When we lowered it to the deck, we gathered around it and stared.

Gus said, "I'll be damned; you did find treasure."

"Yep," I said as we unloaded the bag and began stacking the ingots on the deck.

The Coms squawked as I heard Joe say they had the second crate loaded intact and were sending it up. I couldn't stop grinning as I looked at Gus's astonished expression.

"Gus," I said, "I'm pretty sure you and your crew are about to get a raise." The second lift bag hit the surface, and we repeated the retrieval process. This time, it was an intact wooden crate. It looked to be about a foot or so square and seven or eight inches high. We grabbed the crowbar and carefully removed the top. Having been Completely buried in the sand the wood on the crate was in remarkably good shape.

As we pried the top up, 12 more gold bars saw the light of day, the first since 1715, more than 300 years ago. I just stared for a couple of minutes and thought this is indeed one of those life-changing moments: viewing something no one has seen for 300 years and of such immense wealth.

Now, Gus spoke, "I can't believe this is really happening; you're just bringing this stuff up one after another, easy as pie."

I broke out of my reverie and said, "It looks that way Gus, but I guarantee you a lot of time and hard work have gone into getting to this point. You happen to be lucky enough to have joined our group just before pay-day."

He looked at me, shook his head and said, "No shit, Captain!"

The Coms squawked again; it was Doc this time, "Colt, you copy?"

I went to the table where the Com unit was set up and keyed the mic, "I'm here, Doc."

"We've gone over the hole created by the second crate and the surrounding area, no more hits with the detectors."

"Roger that, we've got about another hour left of bottom time, continue moving north along the base of the shoal," I said.

"Copy, moving north," Doc replied.

Within five minutes, Joe came over the radio, "I've got a hit, and it's a big one!"

Doc came back, "Colt, Joe's about ten feet in front of us moving north; we're taking the lift to his position now."

"I copy" I said. Now, it was starting to get crazy on deck. Gold bars were being removed from the crate and stowed next to the wheel house; the higher the stack got, the more excited everyone became.

Twenty-five minutes later, Joe's voice came over the radio, "We've got another... no, wait... Holy Shit, we have two more crates down here." I dropped into one of the deck chairs and the mic I had been holding fell from my grip.

Everyone had stopped what they were doing and were just standing, staring at the radio. I don't know how much time went by, but in a minute or two, I said under my breath, "Son of a bitch!"

Now there was serious chatter from below. There were whoops and hollers coming over the radio, and when it finally sunk in, the deck exploded with the same responses, and the celebrations began! One crate was found almost directly on top of the second and around five feet deep in the sand. We surmised that was the way they were stacked in the longboat when she broke up and they fell straight to the bottom, unaffected by the waves or storm.

Within the next hour and a half, we had raised the two new crates, still intact, and had them on board. The three scuba boys were just about out of air, so all divers returned to the surface. We got all the equipment on board and stowed, and once the divers had their gear off, we gathered around the last two crates. Just like the other two, when the lids came off, there were three layers of gold ingots, each ingot was about four inches long, three inches wide and two inches thick, 12 ingots per layer and each crate weighed a little less than 500 pounds. In one day, we had recovered 132 gold ingots, total value somewhere around $44,184,000! Not bad for a day's work!

Once we got things stowed and the deck cleared off, the beer, whiskey, and rum flowed freely. Divvying-up our find eight ways came to a little over five million apiece, and that was only finding four of the crates!

I pulled Gus aside and said, "As of right now you and your men's salary just went to two thousand dollars a day."

He was still walking around like a man in a daze, "Uh, okay," he said with a beer in one hand a bottle of whiskey in the other, "That's just fine, Colt… just fine." With that dazed look still on his face, he turned and walked over to the nearest chair and sat down. I didn't even try to contain myself and went around slapping the other guys on the back and congratulating them with clinking cans, bottles, and glasses. The sun was starting to slowly spread its orange glow in the western sky. Things had settled down a bit as we all sat around on the deck, but the smiles on our faces would have had to been chiseled off. I felt like something should be said so I stood up and looked at everyone, "Gentlemen," I said, "today has been a monumental day, a day I wasn't sure would ever come, especially this soon. We have all worked hard to get here, endured a lot, and now are reaping the rewards of those efforts."

Dimitri looked at me and said "Aw, shit, Colt, don't go getting all philosophical on us."

Everyone laughed, including me, as Doc said, "Let the man finish. I always get a kick out of it when he tries to do this kind of stuff."

Now, everyone roared I knew the moment had passed, so I let it go and finished with, "I just want to thank you all for your efforts and believing in our adventure."

Doc said, "You know there are still six more crates down there and we're going to find them all!" That was followed by a bunch of hell yeahs, damn rights, and a couple of amens!

I doubt that anyone slept much that night. Doc, Joe, and I spent the night on the *Lisa B*, and everyone else stayed on the *Falcon*. We talked quietly until the wee hours of the morning. The excitement finally wore down and sleep crept in for a few hours, but as soon as the sun started coming up, we were wide awake.

We could smell the bacon and fresh coffee smells coming from next door. We had taken the Zodiac last night to our boat, so we motored over to one of Smittys' sumptuous breakfasts of bacon, eggs, hash browns, and some of the best coffee I have ever tasted. We were all trying to contain ourselves, but chores had to be done first and the day's gear laid out on the deck. Once this was done, Lawrence, Dimitri, Joe and Doc suited up and hit the water.

Our shark friends were back, nothing to worry about but the divers had started carrying bang sticks just in case. Using the same plan as the day before, Lawrence and Dimitri continued to work the edge of the shoal with metal detectors while Doc and Joe followed the longitudinal search pattern six to ten feet away from the shoal with their detectors.

As they slowly worked their way northward, it was Doc who came up with the next hit. He reported a moderate signal and began fanning and digging by hand. Luckily, the bottom sand was easily moved, and it wasn't difficult for him to work his way down about a foot and a half to two feet until the glint of gold became visible. He had found a single bar. That confirmed that at least one of the crates had broken open and spilled its contents on the ocean floor. Dimitri and Lawrence had not had any hits next to the shoal base, so they moved a little further out and joined Doc and Joe in the longitudinal search pattern. Within another 15, minutes both Lawrence and Joe had gotten hits and uncovered three more bars about two and a half feet below the sandy bottom. It was slow going, but by the time their scuba tanks were getting low, they had recovered another 16 bars, 20 bars total. That still left 16 out there somewhere.

We were only diving in 20 to 25 feet of water, so there was decent light from the surface. On the bottom, a current was picking up and visibility had decreased from 12 feet or so to 6 to 8 feet. I called the dive, and they put the bars in one of the lift bags and sent it up. It was retrieved by Smitty as the divers surfaced.

Excitement was still running high as we pulled the bag onto the deck. Our stack of ingots continued to grow. The current made it harder to control our broader search area and the lift, so I suggested for the next dive we concentrate back on the edge of the shoal. Although some still wanted to continue our search further out, it was agreed that due to the decreased visibility and the current, searching the shoal edge was our best bet. The shoal helped block some current and made the dive somewhat easier.

After an hour's rest I changed the dive teams and sent Tony, Wild Bill, Smitty, who was chomping at the bit to get below the surface, and Dimitri back down. Gus said Smitty was part fish and would do fine diving with the crew. I told him that was good because I assigned Dimitri as his partner and was sure that Dimitri had gills somewhere on his body. After only 45 minutes, Dimitri called in and said the current had picked up dramatically and visibility had dropped to two to three feet. I had no choice but to call the dive. I wasn't going to risk any of the divers in those kinds of conditions. When everyone was aboard we went through the routine of cleaning and stowing the gear. It was early afternoon, and I decided to call it a day and see what things looked like in the morning. We were going to take the *Lisa B* back in the next day to move the gold to the safety of our facility and to have the scuba tanks filled. I figured we had one more dive session the next morning before we headed back in, current and visibility permitting.

As we sat around the deck, we reviewed and discussed the dives so far. Lawrence asked why we thought we were finding the gold so shallow in the sand. The deepest we had excavated had been around four or five feet. I said I have no idea, just figured we were lucky. Junkyard laughed and said that, during the winter, there was a very strong current that passed around the cape. He thought that most of the sand that might get built up over the summer got moved northward with the current during the winter. So, instead of being ten to twenty feet deep in the sand like it probably would be by the end of summer and hurricane season; it was only two to six feet beneath the sand now at the beginning of the summer season due to the shifting currents. That's also why we saw so many dark shapes in the water during our aerial search. More of their physical shape had been uncovered during the winter by the current. Gus concurred with Junkyard. He said he had run into the currents during his years of fishing in this area and heard many other fishing boats telling of the same thing. There you have it, mystery solved, if only the other mysteries surrounding this wreck were that easily explained.

Unfortunately for us the weather took a turn for the worse during the night and the next morning saw gray skies, wind and choppy seas. No weather for diving! We hauled anchors and headed back to port after loading the gold onto the *Lisa B* which was no mean feat with the Zodiac and the current weather conditions. It was a bumpy ride home, but in a couple of hours, we were inside the Jetties of the port and things smoothed out considerably. We watched Gus pull the *Falcon* into the marina where he had his slip. We headed for the locks to make our way into the Banana River and Tony's house. Another hour and a half and we were safely tied up in the canal and beginning to unload dive gear and "other cargo," very discreetly! We had left the dive weights on the boat and replaced them with shiny gold ones in the dive bags. Two coolers and a couple of other cases we had on board helped us move the gold. The CES cargo van was parked out front, and by the time we got our "gear" loaded, its suspension was being put to work.

Everything included we had over a ton of cargo in the van. We headed for our new CES facility. "I refused to call it our Lair," and there we reversed the procedure once the van was in the cargo bay and the outside bay door was shut. We got busy unloading everything, cleaning it, and staging it for re-loading in the van for our next trip out and moving the ingots to the vault.

In retrospect I'm glad the weather turned on us, no one realized how tired they were until we got back. With the gold secured, I said I was heading out, and Joe and Dimitri said, "Hey, have at least one celebratory drink before you go."

I agreed, and after more back slapping, hand-shakings and hell yeahs, I hit the door to be followed soon thereafter by the rest of the guys. We had agreed to meet the next day at four, and I put in a call to Gus to let him know about the meeting. He said he would be there. As I pulled into my driveway, all I wanted was a hot shower, a soft bed and about 14 hours of sleep. Well, two out of three ain't bad!

CHAPTER TWELVE

The next morning, the weather had gotten worse. Cloudy, rainy, and windy, we weren't going anywhere. I contacted Fitz via our secure Com-link, gave him a quick update, and planned for another pickup and delivery. He congratulated me on the fantastic news and asked how long we'd be in port. I told him I wasn't sure. I would look at the long-range weather forecast and let him know later. He said to call him later that afternoon; he might be able to get away for a visit. I told everyone we were standing down till the weather cleared, so they all had a chance to play catch up after spending the time getting ready for our trip and our past three days at sea.

Doc and I spent more time at the Lair, looking at the oceanographic charts laid out on the conference table, and talking over next moves. We both agreed that finishing up the shoal area search should be priority one. Once we were sure we had found everything we could, we would look for the ship. In the meantime, we speculated on its location projecting out from the shoal. The water in our search area was 20 to 25 feet deep. Within a mile east, it went to 40 to 50 feet and stayed between 40 and 60 feet for the next mile or two. We pulled up the telemetry from Fitz's Neptune on the 70-inch LED screen we had installed in the conference room along with the terminal tied into the "Lair's" cutting edge Computer system... Okay, I called it the Lair, so sue me; it sounds better than Main Office, Headquarters, or Home base, at least more dramatic.

As we sat and reviewed our aerial search, we looked more closely at the dark images on the bottom. Having Fitz's data to Compare our video to was great. We were able to either identify what we had seen or mark it as a bogie and log the GPS info for further underwater inspection. The biggest bogie we had turned out to be a large shrimping boat, 70-feet long, that had sunk during a storm in '72.

She was pretty well intact and lying on her side on the bottom in 60 feet of water. Partially covered by sand, she was visible as a big blob from the air but reviewing Fitz's Neptune data, we had a high-definition image of her. The detail Neptune provided was impressive, like an underwater photograph. After we had stared at the image for quite a while, Doc finally said, "There's something strange about that wreck."

"What do you mean?" I asked.

"Not sure." he replied, "what other angles do we have of her?" I moved the digital image around as much as I could to no real revelation I could see. After some time studying the image, Doc said, "There's just something that's not right. I can't put my finger on it, but it's not right."

I said, "Well I can't see anything; let's take a break, and we'll come back to it." He agreed, and we went on to the rest of the images. By the time we finished, two-and-a-half hours had passed, and our eyes were crossing from staring at the big screen in front of us. We agreed to call it a day. We had identified six images or bogies we thought ought to be investigated first-hand. All were around a mile to a mile and a half east or east-southeast of the shoal... the outer limit was the steel-hulled shrimper wreck.

We speculated that the longboat could not have made it much further than two miles at the most from the ship in hurricane seas before she hit the shoal. That narrowed our search area to the one we had just identified with the video review.

I looked at Doc and said, "I hope our guess is right."

He agreed and said, "It's an educated one, but if we find nothing we expand it using the same parameters we have for this area. We know the hurricane came from east-southeast, winds and waves pushing west by north west. We found the cargo of the longboat on the shoal; the big variable in the equation is how far did the longboat get from the ship before hitting the shoal and breaking apart?"

"That's a big variable! We're thinking only a mile or two, but what if they got three to five miles?"

"Well, then," Doc said, "We will be looking in the wrong area by a large margin, as they say… we'll have our dog in the wrong hunt."

"Well, that's a problem for later. For now, we need to concentrate on finishing what we started and as quickly as possible."

Doc concurred, "Another thing, if we are going to legitimize our, what I'll call Phase Two search, we should incorporate Risky Business and get ready to file a legal search claim with the Feds."

"I know, Doc, just when I was starting to enjoy this whole pirate thing."

He laughed. "We should get Lawrence working on that sooner rather than later; it will take time to make that happen." I agreed and asked him to contact him and get the ball rolling. He agreed, and with that, our little meeting came to an end.

The rest of the week was filled with lousy weather and getting our gear ready for the next trip. Tony was still keeping an eye in the sky on the shoal with no visitors to report. Fitz had come by and made a pickup and delivery, personally, without

Ms. O'Reilly, much to Dimitri's and Lawrence's dismay. We refueled and restocked both vessels. We tried to keep Lawrence busy with the legal stuff that needed attending to for our ship search, but he still found time for a little carousing with the ladies. In fact, he announced he would stay in port on our next trip out. He had an invitation to a Napa Valley wine tasting he couldn't turn down. However, he assured us this would not interfere with his assigned task of getting Risky Business legal, and it would be taken care of ASAP.

I said, "Fine, just don't drop the ball on this, and keep quiet about our work, no bragging about being a millionaire or a treasure hunter." He assured me discretion would be his utmost concern.

I said, "Yeah, right."

I told Junkyard to spend more time at the port, since he was a familiar face, and keep his ears open for any scuttlebutt that might be important for us to know. He said he could handle that and would focus on the Sailor's Choice, a watering hole for port workers, charter boat captains, and crews as well as the Coasties from the port's Coast Guard squadron. "I'll let you know if I hear anything, Colt!"

The forecast for Friday and the next three days were clearing skies and flat seas. Gus said he was sending the *Falcon* back out on Thursday with Wild Bill and

Smitty to get anchored in place, then would ride out with us on Saturday morning.

He said he needed to take care of a couple of things with his daughter. "Of course," I said, "No problem. Joe, Dimitri, Tony and I will head out first light on Saturday, and you can just meet us at the *Lisa B*." I felt pretty good about having put a number of things in motion and was ready for some R & R on Friday before leaving in the morning.

The call came in from Gus at three Friday afternoon. "There was a problem on the *Falcon* and they needed help!"

I called Dimitri and relayed the message. He said meet him at *The Pandemonium* in fifteen minutes. It turned out that was the name of the go-fast that he borrowed from his friend. I contacted Gus and gave him the info, and he said he would meet us there. They had both arrived by the time I was running down the dock and were casting off the lines. The boat was warmed up, and we pulled out of the slip immediately. We got lucky that day because, as we were in the channel leaving the port, we were already up to 50mph. By the time we got to the jetties, you could hear the twin superchargers beginning to scream, and we were hitting the high side of 90. It took us 12 minutes to get to the *Falcon* once we got to open seas.

As we slowed and pulled alongside, we could see the damage to the wheelhouse and cabin area. Broken glass was everywhere. Smitty and Bill tossed us lines as we came alongside; they both looked like they had been through a meat grinder. When we finally got on board, we could see that Smitty was limping and had an eye that was swollen shut; Wild Bill's face didn't look much better, another swollen eye and jaw. They both had split lips, and dried blood covered their faces.

Bill spoke first to Gus, "Master Chief, we're sorry. We did the best we could, but there were five of them, and they kinda took us by surprise." As he was talking to Gus, I surveyed the scene in the wheelhouse and cabin area. Every monitor or display screen had been smashed, the radio was lying on the floor, glass from broken windows littered the chart table, and the computers had been ripped out of their mountings and were lying on the deck in pieces. I turned to see Gus helping Bill to a chair that he had picked up from the deck; that's when I noticed the blood on his shirt. Dimitri had produced a first aid kit and was tending to Smitty's wounds as Gus calmed Bill down and asked who did this to them. Slowly, the story began to unfold.

I had gone below and brought water for both the men. The cabin and galley area had been left untouched. I guess whoever did this figured taking out all the electronics was damage enough. I looked in the engine room and saw nothing out of place. As I handed the water to both men, and Dimitri had moved to work on Bill's injuries, he told the story. It had happened earlier that day. A sport fisherman, approximately 40-feet long had eased alongside them with smoke coming out of the engine compartment. Two men were on board waving their arms and hollering that they needed help. Smitty had gone below to get the big fire extinguisher as Wild Bill threw them a line. As they pulled alongside, three other men came out of the cabin area and jumped Bill. When Smitty got back on deck, the other two were on board and jumped him. Smitty put one of them down with a swing of the fire extinguisher, but then got tackled by the second guy. One of the first three had grabbed Bill's arms and was holding him while the other two used him for a punching bag.

Both men had gotten in a few licks but were rapidly subdued and knocked unconscious. Wild Bill said he did remember catching one of his attackers with a sidekick that connected with the guy's knee and he had heard bones break as the guy screamed and fell to the deck. When they came to, the boat was gone and everything was smashed to pieces. Both men were trying to apologize for not being able to protect the boat at the same time Gus was doing his best to reassure them they did fine and the fact they were okay was the most important thing.

After Dimitri finished looking over Bill, he said it looked like a number of bruises, cuts, and contusions but nothing more serious than that, thankfully. Gus asked if they had any idea who the attackers were, and both men said no. Bill did say he remembered seeing one of those bright orange toss-able life rings hanging from the fly-bridge of the boat with the name *Dizzy D* on it, but neither man saw the transom of the boat to confirm its name or remember ever seeing the men before. Gus's face was a bright shade of crimson as he surveyed the men and the damage that had been done to the boat.

He asked, "Engine room?" I told him I had looked in and things looked okay but we should check further. I said that the galley and bunk area looked untouched. It looked like they had focused on the wheelhouse. "Those sons of bitches will pay for this," he said under his breath.

I said "Don't worry about that now. I'll take care of replacing the equipment that was damaged. Let's just get the boat back to port and get the guys checked out by a doctor. We'll decide what to do after that." He agreed and headed below to check the engine as I made sure the throttles and steering were still operational.

Once we were satisfied we could make it back under our own power, I told Dimitri to head back and we would meet up at the *Falcon's* berth. He was tight- jawed and mumbling to himself, not a good sign! "Hey, Dimitri," I hollered over the growl of the go-fast as we released the lines, "Be cool till we get in; don't do anything stupid!" He just nodded and pulled away with a scowl locked on his face. I knew he was thinking the same thing I was. Those dumb asses from the *Carrie Ann* were behind this and retaliated after all or got friends to do it for them. I figured, between Gus and Dimitri, this would get real ugly before it was over. I knew what the crazy Cossack was capable of, and I could only guess that Gus was just as bad. I would not want to be a member of either vessel's crew, no way!

We made it in okay; Dimitri was waiting for us. I immediately looked for blood, but since none was visible, I breathed a sigh of relief. Gus said he was taking Smitty and Wild Bill to the walk-in clinic and he would call us with an update.

"Good," I said," I'll call Joe and Tony and let them know about the damage and get them out here tomorrow morning to get an assessment and plan for repairs." I noticed Dimitri had said nothing and was standing waiting for Gus and the guys to leave.

When they were gone, he said "I found the bastards."

I raised an eyebrow and said, "And...?"

"They're four docks down next to an empty berth that just happens to be reserved for the *Carrie Ann* when she comes out of the boat-yard."

"Damn it," I said, "I was afraid of that."

"Guess we're going to have to do something about that, right?" Dimitri asked through clenched teeth.

"Yes," I said, "but not now."

"Not now?" he growled, "Why not? They're sitting around on board right over there," he said pointing.

I pulled his arm down and said, "All in due time; all in due time. We don't want to cause a ruckus in the port and draw any unnecessary attention to our operation. Don't forget how much we've got to lose if we get involved in a mess like this and other details come to light." For once Dimitri was listening to the voice of reason and started cooling down. He didn't like it but he understood.

I slapped him on the shoulder and said, "We'll have our chance to even the score, not to worry, my friend."

He turned and looked at me with a clenched tooth grin that would scare the shit out of anyone it was directed at and said, "You bet your sweet ass we will!" The good Lord have mercy on the recipients of this man's anger, I thought, because no one else would!

We walked slowly to our vehicles in the parking lot. As we got to our cars, Dimitri turned and said, "I'm buying the boat."

"What?" I said.

"*The Pandemonium*, I'm buying it."

"Really?" I said.

"Yeah, it's been handy to have around, and I have a feeling we may get more use out of it."

"Okay, what brought that on?" I asked.

"Don't know I'm just so pissed right now I need to do something!"

"So, you're going to buy a go fast, because you're pissed?"

"Yeah, I read about it in *Cosmo*; it's called retail therapy," he said with that grin back on his face. "It helps you get over bad times."

A lot of smart-ass comments came to mind, but I decided I'd better keep them to myself and said, "That's cool."

"Yeah," he said with a noticeable sigh, "I feel better already." As he walked to his vehicle, he said, "Catch you later, Colt."

As I got in my vehicle, I thought, well, at least he didn't kill anybody… that's, a relief, but *Cosmo* and retail therapy… Bizarre doesn't even begin to cover it!

The next day, the crew, except for Junkyard and Lawrence, met at the *Falcon*. Gus and the boys had cleaned things up as best they could. Joe and Tony jumped in and started pulling out the broken units and making a list of what was going to have to be replaced. I asked how long it was going to take to make repairs. They agreed five to seven days, providing everything was available locally.

I said, "You have five, bring in extra techs to help with the general equipment installs, and the two of you focus on the computer systems, satellite system, and secure Com-links." They both nodded and got on their respective cell phones.

I walked up to Dimitri and Gus who were engaged in an animated discussion, just in time to hear from Gus, "The hell you will." It was obvious that Dimitri was not happy with his response. Gus continued, "It's my boat, my crew, and my problem no matter what you say, so I'll take care of it."

"But you know our actions are what precipitated this event."

"…Doesn't matter," Gus said, "my boat, my crew, my problem, end of discussion!"

Frustrated, Dimitri turned and said, "Help me out here, Colt."

As I looked at Gus, he said, "Don't even bother, Colt, I'm gonna take care of this, so don't waste your breath."

I shrugged my shoulders and said to Dimitri, "He's the captain".

Dimitri's frustration from last night was coming back, and Gus's attitude was just adding to it. He wanted action, and he wanted it now! It was time to kick some serious ass, and he wanted to take the lead! "Well, just what the hell are you going to do against five of them?" he asked Gus.

Wild Bill had been listening from a distance and interjected, "I'm pretty sure one of them is in a cast somewhere, so there's probably only four." Dimitri turned and glared at him as he went back about his work.

Gus thought before he answered; he understood the situation and could easily see Dimitri's frustration and pent up anger.

"Dimitri," he said "I know what you're feeling, been down that road many, many times. Responding with a knee-jerk reaction right now won't do us any good; it's not time. But know this," as a big ugly grin spread across his face, "when it is time, I promise I will do you proud!"

Oh, shit, I thought, this means trouble with a capital T! "Now, Gus," I started. He held up his hand, palm toward me, and the discussion was over.

He looked at us both and said, "We've work to do," and turned to the pilot house.

CHAPTER THIRTEEN

Joe and Tony met my five-day deadline, and by Thursday morning, the *Falcon* was truly ship-shape again. New windows in the wheelhouse had been replaced with Lexan; radar, sonar, and VHF Coms had all been replaced by Joe's team. Tony and Joe were able to concentrate on the computer "stuff," and we were up and running, encrypted Coms to Fitz and all. Actually, the new systems in all areas turned out to be a significant upgrade since money was no object this time. Tony and Joe were rightly proud of their accomplishments.

Wild Bill and Smitty, although sore, were pretty much over their injuries and both said they were ship shape and ready to get back out on the water. The weather looked good for the next six days, so I said we could head out that afternoon since all was ready. Gus said, "Let's wait till tomorrow morning; everyone's been working hard and could use some relaxation time this afternoon, get a good night's sleep, and get a fresh start in the morning."

I said I didn't have a problem with that and agreed to meet them at the shoal the next morning in the *Lisa B*. That afternoon was spent under the rear deck canopy of the *Falcon* with music coming out of the new 1200 watt stereo system that had been part of her upgrades, and beverages from the new beer/beverage fridge! Dimitri had brought over two bottles of his favorite Russian Vodka, one for the freezer of the new fridge and one for the Grog locker. By six or so, we began saying our goodbyes and heading out, looking forward to the renewal of our adventure the next day. Gus seemed in a very good mood and was as jovial as I had ever seen him. I was glad to see he had shaken off last Friday's experience and was approaching Thursday with a positive attitude! I learned something very important about Gus that day.

We were about an hour behind the *Falcon* the next morning arriving at the shoal site about 7:30. They had already set the marker buoys out and had the dive gear on deck as we pulled into position on their starboard side, lying off about 30 feet or so. The Zodiac came over and picked us up. Once on board, the first dive team of Joe, Tony, Dimitri, and Smitty began suiting up. I helped Gus move our lift equipment into place for offloading. The guys were just about ready to hit the water when the outside speaker of the VHF radio in the wheelhouse crackled with a mayday from a vessel in distress.

The Coast Guard radio operator responded immediately, requesting vessel identification and location. What I heard next made the hair on the back of my neck stand up. "This is the vessel *Dizzy D* three miles south of the port in route to Ft. Pierce. We've had an explosion and are taking on water. We are abandoning ship and request immediate assistance." I turned slowly and looked at Gus. His face was expressionless as he continued getting gear ready for the dive.

The radio squawked again, "I repeat this is the *Dizzy D*. We are abandoning ship; she is going down, request immediate assistance." The Coast Guard operator responded that the rescue boat and chopper were in route and asked about injuries. "No injuries," came the reply.

"Copy no injuries, eta 14 minutes."

That's when I looked at Dimitri, who was staring at Gus, "Boating can be a dangerous undertaking," he said.

Gus looked up, still expressionless "Sure can," he replied and continued with his preparations.

I saw the grin spread over Dimitri's face as he finished donning his gear and I swear I heard him say under his breath, "Nicely done."

I said nothing and helped the divers in their final preparations. Five minutes later, all four were in the water, headed for the bottom. I did my best to put that radio transmission and its implications out of my head and concentrate on the task at hand for the rest of the morning as the radio chattered in the background, but it was difficult.

We did our Com check, and I asked for a sit-rep once the divers were down. The report was good, almost no current, good visibility, but some sand had built up at the shoal base since our last dive. At least it covered all our dredging activities so far, I thought. Dimitri and Joe were teamed up at the base of the shoal that morning, and Wild Bill and Tony were searching further out. They determined the ending point of the previous search and began the same basic search pattern we had used before. Fifteen minutes later, Wild Bill got a hit with his detector and uncovered two gold bars about two feet deep in the sand. This was his first personal find, and he was excited, whooping and carrying on over the Coms. We all had to smile, even Gus.

Doc was grinning and said, "So it begins again; that only leaves 14 bars from the broken crate still unaccounted for." The day was starting out well, I thought.

Unfortunately, that was the extent of our recovery for the morning dive. Once all the divers were back on the boat and were rehydrating and resting, we discussed the lack of further discoveries in the morning's search. There were quite a few long faces, and I was afraid we had all gotten too used to finding a lot of gold with each outing. Not that two gold bars weren't quite a bit, especially at around $333,000.00 per bar, but the large quantities we had found previously and with such regularity were desensitizing us to the significance of the smaller finds.

As I pondered that thought, I realized that thinking that was just freaking crazy. For a couple of hours' work, we had just made over a half million dollars, and we were talking like it was minimum wage, small potatoes! I said to everyone, "Reality check time. Remember, as Dimitri pointed out months back, it's called treasure hunting, and we may have gotten spoiled with the treasure finding we've been doing. There are still five crates out there; we know we are in the right location, and we need to continue to apply ourselves and make sure we search the area thoroughly. The crates didn't get up and walk away, so let's review the chart and see if we've missed anything and, if not, we'll keep following the plan until we're satisfied we've done all we can."

Joe said, "I agree, Colt, it's just things were going so well in the beginning."

"Right" Dimitri chimed in.

"I know," I said, "but let's not forget there is still a ship out there that needs finding! And from what we have found so far, she's a very rich ship."

We spread the chart on the table, and all gathered round. On it, we had marked the exact location of each find with their GPS numbers. As I looked at it, I began to see a pattern and spoke up. "Look at this," I said as I pointed to each of the crate discovery locations and the individual bar sites. "Anybody notice anything?"

Doc was the first to speak, "There's a pattern."

Joe picked up a grease pencil and inscribed a half circle, starting at the base of the shoal and encompassing all our finds, terminating back at the base of the shoal.

Dimitri jumped in, "All our finds have been in this area," he said as he pointed to the half circle on the map. "Where we started at the south end of the shoal, we found nothing till here, where we found the first crates, then more up through this area," as he traced his finger along the base of the shoal. "Now, we've covered another 75 yards beyond Smitty's find this morning with nothing more than a small fishing boat anchor and a piece of an old metal ice chest."

Doc had been studying the map and spoke up, "I think we have made an erroneous assumption."

I said, "Go on, Doc."

He pointed to the center of the half circle and said, "I believe we have assumed the longboat hit the shoal broadside, broke up, and sank here."

"Agreed," I said.

"That may have been our mistake," Doc replied.

I was looking intently at Doc now and said, "I think we may have the same idea; go ahead."

"We know the longboat was somewhere in the 35-foot-in-length range, possibly longer. If one end of it was pointing almost due east when she hit the shoal instead of broadside, it's possible that when her keel hit the coral, it broke her back, in essence breaking her in half and very possibly dumping half her contents on the east side of the shoal and the next wave along may have picked up the other half and deposited it on the western side."

That was what I had thought as I looked at the distribution of our finds on the map. That could account for the concentration of bars in this area and nothing north or south of it. Now, the buzz started again. Once it settled down, Doc suggested we go back to the center of our half circle and start working our way over the shoal and down the other side. We should be able to determine the validity of our new hypothesis fairly quickly. If we found nothing, then it would truly be back to square one. It was decided the next dive team would work their way up the side of the shoal, starting from the center point of the half circle, checking out the crevice's and cracks, then across the top, which was only about 10 to 12 feet below the surface and 30 to 40 feet wide, and then back down to the bottom on its western side. Doc and I would move the *Lisa B* to the other side of the shoal to be the tender for the divers, and Smitty would have the inflatable in the water between us and the shoal.

The excitement had returned as the divers donned their gear and Gus repositioned the *Falcon*. The same dive team hit the water and made a four-man line moving up the face of the shoal, peeking and poking every crevice with detectors and hands.

They were a few feet below the crest of the shoal when Joe came over the Coms, "I've got something,"…a couple of minutes later, "It's another bar," he shouted.

I looked at Doc and said, "Damn, you may have figured this one out," and slapped him on the back.

He smiled and said, "I hope so."

As the divers crested the shoal, Dimitri sang out, "Got another one!" Now, the excitement of our earlier discoveries had returned, and there was a constant flow of chatter between the divers as they crossed the top of the shoal and began their descent down its other side.

Wild Bill chimed in next, "I need a pry bar. I've got two wedged in a crevice and can't budge them." Tony replied he had a small pry bar and would bring it to him. Together, they worked for about ten minutes, finally freeing both bars. That only left ten bars out there from the broken crate, that is if only one crate broke. They found one more bar on their way to the bottom, down to nine now.

Once on the bottom, they used the same search pattern as we had on the other side, two divers close to the base and two 10 to 12 feet out. We had sent them over in the middle of our eastern search area and told them to move south first till they got to the edge of our half circle, which we know continued to the other side to make a full circle; they would then return to the center and search north. Getting close to the end of the second dive, Dimitri said he had a hit, much stronger than the single bar hits they had been getting. A few minutes later, he called for the lift to be sent down.

He had hand-fanned his way down about a foot or so and the signal was getting stronger but he needed to move more sand. Gus loaded the lift gear and a couple of lift bags into the Zodiac that we had sent around to the *Falcon* and brought them to our side of the shoal just as Joe was surfacing to take delivery.

As Joe dropped below the surface with the lift, I could sense Doc's excitement; it was looking like our broken in half theory may have been right! Twenty minutes and a large brown cloud of dredged sand covering the area, Dimitri exclaimed, "Two more crates, one almost directly on top of the other."

"Son of a bitch, we were right," I said to Doc.

He had a Cheshire cat grin on his face as he said, "We're back in business!"

As the crates were brought to the surface by the lift bags, one at a time they were slowly herded over the shoal to the *Falcon* and its winch and pulled on board. The guys were running low on air, and no additional discoveries had been made, so all divers surfaced. Once they swam over to the *Falcon* we maneuvered the *Lisa B* back into a rafting position. Tying the *Falcon* right up against the *B* with only large fenders between us made our going from one vessel to the other much easier, and in these calm seas, not the least bit dangerous.

Once on board, we examined the crates and found them to be identical to the ones we had previously found. When we opened them, we saw the same bar configuration as in the others. Three layers of 12 ingots each for 36 bars in each crate. We unloaded the crates and placed the bars on deck. I tried to do the mental math for our find thus far, and it totally escaped me. I'm sorry; I just have a hard time dealing with numbers that large in my head, not to mention I kept thinking, "We're multi-millionaires, every one of us, Freaking multi-millionaires!"

We agreed to call it a day and get a fresh start in the morning. According to the weather reports and radar scans, we had good weather for at least two to three more days. The routine kicked in, gear cleaned, checked, and stowed. Ingots hidden under cover and music rocking out of the boat's exterior speakers made for a very festive atmosphere. Beverages were passed all around, and the toasting started again. From the lows I saw on the crews' faces this morning to the high-pitched level of excitement now, I figured tonight would be one hell of a celebration on the *Falcon*, and I had no intention of putting a damper on it! As the afternoon progressed and everyone started to relax some, I noticed Gus had moved to the gunwale of the boat and was staring into the distance. I really had kept this morning's incident with the *Dizzy D* at bay, but it was like an itch that couldn't be scratched, and I really needed to scratch it. I walked over to Gus and leaned on the rail next to him, handing him a fresh cold beer.

He accepted it without looking at me, took a long swig, and said, "Okay, Colt, we might as well get this over with."

Without looking at him, I asked point blank, "the *Dizzy D*, was that you?"

He took another long hit on his beer and said, "Yep."

I said, "Jesus, Gus, you could have killed someone!"

He turned to look at me and said, "No, I couldn't have."

I said, "What the hell do you mean you couldn't have? You sank the freaking boat."

"I know," he replied.

I said, "Someone could have died."

He turned and looked at me with a face I had never seen before, anger, strength, and disdain all in one. "No one dies unless I want them to."

"You can't be sure of that," I said.

"Yes, I can," he replied.

"How so?" I asked."

He said through clenched teeth, "I have been blowing up shit all my life Colt, big shit, little shit; been trained by the very best. I know what I'm doing and I'm VERY good at it! Like I said earlier, my boat, my crew, my problem…My Solution! This conversation is over; don't bring it up again," he said as he turned and walked to the guys sitting around the table on the rear deck and immediately joined in the jovial conversation as if nothing had just happened.

I just stood there. Holy shit, I thought, this is one tough, dangerous son of a bitch, talented, but dangerous. I'm sure as hell glad he's on my team I thought as I filed away the, "never mention the *Dizzy D* incident to him again," note to self. I hoped I hadn't screwed up our relationship with my questioning. I really liked and respected Gus; screwing up now could be disastrous for the team and the work ahead of us. After a few more minutes, I joined the group and put a smile on my face. Dimitri looked at me with that, "What's going on?" look. I almost imperceptibly shook my head, and he nodded slightly, put his smile back on, and went back to the celebration.

As I stood there with a thousand things swirling in my mind, Gus walked up and slapped me on the back with a huge grin on his face and said, "Damn, Colt, in all the excitement, I haven't even said Congratulations," and stuck out his hand.

I took that firm grasp and returned it, saying "Thanks, Gus," with a real smile making its way to my face.

He said, "Since we've hit it big again, I don't suppose me and the boys could talk you into another one of those raises?"

I looked at him still, grinning, and said, "We'll talk."

He broke out in a big laugh, slapped me on the back again, and said, "That's good enough for me, Colt." He turned and walked away, singing some sea shanty something or other, and I thought, well, I guess Gus and I are okay. What a freaking relief!

The next morning dawned bright and clear with a few Cirrus clouds spreading the golden glow of the sunrise across the horizon and a light salty breeze the parfum de jour. I had slept better than I had in weeks and awoke refreshed and ready to seize the day. I was energized and anxious to get divers in the water, but the smells coming from the galley of the *Falcon* soon sidetracked me, and I realized a good breakfast was the best way to start the day.

I didn't realize how hungry I was until I sat down with the rest of the guys and had my second helping of Smitty's pancakes, eggs, bacon, hash browns, and coffee. Smitty was an exceptional ship's cook, but for some reason, today everything tasted better than any I'd had before, and I savored every bite. Within an hour, we had divers ready to hit the water and continue our search.

As they swam across the top of the shoal, Doc and I once again maneuvered the *Lisa B* into position on the west side of the shoal. We had secured the lift to the bottom last night, figuring we would be using it again today, and the seas and weather posed no threat to us losing it during the night.

They found it where it was left, and the two teams started their sweep south toward the edge of the search perimeter we had laid out on the chart. Nothing new came up by the time they reached the edge of the search area, and I told them to go back to the center point and now work north. Once there, they started moving along the base of the shoal; they got a couple of minor hits which turned out to be bottom junk but continued on.

Halfway through the morning search, Joe said he had a hit. He and Dimitri were working the outer area of the search grid as Tony and Wild Bill worked close to the shoal base. The lift was employed, and the first gold bar of the day came to light under three feet of sand. Fifteen minutes later, I heard Wild Bill calling Tony to come to his location about ten feet away from the shoal base. He said he was getting a strange reading on his detector.

Tony replied, "On my way," and all was quiet for another ten minutes.

I picked up the mic, keyed it, and asked Tony what was going on. In a minute, he replied, "Bill has got a pretty strange reading down here, it's varied in depth and strength, and the area where we're getting it is about 10 to 12 feet long."

Tony said "We're bringing the lift in and going to start moving sand." Soon after, I saw the brown cloud forming in the water. Twenty minutes later, Tony reported they were down about two feet and still getting strong readings. After another ten minutes, Tony said they were down about three feet, and he'd found broken pieces of wood that looked like part of another crate. Dimitri came on and said he and Joe were there and helping with the sand removal. The brown cloud was getting much larger and spreading; it was obvious these guys were excavating with their hands as well as the lift and really stirring up the sand.

"Holy shit," I heard Dimitri exclaim.

Then Tony added, "Son of a bitch, Colt, you better get down here. We've found another crate that's busted up."

"Great," I replied.

"Yeah, I mean, No," Tony said.

"Say again," I said.

"Colt, get your ass down here. The crate and gold ingots are laying on part of a skeleton; you've got to see this!" I don't think the entire message had a chance to register in my mind as I threw on the third rebreather and grabbed my fins. I was putting my mask on as I flipped myself backwards over the side. The last thing I saw was Doc's hand signal for me to turn on my radio. I slipped on my fins as I headed down; visibility was marginal with all the sand in the water, but I found the guys huddled around the end of the lift pipe.

I heard Doc say over my radio, "Colt, Com check."

"Five by five," I said.

"Roger that," came the reply. As I swam up, I saw where the sand had been cleared, revealing a broken crate with gold bars scattered around on top of what appeared to be white sticks protruding from the sand. When I got closer, the white sticks turned into the femurs and tibias of two legs of a skeleton. I couldn't believe my eyes. In all our searching and recovery, we had never come across anything this sobering. It had been easy to accept the fact that lives had been lost trying to save what we had been finding. The only direct contact we had to those individuals had been the gold. No faces, only names on paper 300 years removed from us. And now, right before our very eyes, was the remains of a person who had been on that ship, who had tried to save his life and given it in the name of king and country. The excitement drained away, and I felt like I had just become a grave robber, and it sent chills down my spine. No one spoke for the longest time till Docs voice came over the Coms asking what the hell was going on down there and was everyone all right?

"Yeah," Joe replied, "we're all okay just a little freaked out by what we found, an actual member of the crew of a 1715 treasure ship; that's all."

CHAPTER FOURTEEN

Once the shock of our discovery wore off, I picked up the lift tube, Tony had dropped and removed more sand from the area around the crate. It was then we saw that both legs were broken where the crate was resting. There was no way to know if this had happened in the original accident, or over time as the body deteriorated. I moved up the skeleton, revealing the pelvic, area and then the corner of another crate. The skeleton was lying face up, and, once we removed more of the sand, we found his chest had been crushed by the weight of a second crate. The skeleton's left arm was wrapped around the crate, its boney fingers grasping its edge, as if in an embrace. But it was a deadly embrace. The only way this could have happened was while the person was still alive. He must have been trying to move the 500-pound crate off his chest with one arm while being pinned to the bottom by its weight. Once again, silence.

I heard Dimitri say, "What should we do, Colt?" I knew there were strict legal protocols that went into effect when human remains are found at a traditional archaeological site, but this excavation was neither traditional nor an archaeological dig.

After a few minutes, I told the guys to remove the scattered gold bars from the skeleton and the area around it but not to disturb the remains.

No one questioned the order and began the removal. I told Dimitri and Joe to remove the contents of the broken crate until they could lift it off the legs.

"I'll continue removing sand around the torso rib cage area, and when it's cleared, we'll attach a lift bag to the crate on his chest and lift it off."

Work was progressing at a good pace but with caution and reverence. I had the area of the chest cleared and had backed away while the lift bag was being attached to the crate sitting there. The left arm was moved and placed alongside the skeleton. All the gold and debris had been removed from the legs, and Wild Bill had come over to help with the crate on the chest. He laid his metal detector next to me on the bottom as he helped with the delicate operation. The lifting bag was filled with air ever so slowly, so that, as it rose, its movements could be controlled by Dimitri and Joe. The bag lifted the crate two inches, four, then ten inches; when it got to about 12 inches and cleared the remains, they guided it away from the skeleton until it was clear and moved out of the way.

We looked at the white bones, and for the first time noticed that where the crates had been sitting on the legs and the chest, there were scraps of cloth lying in place remnants of trousers and shirt I guessed. As the crate on his chest was moved, the unmistakable glint of gold was revealed. A heavy gold chain with a large gold crucifix on it encircled the skeleton's neck. The crucifix was jewel encrusted and glittered even in these silty waters. Wild Bill moved forward hand outstretched, toward the necklace.

As I grabbed his wrist, I said, "No, leave it there."

"But it's worth a fortune," I heard him say.

"I know, but I believe it needs to stay right where it is." Call it superstition, respect, intuition, whatever you want, but I knew we had to leave it.

Dimitri's nodding head was followed by, "I agree." As I looked around, I saw they had removed the gold and it had been placed in the net bags of the lifts waiting to head for the surface.

I said to no one in particular, "We need to re-cover him before we go." I reached down to move the detector that had dropped next to me while the bags were being filled with air and noticed the LCD display was going crazy. Going full bars then nothing, full bars then nothing. I picked it up, and it continued doing the same thing. A malfunction I guessed and shut it off and turned it back on as I moved further away while the body was being re-covered. The display resumed normal operation, and when I got it close to the gold in the bags, it deflected as it should. I swung the detector back around to the area where I had been kneeling in the sand, and the display went crazy again. What the hell, I thought as I moved the detector over the bottom and the signal stopped and started again. That's when I noticed the deflection was occurring whenever I passed it over the area where the skeleton's outstretched right arm disappeared into the sand. I said, "Guys, look at this." They stopped covering the skeleton and came to look.

"That's weird," Joe said. "That detector has been working fine all day. What the hell could cause that kind of reaction?"

"I don't know," I said, "but whatever it is, it's right in this area," pointing to the bottom where the half-buried arm and hand of our skeleton would be. Dimitri got the lift turned on and began vacuuming the sand away. Everything below the elbow was still covered with sand, so he began a sweeping motion clearing the sand from the bones of the forearm. At two feet deep the bones of the hand came into view and, as the fingers were uncovered, we saw that they had a loop of black rope or line in their grasp and on the index finger of the hand was a large gold signet ring. This was no ordinary seaman we had found, not wearing that golden crucifix and a ring like that!

It was then that Tony said, "I just went on reserve." He was using scuba gear on this dive. Wild Bill followed up with, "I've got about 100 psi before I hit it too." Joe, Dimitri, and I had the re-breathers on, so we didn't have any air issues. I sent the two scuba guys up with the lift bags, telling them we would follow in a few more minutes. As they rose to the surface, we continued clearing sand around the hand and looped rope, uncovering part of one side of a chest that had the rope attached as its handle. I took the detector and held it close to the blackened wood, and it went nuts again; when I moved it away, it was fine.

Joe said, "What the hell?"

"I don't know, but whatever is in this box is having a screwy effect on the detector." Dimitri had shut off the lift, and the slight current was helping clear the water. We knelt there, looking at the hand and the side of the box.

"Well?" Dimitri said.

"Yeah," Joe replied, "What now?"

After a moment's hesitation, I replied, "Doesn't make sense to leave it here; I say we dig it out."

"Hell, yeah," Joe replied.

Doc had gotten an update when the divers reached the surface and had been following our conversation over the Coms. His voice broke in, "All right, guys, what have you got going on down there? I'm jumping out of my skin up here."

We all three chuckled. I gave Doc the details of our find and told him we needed the two foxhole shovels from the storage locker on the boat. "Roger that," he said.

Within five minutes, I saw a diver heading down from the surface; it was Wild Bill, and he was making a free dive to us with the shovels. He handed them off, we gave a thumbs up, and he took a quick look at what we had found. I saw his eyes widen through the glass in his face mask as he took in the scene. With a grin and big okay signal, he headed for the surface, exhaling as he went. Those Navy divers, with just a couple of good breaths of air at the surface, could free dive to depths of 60, 70 feet easily, hang out for a bit, and then return to the surface.

With shovels in hand, Joe and I unscrewed the locking ring at the top and flipped the shovel blades 90 degrees to the handle, making them perfect trenching tools. Carefully using them like a pick, we would dig in the sand and then pull it away from the box. Dimitri had turned on the lift again and, as we stirred up loose sand, he would suck it out of the hole we were creating around the box.

Once we got one side fully cleared, I stopped digging to inspect it more closely. It was black and covered in a substance that looked like tar. Over time, it had hardened, and I guessed it was pitch, used on boats for centuries as caulking and waterproofing. I realized my breathing had increased and my heart was pounding. We had found a crate or box that had been sealed and waterproofed in 1715 to protect something inside. If the waterproofing had done its job, whatever it contained might still be in as good a shape as the day it was placed there 300 years ago.

I resumed digging with renewed enthusiasm and within 15 minutes we had uncovered the entire box. It was about the same size as the crates that had contained the gold bars, maybe slightly larger. I reached down and removed the rope handle from the skeletal hand. I told Joe to get his hands underneath his side of the crate, and we would try to slide it as far as we could away from the skeleton.

Expecting the weight of the previous crates, around 500 pounds, we were surprised when we could not only slide it but pick it up and move it. Once out of its hole, we examined the entire surface of the container and could see no cracks or disturbed sections of the pitch covering. It looked as if the seal was still intact. Dimitri had shut off the lift again and was observing the box when two more divers arrived. It was Wild Bill and Tony; they had gotten new tanks and had come back down to help. I put them to work finishing covering the sailor's remains with sand as Dimitri and Joe placed the black box into the net bag of the third lifting device. I filled the hole the box had come out of and was covering the extended appendage when I saw the ring again.

Carefully, I reached down and removed it from its skeletal resting place and put it in my vest pocket. Taking the ring that might help us identify this person differed completely from taking his crucifix, I rationalized, as I continued helping cover the remains. When we finished, I surveyed the area and was satisfied. Not only had we covered our excavation tracks, but we had covered the remains of this unknown individual in his original resting place.

As we paused, Wild Bill asked over the Coms if we should say something over the remains. I had no idea what to say and since no one else responded, I guessed they didn't either.

So, I said, "Bill, what do you suggest?"

Bill was kneeling in front of the burial site and bowed his head.

After a couple of minutes, I heard "Lord, we commit this body to the deep, to be turned into corruption, looking for the resurrection of the body when the sea shall give up her dead and the life of the world to come, through our Lord Jesus Christ, Amen."

Through the Coms, I heard the amens, even Doc's from topside and so added my own.

With our impromptu ceremony completed, we gathered our gear and our mystery box and slowly made our way to the surface.

On the way up, I said "Thanks, Bill, well spoken."

He replied, "Thank you, Sir. It wasn't much, but I just thought, from one sailor to another, we needed to do something for him."

"You were right, Chief; I'm sure it was appreciated."

I could hear the smile in his voice as he said, "Yes, Sir."

We got the equipment on board the *Falcon* and then all worked to hoist the black box on board. It was the center of attention as soon as it hit the deck. Those of us who were helping from the water clambered out, tossed off our gear, and went to get a better look at the mysterious box.

Doc was kneeling next to it when I got there, and I said, "Well, what do you think?"

His reply was no help. "I don't know, but whatever it is, it's lighter than the other crates and was sealed in a way to be watertight."

"Agreed," I said, "But why?"

"That we won't know, dear Colt, until we open it and examine the contents."

Most everyone was eager to do just that, but Doc said, "I recommend we not touch it until we get it in some kind of a conservation laboratory environment."

Dimitri said, "But we don't have anything like that at the Lair!"

We cringed at the name but agreed and simultaneously, four of us said "Fitz!"

Doc said, "I think that's a wise choice; I'm sure he has a facility that would meet our needs. We need to contact him immediately."

"Tony…" I said.

"On it, Boss," he said as he headed for the wheel-house and our communications center.

Doc said, "Let's get a cover over it and get it on the Lisa B for transport." After moving all the ingots and the black box over, we gathered around the table for our informal debrief. The guys who had stayed on board were all ears and wide-eyed as we told of the skeleton and the other discoveries.

When we had finished, Gus said, "Son of a bitch. This is the shit they make movies out of."

"Yeah," Smitty concurred, "movies!"

"Maybe so," I said "but right now we have one hell of a mystery on our hands and I, for one, can't wait to get some answers." I reached in my pocket and pulled out the signet ring I had taken from the skeleton and passed it to Doc. It was gold, large, and encrusted with I'm guessing precious stones around the center crest, "Another research project for you, Doc."

"You find this down there?" he asked.

"I took it off a finger of the hand that was holding the black crate."

"Oh, I see," he said, eyeing it closely.

"I was hoping you could research the crest and maybe it would give us a clue to who that guy was."

"Maybe so; maybe so," he said, still eyeing the ring intently.

It was getting late in the afternoon, so we decided to take the *B* and head in. I asked Gus and the guys to spend one more night out there just to help maintain our cover. I told them we would meet with them as soon as we got word from Fitz as to what our next move would be with the crate. Gus said no problem they would do some fishing and head back in tomorrow afternoon and wait at his slip for our call.

"Sounds good," I said as we cast off the lines that had held us rafted together the last two days. They manned boat hooks, and we pushed ourselves away from the *Falcon* as Dimitri fired up the diesel. After the initial belching of black smoke settled, we made a wide turn and headed west-southwest toward the mouth of the port at a sedate six knots. No time to draw any attention to our activities, I thought. The seas were calm, just a moderate chop with a nice breeze at our backs. Doc walked up to me in the wheelhouse as the rest of the guys opened beverages and sat around on the rear deck.

"I've got an interesting fact for you."

"What's that?" I asked.

"Something I bet you haven't thought about."

"Go on."

"You realize we have found ALL ten crates," he said with a huge grin.

"No shit!" I exclaimed. I hadn't thought about it; I was so wrapped up in our discoveries, I hadn't bothered to count.

"Yep," he said, "not bad for a bunch of amateurs!"

Now, I was grinning from ear to ear, "Not bad at all, Doc!"

We followed our usual procedure, and this time we eased up to the dock behind Tony's house instead of our slip at the port. We cleaned all our gear and stowed it, waiting for the sun to go down before removing the gold bars from below decks. Once again, we stuffed them in dive bags, coolers, and other mundane carrying devices. By the time we had everything loaded into the CES van, it was getting dark. Time for one cold celebratory beer and a little conversation before it turned dark enough to load the black crate onto our dock cart and roll it out to the van.

We agreed to meet the next day, said our respective goodbyes, and Dimitri, Joe, Doc, and I headed for the Lair. When we arrived, we pulled the van into the loading bay, and when the door was closed and all security systems reset, we began unloading. As we stacked the new load of gold bars in the vault, I surveyed the scene and thought, man, this looks like freaking Fort Knox! We had five stacks of gold bars about two and a half feet high and a shelf full of bundles of 100-dollar bills. We set the crate on the metal table inside the vault and gave it a once over under the overhead lights. There was still no sign of a seam or break in the pitch coating anywhere. What the hell was in that thing, I thought. The crate weighed a few hundred pounds, not as much as the gold crates, but not light either.

Joe said to the group what I had been thinking, "What do you think is inside?"

Dimitri shook his head and said, "I don't know, but it must be important for them to take this much trouble to protect it from the elements... and the way that guy had a grip on it... even after he was dead, that's pretty freaky!"

"I know," I said. "Hopefully, we'll get some answers tomorrow when we get it to Fitz's place and get it opened." We turned off the light, closed and locked the vault door, and headed for our vehicles.

CHAPTER FIFTEEN

The ringing phone pulled me out of a deep sleep at 6:30 the next morning. "Colt," the voice said.

"Yeah, Fitz," I mumbled, "who did you expect at this number, the friggin' Easter Bunny?" I'm very grumpy when I'm jarred awake by loud noises. "Well, good morning to you too, sunshine," he replied. "Got your message yesterday and wanted you to know I'm flying in; be there by 7:30."

"Great," I said. "Start the coffee if you get there before me," and I hung up on him. Like I said, grumpy. I got up and hit the shower. Luckily for me, the Lair was only ten minutes from my place. I made it there by 7:15; the chopper had landed out back, and when I got inside, Fitz had put the coffee on! Thank goodness for small miracles. Doc, Dimitri, and Nils were there, and Joe came rolling in on his BMW GS1100 five minutes later, with donuts! Ah, it was a miracle!

Everybody was in the conference room when I joined them and as always Fitz got straight to the point. "Okay, so fill me in," he said. "What's this about a skeleton and a black box?" I hadn't even finished pouring my cup of the rich Columbian coffee, whose magnificent aroma filled the conference room.

"Just a minute," I said, "I'm not talking to anyone until I get at least one swallow of caffeine."

He laughed and said, "Grumpy bear. Slide the donuts this way, sit your ass down, and let's hear this story. Oh, congratulations, now get on with it."

I smiled as I pulled out a chair grabbed a jelly donut and took a large sip of coffee.

Things were getting better. "Okay," I said. Thirty minutes later and numerous questions, and Fitz was up to speed, including the incident with the *Dizzy D*.

He let out a low whistle and said, "My, my, you boys have been busy. So, you want a clean room to open this mysterious box in."

"Yes" I replied. "Since we have no idea what's in it, I want to make sure whatever it is doesn't get contaminated by the environment, or we get contaminated by it. Also, we may need to implement preservation protocols for what's inside. It has remained sealed, as far as we can tell, since 1715, and we may need some of your high-tech toys, depending on what we find inside."

He got up and poured himself another cup of coffee and over his shoulder said, "I've got just what you need. I'll alert my people, and we can fly it out when you're ready."

"Great," I said.

"I'm guessing," he said, "that you will want to make another conversion while we're at it."

"That would be nice," I replied between sips of coffee.

"I've got room for four of you, the crate, and "other" cargo. Colt, you can sit co-pilot this time."

"No problem, just as long as I don't have to fly that thing."

Shaking his head, he said, "How much do you want to convert, and FYI the two million limit has been lifted for you guys, so what's your pleasure?"

I looked around the table at those there and said, "A crate?"

"Sure, why not?" Dimitri replied. I got nods from Joe and Doc.

"That will be around 11 mill, Fitz," I said.

He said fine and didn't blink an eye. "It's like I told you," he said "you have made some powerful new friends, and they're ready and willing to help." This was still unbelievable, absolutely unbelievable, I thought. "So, the crate weighs approximately 500 pounds and the other one?"

"Around 200," I answered.

He thought for a moment and then said, "We should still be okay, close but okay. Now, where's this mysterious black box of yours?"

We headed to the vault and rolled out our crate of gold and then the black crate/box. He looked it over, mumbled to himself, then said "Okay, let's get it loaded and get to my lab." Thirty minutes later, we were walking across the tarmac to the main building at Acme Corp. with techs rolling both crates under cover behind us and four armed men flanking us. Tony and Junkyard arrived by car 20 minutes later.

We had taken the elevator to the secure lab and were watching as two techs were setting the black crate on a table in Fitz's clean room. He laid out a plan for our approval: first, scan the box to get an idea of what was inside. Next drill a small hole with a device that was an airtight system and take an interior air sample. No sense in letting any 300-year-old bugs or bacteria, out and third, insert a fiber optic camera to view the interior. Only the two techs would be in the room; we would monitor everything through a large safety glass window and Computer screens from the next room. I agreed that his plan and precautions were fine and gave the go-ahead to proceed. The techs were meticulous in their work and soon had the scanning machine moving over the box.

We watched on our monitors as the interior image appeared. There appeared to be blocks or ingots on the bottom, what looked like an open space and then two pouches and some kind of a packet on top of the empty space above the ingots. That was weird. How could the packet and pouches be floating in space six or seven inches above the layer of ingots? We then saw images from a side view with the same weirdness, packet and pouches sitting about six or seven inches above the ingots with nothing in between. I looked at Fitz as he looked at me, "Hell if I know," he said as if reading my mind. He punched a button and activated the intercom. "Is the equipment functioning properly?" Fitz asked.

The lead tech said all systems were in the green; it was working.

"Start drilling," he said. The techs both in hazmat type suits, breathing purified exterior air, moved another machine in place and began drilling in from the top in a corner of the box. It was a slow process… any material that was brought to the surface by the drill was sucked into a special sealed container, just in case. When they had drilled through, they inserted another device that sampled the interior air. The techs looked at computer readouts for a couple of minutes and then pronounced it all clear, no anomalies. A vacuum device had been used to evacuate the interior air into another sealed container and replaced it with air from the lab. A fiber optic camera was being inserted as we entered.

When we approached the table, there was an image on the large screen in the lab. We could make out what had looked like the packet and as the camera slid further in, we could see the pouches. But what puzzled us was what they were sitting on. It was wrapped in a material that had a sheen or gloss to it. The scans were still up on another screen, where there appeared to be a void in the place we now saw the wrapped object that the packet and pouches were sitting on.

Now, Doc said, "What the hell?" The camera moved further, and we could tell that this looked like a normal wooden box on the inside and there was nothing that would cause us to hesitate opening it.

The techs removed the fiber optic camera, and began the process of looking for a seam, where the lid on the box met the box itself. It took a few minutes, but they found it and made a cut through the pitch, following the seam around the box's perimeter. Once completed, they used thin stainless prying devices to work the lid loose. This took time since we didn't want to destroy any part of the container.

Now, there were four of us working on the lid, Fitz on one side, me on another, and the techs on the other two. The lid had a great seal. This was a precision-made container, but slowly the lid rose and in a few more minutes was lifted off and set on the table. We cautiously moved forward to look inside. There were the two what now looked to be leather pouches; there was a packet in there also wrapped in what looked like leather, all sitting on top of something covered in what appeared to be shiny Mylar fabric.

I reached in with my white-gloved hands and lifted out one of the pouches, fearing the leather would disintegrate as I moved it. Amazingly, instead of being brittle and hardened by time, the leather was supple and pliable. I set the pouch on the table and then removed the second in the same condition. They were each about the size of a large grapefruit, and I could feel their contents moving around like marbles in a bag. I next removed the packet, also wrapped in leather, but just as supple as the pouches. I would examine them all more closely, but for now my gaze was locked onto the Mylar-looking wrapped cube they had been sitting on.

I reached in and got my hands around it and lifted. There was weight to the cube, and I asked Fitz to take one side and help me lift it out. We could just get our fingers down the sides between the wooden box and the sides of the cube and lifted it out and set it on an adjacent table. I heard Doc, Joe, and Dimitri all gasp at once and turned to look back into the box. On the bottom were ingots of not gold but of silver, I thought, glistening in the lab's lights, untarnished? What elicited the gasp was that each ingot was engraved with a strange set of hieroglyphics or writing of some sort.

As we looked at each other, our respective eyes the size of saucers, Doc said, "Holy shit, Colt, what the hell have we found?"

I felt like a kid in front of those big department store display windows at Christmas time with all the animated scenes and decorations vying for your attention. Where to go first, the box, the pouches, the packet, the strange cube…? I chose the cube. Fitz was standing there, staring at the wrapping as if afraid to touch it.

I walked back to the table and said, "Well, let's see what we've got," and removed the shiny wrapping. It was lightweight, very light but with substance to it. Not like tissue paper used for gift wrapping but unlike any other material I could describe. As I removed it and lay it aside, I uncovered a silver cube that took my breath away. I felt light-headed and took a half step back at the same time Fitz did. We both were awestruck by the sight before us, a gleaming silver cube about six inches high, and 10 to 12 inches square.

The cube was covered in what looked like embossed or engraved designs, pictures, and writings. I didn't recognize any of the designs. Now, I put both hands on the table to support myself as my mind swirled. "Doc, get over here," I said He was still looking at the silver ingots in the box. He turned and hurried to where I was standing and looked down at the silver cube.

Quiet for a moment and then, "What the freaking hell is this?" he exclaimed loud enough to draw everyone to the table. By now, we were all standing around in shock or a reasonable facsimile of shock.

Fitz hadn't said a word yet, but he finally spoke. "Colt, I think we better sit somewhere and talk," he said in an even tone that did not reflect the level of emotion he was experiencing.

Joe had moved to the pouches and had untied the leather thong that held one of them closed. He said, "Guys, before we do that, I think you may want to see this," as he poured its contents on the table. Dazzling dark green and light green irregular shaped stones fell out in a pile, most the size of marbles, some smaller and some larger. There was no doubt we were looking at raw emeralds. He had untied the second bag and, as he opened it to pour its contents out, he uttered a very elongated, "Ssshiiiitttt," and poured out an assortment of red, blue, white, and green faceted stones that lit the room with their reflected colors. Once again, the size of marbles but with some much larger, they were cut in triangles, diamond shapes, smooth half circles and others were just smoothed in their natural shape.

The silence was deafening; it felt like it was getting hard to breathe when I said to no one and everyone, "Yeah, let's sit somewhere and talk." We followed Fitz to the door, pulling ourselves away from the tables that held our amazing discoveries.

As Fitz got to the door, he pressed a button on the intercom, and a voice came back, "Go ahead, clean room B."

"This is Fitzsimmons. Place this lab on security level Alpha. The only personnel allowed entry are Johnson and Stevens, who are on site now, and Dr. Burnett's team. You have their badge and biometric info."

"Yes, Sir, Colonel," the voice replied, "security protocol Alpha at clean room B now initiated."

As we opened the door to move, the large viewing window in the clean room and exit door window darkened. By the time we were out of the clean room, the window was black, and two armed guards came through the entrance/exit door. They took up positions next to the entrance to the clean room. As we walked into the hallway, two more armed guards were standing outside a doorway down the hall. Fitz led us four doors down the hallway between the two guards and into a medium-sized conference room. The door closed with a soft click and a voice came over hidden speakers saying, "Room secure.

Fitz pulled up a chair and fell into it. I couldn't sit down and began pacing as the others took seats. Everyone had a glazed look in their eyes, and no one spoke. They were trying to process what they had just seen in their own way. Finally, Fitz said, "So?"... "I think I know what I saw, but I'm not sure."

Still pacing, all I could say was, "Holy shit... Holy shit... shit!" I was having a hard time wrapping my mind around what we had just seen. There was a lot to grasp, and my mind was bogging down trying to process it.

Doc said, "Sit, Colt, for Christ's sake, you're driving me crazy with the pacing," as he replaced his head in his hands looking at the table. Junkyard was staring into space; Joe was looking at his hands clasped on the table, and Dimitri had the biggest shit-eating grin on his face I have ever seen. I pulled out a chair and sat down, scanning the group. I don't know what I was looking for, but I couldn't stop looking at everyone.

Fitz said, "Okay, will someone please tell me what we just saw!"

After a short pause, "Yeah," Doc said. "I'll tell you what we saw, something that was freaking impossible; that's what we saw!" A few seconds later, a chime sounded and Fitz hit a key on the computer that was built into the conference table. One of the tech's voices from the clean room said, "Colonel, pardon the interruption, but I think you will want to see this."

Fitz hit a couple more keys on the tabletop, and a large screen appeared in the wall, and the face of Johnson was looking at us. Fitz said, "Go ahead, Johnson."

The tech looked flustered as he began. "I figured it was

better to show you this than try to explain it... because... well... I can't."

"Get on with it, man," an exasperated Fitz responded. Now, the emotion was showing itself.

"Yes, Sir, we wanted to try and determine if the silver cube was hollow, so we ran another scan on it." There was a pause.

"And?" Fitz said.

"And this, Sir," an image from the scanner appeared on the screen, showing nothing!

"What the hell is this?" Fitz exploded, "Some kind of joke!"

"No, Sir; No, Sir, let me show you." Now the screen split, and two images appeared, one with the cube sitting under the scanning device, and next to it, the same view with the box removed. "Sir, the cube does not show up on our scanner. This is a live shot with the video camera on the scanner, the other with the scanner image, Sir."

"What?" Fitz exclaimed.

"Colonel, we have run every diagnostic on the equipment twice and everything is functioning properly. Plus, we have used every scan mode we have with the same results, NO IMAGE of the cube shows up!"

"That's impossible!" Fitz exclaimed.

"I know, Sir, that's what we thought, but I have something else." The tech turned to Stevens and told him to remove the cube and place the pouch under the scanner. He did so, made an entry into the computer, and the pouch showed up on both screens, a video image and a three-dimensional MRI scan type image. The tech faced us again and said, "Now, watch this," he turned his head and said, "Go ahead," and Stevens draped the silvery cover material we had taken off the silver block over the leather pouch, the pouch disappeared from the scanning image, but we could still see the silver material covering it on the video.

Our collective jaws hit the floor; this was insane, not possible, and freaking unbelievable! "Sir, there's one more thing," Johnson said. "We ran the cube through Big Mo, and we get a flat line; nothing on our periodic chart shows up."

Fitz stared at the tech for a minute and then said, "Keep checking. I want to know everything about all that stuff, and I want it yesterday!"

"Yes, Sir Colonel," and the screen went blank.

Joe looked at Fitz and asked, "Big Mo?"

Fitz said, "Yeah, that's our name for a piece of equipment we developed; it's like a mass spectrometer on steroids."

"And it picked up nothing?" Joe asked, "Nothing?"

"That's what the man said," Fitz replied.

"How is that possible?" Joe asked.

"Hell, I don't know how any of this can be possible," Fitz replied, looking around the table at all of us, waiting for someone to speak up. "Why can't we figure out what the cube is made of, why does that material make shit disappear in the scanner, why was the leather in perfect shape on those pouches after 300 years, what were those markings on those bars, and what was that writing on top of the block?" he finished. "We need answers."

I looked around at everyone and said, "And that's the one thing we don't have."

CHAPTER SIXTEEN

Fitz got up from the table and walked to the wall, pushed a button, and a panel slid back, revealing a full bar.

"I don't know about you guys, but I need a drink," he said as he took a bottle of Wild Turkey 101 off a shelf and poured a glass half full. I got up and walked to the bar and retrieved a bottle of 12-year-old single malt scotch, got a couple of ice cubes from the dispenser there, and poured myself a healthy drink. As we sat back down, the rest of the guys had gotten up and were doing the same.

Jack Daniels, Vodka, and Gin filled glasses; the sound of ice clinking was the only sound in the room.

Once we were all seated at the table, I said, "Doc, did you check out the leather packet?"

"I did, and it's a leather bound-journal. I only looked at it briefly; it's handwritten in Spanish."

"Then you need to check it out; that's the one thing we haven't examined."

Doc replied, "Right, Colt, I'm hoping it will give us some answers, plus I want to inspect the crate itself."

"Good idea," I said.

Joe looked around the table at all of us and said, "I don't want to sound like a crackpot or anything, but there is no way that what we saw could have originated in 1715!"

"Yeah, I was thinking the same thing," Dimitri said.

Our resident rocket scientist, Nils, chimed in, "In all my experience at NASA, I've never seen any materials exhibit characteristics like that, and I've dealt with a lot of exotic metals." Everyone around the table nodded, including Fitz.

I said, "I've got a feeling we just opened Pandora's Box, and I don't think she was from around here!"

Doc tossed down the rest of his drink and got up, saying, "I'll get the book," And left the room. I asked Fitz to pull up the images of the cube that the techs had saved to the hard drive during their investigations. A 3D image of the cube appeared on the screen and, as it rotated, I told him to zoom in on the top, so we had a full-screen shot of the amazing graphics on it.

After staring at the image for a few more minutes, I said, "There's no doubt about it; those engravings bear some resemblance to Egyptian and Maya hieroglyphs, and that looks to be Sumerian cuneiform next to them. There is something about the glyphs that seemed strange, just not sure why and those other markings... I have no idea what they are. Maybe Doc can give us a clue when he gets back."

As we stared at the image, Tony said, "Can we get a closer view of the sides?" Fitz ran his finger over the tabletop, and the image rotated again and zoomed in on one side covered with additional carvings. Tony was gazing at the screen now and stood up, "Can you zoom in on the top edge?" As the image grew larger, he said, "Stop, there. Now, rotate the image 360 degrees, slowly." The cube rotated 360 degrees, "Again," he said... and then, "Again."

When the image stopped after three rotations, Tony stood

silent, staring at the screen. He slowly turned with a stunned expression on his face. "This thing is from 1715, right?"

"Yes," I answered, "as far as we know."

"Over 300 years old."

"Yeah," I said.

Tony paused before he spoke again, and then said, "If that's so, then how in the hell did the entire top edge of that thing get covered with binary code?"

Stunned silence filled the room. "What…, your shitting me," I said.

"I will have to study it more closely… but I believe it is a form of binary code," he said.

Dimitri said, "Son of a bitch…"

Junkyard spoke, "Are you sure, Tony?"

"I'm not positive, but if I had to guess, I'd say yeah, I'm pretty sure. I'll know more when I have access to my Computer and can study it more closely."

I looked at the image and then everyone in the room and said, "This is impossible-just freaking impossible."

By now, a little over an hour and a half had passed since Doc had left to get the book. I looked at Fitz and said, "Is Doc still in the lab?" Fitz hit the keys on the Computer in the table-top, and the cameras in the lab came up on the screen.

Fitz spoke, "Johnson, is Dr. Greene in there with you?"

"Yes, Sir, he's been sitting in the corner with the book we took out of the box. He's acting kind of strange; he keeps mumbling to himself, and when we try to talk to him, it's as if he doesn't even hear us, so we left him alone."

"All right," Fitz said, "tell him we need him back in the conference room, NOW, and make sure he hears you."

"Yes, Sir," Johnson replied as Fitz cut the connection. Five minutes later, Doc came back into the conference room with the book in hand and pale as a sheet. He walked to the table, pulled out a chair, and sat down, laying the book in front of him.

He looked at me and said, "You remember that Hunter S. Thompson quote we liked so much?" "'No matter how weird it gets, it never gets too weird for me.'"

"Yeah, I remember," I said.

"Well, that doesn't apply anymore because I'm weirded out right now!"

"Jesus Christ!" Fitz exclaimed. "Will someone please tell me what the hell is going on here!"

"Okay, Fitz, as far as I can tell," I said "from a shipwreck in 1715, 300 plus years old, we have found a cube or something made of a material not on our periodic table. It was covered by a flexible metallic-looking cloth-like material that renders objects invisible to our modern technology. The cube seems to have writing on it from three separate ancient cultures that modern archaeology says had no contact with each other. Only two of which were possibly contemporaneous. It also includes writing or symbols we have no idea of their origin surrounded by some freaking type of binary code!" Somewhat breathless I looked around the room and said, "Well?"

Joe said, "That about sums it up in a *Reader's Digest* version."

Doc said, "Binary code?"

"Yeah, that's what Tony thinks," I said.

"Okay the weirdness meter just got pegged!" Doc said. "And I'm about to wrap the needle around the peg."

"What did you find in the book?"

He took a deep breath and let it out and said, "It's not a book; it's a journal. It was written by a Jesuit Friar , Fr. Raul Antonio Dominguez, somewhere around 1703 or 1704. I can't believe how well the writing and pages are preserved; they look like it was just written yesterday. In that respect, it's easy to read, but the vernacular and structure are a little ponderous. I've only scanned some of it, but I can give you the gist of it so far. Believe me, there is a lot more here that will require study."

"Fine," I said, "what have you got?"

"I'm giving you this in my words, not a direct translation, so bear with me. It seems the friar set out with a contingent of soldiers into the eastern Andes. He was looking for natives to convert, and they were looking for gold. It was an arduous journey, and they lost many men to sickness and accidents. Toward the end, there were only five men left, and they turned back. They had found no gold, were low on food, and weary of the torturous mountain terrain they had to traverse. Four months had passed since they had left their main camp. The friar , however, said he would not turn back and continued on by himself, driven by God's word and his religious zeal.

"Three days after the departure of the soldiers, while climbing a narrow rock-strewn trail, he came upon a child of eight or nine years old lying on the ground. He was unconscious and had a broken arm. The child had fallen; he was not sure when but must have succumbed to the pain and passed out. Having also been a student of the medicinal arts while he was studying at the Jesuit monastery in Spain, he tended the child's wound. He set the arm with a crude splint and shared his water and his food once the child regained consciousness. He noticed the child had a strange look about him, rather tall and slender but not in an undernourished way. The child's head was elongated with no hair. He had large grey eyes with a sloping forehead.

"At first, the child was too weak to speak or try to communicate. He seemed very fearful of this man in black robes. After two days of rest and sharing food and water, the child seemed to lose his fear and responded to the friar s attempts at communication. Although he understood nothing of what the child was saying, the language was unknown to him, the child seemed to understand what the friar was saying. So, through a series of hand gestures and pointing at objects, they established a rough line of communication."

"Once the child seemed well enough to travel, the friar

encouraged him to lead the way, hopefully, back to his people. The child seemed hesitant at first but finally gave in. They embarked on a two-day journey through the mountains. The trails they were on were well hidden and would have been easily missed by someone unfamiliar with them. Eventually, their journey brought them to his village.

Upon arriving, two things became apparent to the friar. One, this was a tribe of headhunters, as he noted the shrunken heads hanging from trees and make-shift display racks at the entrance to the encampment. Two, the boy he had helped was the son of someone of importance within the tribe. He was immediately surrounded by members of the tribe, speaking and gesturing excitedly. Because of the latter, he surmised, he was not killed outright but bound to a stake in the center of the village.

"Serious discussions were held amongst the tribesmen, with several comments being interjected by the young boy. After a time, the friar was untied and offered fresh fruit, some kind of cooked meat, and water. This being the first real meal he had had in many months, after a short prayer, he attacked the food satisfying his ravenous appetite."

As if on cue, the door to the conference room opened, and a cart of sandwiches, cold beverages, and pastries was rolled into the room.

Fitz said, "I ordered food since it looks like we will be here for a while." I looked at the clock on the wall and saw that four hours had passed since we had started this discussion. Without hesitation, we attacked the tray of food with similar gusto to that of the friars.

Once we had finished, Fitz said there was no reason to curtail our investigation, and we could all stay as long as we liked. He had already planned for sleeping accommodations at the on-site "barracks" for us. Meals would be provided, and any personal needs we might have would be taken care of. With that out of the way, we turned our attention back to Doc and told him to continue his story.

Settling into his seat, he continued, "The next day, they took the friar to a hut set apart from the rest. It was a strange design, not like others in the village, and seemed to be made of some kind of metal. He was ushered inside. There, he found the boy he had helped and a man who he guessed to be his father. He had not seen him the day before. The first thing he noticed as the man stood was that he was much, much taller than the other tribe' people. He was also slender but in a graceful way. The elongated head was more pronounced, and his grey eyes were larger. His clothing was of a different design than that of the other tribesmen. He offered the friar a seat on a rug in the center of the hut, and he sat down.

"In one fluid move, the father and then the son did the same. It was then that the friar noticed that the child was not wearing the splint he had attached days earlier; in fact, the child seemed to have full use of the arm with no ill effects of the recent break. While staring at the arm, the father spoke, and while the friar did not understand the words being spoken, he had an understanding of what was being said. This set him back and, wide-eyed, he stared at the father who had an amused smile on his face.

"As the conversation continued, he came to understand that the father was the spiritual leader and healer of this tribe. A shaman, the friar thought and immediately, a thought entered his head, 'Not Shaman, much, much more.' He looked at the father as the smile widened. He spoke to the father in Spanish, asking him what was happening, and as the father replied in the language of the tribesmen, the thoughts came to him 'that all things would be answered in due time, but he thanked him for bringing his son back to him' and nodded toward the child, who was smiling during this entire exchange."

We stopped Doc and said, "Whoa, wait a minute; this sounds

like some kind of telepathic communication. Is that what you're saying?"

Doc replied, "I'm only recounting what the friar wrote in his journal as best I can. However, as I read it, I thought the same thing. I don't know, but like I said, the weird meter is now officially pegged! And it gets better... With that, the discussion with the father ended, and the son led him out of the hut back to the waiting tribe. Moments later, the father emerged and said something to the gathered crowd. There was more discussion and some raised voices, but the boy's father spoke again in a stern, voice and all before him bowed and seemed to accept what had been said. The father returned to his hut, and they led the friar to another hut that was unoccupied.

"Inside, he found blankets, a small fire pit, a makeshift table and his backpack that had been taken from him when he entered the village. Moments later, a woman entered with bowls of water and fresh fruit. She had a woven pull over garment and sandals which she laid next to what he thought was his sleeping area, covered with blankets and a fur skin of some sort. She bowed and backed out of the hut, leaving the friar alone. He sat down next to the table and as he ate, tried to make sense of these recent events."

"Over the next few days, they gave him his freedom to explore the village, although it was obvious he was being watched at all times. One afternoon, he was summoned from his hut by a young girl and brought to a gathering in the center of the village. It looked as if all the villagers were there and, standing to one side were the father and son. It was obvious they were presiding over this gathering. When he arrived, the father nodded in his direction and addressed the group. As he spoke once again, the friar could follow what was being said, not through the language, but through his thoughts. The father, whose name he had found out was Anutu and his son, Theos would be leaving the village.

"Anutu then pointed to the friar and told the group the man in the black robes was the chosen one and was to be kept safe and obeyed. There was mumbling, but at a hand gesture from Anutu, they all turned and bowed toward the friar and accepted his word. The friar was stunned and looked at Anutu, who held up a hand halting any question that he might have spoken. More was said, but the friar didn't quite get all of it. The group dispersed and left Anutu, Theos, and the friar standing alone. Once again, he was led into Anutu's hut and invited to sit down. When all three were seated, Anutu spoke again, and again the friar understood not the words but the thoughts.

'You must take care of these people now, nurture, protect, and teach them. They will listen to you and protect you.'

"The friar spoke in Spanish, '"Why me?"' he asked."

'We have been waiting for you for a long time, and now you are here, and our task is completed; yours has begun,' Anutu said."

"The friar asked, 'Waiting, for me, what do you mean, for how long?' The multiple questions tumbled out in a rush."

"Anutu smiled and said for 'many thousands of your years' and handed the friar a book with a metal cover and binding. 'This will help you along the way. You will find many answers within, and know this, your people will reward you for your efforts from this day forward. Now, go, we must prepare.' And with that, they rose, and the friar left the hut more bewildered than ever.

"He went back to his hut and sat down to study the book." Doc paused, "What happens next is where the weirdness really begins. The friar doesn't remember reading the book or falling asleep. He remembers waking, and it was the next day. He went outside, and life in the village seemed normal, except now people acknowledged him with a smile and a slight bow as he made his way toward where Anutu's hut had been with a thousand questions on his mind. However, when he got there the hut was gone. There was nothing left, in fact, you could not tell that any kind of structure had ever been there. He stood in awe and turned back toward the village and thought, "'I have been touched by the hand of God, and his angels have shown me my destiny.'"

CHAPTER SEVENTEEN

We sat there in stunned silence. Doc got up and headed to the bar and spoke over his shoulder, "I have been giving you a close translation so far, but I skipped forward through the journal here, and so will give you the highlights of what I saw as I went through. This guy was one hell of a chronicler, and there seems to be a lot of detail I want to go back and study, but I need to tell you about the part I found in here that pertains to our current discoveries." He sat back down with a large tumbler of Jack Black, neat, and thumbed through the journal for a moment. When he stopped, he took a large swallow of his drink and started again.

"Okay, so this guy stayed with this tribe for years. He learned their language, their customs, in fact, everything about them except for one thing." We all looked at one another and then back at Doc. "As close as I can tell, after about five years, say around 1709, he had earned their trust and was accepted as part of the tribe. He had healed many of the tribe that had gotten ill and taken care of many injuries. After that, members of the tribe began bringing him gifts much like payment for his services or offerings. He received gold and silver statues and sheets of hammered metal with strange markings or writings on them. When he questioned the chief about them, he said they were special offerings for him from the gods. Having seen none of the tribesmen doing any kind of metal, work he asked where they came from and was told the gods' holy city. When he questioned the chief, he refused to answer any further questions."

"This went on for over a year with no additional information coming forth about the location of the holy place, but he found out it housed many wondrous things made of metal the color of the sun and others the color of the graying sky and glistening stones of many colors. He thought this could only mean gold, silver and other valuables. Sometime around 1710, he sent a message to the king through a network he had developed of tribes and traders, telling him of the immense wealth that lay at his fingertips and said he would send examples to Havana to be delivered to the Flota and taken to the king." "I'm sure the king got the message, and now, I believe he sent the ship we're looking for to pick up the package," Doc said. We nodded, and he continued, "All right boys put on your aluminum foil hats and get out your Reese's Pieces."

There was a collective "Huh" around the table as Doc continued.

"Later that year, the chief took him into the mountains. After almost a full day's climb, they came to a significant clearing where a monumental building complex was being repaired. There were 200 to 300 workers moving about the area. The friar realized that this workforce must be individuals from multiple tribes since in his village there were only 150 members, including men, women and children. This showed a level of cooperation between tribes in the area he had not seen before. When he asked the chief about it he said they were working to restore the city of the gods. As the friar looked around, he saw that the site was much larger than he had first noticed and that many of the structures were covered by jungle growth or hidden by trees. The structures were immense, many of them pyramidal, but looking as if some disaster had ravaged them. There were huge stones lying around in a jumble as if kicked over by a giant foot in a fit of rage and many of the other buildings looked to be in serious disrepair. As he peered into the jungle down what must have been the main colonnade, he saw that it led into a canyon of sorts. Inward sloping sides of immense height blocked out much of the sunlight. In the mists above, he could see the opposing sides never touched, thus creating a shining slit high above. Buildings and their remnants lined the sides of the colonnade, and in the misty distance, he saw what looked to be gigantic carved figures, carved into the natural sloping sides of the walls. He stood in awe of the spectacle before him. It was then he saw two men standing next to a carved block of stone that must have weighed at least ten to 15 Quintals (2,000 to 3,000 lbs.). From where he stood, it looked like they placed a shiny object on top, made some kind of change, and then pushed the stone forward as if it weighed nothing.

"The friar was awestruck and asked the chief how the men were moving such an immense stone, and the chief replied that the men weren't moving the stone... the gods were with the sweat of the sun. As the friar moved forward to get a better look, the chief stopped him and said this was a very sacred place and he could not enter... yet. The friar watched as the stone slowly glided along and then was pushed into place by the two workers. Once in place, they removed whatever it was they had placed on top of it, and there was a thud as the stone settled. The two workers went back toward another huge stone." Doc paused and looked around the room.

Fitz was the first to speak, "Doc, are you telling us these guys some kind of anti-gravity device?"

"Not at all," Doc said, "I'm just telling you what I read in the friar's journal; the reality of it remains to be determined."

Nils said, "It sure the hell sounds like that's what he saw."

"I know," Doc replied. "But these are just words on paper; we have nothing to substantiate it."

"There may be a plausible explanation," I added.

"Yet…" Joe said, "This has gone from *Indiana Jones* to *E.T* to *Close Encounters* in a matter of minutes."

"If," Fitz said, "and that's a big if, we can document what he is saying somehow…" he left the sentence unfinished.

"I was hoping someone would say that," Doc replied. "Let me skip ahead toward the end of the journal. Remember, years have passed since that passage. The friar now states that, along with his journal, he is including material and 'devices' (my words, Doc acknowledged) from the Holy City and a sacred place under the earth. From what the chief said, he thought it was a cave of sorts. While he is still not sure what these things were, they told him they were devices (my words again) or tools of the gods. The friar tells the king that his next communication with him will have the location of the cave. He was told by the chief he would be shown its location soon. He would describe its contents, which he was assured by the chief is immense and fills many rooms of great size. He signs it and packs it away in the box."

A pause, and then Doc continued with a laugh, "Eat your heart out, Steven Spielberg!" As had happened so many times within the last 24 hours, we sat, dumbfounded by what we had just heard. The room was electric; we had discovered what sounded like a record from the 1700's, describing what can only be called advanced technological devices. Anutu and Theos… could this be evidence of possible contact with another lifeform not from this planet? Impossible, or was it?

I leaned back in my chair to a room as silent as a graveyard at midnight and looked at the clock. It was three a.m., and no one seemed to notice; we all sat there, not saying a word.

Doc spoke up, "Gentlemen, I thought our discovery of the gold from the longboat was the pinnacle of my career, but I see now that that seems to be just the tip of the iceberg. I think you'll all agree that with our discoveries today and with those that I know we will make," he said with a chuckle, "we are about to change the world." He raised his half-empty glass as our own glasses left the table in salute, "Here's to a bunch of regular guys who just changed the freaking world." Hear, hear we chorused.

As I looked around the room, I realized the only person who hadn't raised his glass was Nils. He was just staring into it, head down.

I said, "Nils what's, up, man?"

He looked up from his glass with a distant look on his face and said, "All the years I worked at NASA, there was talk about this discovery, this moment, by the Astrophysicist and Planetary geologists, the astronauts, and all their buddies, but a lot of them never sounded convinced of the things they said. It was like it was a rehearsed speech for a sound bite, and the whole time, I believed it. I mean, I really believed, wondering if I would live long enough to see it happen, and now, not only did I live long enough, I'm part of the group that just confirmed it's true, we are not alone!"

As I looked at him, I thought I could see him getting misty-eyed and right, then I knew why I called him a friend. He never strayed from the path of his beliefs, and I guess he kept a lot of it bottled up inside.

"Well, old friend, it looks like you were right," I said, "Now, we take a few minutes to celebrate and then work on what the hell to do next!"

He looked at me, smiled raised his glass, and tossed his drink down in one swallow and said, "Hell, yeah!"

It was five a.m. when we wound down and headed to the dorm for some much-needed sleep. Fitz said he would rouse us no later than 10 a.m. and breakfast would be served in the dorms, cafeteria till 11, so no sleepy heads! By 9:45 the next morning, we were in the cafeteria all trying to speak at once.

Nobody was sure if they had slept or not, but everyone was, "Bright eyed and bushy tailed," as my grandpa used to say, that morning and ready to get back to work.

Over breakfast, Joe had said, "Boy, I know somebody who's going to be pissed!"

"Who?" I asked.

"Lawrence," he said. "I sure hope that Napa Valley wine was good, and the company was better because it will take a lot to top this!"

Shit, in all the excitement, I had forgotten about that. "When is he due back?" I asked.

Joe said, "In three days."

"You better get on the phone and tell him to drop everything and get his ass back here, NOW! And for God's sake, don't tell him why over the phone!"

"Roger that," Joe said as we were walking back to the lab area. A few minutes later, I heard Joe arguing with someone on his cell and thought with a chuckle, "Yeah, he's gonna be pissed!"

We passed the conference room and its guards and were let into the lab by what I guessed were the dayshift security. Johnson and Stevens were inside, still busy doing their science thing. I'm not sure if they even left last night and were obviously very excited about something.

As we entered, Stevens spoke up first and said, "Colonel, glad you're here; you will not believe what we found."

"Jesus Christ," Fitz said. "I've heard that phrase more in the last 48 hours than I have in my entire life; now what?" Stevens didn't know whether to take that as a rebuke or just an exclamation by his boss who had been continuously overwhelmed in the last two days. "Go ahead, Stevens; don't mind me," Fitz said.

With a sigh of relief, he continued, "Sir, you know the hole we drilled in the box yesterday?"

"Yes," Fitz replied.

"Well, Sir it's, gone!"

"What?" Fitz exclaimed. "What the hell do you mean gone?"

"Yes, Sir, it's gone; look for yourself," he said as he handed Fitz the top of the box. We observed where we had disturbed the tar or pitch with the drilling device on the outside, but once we got through it, the surface beneath was smooth as if we had never disturbed it.

As we studied it, he said, "What the hell kind of wood is this thing made of?"

"That's another interesting thing," Johnson chimed in. "When we discovered this, we ran the test on the particles of the box we caught when we drilled the hole… It's not wood, Sir, but some kind of polymer-based material as far as we can tell."

"Well, what kind of polymer?" Fitz growled. It was obvious these two scientists were not used to NOT having answers to their boss's questions.

"We're not sure, Sir. Big Mo couldn't give us any answers."

"Jesus, just when I thought the weirdness might be winding down," Fitz said. "Okay, drill another hole and monitor it; I want to know what happens!"

"Yes, Sir," they both responded.

"Where are we with the other items, the cube and cloth stuff?" Fitz asked. Both scientists looked at each other rather sheepishly and mumbled, "Nowhere Sir, we have nothing new to report." That's not what Fitz or any of us wanted to hear.

I said, "Now that we have the information that Doc gave us from the journal last night, let's check out the cube again." We walked over to the table where it sat and examined it closely.

I said, half-jokingly, "Anybody see an on or off switch?" with a chuckle. My attempt at humor was not well received. "Are we guessing that this is the device that the friar saw being used?"

"Maybe," Doc said.

"But if this is the same type of device that the friar saw in operation in the jungle, there has to be a way to activate it," I said. We continued to examine the cube from every angle and all sides. Nothing...! I spoke to Johnson and Stevens and asked if they had run a test that would identify any power or magnetic signature this thing might have. They said yes to both questions and came up with nothing much; some of their instruments gave them some inconsistent, wacky readings, but nothing concrete. Okay, back to square one. What if this wasn't what the friar had seen being used? Maybe it was just an ornate artifact he included for the king's pleasure. I turned to Doc and said, "Wouldn't you think the journal and what was included in the box would have some kind of relationship to one another?"

"I would think so... if you're trying to impress a king and you had made some amazing discoveries, you wouldn't want to be sending him trinkets. If you could call all this cool stuff trinkets," Doc said.

Joe added, "Yeah, if you're trying to impress him, that would be like sending the king a transistor radio and not including the batteries. Unless of course he had no idea what this stuff did either."

"Didn't the friar say the natives were doing something to the box on the stone before they moved it?" I asked.

Doc said, "Yeah, but he couldn't see what they did from as far away as he was."

"So, let's take a closer look at the top; we may have missed something," I said. As we scrutinized the surface of the cube, there was nothing that looked like a switch or activation device.

While we were looking at it, Doc said, "You notice anything strange about these hieroglyphs, Colt?"

I said, "Maybe but I'm not sure what it is."

"Both seem to resemble proto-Egyptian and Maya hieroglyphs. From what little we know about this era, we estimate it pre-dates what we normally observe in carvings and wall paintings by up to three to four thousand years."

"No shit," I said. "I thought there was something kind of different about them but had no idea that's what it was."

"Yep," he said, "I would guess these texts, as unbelievable as it may seem to be somewhere in the five to seven thousand BCE range."

I let out a low whistle. "I thought the Maya said their calendar and civilization started about 3,600 BC."

"They did," Doc said. "But we now believe the Maya may have copied their writing, calendar, and math systems from the Olmec, who could pre-date the Maya by thousands of years."

Everyone had been listening to our conversation with interest, and Dimitri said, "So, this is not regular Egyptian writing or Maya?"

Doc said, "No, this is much older than what we're used to seeing."

Joe said, "So, that means that this cube could be nine thousand years old?"

"Possibly, possibly more, or else someone was very well versed in these ancient languages and carved them on here," Doc replied, "and I don't have a clue why someone would do that. As a matter of fact, I don't believe they were carved by hand anyway. This looks more like machine engraving."

I looked more closely at the top and said, "You're right, Doc, it's all too perfect to be hand carved. Can you read the text?" I asked.

"Not really," Doc said, "I can pick out a couple of things, but trying to understand what they say or mean will take time and research, and that includes this early version of cuneiform if that's what it is."

Fitz said, "Okay this keeps getting stranger and stranger."

Doc looked at him, grinning, and said, "Told you I would wrap the needle around the peg of the Weird-meter!" Stumped by what we knew or rather didn't know about the cube, I shifted my attention, for the time being, to the one thing we hadn't discussed, the carved ingots that were in the bottom of the box. The techs had removed them and had them sitting on another table in the lab.

I walked over to it and said, "Doc, what do you make of these"? As he walked over, I asked Stevens if they had any info on them and he shook his head.

"No, Sir, not really, we think it may be a similar material as the cube, but they showed up on our scan, so we have no way of confirming it since neither of them gives us any readings on Big Mo. We're only basing that guess on outward appearance, but we know they're damn hard. When we got our sample for Big Mo, we tested for hardness and got numbers on the Rockwell and Brinell scale that were amazing."

I picked up one ingot and looked at it closely. It wasn't heavy like the gold we were used to handling, but it wasn't light. The carvings didn't look like carvings either as I examined them more closely; they appeared to be precision engravings. I Compared it to the cube and saw the same precise cuts. Nice, sharp, clean lines, exactly like an engraving. When I pointed this out to Doc, he said he agreed and, if that were the case, since the engravings varied from ingot to ingot, they might provide specific information about something on each one. Hmm, he could be right.

"But, if so, what were they telling us?" I said. "Tony, can you take a look at that binary code on the cube and these engravings on the ingots and cube and see if you can come up with anything?"

"Sure, he said. "I'll need a terminal that can access my server."

I said, "Fitz?"

"No problem; use the one in the conference table. I'll get you access to our system, and you can use the encrypted link we set up with your machine."

Tony headed for the conference room, saying, "That would be perfect. I'll already have the images in the system and can get right on it." Fitz touched his ear and gave orders for access for Tony to someone on the other end of his personal Com link.

He turned and said, "Done."

I nodded and turned my attention back to the tables in the lab thinking, okay, now we are approaching this problem from multiple fronts. I just hope we can start making some real progress and come up with some answers.

CHAPTER EIGHTEEN

I turned to Fitz and asked, "Do you have another room we can use for a Pow Wow? I've got some things on my mind I need to hash out with everyone, and I don't want to disturb Tony in the conference room."

"Sure," Fitz said "We'll use the observation lab next door. It's got a small conference table set up. Plus, we will still have access to our computers and communications from there."

"Great," I said as we headed for the door. Once we had settled into the new space, I said "Okay, scientific-test-wise we have no answers on our discoveries; let's approach it from another direction. Let's apply some deductive reasoning to this whole thing and see if that gets us anywhere."

Dimitri added "So, we go from Mr. Spock to Sherlock Holmes."

"More or less, yes," I said. "Open discussion float any idea no matter how off the wall it may seem. We're dealing with some strange shit here, and we need to find answers and soon."

Fitz had taken his usual seat at the head of the table and chewed on one of his unlit Cuban cigars and nodded. "Okay, so what do we know?"

"Well," I said, "we have a crate from a 1715 shipwreck." As I spoke, I realized my words appeared on a screen built into the wall and Fitz was tapping on the table-top.

He smiled and said, "Go ahead; there will be a recording and text displayed on the screen as you speak." Ah, modern technology at your fingertips, he has all the toys, I thought.

"The crate contains objects that we haven't been able to identify, placed there by a Jesuit Friar. The crate was destined for King Phillip of Spain," I said. "The friar says he found or was given these things by the tribesmen he was living with in the Andes Mountains around 1709."

Doc added, "Right, somewhere on the eastern side in Ecuador."

I added, "They were being sent to the King of Spain under special guard and transport."

Dimitri jumped in, "And we've got a journal describing the adventures of this Jesuit Friar who lived with the indigenous people of that time for several years."

"Right, so we are dealing with three points in time; the time the friar lived with the natives, the sending of the package to Havana, and the sinking of the ship and loss of the package in 1715."

"What about the skeleton holding onto the package?" Joe said.

Yeah, I had all but forgotten about him. I turned to Doc, who reached into his pocket and pulled out the large signet ring I had taken off the skeleton.

"I haven't forgotten," he said as he held it up, "but with all the excitement of recent discoveries, I shoved it to the back burner. I'll get some of my people in Spain on it and see if they can bird-dog this for us."

"Good," I said, "and get back into that journal. We need every scrap of information we can get our hands on." He nodded in agreement. "Okay," I said, "the stuff in the box, the metal cube, the journal, the jewels, the ingots, and the silvery invisibility cloth: place of origin?"

Joe said, "I would say the rough emeralds came from South America, the diamonds, rubies, and sapphires could be from there as well, I guess, but less likely, and they didn't have such precise faceting capabilities, did they? And the journal is self-explanatory."

"Okay, for now, that's good." I replied.

"The gold we found came from the Mexico City mint," Dimitri said.

"Right, so we have a time frame, mystery crate, place of origin, destination, main characters, the friar, local tribesmen, Anutu, Theos, and our mystery skeleton."

"The next big pieces of the mystery are the contents of the crate, which is hard evidence, and the contents of the journal; is it truth or fiction?"

Doc spoke, "I think what we have in the lab corroborates much of what the friar said in his journal and a friar lying to a king is not likely in this situation."

"All right," I said, and as I looked around the room, everyone nodded their assent. "Then what about the city of the gods that was being re-built and the mysterious underground holy place; were they truth or fiction?" I asked.

Nils said, "I think we have to be open to the possibility that what we are dealing with is something not of this world: possible advanced technology being used by ancient cultures. Plus, we need to find out who this Anutu and Theos were."

Dimitri said, "I think the only way we will get answers to those questions is to get to the source, put boots on the ground in Ecuador."

Joe said, "I was wondering if someone would make that suggestion, Dimitri," and laughed.

"I think you're right; we need to continue to chase down the facts until we have irrefutable evidence and answers. I mean rock solid stuff that no scientist can deny," I said.

Fitz and Doc both said, "Agreed."

"Yeah, the last thing we need is to look like a bunch of loonies on the front page of every newspaper in the world," Dimitri added. "It would be like that Roswell thing all over again."

Nils laughed and said, "Don't scoff, buddy, that Roswell thing may turn out to be real after all!"

"Okay, so what's our next move?" I asked.

"Well, I think we need to get our ducks in a row here first; you know with Risky Business. It would be a shame to drop the ball on the galleon search now since we know it's real and we're close," Nils said. "What's the plan for continuing the search?"

I thought for a few minutes and then said, "I think our best course of action will be to turn the galleon search over to you and Lawrence with Gus and his crew. Since we are going to look for the galleon, we need to finish the incorporation process. File for leases off the cape or whatever we need and establish ourselves as a legitimate underwater recovery company. That also means anything we find from here on out will be monitored by the powers that be."

Dimitri raised his hand with a grin; I said, "Yes?"

He said, "Anything we find?"

I thought for a minute and then replied, "Well, most anything, at least enough to keep us looking legit!"

"Okay," he said, "I like that better." Everyone laughed... that damn pirate mentality, I thought.

"We've got to establish Gus, the *Falcon* and its crew either as part of Risky Business or as a subcontractor and let them take over the on-site galleon search, to protect them and keep us legit. We'll leave the details of completing that whole process up to Lawrence. He can work that out. I want you guys in charge of overseeing that endeavor and staying on top of those details. I'm sure some of us will be out-of-pocket down the road."

Fitz spoke up, "I suggest we bring O'Reilly in on this and I will assign Wilson to handle the financial stuff. He's the best I've got and can move money around in ways it would take any federal agency decades to pick up a trail. Wilson is one of my top accountant types; he also keeps me up on the global money market situation and investment opportunities."

I have to admit; this was sounding better than it had at first. "Okay," I said, "but with this in place, if I need money right away, how long will it take to negotiate this system before I can get it?"

Fitz just laughed, "Colt, you get a request to us and one hour later, you will have a line of credit or cash in hand anywhere in the world, up to a couple of million dollars, guaranteed!" Fitz continued, "O'Reilly is a great analyst, besides being a top field operative and pilot. She did down and dirty field work in Iraq, Afghanistan, Iran, and some other places you don't need to know about. She worked for the CIA until she got severely injured on an Op and had to spend time stateside recuperating. That's when her abilities as an analyst got noticed. She lost some good friends on that Op and never got the chance for payback. It's hung with her ever since. I don't think she's ever gotten over it, but she is totally dependable. Just remember… she does have a short fuse if you know what I mean. You don't want to piss this lady off!"

"Got it," I said.

"She spent the next four years behind a desk with promises of being able to return to the field going unfulfilled. She got fed up with the bureaucratic bullshit, and that's when I snagged her. She's back to full field operations and is still a great analyst."

"So, we could use her as needed?"

"Yep, that is if she agrees… and she will act as a conduit to Wilson on the money side of things."

Dimitri was beside himself and said, "Great idea!"

Fitz looked at him with a slight grin and said, "I thought you might like that."

I said to Fitz, "Okay, then let's do it."

Fitz now touched the table-top, and a voice responded, "Yes, Colonel?"

"Have O'Reilly report to my location ASAP."

"Yes, Sir, Colonel," the voice replied.

Fitz said, "When she gets here, I'll bring her up to speed and brief her on our plans; from then on, she will be a part of your team and under your command Colt, chopper too!"

O'Reilly arrived a few minutes later, took a seat at the table, and Fitz did his briefing thing.

When he finished, she turned to us, smiled and said, "Sounds like fun." O'Reilly said she would contact Wilson and get things moving on the financials. Joe said he would contact Gus on the *Falcon* and bring him up to speed on the plan to search for the galleon. Joe also reminded me that Lawrence would arrive at OIA in about an hour and a half. He had made his excuses to his lady friend and gotten a ride on a corporate charter jet that had left LAX about three and a half hours ago.

It had cost him a full three-day spa treatment for his companion and a first-class ticket home, but he had pulled it off. O'Reilly volunteered to fly over and pick him up once he got in. Dimitri volunteered to tag along, just so he could bring Lawrence up to speed before they got back here.

O'Reilly said, "Fine, if it's okay with you, Boss?" The way the two of them were grinning, rather than get into a protracted discussion, I agreed.

Fitz said, "Now that we know how we will proceed, I think we need to get back into the lab and turn our attention to the contents of the crate." We left the conference room, going our separate ways. Joe said he would join us as soon he contacted Gus and pulled out his cell phone.

Back in the lab, there was not much new. Tests continued to be conducted with everything the two techs could throw at the cube, and I think they were about to go looking for a kitchen sink. No new information.

Joe had rejoined the group and walked over to the table with the stones and blocks on it.

After a couple of minutes, he said, "Colt, come here and look at this." He was standing at the table with the ingots spread out, and next to them, the contents of the two leather pouches were in separate piles.

As I walked over to him, he was staring at one ingot and running his hand through the faceted stones and spreading them out.

"What's up?" I asked as I got to the table.

He never looked up but said, "I'm not sure yet, maybe nothing." He had one finger of his right hand poised over the engraving at the center of an ingot and with his left he was rummaging through the cut and polished stones. In a few seconds, he stopped and said, "Here," as he picked up a ruby somewhat in the shape of an ellipse. I looked to where his finger on his right hand was pointing and saw a similar design cut into the silvery surface.

"No way," I said as he brought the stone closer to the ingot. By now everybody had gathered around and was looking at the table top.

Joe looked up at me and said, "What do you think?"

"I don't know," I said and looked at the faces peering down, including the techs', "try it and see." Joe slipped the ruby into the niche and it slid perfectly into place.

"Well, I'll be damned," Fitz said.

"Nice decoration," Joe interjected, and we were all admiring how it looked when from each side of the engraved ellipse, a lace pattern of silvery spider webs covered the ends, locking the gem in place. It was then we heard the low humming that came from the bejeweled ingot!

"Holy shit," one of the techs shouted, "You turned it on!"

Joe said, stepping gingerly back from the table, "Turned what on?"

"The silver block thing."

The other tech shouted, "Turn it off; turn it off!" The hum was increasing, still low, sounding like a small turbine spinning up. The ruby was glowing ever so faintly, and most everyone was backing away from the table except Joe and me.

"Shit, turn the damn thing off; we don't have a clue what it's doing," Fitz shouted.

Joe said, his voice rising, "Turn it off? I don't even know how I turned it on!" I leaned over the block and pressed my finger against the uncovered center of the ruby and the hum immediately diminished. I heard everyone exhale in one whoosh the breath they had been holding.

"How did you do that?" one tech asked.

"I touched it," I said. At that moment, Joe reached out and touched the stone again and immediately, the low hum began… Joe touched it again, and it stopped.

Fitz said, "Joe will you stop that shit? You may blow us all to hell and back. We have no idea what that thing is."

Joe said, "I think maybe I do." As he touched it, the hum started again. He let it continue a minute, listening intently, as it rose to a low level and got no louder. We also noticed the ruby's glow was back. He touched it again, and the hum stopped; he then slid his finger-tip across the entire stone, including the spider web-lace work at both ends and the lace disappeared, and we heard a very low popping sound as the stone raised up slightly from its resting place in the engraved niche. Joe reached down, picked it up, and looked at us, grinning from ear to ear, "Found the on and off switch, boys!"

We stood and stared in disbelief. Johnson, the tech said,

"You could have killed us all."

Joe, still grinning, said, "Well, we said we needed answers; now we have some!"

"Like what?" Fitz stormed.

"Like, I believe this block is some kind of power supply, and it's activated or turned on and off by placing this stone in the engraved niche on it."

"Yeah, but what does it do?" Fitz bellowed.

"Hell I don't know, This shit didn't come with instructions," Joe replied.

I stepped in then and said, "Okay, guys, take it easy." Everyone's adrenaline was running wild. I mean how often do you get a chance to start up an alien device, not knowing what it does and having no idea how to shut it down... Okay, that was pretty scary for a minute or two... or maybe three. All right, it scared the shit out of all of us for a time, but nothing happened, and we came away with some answers without destroying the world as we know it. I'd say that was a good thing!

Joe was now looking at the other blocks of silver metal. He picked up a cut sapphire and placed it into a corresponding niche on one of them, and the same thing happened. A spider web of silver threads encased two-thirds of the stone, and a low hum started again. Joe touched the stone, and the hum quit, slid his finger across the stone, and the silvery threads disappeared and there was the slight pop as the stone left its resting place.

Joe, looking very pleased with himself, said, "I think we have just found our first hard evidence concerning these stones and ingots. The stones activate the blocks. How? I have no idea, and the blocks generate something. I'm guessing some kind of power or energy based on the humming sound we heard. That's providing we can apply our world knowledge of power and physics to this stuff, which I'm not sure is entirely possible." With that, he turned, rubbed his hands together, and with a Cheshire cat grin on his face said, "Now, for the cube."

CHAPTER NINETEEN

Unfortunately, the cube proved to be more problematic than Joe had expected, and after four days, we were no closer to having any answers about it than when we started. Fitz had brought in two new members to our team from his Skunk Works division, a theoretical physicist and an electronics engineer. They had been given the invisible cloth to work with as well as assisting Johnson and Stevens as needed. Stevens was working on the silver ingots and gems while Johnson worked on the cube dilemma. Fitz had expanded our work space to an adjacent lab, and it had become a beehive of activity.

Lawrence had gotten in, and Joe was right, he was pissed that we didn't contact him right away with our discoveries. Too bad, we all agreed, maybe next time he will stick around a little more and arrange his personal schedule to accommodate the important stuff. True to his word, though, he had followed through on all our legal paperwork and we were incorporated and would soon receive our permits/leases in the area we wanted to search for the galleon from the feds. We had brought Gus up to speed, and he was adding another crew member to the *Falcon*, another one of his shipmates from Nam. In the meantime, I had put Junkyard (Nils) and Lawrence in charge of the galleon recovery efforts. The rest of us focused on the contents of the crate and the story in the journal. It became obvious that a trip to South America was in our future if we were ever going to get to the bottom of this.

We had spent a week at Fitz's compound eating and sleeping in the dormitories; the rest of our waking hours were in the labs. Lawrence and Nils had headed back to the coast to gear up the search operations for the galleon. They were closing down the ecology company cover we had been using, thanks to Fitz, and replacing it with our Risky Business Ltd. information. Thus, making us a new legit salvage operation based out of Port Canaveral.

Wilson had set up our finances, and our company was solvent with a nice bank account, holding donated funds from numerous sources, many anonymous but all legal, more or less. It was from a part of the gold we had already found and an untraceable conduit to replenish funds when necessary was set up.

Things were coming together on most fronts, but the cube still had us stymied, and the frustration was building. The techs all agreed that the smaller cubes were generating some kind of energy or power when activated by the gems, but they couldn't figure out what kind or how the stones activated them. I kept hearing, "But the laws of physics don't allow for that."

I came into the lab a week later to find a heated discussion going on amongst the techs over the laws of physics topic with Joe sitting on a stool at a distance, taking it all in.

As I entered, he looked at me with an exasperated expression, shook his head, and stood up from the stool and said in a loud voice to the techs, "Gentlemen, I know you have over a half a dozen PhD's between you from many prestigious institutions. I have been listening to the same laws of physics bullshit discussion for the last four days, and I'm fed up with it. It should be obvious to guys as smart as you that our laws of physics may not apply here or at least physics as we know it. So, maybe it's time to break out the old copies of *Star Trek* and *Star Wars* and build a new paradigm of physics, taking into consideration something other than Our laws and start thinking outside the Goddamn box for a change!"

He turned and stomped toward the door and, as he passed me, he said, "Shit, I only have a master's degree, and I figured that shit out two days ago," and left the room.

The techs all looked at one another and, after a minute or so, one said, "Was he serious?" to his colleagues.

I spoke up and said, "Dead serious, let me see if I can help you understand where he's coming from. One, we pretty much know this stuff is alien in origin, and I mean alien as from out there," I said as I pointed to the ceiling. "Two, it was brought to this planet, not just dropped out of the sky by the aforementioned aliens. Three, since they came to our planet and brought this highly advanced stuff, that means they must have developed some type of interstellar ship and drive system or created some other technological way to get them here. Four, if their technology accommodated that, then their tech must be far beyond what we now know and understand here on Earth. So, five, the laws that govern their physical universe are either very different from ours or quantum leaps ahead of where we are now. Therefore, we need to explore science fiction more as science fact and start coming up with new theories on all this stuff without the constraints of our laws of Physics. Does that help you guys?" I asked.

They stood there with their collective mouths open. "Yes, Sir, I guess so," one of them finally said.

"Good," I said, "then I'll let you geniuses get back to doing your genius stuff," and as I turned to leave the lab, I looked back over my shoulder and said, "Oh, and by the way, May the Force be with you."

Doc was still busy with the translation and analysis of the friar's journal; working on the translation of the text on top of the cube and monitoring his people in Spain who were trying to track down the owner of the signet ring. Luckily, he had some superb contacts in Seville to help with the archive search and so he was concentrating on the first two items.

Tony had his face glued to his computer screens, working on the binary code mystery he had found on the cube, and Fitz's nerds were laboring over their physics quandary. This meant Dimitri, Joe, and I didn't have a lot to occupy our time, so we headed back to the coast to work on a plan for our inevitable expedition to Ecuador.

Since O'Reilly was now part of our team, she flew the chopper to the Lair and met us there. I think we all were ready for a good night's sleep in our own beds, and once we got O'Reilly settled in an office at the Lair that we had converted into a bunk room, we all headed our separate ways. We planned on staying in touch with everyone at Fitz's base through our video and Com-link, and they all assured us they would let us know if they came up with anything.

Sleep tried very hard to elude me, but a hot shower and a pair of Scotch's later, I dozed off. After a decent night's rest, I met up with the rest of the team at the Lair the next morning. The smell of freshly brewed coffee, fresh pastries, and hot breakfast sandwiches bought by O'Reilly during her morning ten-mile run really kicked us into gear, and we began laying the groundwork for our trip.

Of course, O'Reilly told us not to get used to the breakfast service; we were just lucky she was hungry when she got up and hit the pavement.

"Next time, Boss, it's someone else's turn," she said in a rather loud and fake gruff voice, as she handed me the bill for the food with a wink and a slight smile. No one would take this lady for granted, that's for sure, I thought.

With the information Doc had provided us from the journal, we identified the location for the start of our South American investigations. It was in the Tayos region on the eastern side of the Andes in Ecuador. It was a very mountainous, jungle region of the country. O'Reilly jumped right in, and her skills in research and data analysis proved invaluable. There were a number of stories about the Metal Library or Golden Library in popular media. We read about a number of past expeditions that had gone in search of it. We sifted through everything we could find on-line and compiled as much information as we could.

However, trying to pull out the kernels of truth from the copious amounts of fiction out there proved to be challenging. With what we had already discovered, we found that a lot that would be considered Sci-Fi fantasy before our discoveries was, in fact closer to the truth, and much that was presented as fact was closer to fiction. This was a strange twist for internet information. Slowly, we built a picture of the mysterious caves at Tayos and the past and current investigations into the library's whereabouts.

The Hall expedition back in '76 had been the most extensive investigation of the Tayos caves to date. Stanley Hall, a Scotsman adventurer, put together a large expedition to the Tayos region. Cavers, the military, and others joined forces, and they did a good job of exploring and mapping the supposed cave location. He received quite a bit of international press coverage and funding, primarily because one of the team members was astronaut Neil Armstrong.

After an extensive search of the cave, they found nothing remotely resembling a library. So, the question became, where do we go from here? We knew our true mission information had to be kept a secret, and we had to use the information we had to find the real location of the library. This would take detective work and a fair amount of acting on our part.

We decided our trip to Ecuador would have to appear just

like any other group of treasure hunters or adventurers hoping to find the library. That shouldn't be hard because that's just what we were. The only difference was that we knew the library was real. After gathering as much information as we could, maps, expedition stories, supposed first-hand narratives, we made a list of supplies and equipment we would need. We had to be careful not to go over the top with this and draw any more attention to ourselves than previous groups of adventurer/vacationers had in their searches.

After ten days of work, we had a plan, supplies, and equipment in hand or on order, and were planning to enter the country quietly and legally. To maintain our cover, we decided not to use any of Fitz's offered travel resources but use commercial travel and purchase anything else we might need once we arrived in country. This would include setting up a base of operations and purchasing a used four-wheel-drive SUV for transport. We had all agreed, much to Dimitri's dismay, not to try and bring firearms into the country, and also to minimize our carrying of all the high-tech toys that Fitz offered. Keep it low key and try to fly under the radar was my mantra. Fitz was concerned for our safety, based on some recent Intel he had received about the area we were heading into, hostile actions against tourists and travelers by the local bad guys or Banditos. He also had it on good authority that the Columbian drug cartels had routes through the mountains in that area to move their product. They reportedly had been responsible for several deaths of those that had been traveling in the wrong area at the wrong time, both locals and international tourists.

He finally relented when we agreed to take two encrypted SAT phones at least. He said there is a number hidden in their electronic memory that would immediately put us in touch with him, directly, and also that we would be contacted by Uncle Harold once we were established at our base of operations.

When we asked who the hell Uncle Harold was, he said,

"Never mind, just call the second number in the phone once we were in place." It was our turn to relent and agreed. That seemed to satisfy him and added a worry to our list. The site of our base of operations we decided should be Cuenca, south and west of the Tayos region. It was a fairly large city with a colonial atmosphere. It seemed to be the starting point for most of the previous expeditions and a repository for information pertaining to the legend of the library and those that had searched and currently searched for it.

Joe had been sequestered in the small electronics workshop he had set up in the loading bay of the Lair and was putting the finishing touches on what he said would be some very cool personal locating devices for the team members to carry. Very unobtrusive, they would pass for portable GPS units, which they also were but with more functionality and extended range due to his modifications. It had been almost two weeks since we left Fitz's land of magical wonders when a Vid call came in from Doc. His face, voice, and arm-waving were a dead giveaway that he had found something.

When he finally regained some semblance of control, he said we needed to get over there as soon as possible. When I asked what was going on, he said, "Get your asses over here, NOW!"

O'Reilly said, "We can be there in less than 15 minutes. I'll get the chopper ready," and left the conference room at a run. We relayed the news to Doc, signed off, and headed for the back parking lot where the chopper sat, hearing the turbine spinning up as we left the building. Twelve minutes later, we were touching down at the Helo pad at Fitz's facility where a golf cart was waiting to take us to the main building. When we got to the conference room in the lab area Doc was pacing like an expectant father.

"Oh, good, you're here," he said.

"What's going on?" I asked.

He said, "Sit down, and I'll explain, and then we'll go to the lab." As we sat around the conference table, where Fitz was already seated, Doc began his explanation. "Okay, I've been working on the translation of the journal, as you know, and Fitz's team has continued their work on the cube with little success."

Joe said, "Yeah, we know that, Doc."

"Well as I've been translating the journal, I have been finding many references to Incan culture. Things the friar was told by his tribesmen as well as others he came into contact with later. Now, the Shuar language and ancient Incan are not the same at all, but some references that were made in the journal were straight from the Inca language, and that got me to thinking. What if I had read something and had translated it in the context of the Shuar language without considering the reference, statement, or word as possibly being from the Inca language, not Shuar!"

"I don't follow, Doc; you said his journal was all in Spanish."

"It is; it is, but some of what he is saying is right out of the language of the Inca. This is tough because the Inca didn't have a written language; it was a technologically sophisticated culture, and it was a huge empire. The largest in the Western Hemisphere and it's the only Bronze Age civilization that didn't develop a written language! It's called the Inca paradox. So, everything in the journal is a translation from what the Shuar are saying in their language to the friar with Inca words and phrases they have learned thrown in and written in Spanish. Once I understood that, that's when I figured it out."

"Hold on, Doc," Dimitri said, "now I'm completely lost; what the hell are you talking about."

Doc, still wound tighter than an over-wound clock spring, was pacing around the room like a caged tiger. He stopped at the end of the conference table that had the table top keyboard and touched it a couple of times. A portion of the journal came up with the original Spanish, underscored by the English translation. I immediately recognized the section as the one we had discussed when he first began translating the document as being the section about the friar and the chief's visit to the ruins that were being repaired in the jungle.

He went to the screen, "Here, see where the friar asks him how the two natives are moving the giant stone?"

"Yeah," I said.

"And the chief says they're not, it's the gods moving it… with the Sweat of the Sun!" He was looking at us with a huge grin on his face our blank looks must have driven home the point that we still didn't get it. He said, "It's not Sweat of the Sun, it's tears of the sun; that's not a Shuar phrase, it's an Inca one… it's what they called gold."

The light bulb in my head went on, and I said, "So, that could mean the natives added something gold to the silver object he saw on the stone and that's what activated it?"

Doc was already headed for the door as he said, "We have a winner; follow me to the labs," and was out the door. We catapulted from our seats, except for Fitz, who just sat there smiling. We got to the lab, and all the geniuses were standing around a work-table, grinning from ear to ear. On the floor was a group of six concrete blocks neatly stacked in a pyramid, three, two, then one on top. On top of them sat the silver cube. Once we gathered around, Doc picked up one of four small pieces of gold that were on the table next to the blocks, about the dimensions of half a credit card and about as thick. Like a magician about to perform a trick, he held the metal up for us to see, and then placed it on top of the silver cube and stepped back.

For a few seconds, nothing seemed to happen, and then we detected a faint hum and the slightest bluish glow emanated from the cube. As that happened, Doc took one hand and pushed the top three blocks off the bottom three. We were awestruck as the three concrete blocks on top slid effortlessly off the stack and slowly floated in the direction Doc had pushed them and hung suspended in space about 7 inches off the floor.

He was obviously very pleased with himself as he pushed them back on top of the remaining three blocks, then removed the piece of gold. We heard the blocks settle back on top of the others with a slight scrape. He now picked up two pieces of gold and laid them on top of the silver cube. Once again, a few seconds passed, and the slight hum returned; this time, Doc pushed the entire stack of six blocks with one hand and we watched as they hung suspend in space a couple of inches off the floor all still touching one another, and moved a couple of feet away from the table. Doc then walked up to them and pushed one end, and they slowly rotated 360 degrees in thin air.

No one had uttered a word till Joe said, "Son of a bitch; it's an antigravity device activated by gold!"

Doc exclaimed, "Precisely, and the more gold you add the more it will suspend, as long as what you want suspended is somehow in physical contact with the silver block when the gold is applied. Multiple pieces, such as these blocks, have to be touching each other to lift as a group. With the right amount of gold placed on the block, I believe it can suspend anything!"

"I'll be damned," I said, "Tears of the Sun!"

CHAPTER TWENTY

An hour later, we were all sitting around the conference table, listening to Doc give us a full explanation of his discovery in the journal. As we slowly digested the information, the excitement continued building.

Dimitri said, "So, if these guys had a bunch of these things, they could move hundreds of huge blocks of stone and place them wherever they wanted?"

"That's right," Doc replied, "and we haven't even determined the maximum limits of their lifting capabilities yet. For all we know, with a few of these devices, or maybe just one and the right amount of gold, lifting a 100-ton block of stone could be as easy as lifting a loaf of bread. Hell, we don't know if there are height limits to their lifting capabilities! For all we know, this could be the basis for some kind of propulsion system." We sat and stared; he went on, "We haven't even scratched the surface on this. The possibilities are mind-boggling; I mean if these people had contact with other civilizations, it could explain the structures in Peru, Mexico, Honduras, Sumer, Guatemala, Egypt, and God knows where else. Hell, if they have been on earth long enough, it could go back to Stonehenge or even earlier. We're potentially talking tens of thousands of years... if not more."

Stunned silence accurately described the environment in the room at that moment. I mean, we had already discovered and seen enough evidence to make us all question our version of ancient history, but this...

I looked around the room at the faces at the table and slowly said, "I guess we're really onto something here."

Fitz just snorted and said, "Colten, you are the master of understatements!"

That broke the stunned mood of the room, and multiple discussions erupted around the table as Doc just sat there and grinned.

"But what powers these things?" I asked.

"Colt" Doc said, "that's the 64-thousand dollar question!"

We had made these discoveries from what was on the ship, so who knows what awaits us in the mountains and jungles of Ecuador. A few hours later, we left the continuing research into the block in the hands of Fitz's people and, still stunned by our discovery moved forward with our plans for our trip to South America.

The next few weeks were filled with furious activity, not only on the part of the Ecuadorian group, but Nils and Lawrence along with Gus and his crew were making real headway on launching our search for the Black Galleon. Tony would provide tech support and use his satellite hacks to provide overwatch of the search area in our absence. Lawrence had been assured all permits were approved for the search and would be in their hands in the next three to five days. Gus had added his new crew member, Petty Officer Wilson LeMasters, another crew member that had served with Gus's team in Nam.

A demolitions expert, excellent diver, and a mountain of a man, at 6'6" and 330lbs., he was no one to mess with. Gus assured me that his size was deceiving; he was as quick as a cobra and as deadly on land and as agile as a ballerina in the water. I had no reason to question his decision and let him get on with his preparations. By the end of the third week, we were wrapping things up and getting ready for our departure.

We held our final meeting as a full group and set up our communications protocols between ourselves and Fitz reviewed our individual operational plans, planned for every contingency we could think of, and set up our funding streams. This was so the Galleon Group and the Library Group, as we called ourselves, could access funds in any amount as necessary. An international letter of credit had been sent to the largest bank in Cuenca, so we could easily access money while anywhere in South America. We would travel as a privately funded group of "Adventurers" looking for the Golden Library. There was an extensive back story about us and history of other expeditions on the internet and in certain electronic periodicals, thanks to Tony's computer expertise. We were pretty sure we had covered our bases as best we could, considering the unknown circumstances that both groups were about to face. We agreed to take the next three days off from direct involvement in preparations and let the things we had put in motion move forward on their own. We all needed to step away from the monumental task before us and take a deep breath, try to relax as much as we could, and mentally regroup before putting on our game faces and hitting the field, metaphorically speaking. It was decided we would meet in three days, but till then, we were on our own. We could contact one another if the need arose, but only if it were vitally important. With that decision made, we left the Lair and went our separate ways for the next 72 hours.

I drove back to my place hit the opener for the center door of the three car garage, pulled in, and listened as it closed behind me. I entered the house and disarmed the security system and poured myself a hefty glass of 12-year-old Scotch before flopping down on the leather couch in my living room. I kicked off my shoes, picked up the remote for my sound system, and started one of my favorite playlists, a combination of classical and relaxing new age electronic music, took a long swallow from the glass, laid my head back, and tried to let the music and alcohol relieve some of the tension that had every muscle in my body quivering uncontrollably.

My mind was racing, and I felt like I was about to go over the edge of a bottomless waterfall… another swallow and then another. Did I get the relief I was looking for? No, but there was a slight ease in the knot in my stomach, just not much. After 30 minutes, I got up and went to the bedroom got out of my clothes and stepped into my shower, turned on every jet in it, and let the hot water bombard my body from all directions. After 15 minutes of this hydro therapy, I shut it down stepped out, toweled off, and fell onto my bed. I set the A/C on stun, so between the hot shower and the cold breeze on my body, I finally felt some relief. It was three o'clock in the afternoon when I drifted off into a fitful sleep.

I awoke with a start. The dream I had been having, while foggy and unclear, was filled with conflict and danger. As my head cleared, I realized I was safe at home, and my breathing and heart rate started returning to normal. I looked at the digital clock on my headboard, 12:15 a.m. I had slept for around nine hours and still felt tense and tired. I slid out of bed and put on a pair of old sweatpants, a T-shirt, and my old deck shoes, and headed to the kitchen. I wasn't starving; God knows why not… I hadn't eaten in 18 hours. I grabbed a Gatorade from the fridge and started pacing, my mind whirling. How had this all happened, and more importantly, what had happened and what would happen, to me, my friends, my crew, hell, the world?

I was knowingly putting us all in harm's way in one way or another. Sure, we were getting rich; hell, we were already rich. Why not stop now…? After a moments pause, that little voice in my head said…Well, that would be just stupid. We are on the verge of who knows what; the discoveries we have made are beyond belief, the stuff of science fiction, and yet all the evidence seemed to be pointing to discoveries far greater lying ahead. Discoveries literally out of this world, I thought with a wry smile, pun intended!

I realized I had made over 20 circuits of my living room and was holding a crushed empty drink container in my hand. I am wound way too tight, I thought as I tossed the plastic bottle toward the sink in the kitchen, heading for the garage door. I took the set of keys off their hangar next to the door before entering the garage. I didn't turn on any light as I hit the door opener, and its dim safety bulb illuminated. I walked past the other two vehicles parked there, Tessa's Jeep and my SUV, to the other side of the garage. I stood before the gray-car covered vehicle, reached down, and slowly pulled off the cover. The glistening metallic deep burnt orange paint shone even in this dim light. I stood for a moment, admiring her sleek lines for the thousandth time, a classic in her own right.

Not a Ferrari, or Porsche, nothing so mundane. Her mildly flared front fenders and slightly wider ones at the rear, like the hips of a beautiful woman, seemed like a siren's call to a lost sailor; the low-profile tires and wheels beckoned with the promise of precise handling and traction and kept her only six inches off the ground. I slid my hand across the smooth surface of her roof as I reached down for the door handle, the glistening circular emblem with the Z in the middle shown on the slope of her fastback like jewelry on a beautiful lady. I was immediately bombarded by the scent of rich leather as I opened the door, a scent headier than a fine perfume. I slid into the leather-covered Recaro seat and closed the door. This is what I needed, an escape from the craziness I had been subjected to these last months.

I could feel the tension slowly melting away as I inserted the key and brought this beautiful beast to life. The red glow from the fully digital engine gauges and the sound of the custom Borla exhaust system dispelled any idea she was "just another pretty face." Beneath her glistening exterior lurked a beast just waiting to be unleashed. I blipped the throttle a couple of times and heard the three dual-throated Weber's intake of air feed the 390 + horsepower under her hood. As the operating temperature came up, I eased the vehicle into reverse and slowly backed out of the garage into the dark moonless night. I strapped myself in with the five-point harness and felt the vehicle's warm embrace as I pulled them tight. I eased out of the driveway slowly watched the tach climb two thousand, three thousand RPM's, then a solid shift to second gear and the numbers continued their climb. I slowed my acceleration when the speedometer hit 70 mph. No sense in rushing things. I scanned the gauges in front of me, all digital but with the look of analog, pointing indicators and all; a piece of modern magic, I thought, a nice addition to a 48-year-old vehicle. The gauges showed everything was as it should be, and I settled in, windows down, air rushing in, no music other than the soothing growl of the exhaust. I had spent years working on her, keeping her mostly stock appearance but adding the newer technology where it was necessary, but not obtrusive. Six-piston disc brakes with carbon fiber rotors front and rear, a balanced and blueprinted engine with an updated camshaft that allowed the engine to breathe properly. Her exhaust was a six into two header, capped off with the custom Borla exhaust system. The four- speed gear box and rear end had been rebuilt with ratios that gave this lady very long legs, meaning first gear was a quick trip to 65mph second 110, third 145, and fourth, well, let's just say fourth was the "holy shit" gear!

 By now I had reached the on ramp to I-95 North; down shifting from third to second, I watched the revs come up. With no headlights behind and no taillights in front, I held the speed at 70 as I merged onto the interstate, only 25 mph over the posted ramp speed limit. With nothing but darkness in front of me, I said, "Okay girl, let's see what you've got," and pushed the loud pedal to the floor. Like a thoroughbred leaving the gate, she leaped forward and quickly passed the century mark on the speedo, still 2,500 rpm's below her redline of 8,700. Third gear followed quickly, and as the wind in the cabin and exhaust note increased, I could feel it tearing away my tension and replacing it with elation. I felt the ground effects I had installed on the body coming into play as we reached 135 mph; she was hugging the highway like she was on rails. With only a moment's hesitation, I decided what the hell, clicked the gearshift back into fourth, and kept the accelerator firmly slammed against the floor. My tiredness had evaporated, replaced by adrenaline. I could think of nothing but the highway ahead of me and handling the beast I had unleashed. My mind had cleared, and I was living only in this moment, this place, reveling in the joy of that experience!

    I took a deep breath and let it out slowly, becoming aware of my surroundings once again, and realized I had blown past the Titusville exit, my usual turnaround point. I saw taillights off in the distance and, in the rearview mirror, a set of headlights some distance back. I looked at the speedometer and saw it sitting at 155 mph. I quickly calculated my next turnaround should be Hwy 46 and figured it was coming up quickly, but I had a couple of minutes, so I let her climb to 160 before slowly backing down. I got to the Rt.46 turn off at about 100 mph, got on the brakes, and flicked the wheel to the right and hit the off-ramp perfectly. Getting on the brakes hard, I pulled in the beast to 50 mph before getting to the stop sign, which I didn't slow down for, but seeing no traffic in either direction, saw no reason for a complete stop. Sorry, Officer. I accelerated into a left turn four-wheel drift under the interstate and made an immediate left under power onto the southbound on-ramp, easily keeping the drift under control, shifting out of second and into third at about 110, once again merging onto I-95 south this time.

By now, my adrenaline had reached a more normal level. My muscles had lost their tightness and was replaced by a wonderful fatigue. I slipped the transmission into fourth gear, slowed, and headed south at a sedate 80 miles per hour, more relaxed than I had been in weeks. There still wasn't any traffic south bound, but I noticed the north-bound vehicle as it went by was an FHP Dodge Charger, now with its red and blue lights on. Oops, I thought and watched in my mirror as he blew past the Rt. 46 turnoff, still heading north. Phew, maybe he was headed to an accident or after someone else, not me... hmm, not likely, I thought, as I passed the Titusville turn off. I was thinking the luck I had been having lately was continuing when I saw the blue flashing lights in my rearview mirror. I immediately looked at my speedometer, sitting right on 80. Well, better than 160, I thought, as I turned on my right-hand turn signal, slowed, and headed for the shoulder.

By the time the trooper was getting out of his car, I had my license, registration, and insurance card in hand. Being so low to the ground, I could only see the officer from the waist down as he approached with his flashlight.

"Do you have any idea how fast you were going?" the trooper said.

"Yes, I do," I replied as I realized there was something familiar about the voice, "about 80," I said.

"Not just now," he replied in his best trooper voice, "the first time, northbound, about 20 minutes ago?" There was a lengthy pause, and he continued, "You know, when I was in college, I always wanted a 240 Z but could never afford one."

I was startled for a moment as I finally recognized the voice and then said, "Trooper Connors?" leaning my head down so I could look up at the man standing by the door.

He had turned off his flashlight and said, "Hello, Doc, mind stepping out of the car?" James Connors was a big guy at about 6'3" and right around 240 lbs. We had crossed paths a few times on some of my previous highway excursions. He'd given me a couple of warning citations, but the most recent contact with him was on a return trip from Gainesville when I saw a minivan go off the road in front of me and burst into flames. I pulled over and ran to the vehicle and began pulling people out. It was a family; the mother was the driver, and the father had been asleep in the passenger's seat when a front tire blew and caused the accident. Trooper Connors was the first officer on the scene. I had just gotten the wife out and was working on the kids when he arrived, and we worked together to get the rest of them out before fire engulfed the vehicle. Mother, Father, and three kids, they were banged up, but all had been belted in, so they got lucky.

We pulled them to safety minutes before the van turned into an inferno and Connors went out of his way to make sure the authorities knew he had helped me save their lives, not the other way around when he filed his report. He had proven himself to be an honorable man and a real hero as far as I was concerned, and I considered him a friend.

Guess if I was going to get busted, it might as well be by one of the good guys, I thought. As I stepped out of the vehicle, I said in my most innocent voice, "Sir, I have no idea what you're talking about." There was a moment's pause, and then he laughed and said, "You're a lousy liar, Dr. Burnett," as he extended his hand. As I took it, I said "Colten, and I thought I did a pretty good job," and laughed myself.

"Well, you or someone has Simpson chasing his tail up around Mims, still headed north."

"Is that so?" I said.

"Yep, he was on the north-bound I-95 on-ramp at Port St. John, when some sports car blew by at over a hundred miles per hour."

I looked at him with a straight face, and said, "You don't say? A hundred miles an hour, wow."

"I was on my way back from Daytona when I heard the call. The BOLO said a sports car was headed north at a high rate of speed. I figured I'd see it, but you know what? I saw nothing but an 18-wheeler between me and Simpson heading north... but I did happen to see a sports car heading south traveling slightly over the speed limit."

I held up my hands and said, "Guilty, I admitted I was doing about 80, remember?"

"Yeah, well, that's not going to get you a ticket tonight. Besides, Simpson lost sight of the vehicle somewhere just north of Titusville, so he should have broken off pursuit by now. He just got one of those new Chargers with the police Hemi in it, and I think he wants to show off."

I said, "Well, hypothetically speaking if the vehicle he was pursuing was doing over a hundred mph as he was coming onto 95, the laws of physics were against him from the beginning. I don't care what kind of Hemi he had."

Connors chuckled again and said, "Last I heard, he was running about 120-125.

I shook my head, "Wouldn't be enough."

"Really?" Connors said.

"Nope," I replied.

"Well, hypothetically speaking, how fast would he have to have been going to catch this vehicle?"

"Well, saying the vehicle in question was still accelerating when the pursuit began, and say it got up to 150 or 155, that would have happened long before Trooper Simpson hit 120; then it would have been almost impossible for him to catch it."

Connors looked the 240 Z over from front to back slowly, I think with a new respect for the elegant lady, "Hmm, 150 I'll have to remember that" he said, obviously rolling the data around in his head.

"I don't think you have any worries about that, though," I replied; "I'm sure whoever it was won't be back this way anytime soon."

Connors looked at me a little more sternly and said, "I hope not, Colten, at least not on my watch," as he stuck out his hand and said, "be safe."

I took his hand and said, "I'll do my best," as he handed my license and registration back. As he was walking away, I said, "Actually, it was closer to 160."

I saw him pause; he never turned around, but I heard him say, "Impressive," as he kept walking. I got home and pulled into the garage and took one last look at my beauty with a smile on my face and as I gently slid the car cover back over her said, "Till next time…" and headed to bed.

I slept for 12 hours and felt like a new man when I awoke the next day.

CHAPTER TWENTY-ONE

We had been in Ecuador for the past three weeks, getting ourselves acclimated to the environment and altitude. Coming from sea level to around 8,400 feet altitude impacted our breathing as we learned our way around Cuenca, putting our feelers out for any information that might be floating around about the library and finding ourselves reliable transportation. We had rented an old Range Rover that had seen better days around 15 years ago, but it beat walking, barely. I had gotten rooms at the Condor Hotel, a moderately priced place outside of the tourist zone but close to the main roads leading out of the city to the mountainous countryside.

The idea was to establish ourselves as "just" another group of American adventure/treasure hunters looking for the fabled Lost Golden Library. We soon found that we were just one of several groups tromping through the mountains and caves of the Tayos region looking for the same thing. Not far from the hotel we found an excellent bar, restaurant, hang out called Diego's Place. It was run by an American Ex-Pat from California who had volunteered as part of a privately funded library expedition in the mid '90s. They didn't find much of anything. So, they soon ran out of money since their backers saw nothing in return for their investment and pulled their funding. Once the search was disbanded, he and a friend of his decided to hang out for a while in Cuenca. Of course, there was a woman involved; she had also been part of the expedition, a local who had a degree in archaeology and whose father taught at the local university. The Americans name was Douglas Robbins, and his lady friend/partner was Theresa Sanchez. Both were delightful and full of information, history and folklore they were willing to share. I refrain from using the term legend, or tall tales, using folklore instead since we came here knowing there was truth behind many of those stories.

Theresa oversaw the food portion of the establishment while Doug took care of the bar end of things. Dimitri proclaimed it our HQ while in Ecuador, when Doug pulled a chilled bottle of his favorite Russian Vodka from behind the bar and started pouring shots. I had to agree; the environment was perfect, the walls were covered with photographs, newspaper, and magazine articles about the history of the local area and of searches for the Golden Library. The food was excellent, hospitality was genuine, and the bar… well, the bar was the bar and well stocked. We made it our main place for eating, drinking, and just hanging out talking and doing a lot of listening.

According to Doug, most people looking for the library made at least one stop at Diego's Place while in town. Others, like us, became regulars, put down squatter's rights on certain tables within the spacious bar/dining room, and showed up on a regular basis. It wasn't long till we blended in with the clientele and made new friends and connections. First stage of the mission accomplished!

While we all spoke some Spanish, Joe, Doc, and O'Reilly were truly the best of the group. What was interesting was that not being a strong Spanish speaker didn't turn out to be that problematic at Diego's. English was spoken most widely, and on any given night, you might hear conversations in German, French, and Italian in addition to Spanish. We spent most of our days driving into the countryside and the thickly canopied mountains, getting a feel for what we would be up against when we started our search in earnest. While it was breathtakingly beautiful, and the main roads were paved and maintained, our short excursions onto the mountain roads showed them to be narrow, hard to traverse, and at times, extremely dangerous, with three-to four-hundred-foot drops at the edge of the one-lane rocky roads.

We all developed a healthy sense of caution when driving. Blind corners, wash outs, and rock slides were not uncommon, although the locals seemed to take it in stride. When mud or rock slides made it necessary, they would dig into the mountainside just far enough to create a new narrow passage for the vehicles that plied these treacherous roads. We soon discovered our geriatric Range Rover to be woefully inadequate for our needs.

After one such day we sat at Diego's, bemoaning the limitations of our current transport when Doug, who had been talking with us from behind the bar, asked if we would be interested in purchasing a vehicle. When we asked for more information, he explained to us he still owned the vehicle they had used on the expedition he had been on and would be willing to let it go for a very reasonable price. Our interest piqued, we asked for more details; it was a four-wheel drive 1975 Suburban he affectionately called "The Beast." He said he had it stored at a buddy's auto shop and, if we were interested, we could go look at it the next morning.

Dimitri piped up, "That's 20 years older than our current rental vehicle that we were just complaining about."

Doug assured us the age didn't matter; the vehicle was tough, it had rarely left them stranded, and covered some serious mountainous terrain in its time.

With a certain amount of trepidation, we agreed to have a

look the next day. He had gotten so excited when extolling the virtues and ruggedness of this thing we didn't want to hurt his feelings and take the chance of ruining what was turning into a great friendship, so we agreed to meet him out front at ten the next morning and have a look at his "Beast."

We picked up Doug the next morning and after a short drive found ourselves in front of a two-story warehouse-looking building with two large roll-up bay doors on its front. It was located in what at one time had been an industrial business area. It was still busy, but the buildings had seen better days decades ago. We parked out front and went in the one open bay door and found ourselves in a large open bay with various cars and trucks littering the interior. Most had their hoods up or were jacked up, sitting on cinder blocks, and we saw several young men and boys with their heads stuck in the engine compartments or lying on their backs underneath, busy at various tasks on each one.

As we walked through the beehive of activity toward the back of the building Doug shouted, "Hey, Sean, you in here?"

To which a young man under the pickup truck we were standing next to replied, "Senor Sean is in the back." Doug thanked him, and we wound our way through a maze of vehicles in various states of repair/disrepair toward the rear of the building. There must have been 12 to 15 vehicles being worked on by as many men and boys and even a few young women. I would categorize it as organized chaos, but the work area was clean and well-lit with fluorescent light fixtures hanging from the 15-foot ceilings and the sounds of air wrenches, hammering and other power tools being used echoed around us.

We neared the back of the cavernous room and were surprised to see two men in coveralls under the hood of a 1969 Dodge Super Bee, looking to be in pristine shape. It was parked next to a 69 Chevy Chevelle Super Sport, equally beautiful. There were four or five other cars lined up under car covers, hiding their identity, next to them. Doug said, "Sean," in a loud voice and one of the two individuals came out from under the hood and responded with a huge grin.

"Hey, Dougie, what brings you to my neck of the woods?" Doug was around six feet tall and the mechanic that greeted him was at least three inches taller, and had a bandana tied around a head full of curly blond hair. They approached each other and did the bear hug thing, slapping each other on the back as longtime friends would do.

As we walked up, the mechanic acknowledged us and stuck out his hand, saying, "Sean Jamison," as Doug introduced us. We immediately began admiring the Dodge and commented on its fantastic condition compared to most older vehicles we had seen on the roads.

Joe had walked up to the front of the car and, as he looked under the hood said, "383 Magnum, very nice."

Sean was beaming; he was proud of this vehicle, "Yep, all original, matching numbers, four-speed with a posi-rear end."

"Sweet ride," Dimitri chimed in as he checked out the perfect interior.

"Yeah, I've made sure she was taken care of since the day I bought her."

After we talked cars for a bit and found out he had a few more classics under the covers, either restored or on their way to restoration, Sean asked, "So, what's up, Dougie?"

Doug grinned at the use of his personal nickname and said, "These guys might be interested in buying the Beast."

"No shit," Sean replied.

"No shit," Doug said.

"Well, hell, let's take a look at it I haven't seen it in a couple of years myself," as he turned and headed to the far end of the row of covered cars. As we got to the last vehicle, we saw it had a tarp over it, not a real car cover, and had been used as a repository for all kinds of loose parts sitting on the hood, tires and wheels on the roof, axels and radiators leaning against its sides. It took us ten minutes to remove all the junk just so we could pull the tarp off.

What we saw was indeed a 1975 Suburban that had seen better days. Three of the four tires were flat, and it was covered in dirt and mud that must have been on it when it was parked, no telling how long ago. The interior wasn't in bad shape but could use some work. It had a light bar across the roof with a couple of busted driving lights hanging from it, and the homemade front bumper had obviously done its job and come in contact with some large semi-immovable objects. The body was in surprisingly good shape, no major dings or dents.

"What's it got for a motor?" I asked.

Sean popped the hood and said, "A small block Chevy we got from a donor car back in the day, but it's got over a hundred thousand miles on it and was on its last leg when I brought it in here and parked it."

I looked at him and said, "That's not much of a sales pitch."

He smiled and said, "If you really want to buy this thing, I want you to know what you're getting for your money. When it comes to automotive stuff, I'm as honest as they come. I've been screwed a few times and learned my lessons the hard way. I do believe in karma, and I want to keep mine in good shape as long as I can."

Dimitri and Joe had been crawling over, under and around the Beast the whole time Sean and I were talking. I waited until they finished and walked over to us, I knew I would get a full report from them.

"Well?" I asked.

Joe spoke up first, "Frame looks in good shape, the front transfer case seal is leaking, floor panels are good, but suspension looks shot."

Dimitri followed, "Body is in good shape, interior doesn't look bad, but I wouldn't want to ride on any of these roads in it;

lights and wiring seem a little worse for wear but nothing that can't be fixed." Joe nodded in agreement.

Doc spoke up and said, "It has quite a bit of cargo space, and its four-wheel drive."

Joe interjected, "Maybe once, but I wouldn't be too sure about that now."

I looked at them and said, "So, what you're saying is that we would be buying a frame and body, and that's about it." They nodded in agreement.

I turned to Sean, and he grinned again and said, "They're right, but I can say the four-wheel drive is working." About then, one of the younger kids working in the shop came up and asked Sean a question about the fuel pump he was holding. Sean, in fluent Spanish, answered; the boy nodded and headed back to his project. Sean turned back to us and said, "Kids pick up on stuff pretty quick, but they still need a little guidance now and then."

"I saw a lot of young kids and teenagers working in the shop," I said.

"Yeah, most of them are street kids I've taken in and started teaching them basic auto mechanics to give them a trade they can use when they get older."

"Really?" I said as I looked between him and Doug.

Doug laughed and said, "Yeah he's like the Pied Piper; he helped one or two, and next thing you know, he has a whole flock of them wanting to learn. He even lets them live upstairs."

"We've turned it into two dormitories-girls and guys, got a kitchen, and everything."

I looked at Sean, "So, do you pay them?"

"Some of the older ones, I try to pay a little. The younger ones come here and have a place to sleep and food to eat instead of stealing or prostituting themselves and living on the streets. For them, that's more than they had. Plus, I have two older full-time mechanics and a business manager that help with the training part while they are doing repairs for customers. Doug helps with the food through Diego's when he can."

"I live upstairs and kind of keep an eye on things. One of my mechanics lives there too with his wife; she handles the cooking and stuff and watches over the girls." I was totally blown away as were the rest of my team at what we had just heard. These two Americans, living in Ecuador, one running a thriving business and helping his best friend who is running an automotive trade school for street kids, amazing. Teaching them a trade they can use wherever they go and on top of that, giving them a place to live while doing it.

I was impressed, very impressed, and knew I wanted to help them. But I had partners to consider too, so I asked Sean and Doug if we could have the night to think about it and get back with them tomorrow with our decision. They said that would be fine; we all shook hands and left Sean's automotive training facility and home for wayward kids.

We dropped Doug off and headed for the hotel. It was quiet for a bit and then Joe said, "We are going to buy it, aren't we?"

I said nothing, and Dimitri said, "We can fix it up."

It was Doc's turn next, "You know, we really need to help Sean if we can, and if purchasing that Beast will help, I'm all for it. I have never seen someone so selfless giving back to the community the way he is." I guess they took my silence for indecision on the purchase because they all started coming at me with reasons for buying the vehicle.

As we pulled up to the hotel, I held up my hand to stop the chattering and said, "Enough already, of course, we're buying the vehicle, and when we get with O'Reilly, I want to discuss some additional ideas I have about the larger situation."

We met up with O'Reilly in the patio restaurant at the hotel. She had been following up on a few leads we had gotten on the suspected location of the library in the Tayos region, all of which turned out to amount to hearsay and speculation, nothing of any consequence. We filled her in on the vehicle inspection and told her of the plan to purchase it.

"You're going to do what?" she exclaimed, choking on her beer.

I calmly said, "We are going to buy the Suburban."

"But it's a piece of junk; you all said so."

I leaned back in my chair and took a long pull on the cold bottle of beer and then said, "I prefer to think of it as a diamond in the rough." Before she could offer any further protests, I said, "Let me explain. The Suburban is structurally sound, therefore giving us a good foundation to build on." I saw Joe and Dimitri smile as they figured out where I was going with this. I said "First we need to make a shopping list and get it to Fitz as soon as possible, so he can start gathering the things we need. I suggest we buy the vehicle and then get Sean and his crew to refurbish it for us. We will fly in all the parts necessary and then pay him to put the Beast together."

I received nods and smiles from everyone except O'Reilly. "Are you sure about this?" she asked.

"Absolutely," Doc replied before I could. "Not only will we get a vehicle built to our specifications, but our payment for his work will help his business and all those kids." There was a good vibe going around the table as we grabbed a napkin and started making our list. Since price was no object, we decided to do it up right and resurrect the Beast in style. Full suspension upgrade, four-inch lift kit, which would give us about a foot of suspension travel, 30-inch wheels and off-road tires, new rock crusher transmission and transfer case, new rear end with larger axels, a 454 big block crate motor, which we would have modified for more torque and horsepower without sacrificing long term reliability. New off-road bumper/brush guards which would hold a Warn 25,000 lb. pull winch on the front and a 20,000 lb. pull winch on the heavy-duty rear bumper. Heavy-duty electrical system with multiple gel cell batteries, new lighting all around with the latest LED high-powered driving lights, a computerized satellite communication/navigation system, and Dimitri added "A kick ass stereo system."

    It took us a couple of hours to talk through the details, come up with a solid plan, and complete our list, which we would send to Fitz right away. We all adjourned to our rooms planning to meet at 5:00 in the lobby and head over to Diego's for dinner. Walking to the elevator, I was feeling good about what we had decided to do and how we planned to accomplish it. The mood was jovial, and Joe and Dimitri were discussing watts, speaker size, and in what format we would access music; Doc was smiling, and O'Reilly's expression was unreadable.

    As we got on the elevator, I heard her mumble "Boys and their toys" under her breath. All I could think was what a great vehicle we would have and what a good start to building some good karma for us in Ecuador.

CHAPTER TWENTY-TWO

Joe, Dimitri, and I met up with Doug at his place the next morning, and from there, headed to Sean's garage. Upon arriving we found a scene similar to yesterday's except Sean was moving among the workers, providing instruction and encouragement to his staff of young mechanics to be, smiling and laughing as he went.

When he spotted us, he left his rounds and came over grinning and greeted us with a hearty handshake and smile. "Well," he said, "did you decide on the Beast?"

I turned to Doug and said, "How much you want for it?"

He looked at Sean and then said, "We'd like to get 500 dollars U.S. if we could."

I saw Sean cringe slightly as he said in a low voice, "Doug, don't you think that's a little high? I mean she's pretty much just a shell."

Doug turned to him and in a friendly exasperated way said, "Dude, we can always come down, but once we've set a price, it's hard to raise it, man!"

I spoke up, "Obviously, it needs a lot of work," and Joe said,

"Obviously." "But we talked it over, and the deal hinges on your mechanical abilities, Sean."

He looked a little shocked, and hesitatingly said, "Well, with enough time and money for parts I think I could get her running again, but it wouldn't be easy."

I laughed along with my two guys and said, "That's an understatement, but if you're as good a mechanic as I think you are…" and let the sentence trail off.

Sean jumped in, "Hey, I'm that good, ASE certified, got quite a few years' experience, and I would love to see the Beast back on the road again as much as anyone."

I smiled, "That's good to hear. However, we have some specific accommodations and alterations that would have to be made to it to meet our needs."

Now, Doug jumped in, "Sean is good, but you have to realize, we are somewhat limited in our ability to get specialty parts down here." Sean nodded in agreement.

I continued smiling and said, "That may be true, but we're not!"

"First," I said, "I will not pay one penny over two thousand dollars for your vehicle." They both gaped at us as I pulled the now typed list out of my pocket that we put together last evening. It listed all the modifications and parts we wanted, and I handed it to Sean. He took it and read it with Doug looking over his shoulder. I almost laughed out loud as their eyes got bigger and bigger the further down our list they got.

They finally looked up at us like we were six-headed monsters and Sean said, "Is this some kind of joke…?"

"Nope," I said, "but there's a catch. How long would it take you to do the job?"

Sean scratched his curly blond hair and said, "Well, if, and that's a huge if, I could get the parts, that would take the better part of a month and a half and then everything you have on this list at least another month or more to get it done!"

I put on my best disdainful look and said "I thought you were a good mechanic…" Now Sean turned red.

"Do you have any idea how expensive and hard it would be to get some of these things on this list? Even if I went to Quito, my suppliers wouldn't have half this stuff in stock, and they sure wouldn't order it without payment up front, and it would have to come from the States, and that would take…"

I held up my hand to stop him. I said calmly, "Sean, here's the deal, today is Tuesday, by next Monday I can have everything on that list sitting on this shop floor ready for you to go to work. I will need that vehicle done to the specs we have given you within two weeks from that day and, when delivered I will pay you thirty thousand U.S. dollars in cash or bank transfer, your choice. Additionally, if you run into the situation where you need something we've missed on our list or if during this week you determine you need anything here in the shop to complete the job, let me know and I will make sure you have it within 24 hours at no cost to you. Miss the deadline and the deal is off."

"So, Sean, can you do it?" I asked. I can't say I've ever seen a ghost, but these two guys had turned a ghostly white, if there is such a thing as the blood drained from their faces. I stood there with crossed arms and waited. Sean, walking like a man in a dream, pulled up an old wooden chair and sat down, staring at the list. Doug just stood there, arms at his side.

Finally, Sean looked up and said in a halting voice, "You're serious, aren't you…?"

"Yes, I am," I replied, "and no matter what you decide, here's the two thousand dollars for the Suburban," and handed him an envelope.

He stared at it for a minute and then said, "Even if I say no?"

"Yep even if you say no," I replied.

He slowly reached out and took it. "You're not shitting me?"

"No, Sean, I'm not."

I could see it was sinking in as he sat up a little straighter in the chair and in a loud voice called, "Fernando" over his shoulder. Moments later, one of the men he had working for him came running up and, after a few minutes of animated discussion, Fernando called out and another man and teenage boy showed up and began an earnest discussion with Fernando.

A couple of minutes later, with all of them staring at the list and us, Fernando walked up to Sean, still seated, and with a determined look on his face and a strong voice said, "Si, Senor Sean!"

With that, Sean slowly stood, took a step toward me, and said, "By next Monday, here in the garage, all the parts?"

I said, "Yes, no later than next Monday."

"Make it two-and-a-half weeks," he said.

I paused for a moment, then said, "Done, two-and-a-half weeks."

With that, he stuck out his hand and said, "Well, then, Dr. Burnett, I guess you've got yourself a deal!"

As I shook his hand, all the helpers grinned from ear to ear and Doug, under his breath, said, "Holy Shit!"

I said, "Sean, its Colten." I handed him a card with our hotel contact information on it and said, "Stay in touch."

"Oh, I will," he said, "you better believe I will!"

"One more thing," I said, "this build and this vehicle is between us. It's private business. I don't want word of it getting out to every gear-head or the general population until I'm ready, understand?"

He furrowed his brow and said, "Not really, but okay by me. What we do here is nobody's business but our own, and I can vouch for my people. It will be our secret." I smiled nodded and, with that, we headed back to Doug's place to drop him off. He was still shaking his head as we waved good-bye with promises of seeing him later and headed back to our hotel.

On the way, Dimitri asked, "What if he had said no?"

"He wouldn't have," I replied.

"But what if he did? We already ordered all the stuff on the list from Fitz last night, and it will be here on Friday, not Monday!"

"That will give him a few extra days to get the project done," I replied. Again, the question, "But what if he said no?"

"Then I guess we would have had one hell of a garage sale!"

Joe chuckled, and Dimitri said, "That was a hell of a risk, you know."

"I know," I said, "but I also know people, and this will work."

I stopped in to speak with Sean on Thursday and was pleasantly surprised to see the Beast taken apart. The body was sitting on one lift, and the chassis they had separated from it was being high-pressure cleaned out back by three of the younger workers, including two of the girls I had seen on our first visit. The engine and transmission had been removed and the interior gutted from the cab. There were two more workers cleaning it out, each group under the supervision of the older men I had seen working there.

The place was still a beehive of activity, but a large space had been cleared near the back of the building for the Beast to be worked on. I found Sean back there talking to Fernando about some aspect of the build. When he saw me, he grinned and said, "Well, what do you think?"

"Looks good," I said, "and good thing too."

"What do you mean?" he asked, and I told him about the early arrival date of some if not all the parts.

"That doesn't cut my build time, does it?"

"No, you still have two-and-a-half weeks from Monday."

"Then, that's good news. Now, I have a couple of additional days." I could tell he was happy with the news.

"Yep," I said, "and I'm sure you can use them."

"Damn right," he said with a grin. About then, a young boy

around 14 or 15 came up and stood quietly, waiting to speak to Sean.

He turned to him and said, "What is it, Eduardo?"

The boy spoke in English, "We have finished cleaning the chassis and are ready to take the body out back and clean it."

"Good," replied Sean, "Get your guys and lower the body onto the body dollies and move it out once the frame is out of the way."

"Si, Jefe," he said and turned, running and shouting orders to the other young workers as he went.

Sean chuckled as he turned, "He's one of my best mechanics and has really taken an interest in this project."

"Doesn't sound like he's afraid to step up and be a leader either," I said.

"Not at all," Sean replied. "The other workers respect his knowledge and expertise and follow him willingly. He's also a good teacher and takes time with the younger ones to help them learn."

Fernando chimed in, "He is a very good boy, Senor, and will make a fine mechanic one day; I have no doubt."

"Very commendable," I said, then I told Sean to let me know when the parts arrived and if he needed anything more and headed back to the hotel.

Since we had some downtime, we used it doing local research on the library, the Shuar Indians and the mountainous area we had kind of identified as our starting point, gathering information as we moved eastward. Taking this tack, we thought we would have a better chance of finding "something" rather than just sticking our heads in every cave we might find. We had been staying in touch with Fitz and the galleon crew with no new developments on either front.

Our permits had come in, and Gus and his crew had started doing side scan sonar runs over our search area using the Neptune information from Fitz to help guide them, nothing so far. Tony was still watch-dogging our permit search area with his satellite hacks, but he had spotted no unusual activity. We were all getting a little frustrated at the lack of progress on either front, so we were thrilled to get the call from Sean that the Beast was done.

The two and a half weeks had gone by quickly, and the build had gone well. Sean had beaten his deadline by almost a full day, and the vehicle turned out exactly as I had hoped. One of the hardest parts was keeping Sean from putting a fancy paint job on it. He couldn't believe I wanted it left in is original faded and chipped greenish brown with sanded and primer spots on it.

My only other paint stipulation was a matte clear coat over the entire vehicle, which he was happy to do. He had been curious as to the need for somewhat hidden storage areas within the vehicle's sides, floors, doors, and dash, until I turned Joe loose in his shop installing the batch of GPS, satellite communications gear, and other toys we had received from Fitz, and, yes, it included a kick-ass stereo as Dimitri had requested. Eduardo, with the excellent upholstery skills of some of the girls, had insisted on helping Joe and had overseen the installation of the interior and a number of other aspects of the build, according to Sean, and had done a super job.

Sean and I went to the bank, and I made the transfer of ten thousand dollars into his shop account for the vehicle purchase, and he asked for the rest in cash, which I provided. He said putting that much money in his account might draw unwanted attention to us, our project, and its ties with his shop. I thought this to be a prudent suggestion and was happy to oblige.

Over these past three weeks, Doug, his wife, and Sean and his crew had become almost part of the expedition, certainly part of the family, and provided us with a wealth of local knowledge. They had put us in contact with others who provided additional information that we hoped would help in our quest. We found out from Doug's girlfriend, Theresa, that her father, who taught at the university, was a true believer in the Metal Library and had told her he had seen artifacts supposedly from it, books with metal pages of gold and what looked like silver, with strange writing on them unknown to him.

They had been given to a Father Crespi, a friar who had also lived with the Shuar for many years and ministered to their needs. He had moved to Cuenca as he was getting up in years and spent his final years at a church in the city where he had become friends with her father.

We had seen his name on the internet many times and referenced in books. Unfortunately, many of the fantastic artifacts he had disappeared after his death. There are those who have called into question their very existence, but we now have a first-person eyewitness account that can vouch for their being real. We were making progress, albeit slow; progress none-the-less. We asked to meet with Theresa's father, and she agreed to set up a meeting soon.

We continued to familiarize ourselves with our environment, and our forays into the mountains built our confidence in our new vehicle, its reliability and ability to handle the dangerous mountain roads if you could call them roads- many times not much more than trails barely wide enough for the Beast. We felt confident we could extricate ourselves from pretty much any situation we might run into. Wrecks and overturned vehicles had become an all too familiar sight in our travels as our trips were taking us further and further into the mountains.

We had been in country for over three and a half months and this Wednesday started out like most of the previous days but with a slightly more positive air. The night before, while having supper at Diego's, Doug had told us of a village he had just heard about that supposedly had two Shuar elders living there who had come from another village high in the mountains. He said it was about five hours' drive and then maybe another two to three-day hike. It was in a section of mountains rarely traveled.

They had been visited by Anglos before and were not unfriendly to them as some villages were. We got the general location, thanked Doug and made our plans for a four-day trip into the mountains, leaving the next morning. As we sat there digesting this new information, I said, "We have a conundrum here, folks," as I got stares from the group.

"What do you mean, Colt?" Doc asked.

"Well," I started, "all the stuff we are hearing about the library is based on this guy Moricz's claim to have found it in the Tayos cave. All the expeditions to the cave, as far as we know, have turned up nothing, right?" All agreed. "Now, we have the friar's journal, which seems to indicate he was living in a Shuar village with connections to the library pretty high in the mountains AND his trek to this place of the gods took him even further up into the mountains."

"So?" Dimitri asked.

"So," I said, "these accounts seem to be mutually exclusive. The Tayos region is further southeast from here and at a lower elevation. We know from our research the Shuar region ranged from the Amazon basin to about 3,500 to 4,000 feet altitude in the Andes. But it seems the friar is talking about a village at a much higher altitude. Now, Doug tells us about these elders that may be living in a village in the mountains, and they may have come to that village from a place even further up in the mountains. It would seem that all this stuff about the Tayos cave is wrong and, if our friar's account in his journal is accurate, people have been looking for the library in the wrong place!"

After pondering my statement for a minute or so, O'Reilly said "Seems to make sense, but that is speculation based on a vague description of location in the journal."

"I know," I said "but I've got a gut feeling that it is right. What do the rest of you guys think?" After more discussion, it was decided that we should follow the lead we were getting from the journal for now and see if we came up with any more promising clues. For now, we put Tayos on the back burner and prepared to track down the Shuar elders if they existed.

We came out of the hotel early the next morning. We had packed our gear the night before and headed to our vehicle that was kept in a secure parking area at the side of the hotel. We had to pay extra for the two guards keeping an eye on the vehicle but felt it was well worth it. You can imagine our surprise when we approached the vehicle and found Eduardo wiping it down with clean rags, removing the morning dew and talking and laughing with our two guards.

"What the heck are you doing?" I asked Eduardo in my sternest voice, and, "Why did you let him near the vehicle?" I said to the guards.

Our guards spoke passable English and sheepishly replied, "Senor Burnett, we have known Eduardo for years, and he said he worked for you now and was getting la Bestia ready for your trip into the mountains."

"He said what?" I blurted.

Eduardo jumped in and said, "Please, Senor, it is not their fault; I just wanted to help a little more, and besides it needed some cleaning."

"That's not what I meant," I said. "You told them you work for me?"

"Well, Senor Burnett I would like to, and Senor Sean said it would be okay with him if I were gone for a few days, and I know the mountains where you are going well, and I could help translate for you and…"

I stopped him there. "I appreciate your enthusiasm, I really do, but Doc here has a good handle on the language." I turned and looked at Doc who promptly said something in the Shuar dialect to Eduardo, who promptly replied in Shuar, and then continued the conversation, much to Doc's surprise.

After a few minutes of back-and-forth Doc looked at me and said, "He's good, very good. He has the language down perfectly, better than me."

Eduardo heard this and said, "I am Shuar, my whole family was Shuar, and before I came to the city, I lived in Shuar village high in the mountains. In the same area you are going today."

"What? How do you know where we are going today?"

"Senorita Theresa told me last night when I went by Diego's, so I knew I had to be here early." Now, he was looking very sheepish, eyes down and shuffling his feet. I looked at Doc, and he shrugged; Dimitri and Joe just grinned as Eduardo spoke again, not looking up... "...and, Senor Burnett, I worked very hard on your Beast, and I worked with Senor Joe and was hoping to have at least one ride in it." I guess that did it; call me a softy or whatever, but the kid did deserve a lot of credit for helping with the vehicle.

After expelling an exasperated breath, I walked toward the vehicle and said, "Okay get in back, but the first bit of trouble and you're back at Senor Sean's, comprende?"

He almost jumped out of his skin, "Si Jefe," and was in the back sitting on our backpacks before the rest of us could get in the vehicle.

I looked at the guards and said, "Don't worry about it; you did fine." They both grinned with a sigh of relief, nodding, but I said, "NO ONE gets near this vehicle except my crew, understand?"

"Si Jefe," they both responded and then opened the chain-link gate and we headed out of the city with our newest team member excitedly jabbering to Doc in Shuar and grinning from ear to ear. I hope I don't regret this I thought as we left the city behind and began climbing the mountain road.

Darn Kids!

CHAPTER TWENTY-THREE

O'Reilly had stayed at the hotel. She had planned to download some new real-time satellite images of our search area, through Fitz's connections. Little did we know what a stroke of good fortune that was. The roads were bad; it had rained the night before, and the mud and slippery rocks made for even more dangerous driving once we left the blacktop. After about an hour and a half's drive, we left the main gravel road, which had had traffic on it... old trucks, and busses mostly, a few horse-drawn carts, and some foot traffic and started up a single lane mountain road that was in worse shape than the one we had just left. We were lucky to run 15 to 20 mph on this track and that even slowed when we came to the blind 90-degree turns that were numerous.

Dimitri was driving. I had shotgun and the view out the passenger's window was breathtaking, literally. The valley below dropped away over 700 feet, almost straight down, and the driver's side was a sheer wall that had been cut, dug into the side of the mountain. Beautiful, yes; relaxing, No! We had been on the road for about an hour when we rounded a blind hairpin turn and came upon a sight that made my stomach wrench.

Hanging over the edge of the road was an old gaudily painted school bus filled with people and still moving slightly as it dangled over the precipice. A small sapling had caught between the rear bumper and the body of the bus as it had gone over the edge and was the only thing keeping it and its occupants from a 700-foot drop into oblivion. As we pulled up and jumped out, we could hear the screaming and crying coming from the bus; we ran over, and our hearts sank even further.

We all know school busses have emergency rear doors. However, this one was covered with luggage and boxes. They had been strapped to a frame welded over the rear of the bus, making more room for passengers inside. The luggage was barely sticking above the edge of the road as the bus hung at a severe angle from the small tree. Doc and Eduardo had run to the edge of the drop off and were shouting to the passengers inside, trying to calm them. They were trying to get them to be still as their efforts to escape were stressing the tenuous grasp of the small tree even further.

Imagine a clock pendulum swinging back and forth… well, this one wasn't swinging, yet, but if it started, that tree wouldn't hold, and there would be no hope for anyone's survival. I quickly assessed the situation and saw small clumps of dirt and rock falling away from the tree's shallow root structure and knew we had just minutes to do something. I did a quick survey of the surroundings and spotted another tree on the uphill side of the road about twelve to eighteen inches in diameter, twenty feet up the side of the mountain. It was almost directly in line with the back of the bus.

They say necessity is the mother of invention, so I guess that's what kicked in as I shouted for Dimitri to back the Beast up about 30 feet and start un-spooling the front winch cable.

"Roger that," he responded, jumped into the vehicle and got it into position.

As he was working on the winch, he shouted, "You know we can't pull that bus back up with this winch, right?"

"We don't have to," I shouted, "we just need to help that tree hang on a little longer! See that tree up there?" I pointed up the slope to the one I had spotted, "Get the cable played out and throw it around its trunk and get it down to the back of the bus." He understood what the plan was and, before I could tell Joe to grab the cable and climb the side of the hill to the tree, Eduardo had grabbed the cable hook and was halfway up the slope. He had heard my call to Dimitri and figured out what we were going to try to do. Damn smart kid! "Stand by the winch, Dimitri."

"Standing by," he replied.

"Doc, how are they doing?"

"Best I can tell, we have two unconscious with possibly severe injuries and a pregnant lady who is injured."

"Got it," I shouted as I reached the Beast and grabbed the SAT phone and punched in O'Reilly on speed dial.

She picked up on the second ring, "What's up, Boss?"

I quickly filled her in on our situation and the info I had from Doc, told her I was turning on our Vehicle GPS locator and said we needed Medevac here ASAP.

"Copy," she said as the line went dead.

Eduardo was draping the cable around the tree.

I shouted to Joe, "You ready to play Tarzan on that luggage?"

He looked at me and grinned "As soon as I get the cable secured, I'll be good to go!"

I realized that Doc was making headway with the passengers as most of the screaming had stopped and mainly crying and sobbing along with some shouts were still coming from the bus.

I shouted, "Doc?"

"Making progress but the injured passengers need help now; the bus driver is unconscious along with a young girl that hit her head on a seat rail or something."

Shit, I thought.

"Oh, and by the way the woman, who is about eight months pregnant on board, got slammed around pretty good, and is in serious pain."

Double Shit... Eduardo had gotten the hook and cable to Joe by now, and he was hanging over the edge trying to find a solid connection point on the bus.

A couple of minutes later, I heard Joe shout from over the edge, "Good to go, Colt!" I gave Dimitri the hand signal for taking up the slack in the cable.

As the cable drew taught, I stopped him and called, "Joe?"

"Still looking good here, Colt."

I gave the signal to take up more of the cable, slowly; I could hear the cable tighten and heard the singing sound steel cable makes when it's put under extreme stress. Hang in there damn it; hang in there I thought. I was watching the little tree hooked to the bumper for any sign of stress relief when I heard rocks and dirt falling from the up-side of the road. I didn't want to look and called, "Eduardo?"

"We are good, Senor, still holding."

At that moment, I saw the little tree begin to straighten by about an inch. I gave Dimitri the sign for a halt and called, "Lock it down!"

"Roger that," he replied.

"Joe?"

"Looking good here I got a good hook up on the frame where the bumper connects, and we're good to go!"

"Okay, Tarzan, do your thing." As I watched, he pulled his six-inch Gerber from its sheath and put it in his mouth, pirate style as he used both hands to inch his way up onto the luggage tied to the back of the bus. Within seconds he sliced the ropes and began shoving boxes, bags, and suitcases over the side of the bus, watching as they fell the 700+ feet to the valley below.

In minutes, he was down to the last crate and hanging on by

one piece of rope still tied to the bus. The razor-sharp edge of the Gerber had made short work of the ropes. "Okay last one going," he called, sliced through the rope, and watched as it fell away. "Colt, bad news; there's a rebar frame they welded to the bus to hold all this shit, and it blocks the door."

Triple shit, I thought. "How thick is the rebar?" I called.

"Not bad, but I think cutting at the welded points would be our best bet. Cut a couple of them and looks like we could bend the frame out enough to get the door open."

"Doc, how are things?"

"Holding steady, but you need to hurry every chance you get…"

"Copy that!" While I had been talking to Doc, Dimitri had gone into the back of the Beast and pulled out our 24-volt-battery powered side grinder/cutter, part of our tool stash that could cut cable, chain, or steel re-bar as needed and was running to Joe. A million things were flashing through my mind… would the little tree hold? Would the bumper on the bus hold? Would the bumper on the Beast hold? And would the tree on the mountain-side hold? The only thing I was sure of was that the 25,000 lb. pull Warn winch would hold; it was just everything that it was attached to or wrapped around that worried me!

In the few seconds it took me to run that through my head, Joe had already cut through two welds and was working on the third. "Can we bend it now?" I called.

"Naw isn't going to work; the door wouldn't have opened wide enough to get them out. I've only got two more welds to cut, and the whole thing will be off."

"Dimitri?" I called, he had gone back to winch duty at the Beast, "Still good, Colt."

"Eduardo?"

"Tree is still holding Jefe."

"Joe?"

"Crap, I'm going to need the small crowbar to get this door open."

Eduardo was at a dead run to the truck, "I'll be right there, Senor Joe."

"Doc," I said, "tell everyone that when we get that door open, we need people to work their way slowly to it and, if I see anyone other than women, children, and the elderly trying to get out first, I will personally throw their asses over the edge. Anyone that is healthy and unhurt needs to help get the others out first."

"Got it, Colt," and I heard him burst into a Spanish tirade loud enough so all on the bus could hear. There were comments that came back from the bus that I couldn't hear, but I understood Doc's response, "Just try it!"

Joe, moving very carefully, was prying the door open with the help of Eduardo, both on the back of the bus, hanging in space. Oh, shit, I thought; well, at least it's the two lightest guys in the group, as I saw the door slowly creak open. You could step from the rear bumper of the bus to the road's edge, but there was about a four-foot gap between the two that you had to step/jump over to make it.

Dimitri had come up behind me with one of our climbing ropes and said we could tie it to the door; he would hold it on this side, and they could use it as a hand-grip as we reached to help them across the gap. Not the best idea, especially for the children and elderly, but I couldn't come up with anything else, so we tossed the end of the rope to Joe and told him to tie it off and start the people across. We told them to use the cable attached to the bumper of the bus stretching across the opening as a step if they needed to while holding onto the rope. Eduardo was translating the plan and encouragement to the people coming out the door. I was holding onto the rope with Dimitri and reaching out to the people, helping, pulling, or jerking them across the opening as necessary, all the time keeping an eye on our little tree.

In what seemed like hours, but was only twenty-five minutes, we had all the children and elderly across and were helping the adults. Doc was moving the group around the curve in the road and getting them seated and getting water from the Beast. We wanted them out of the way in case the cable connection came loose, and we had a steel whip flying through the air. There were four young men in their 20's who had been helping everyone out of the bus. Now, the only ones left were the pregnant woman, the unconscious girl, and the bus driver.

They had no idea what to do next as Doc came over and said, "I'm going back in the bus to help get the injured out."

Before I could protest, he had crossed over and dropped through the open door and was talking to the men inside.

The first out was the pregnant woman, who was obviously in pain. Doc did a quick exam and talked with her, then called out, "When you get her over there, get her lying down as soon as possible and get her some fluids."

"Got it," I said, and one of the young men helped her climb out the door to Joe and Eduardo. She was wobbly but determined to make it. She came across with the help of the young man, and once on the road, immediately collapsed.

Doc had briefed him, and he called to some of his fellow travelers, who helped carry her to the others and they began tending to her. Next, they moved the unconscious young girl, approx. twelve or thirteen, to the back door. She was being carried by another of the young men, whose name we found out was Paco. As he exited the back of the bus, I heard a popping sound coming from our little tree and saw a couple of small roots breaking.

Oh, shit. "Doc, the bus is shifting, and we're going to lose it; hurry your ass up."

Paco was poised on the rear bumper of the bus with the girl

in his arms, no free hands to hold the rope as I moved closer to the edge and extended my hand.

He said, "No, Senor," and as graceful as a ballet dancer, launched himself and the girl across the gap and landed one step beyond me. The bus never even moved. Holy Crap, using only the muscles in his legs and not pushing off the bus bumper, he made a six-foot jump, carrying at least 65 lbs. of dead weight.

"Nicely done," I said not expecting an answer.

"No problem, Senor," he said in English and continued carrying the unconscious girl to the waiting group. Doc and the last young man named Raoul were straining to get the overweight driver to the back of the bus. Joe, looking in from the back door, saw their dilemma, untied the rope, and slid through the back door down towards Doc. They were close to the door, and I could hear their conversation.

Doc said, "We can't tie the rope around him; he's got crushed ribs and probably has internal bleeding. It could kill him!"

Joe added, "I know but we can tie it around our young friend here. Let him get the driver's shoulders, and Dimitri and Colt can help pull him along with the driver while we get his legs. It should help us move him. It's worth a try. I'm ready to get out of here anyway; I never liked buses…"

"Did you hear all that, Colt?"

"Sure did, Doc, We're ready when you are; just let us know when to pull." Within another five minutes, we were easing the driver across the gap and getting him to safety. Eduardo had jumped to the road, and Joe had his ass in the air, trying to unhook the cable. Dimitri had slowly let off on the tension, and the bus had started slowly pulling our little tree over again.

Joe said, "The cable's jammed," and was using the small crowbar to pry it loose as he hung even further over the precipice.

Suddenly, there was a loud pop and the little tree that

could… couldn't anymore and broke off as the bus vanished from sight along with Joe. Not realizing the cable had gone slack, I ran to the edge and looked down. The bus was still falling and hit the bottom with a loud crash, and then a giant fireball formed as the fuel tank exploded, rocking the valley below. There, hanging by one hand from the hook on the end of the cable, was Joe, holding on to the crowbar in his other hand.

"You think you guys could give me a hand?" he said with that wise-ass grin of his. As Dimitri and I pulled the cable up and Joe cleared the edge of the precipice, he said, "Sure am glad I got the cable off before the tree went; otherwise that would have been ugly."

Dimitri said, "Obviously, I should have left your little wise-ass hanging there a little longer," and then broke into a grin and gripped Joe in a bear hug.

"Naw," Joe said when he could catch his breath, "I would probably have dropped the crowbar, and you know how Colt is about losing tools."

"Jesus, all right, you two jokers," I said as I smacked Joe on the back of the head and threw my arm around his shoulder, "let's check on these people. We're not done here yet," as we walked to the waiting group of survivors.

When we approached, we saw Eduardo walking amongst the passengers seated on the road, handing out bottles of water, patting kids on the head and shaking or holding the adults' hands while speaking to them with a smile on his face.

"What do you think?" I said to my two companions.

"Kids got some balls," Dimitri said.

"And he knows what to do and when to do it without being told most of the time," Joe added.

"Yeah, I noticed all that and agree. I think we could use somebody like that on the team."

"You mean permanently?" Joe asked.

"I mean while we're in Ecuador at least."

Joe said, "You'll get no argument from me," as we saw Eduardo move to where Doc was tending the young girl.

"Hell, yeah!" Dimitri replied.

"Well, guess it's settled then; we'll talk to him later," I said as we got to the group. Joe helped Doc, and Dimitri started the cable retrieval on the winch. I dug out the SAT phone and called O'Reilly again; she answered on third ring.

"Well?" I asked.

"Working the problem, Boss," she replied.

"The big trouble will be finding a spot for a bird to set down," I said, "Not sure we can. We may have to go to Plan B."

She said, "And what's Plan B?"

I paused and said, "I'll have to get back to you on that."

"Shit, I knew that was coming. I got your location; you're out in the middle of bum freakin' nowhere or should I say UP in the middle. I'm showing your altitude to be about 10,000 feet."

"Bout right," I said.

"How much time do I have?" she asked.

"None," I replied. I looked at Doc's face as he was working on the little girl. "Turn on your personal Coms and keep the SAT phone handy, now, move your ass."

"Roger that," she said.

I went back to where Doc and Joe were working on their patients. I noticed the driver was breathing raggedly and had dried blood around his mouth.

"Doc?" I asked.

"Not good, Colt, driver definitely has broken ribs and probable internal bleeding. The girl is pretty bad, head trauma, surely some swelling of the brain and possible fluid in the cranial cavity. Our expectant mother is doing well, but I'm worried about the baby since she took a hard blow to the stomach when the bus went over. I just don't know. I still have a good heartbeat on the baby but..." he let the statement trail off.

I looked around and said, "The rest of them?"

"Not too bad," he replied "bruises, contusions, one broken arm, and probably a few fractures, but nothing as bad as these three."

"How much time do we have?"

He stood up, "With the limited resources I have, I can probably deliver the baby if I have to, but if we run into complications or it needs special treatment or if there's internal bleeding," he shrugged and shook his head. "The other two are very serious; maybe an hour, hour and a half, no longer I would think."

"Shit." I reached out and put my hand on his shoulder and said, "I know you'll do your best. I just talked to O'Reilly; the Cavalry is on its way."

He gave me a half smile and said, "I hope to hell they have fast horses," and went back to his patients.

CHAPTER TWENTY-FOUR

As O'Reilly was hanging up the SAT phone from our first call, she had grabbed her Coms and was heading out the door. Downstairs, she flagged down a taxi and handed the driver 50 dollars U.S. and said get her to the airport in less than five minutes. There were no questions asked as he pulled into traffic with horn blaring and foot to the floor. Four minutes later, he came to a tire-screeching halt in front of the operations building on the private side of the airport. O'Reilly threw another 20 dollars his way, blew him a kiss, and thanked the young driver in perfect Spanish. He had just had his day made as the good-looking redhead jumped out of the cab and hit the front door of the Ops building at a dead run.

Inside it only took her a minute to locate the flight operations counter, and she approached the man behind it who was writing on a clipboard. In Spanish, she asked for the director of operations, and when he identified himself as that person, she quickly relayed her story and request to him. His eyes widened, and his mouth dropped open slightly as she finished. There was a pause, and then he apologetically said they had no commercial medical evacuation helicopters at the airport and the local hospital had none. The closest thing they had to that was the military helicopter unit stationed there under the command of Captain Eduardo Montego. O'Reilly looked at his name tag and said, "And where can I find Captain Montego, Senor Gutiérrez?"

He responded, "Outside and two doors down." She thanked him and blasted out the door at a dead run.

In less than a minute, she burst into the military operations HQ office where a young enlisted man was sitting at the front desk. She asked for Captain Montego and, when quizzed as to who she was and what was the nature of her business with the captain, she replied that there was a medical emergency in the mountains, and there were three people critically injured who might die if they didn't get to a hospital right away. The young sergeant asked again who she was and how she came about this information. By then, adrenaline pumping, O'Reilly had had it and in a loud voice said she needed to see the captain immediately.

An inner office door opened. An officer came out and walked slowly to the desk standing behind the sergeant sitting there. O'Reilly, seeing the officer's rank and then his name tag addressed herself to him and tried to explain the situation calmly. A slight man in an impeccable uniform stood there listening and when O'Reilly finished, he turned to the sergeant and told him to get the request forms for this young lady to fill out.

When she said, "Request forms?"

The captain replied that the forms would have to be sent to headquarters for approval before any action on his part could be taken.

"What!" she exploded. "And how long will that take?"

He paused for a minute and said, "Two to three days."

That did it. She looked at him and through clenched teeth said, "I don't have two to three hours, let alone days."

He seemed nonplused at the whole situation and stated that

taking on a flight of this nature into the mountains required permissions, planning, and certain flying skills she probably wouldn't understand, and could not be implemented on such short notice.

By now, a small crowd had gathered of other officers and enlisted men in flight suits. They were looking on with somewhat amused expressions as their commander put this gringo in her place. That was the final straw; she had been at the airport for 17 minutes and that was seven minutes too long. She looked at the captain's uniform and saw no flight wings and looked at the young faces around the room and then back at the captain.

She leaned forward against the desk, about two inches from the captain's nose (she was around four inches taller than him) and said slowly, "You don't even fly." Her voice low, and ice cold as her crystalline green eyes, conveying her disdain for him, bored holes into his soul. She looked around the room again, making eye contact with everyone in a flight suit and then back at the captain, his eyes wide and mouth agape. Speaking slowly, and low, through clenched teeth she said, "Are you going to help me or not?"

The captain was beside himself and took a half step backwards. He had never met a woman that could invoke this level of intimidation in him. He felt as if he were staring into the face of some predatory beast. He had no idea that was exactly what he was doing. He stuttered, "I...I, cannot help you... Senorita."

O'Reilly stood up ramrod straight, and said, in an even tone, "then next time you get called for an emergency, you can let your Boy Scout troop take a freaking bus! And take your arrogant machismo bullshit and stuff it." She started to turn then hesitated, she looked directly at the captain and very conversationally said "Oh, and when the shit hits the fan... and believe me it will, I want you to remember one thing... Shannon O'Reilly," she said, driving her finger into his chest at every syllable, "because I'll be the one bringing the shit storm to your door."

With that, she took one last look at the amazed faces and stormed out of the office back onto the flight line.

Her mind was racing as she looked at her watch. She had been there for 19 minutes now and had nothing to show for it. As she looked out over the flight line, opposite where the military Huey's were parked she saw a shiny Euro Gazelle helicopter with a guy in coveralls leaning into the side door. Holy shit, she thought, this may be her last chance as she sprinted toward the parked chopper. As she got there out of breath, the man in the coveralls turned around and was startled by her sudden appearance and good looks.

"Wow," he said, "'Scuse' me, Ma'am, but you kind of gave me a start!"

"Sorry," she said, "listen, I need to rent your helicopter right now. I have cash…"

"Whoa, whoa, Ma'am, I'm sorry, but this isn't my bird to rent; I'm just the crew chief. It belongs to Mr. Mendez, and he doesn't rent it." She easily detected the Texas accent and said so.

"Yep," he said, "born and grew up in Austin," to which she said, "I really love Austin, and I really need your bird."

"I told you, Ma'am, it's not mine."

"Well, can you call Mr. Mendez and let me talk to him?"

"I'm sorry. He's out of the country right now; that's why I'm getting her ready. He has to use it tomorrow."

"So, it's fueled and ready to go?"

"Yes, Ma'am, it is."

"Look, what's your name?" O'Reilly asked.

"James Dobson, Ma'am."

"Okay, James."

"But my friends just call me Tex," he quickly added.

She forced a smile. "Okay, Tex, here's the problem," and quickly explained the situation to him. She could tell she hit a nerve when she told him about the injuries and potential life or death situation.

"Damn," he said, "that is bad," as he turned his gaze down to the tarmac. When he looked up, he said "I did one tour in Iraq and three in Afghanistan as crew chief on Blackhawks, and I've flown my share of Medevac flights. I feel for you and your friends, but I can't let you use Mr. Mendez's helicopter."

She saw his quandary, and it only took a second for her to make her next decision. "What if it got stolen?"

His eyes got wide, "You're kidding, right?"

"No, I'm not," she said.

"Well, if somebody tried to steal it, then I'd have to stop them."

"But what if you couldn't?" she replied.

"Excuse me?"

She said, "I don't have any more time. You can say I knocked you out and stole the bird, and I'll deal with the consequences later." She started for the cockpit door when he grabbed her arm, pausing, and not saying anything for a minute.

"Well, if that's the way it is then... Guess you better make it look good."

She knew what she had to do, so she cold-cocked him with a right hook and knocked him back into the open door of the fuselage.

"Holy crap," he said, as he got back up rubbing his jaw, "where'd you learn to punch like that?"

She said, "I'll tell you when I get back," as she opened the cockpit door.

"No, Ma'am, I don't think so," he said, "you can tell me on the way," as he climbed in, closing the side door and moving into the co-pilots seat. O'Reilly got in and pulled on the headset as she began the turbine start-up procedure.

Tex looked at her and over the internal Com said, "You can fly this thing, can't you?"

"Yeah, Tex, don't worry I've only got a few more hours to complete until I solo." His eyes got very wide!

The turbine came to life, and soon the operating temperatures were coming up as O'Reilly lifted the bird off the ground.

"Hey, aren't you going to call the tower for take-off clearance?"

"Don't have time for that shit," she replied. As she brought the ship to a hover six feet off the ground, she told Tex to get in her bag and pull out what looked like an i-Pad. Tex did as he was told; she laid it on her thigh, and he heard the Velcro attach itself there. She tapped the screen, and a photo terrain map appeared with a red arrowhead sitting at the airport and a blue dot appearing in the mountains north and west of their location.

"Where are we heading?" Tex asked.

She pointed to the blue dot and said, "There," as she began a rapid climb, nose down.

"What about other air traffic?" he began as their radio squawked with a frantic call from the tower. Tex looked at her and said, "Well?"

"Well, what?" she asked as the Gazelle glided twenty feet off the ground toward the parking lot.

"We've got to answer them."

"No, we don't; just hold on." She leaned over and turned the radio off. By now, they had reached the northern perimeter fence of the airport, far away from the active runways, and O'Reilly pulled back on the collective, opened the throttle and said, "Let's see what this baby will do." They leveled off at 3,000 feet and were heading toward the blue dot at 250 k/ph. Once she was sure she was clear of any air traffic, she switched the radio back on and increased their air-speed to 295 k/ph.

Tex was staring at her and said over the Com, "Lady, you're crazy."

She turned and smiled a sweet smile at him and said, "Tex, you haven't seen crazy yet… but you probably will!" The radio was alive with chatter from the airport, calling for the Gazelle's immediate return with all kinds of threats, both legal and otherwise.

O'Reilly saw that Tex was about to key his mic and said, "Ahh, Ahh, remember, you're my prisoner and unconscious in the back; don't screw up your alibi now." He thought for a minute and then realized she was right and resigned himself to watching the terrain and the instrument panel. As they climbed higher in their charge northward, O'Reilly said, "Her top speed is about 310 k/ph right?" Tex said "Yes Ma'am, but at this altitude in the thinner air, it would be a little less."

"She's in good shape, right?"

"Right," he said, "damn good shape. I've been a crew chief for 12 years, and I kept all my birds in top-notch order."

"Good," she replied, "because I'm going to need that 310 and then some to make up for the time I lost with those military dick-heads."

"You had a run-in with the military at the airfield... Oh, shit, we are screwed for sure," Tex replied.

She said, "Don't worry about it now; you're unconscious, remember?" The blue dot was getting closer; while the ground team had taken about four hours to cover approximately 100 miles, they could make it in 35 minutes. They had been in the air for about 20 minutes when her SAT phone rang; she answered, it had a short conversation, and hung up.

She reached in her bag and pulled out a small earpiece/earwig and stuck it in her left ear and said, "Colten, do you copy?"

There was a second pause, and then she replied, "Roger that. Did you ever come up with that Plan B yet? Because I'm about ten minutes out." Another pause and she said, "Copy that; standing by." Tex was staring at her again.

She looked at him, "My boss," she said, "I had to check in."

He shook his head and said, "Who the hell are you? ...No, never mind, I don't want to know."

She reached over and patted his leg, smiled, and said, "Don't worry, Tex. It will be fine; I'll take care of you," and then went back to concentrating on her flying. It was getting a little bumpy, and they were flying through patches of fluffy clouds as they passed through the altitude of the Andes' cloud forest, the red arrow and the blue dot getting closer and closer together. The radio squawked again; this time, it was military call signs, three of them.

Tex said, "Oh, shit, they scrambled the air force unit at the field, and they're coming after us."

She didn't turn to him, but said, "Well… this is going to be fun!"

Things were a little different at the crash site. They had been following the radio transmissions from the airport and Dimitri said, "Hey Colt, looks like O'Reilly has pissed off the local military flyboys and they are in pursuit."

"Great," I said, "that's all we need. Go around the corner and see if you can find a place for her to set down." Dimitri took off at a run around the blind corner where the bus had lost control. I knew there was nothing behind us but sheer rock face and narrow road. I hoped our luck would be better further up the mountain.

A few minutes later, Dimitri came back, out of breath, and said, "We may be in luck. The rock face goes from vertical to about a 40-degree slope about 75 yards round the bend; there are three trees we will have to take out, but it may give her just enough rotor room to sit down on the road or at least part of it."

I said, "Trees to clear!"

"Not to worry, Colt," Dimitri said, grinning. He then switched to his Boris Badenov voice, "Dimitri have magic rope, wrap around trees, make boom; trees fall down just like that," he snapped his fingers, "then we have nice landing place for whirlybird." I waved him on as he went to the back of the vehicle, his sense of timing for humor was incredible... he called Joe to go with him as he grabbed a backpack and headed back around the corner.

I went to Doc, looked at his patients, and said, "We're going to have to move them around the curve up there about 50 to 75 yards."

He said, "I don't think that's a good idea."

I told him we didn't have a choice. It had already been almost an hour since the call to O'Reilly.

"It's your ride, and she's coming in hot." He nodded in understanding and called the three young men who had helped us get the passengers out of the bus and explained to them what we had to do; two other men came over and offered their help.

Good, they can help our pregnant lady. I asked if she could walk and, although pale, she nodded in the affirmative.

Paco said, "I will carry the girl."

I nodded and said, "The rest of us will carry the bus driver." While we had been waiting for help to arrive, we had made a makeshift stretcher to put him on.

Everyone started to move. As we got to the curve, I stopped them and said, "We need to wait here for the explosions."

"What?" Doc exclaimed.

"Don't worry. Dimitri is just clearing a few tree's so the chopper can land." I heard the bird in the distance and called O'Reilly, "We will clear a space for you, but it's going to be tight."

"Just give me someplace to set the skids, and I'll be fine."

I said, "Plan B may be one skid on the road and try to keep the rotors out of the trees."

"Oh, great," she said. "You just had to make it a little more interesting. I see how you are."

About then, we heard the Det cord go off and I said over the Com, "Popping red smoke at LZ."

"Roger that," she said, "I've got a visual, coming in." I had prearranged the smoke signal with Dimitri and, as we moved around the corner, the road ahead was being blanketed in red smoke. I looked at the angle of the slope and thought, okay, O'Reilly, we're about to find out how good you really are. We carried the injured along the slope side of the road as the chopper came into view. O'Reilly crabbed the bird in sideways, slowly blowing out the smoke enough for us to see there would only be room for one skid on the road before the rotor hit other trees higher up the bank.

I said, "O'Reilly you're only going to be able to set down one skid; any closer and you'll hit trees."

"Copy that; just have your people ready to board when the door opens. I've got extra help here."

What the hell, I thought, but quickly forgot about it as she came in and set one skid down on the road and kept the other hanging in space with 700 feet of nothing below it. The door slid open, and a young guy jumped out in coveralls as we carried the unconscious girl and driver to the door. Doc went in first and took the young girl from Paco and, with the help of the guy in coveralls, they strapped her into one seat, immobilizing her head and neck with an extra strap. Next, we helped our mother to be in and got her belted as best we could, considering her condition. We then slid the driver on the stretcher in on the floor. It was crowded, but we got a thumb's up from our new colleague as he closed the door. Doc had his med kit, and we had agreed he should fly with them to the hospital.

He gave me a thumbs up through the window, and I said, "Okay, O'Reilly you're clear." I heard the power being applied to the turbine, but the lift didn't come as quickly as I thought it should. "O'Reilly?" I said over our Com link.

"We're a little heavy, and the air is thin, but Tex says we can make it; just have to kick the old girl in the ass," she replied. I heard the turbine winding up even further, as more power was applied, slowly the chopper lifted off the road. Once it had, I watched as it rotated and literally fell nose-first over the road edge toward the valley below. I heard the turbine screaming like a Banshee as the rotors worked to beat the air into submission. The young guys gasped as we ran to the edge of the precipice and looked down, sure she was going to crash.

I said, "Don't worry; she's just using the fall to pick up airspeed," as we watched the chopper falling nose-down toward the valley below. At least I hope like hell that's what she's doing, I thought. At around 100 feet from the valley floor, as if on cue, the chopper's nose began pulling up and, ever so slowly, she began to level off and headed down through the valley. Okay Fitz was right; she was a good pilot. In fact, she was a damn great pilot, I thought.

The remaining passengers were resting more or less comfortably on the slope side of the road next to the Beast. Dimitri had secured all our gear, including winch and cable, and had found a place further up the mountain where he could turn the Beast around and drove back to our little survivor's camp. We had been in touch with the local authorities and apprised them of the situation, and they were sending the police and emergency medical teams to our location.

As I leaned against the rock face, I looked at my watch; this whole event

had taken place in less than two hours, yet it seemed like days. I was exhausted, as were the rest of the guys. The only one still full of energy and talking excitedly to the passengers huddled together was Eduardo. I really couldn't hear what he was saying, but there were a lot of waving arms, hand gestures, and pointing in my direction.

Finally, he came over, and I asked him what was going on.

He said, "The people wanted to know who you were. I told them you were a great American explorer and adventurer. You had saved many lives and were known around the world."

I stopped him and said, "What?"

"They are very impressed and appreciative and want to repay you," he said.

"No, no, no, stop telling that story; it's not true."

"But you saved their lives and you are a great adventurer, Senor Burnett."

I stopped him. "That's enough, Eduardo; no more stories."

"Si Jefe, no more stories." I could see his disappointment as he turned, head down and walked back to the group of passengers. Conversations began again and, before long, he was as animated as ever, talking and moving among the people.

It's useless, I thought and turned my attention to preparations for heading back to town. I hoped that everything was going okay for O'Reilly and she was able to get the injured the medical attention they needed so badly.

I should have known better....

CHAPTER TWENTY-FIVE

Once O'Reilly had pulled out of that stomach-wrenching nose-dive into the valley and leveled off, she told Tex to check on their passengers. He looked back to the cabin area, clicked the Com, and asked Doc how everyone was.

Doc replied that his stomach was back in its right place, our expectant mother was experiencing more pain, and the other two were still unconscious.

"How long till we get to a hospital?" he asked.

"About 50 minutes," Tex replied.

Doc said, "I don't think that's good enough."

O'Reilly had heard the exchange and looked at Tex as she keyed her mic "How about 30 minutes, Doc?"

He replied, "Every minute counts, and 30 is better than 50!"

Tex looked at her and said in a lower voice, "There's no way…"

She looked at him with a tight-lipped grin. "I know," she said as she twisted the throttle and the turbine's whine increased. Minutes later, they spotted the three military UH-1's flying in a V formation about 1,000 feet below them. She had brought the Gazelle to 6000 feet and had been cruising at max speed with a slight tailwind. The military must have seen here at about the same time, and the radio crackled to life.

"This is Lieutenant Estevez of the Ecuadoran Air Force; you are under military arrest, and I am ordering you to slow your speed and fall into formation as we escort you back to the airfield." They had slowed and were making an aerial U-turn as she blew right over them, not slowing at all. The radio crackled, "I repeat; you are under military arrest, and I order you to slow your speed and prepare to be escorted back to the air-field."

O'Reilly keyed her mic and said, "You all must be some of those boy scouts dressed up like pilots I saw at Ops. Well, I'm terribly sorry; I can't oblige your request. You see, I'm in kind of a hurry, and besides, I don't have time to play with you kids!" Almost as an after though, she keyed her mic again and said, "Hey Estevez at least I know you guys can fly, that's more than I can say for your commander."

A few seconds later she heard what sounded like a muted chuckle, and then Lieutenant Estevez cleared his throat and said in a professional voice "Please Senorita O'Reilly follow our request it will go much easier on you."

She keyed her mic one more time and said with a chuckle "glad you remembered my name, but sorry boys no can do… Alpha Mike Foxtrot!" She turned to Tex whose eyes were quite wide, he had understood her last transmission, and said, "Remember how you said I was crazy before…"

"Yeah?" he replied…

"You were wrong then." She called to the cabin, "Doc, everybody hold tight…" Looking back at Tex, she said with a huge grin on her face, "NOW you're going to see crazy," as she dropped the nose of the Gazelle, headed for the deck, and twisted the throttle wide open. Without looking at him, she said, "This is a 342 with the Astazou XIV H?"

In a strained voice, she heard, "Yeah, it is."

O'Reilly, still grinning, said, "Then, this baby should be able to take a little more!" The turbine whine turned into a primal scream as the Gazelle leaped forward passing the 200 knots mark and still climbing. At about 50 feet above the treetops, she leveled off and began flying the terrain. Tex was a brave man. He had earned two purple hearts and a bronze star for bravery in combat. But he had to admit that, at this moment, he was pretty much scared shitless! He watched as the taller trees and rock outcroppings of the valley went flashing by. He looked over at O'Reilly, whose concentration was so intense her face could have been carved from stone as she gracefully slipped the Gazelle up, down, and sideways in what seemed like one continuous fluid motion. Eyes straight ahead never once straying, feet dancing on the pedals, her moves on the collective and cyclic were pure poetry. God, she was the most beautiful woman he had ever seen!

The UH-1's were no match for the Gazelle. Their top speed was around 125-130 knots; she was heading down the valley toward the city at about 225 knots. Tex kept scanning the instruments and reported any changes the crazy pilot needed to know as she kept her eyes glued to the onrushing terrain. "Oil temp is rising, turbine pressure has redlined; you can't push her like this for much longer…"

"I know," she said, "I need her to hang in there just a little longer," as she ever so slightly slowed their pace. She tapped the pad on her leg, and another screen came up, tapped again, and a city view popped up with a red cross west of the airport. She asked, "Do you know where the hospital is?"

"Sure," he said, "it's about five miles from the airfield to the south."

"Do they have radio communications?"

"Yes," he replied. She glanced down at the pad, then the dash as she slowed her air speed a bit more, much to Tex's relief.

She said, "Get them on the radio and let them know we have a trauma situation and will be on their doorsteps in about 11 minutes." Tex didn't reply as he switched the radio frequency and called St. Mary's Hospital.

"St. Mary's Hospital, this is helicopter 4569 Charlie Sierra. I am inbound with three individuals onboard needing immediate emergency attention; will arrive your location in 11 minutes." Thank God the person at the hospital was a professional and acknowledged the transmission and asked the nature of the injured. Doc had heard the conversation over his headset and double-clicked his mic. Tex nodded in response.

"Their condition is as follows," and pointed to Doc, who keyed his mic and, in perfect Spanish, delivered their current medical condition to the hospital radio operator. They could hear background noise of orders being shouted and other voices.

"Where will you be landing?" they asked.

Tex looked at O'Reilly and she said, "Right outside the emergency room entrance!"

Tex relayed the message. There was a pause, and the hospital operator came back, "We are moving the ambulances now."

"Which side is the entrance on?" O'Reilly asked.

Tex replied, "Not sure," and relayed the question to the hospital.

The reply was reassuring, "Just look for the red flashing lights we will clear a space for you in the parking lot and have emergency staff standing by."

"They don't have a Helo pad?" O'Reilly asked.

"No, but they have a large parking lot!"

"Good enough for me," O'Reilly said. "Just hope there's not a lot of power lines to dodge."

Tex got a concerned look on his face and said, "No I don't think so, but there are lights in the lot, tall ones."

"Well, if I break your bird there, at least you can have it taken home on a flatbed," O'Reilly quipped.

"Please don't say that," Tex replied. They zipped across the city at about 70 feet and 100 knots. O'Reilly saw the red arrow and Red Cross converge as she spotted the hospital on the ground. True to their word, she saw a circle of about three ambulances and four police cars with lights flashing on the northwest side of the building. There were no cars within the 60 to 70-foot circle they had formed. O'Reilly did a nice banked turn and brought the Helo to a hover dead center. She didn't shut the bird off, but gently touched down and let the rotors slow.

A group of hospital workers and some law enforcement types came running to them. Tex jumped out, opened the cabin door and was waiting when the first gurney rolled up. He helped with the driver, the pregnant woman, and then the young girl. Doc exited last and told Tex he was going in with the injured. He nodded and looked at O'Reilly, who was still sitting in the chopper, watching the scene unfold.

Once the medical staff cleared out, the law enforcement started moving in with what looked like media types and cameras all around. Tex climbed back in put on his headset, and said, "Well now what?"

"Now, we leave," O'Reilly said and lifted the chopper straight up in a slam-you-into-your-seat vertical climb that stopped the law enforcement boys in their tracks. The rapid ascent drew every camera lens to the chopper. As she rotated in the direction of the airport, she said, "Better let the boys at the airfield know we're coming."

"Oh, now you want to talk to them..." he said.

She smiled and said, "Naw... I'll let you do the talking."

As she headed to the airport, the military choppers had caught up, and there was a barrage of verbal communications, orders, threats, and a few obscenities being thrown their way.

Tex looked at his pilot with a grin from ear to ear, "Guess you pissed those boys off pretty good."

"Yep, pretty sure you're right," was all she said. They were approaching the airport as the UH-1's finally caught up and fell into formation around the Gazelle. As they came over the flight line, she saw a crowd out in front of the Ops building. Once again, some media types, law enforcement, and military all mixed together. As they got closer, she spotted her old buddy, Captain Montego standing in front of the crowd. They were still coming in at about 80 feet altitude and 50 yards from the Ops crowd when she dropped the Gazelle straight down out of formation and stopped in a hover, two feet off the ground. The crowd was going crazy, running all around except for the captain who stood his ground. All cameras were on the Helo. O'Reilly slowly moved the bird toward the officer now in a one-foot hover till they were face to face no more than 60 feet separating them.

As the rotor wash created havoc with the crowd she looked at Tex and said, "this thing have a PA?"

He nodded and flipped a switch on the dash. O'Reilly grinned as she keyed her mic, "Hey El Capi-tano, remember that Shit Storm I said was coming…? Just wanted to let you know, it's here!" With that she rotated the helicopter and slowly glided the Gazelle to the exact spot it had been originally parked and set it down. The crowd was now running toward them as she shut down the turbine and pulled off her head-set.

Tex had his off and said, "Well, I guess that's that!"

She turned to him and said, "Not quite," as she leaned over took, his head in her hands, and gave him a really great kiss right on the lips. After a few long seconds, she slowly pulled away and said, "Tex, you're one hell of a crew chief, and I'm proud to have flown with you."

All he could do was stare as the crowd engulfed the bird.

"NOW… that's that," she said with a smile, opened the cockpit door, and climbed out.

The rescue teams arrived at our mountain location about an hour and a half later. An official police officer and a military lieutenant walked up as the vehicles squeezed past the Beast and moved forward as Joe directed them to the place where they could turn around. The medical team had spread out and was assisting the injured. When the two "officials" got to me, they addressed me by name, "Dr. Burnett," they said in English.

"Yep, that's me," I replied, still leaning against the rock wall, exhausted, as the adrenaline was finally getting back to normal levels.

The policeman spoke, "I am Captain Guerrero, and this is Lieutenant Sanchez." I extended my hand and said, "Pleased to meet you and glad you're here."

The policeman ignored my outstretched hand, but the lieutenant took it and shook it firmly, saying, "It is a pleasure, Sir. I have heard much about you from my sister."

I thought for a moment, Sanchez, that was Doug's girlfriend's name, "You're Theresa's brother?"

"Yes, Sir."

"Wonderful lady," I said and returned the firm grip. This interchange made the police captain uncomfortable as he fidgeted and said, "When we get our vehicles turned around, you will accompany us back to police headquarters. We have several questions that need answering."

"Fine," I said, "I'll gladly help in any way I can." The police captain seemed a little surprised at that response. "We will follow you back to the city."

"You will ride with us," the captain said.

"Is that so?" I responded as I looked at them both… there was a pause, "Am I under arrest?"

"No, not, yet," the captain replied. Not yet I thought. There's something I don't know about here.

"Well, then, I will ride back with my team, and we will be happy to follow you," I said rather sternly.

The captain stiffened more when I called to Dimitri and told him to have everyone saddle up; we were leaving as soon as the police vehicles got turned around.

"Gentlemen," I said with a nod and walked toward the Beast. The lieutenant covered up the slightest grin while the captain's frown was its counterpoint.

The ride back was uneventful, but I was worried about what I didn't know. We had followed the Helo radio chatter up to the point O'Reilly landed at the hospital. We had gone off our encrypted personal Coms when we felt things were under control. I got back on our system and tried to raise Doc to no avail, then O'Reilly, no response. I had Joe squawk the Gazelle's radio, nothing. Well, this is a fine kettle of fish, I thought. I wondered what we were riding into as we bumped along the mountain road.

Almost three hours later, I got my answer as we pulled up to the police station to waiting reporters, two TV cameras, and some local onlookers. As we exited our vehicle, the reporters, who were being held back by police barricades, bombarded us with questions. We were taken to a medium-sized conference room and were told to be seated.

"Well, it doesn't look like an interrogation room," I said under my breath.

Joe replied, "Don't count on that, Colt" as the door closed and they left us with an armed guard standing by it. Within minutes the door opened and a large man in police uniform, followed by an entourage of officers and two secretaries, came in and stood at the end of the table, surveying us. He pulled out the chair at the end of the table and sat down; that seemed to be the signal for everyone else to take a seat.

"I am Chief Gallegos, District Chief of State Police for the Cuenca region of Ecuador; which one of you is Colten Burnett?

Leaning forward, elbows on the table, I said, "I am Dr. Colten Burnett, and these are members of my team." I introduced Dimitri and Joe, then seeing Eduardo sitting with his head down, said, "and this is Eduardo, our guide, my personal translator, and assistant to Mr. Sebastiani." Eduardo's head whipped up, his eyes turned as big as saucers, and he grinned. I noticed his posture change as he sat up straighter and made eye contact with those in the room. I continued, "I have two additional team members that are not here. Dr. Ryan Greene is our chief medical officer and accompanied the injured being flown to the hospital. Ms. Shannon O'Reilly, my pilot, flew them there." A rustle went around the room at the mention of O'Reilly's name. Before the chief could respond, I said, "Do you have a report on the condition of the injured individuals taken to the hospital?" The chief was getting a little ruffled at my tone and pointed question.

"That is not of any concern to you, Mr. Burnett."

"Dr. Burnett," I said, getting a little pissed myself, and I guess my voice showed it. "I beg to differ with you, chief since we were first on the scene of the accident and able to get everyone off the bus and to safety. My medical personnel administered emergency medical attention to the injured, oversaw their care while in transit, and my pilot flew them to the hospital while your military were being less than cooperative." I realized my 6'5" frame was sitting ramrod straight in my chair, fists clenched on the table, leaning so far forward I was almost standing, and hadn't taken a breath during that whole outburst. The chief was staring at me intently, as was everyone else. I slowly relaxed my posture and unclenched my fists.

When the chief spoke, I was taken by surprise when, instead of a verbal tirade, he spoke evenly, and his face softened ever so slightly. "My apologies, Dr. Burnett, I was not considering the facts of the situation in my last comments." He held up a hand, and a sergeant handed him a sheet of paper. "Senora Romero and unborn child are stable and, while in guarded condition seem to be doing well. They rushed her daughter, Lily, into surgery and she is still there, as is the driver. We will provide you with more information as it becomes available. Your Dr. Greene is on his way here now and, as for Senorita O'Reilly, she has been our guest for a while." With that, he nodded to one of his officers, who left the room and returned with another officer and O'Reilly in handcuffs!

I noticed the second officer coming in was developing one hell of a black eye. O'Reilly was just smiling. Dimitri leaned over and whispered, "That's our gal," and sat back in his chair, looking at Joe, both trying to hold back the grins spreading over their faces. Oh, shit, I thought, did you have to hit the cop, O'Reilly?

"Hi, Boss," O'Reilly quipped when she saw me and walked to the table. I looked at the chief and back at O'Reilly and said, "Are the cuffs necessary, chief?"

He considered the question for a moment then said, "As long as you keep the Senorita under control, I think we can remove them."

"Oh, I promise; I'll be a good girl, Chief," O'Reilly replied, as the officer with the black eye unlocked the cuffs. "In fact, Ricardo and I have already made up, haven't we?" she said to the officer as she rubbed her wrists and unexpectedly leaned over and kissed him on the cheek. Taken by surprise, he jumped back and bumped into his comrades as he left the room to subdued chuckles. I think the chief even cracked a small smile that quickly vanished as O'Reilly came over and sat down.

"Hi, guys, good to see you made it off the mountain."

I said, "Chief, I think I'm at somewhat of a disadvantage here. Could you explain what's going on?"

"First," he said, "Dr. Burnett, I would like to hear your version of what happened on the mountain." So, I filled him in on all the details of us arriving at the scene of the wreck and the removal of the individuals from the bus. As I spoke, I saw him consulting several sheets of paper, nodding his head. I told him of my call to O'Reilly, requesting emergency medical help ASAP. I specifically asked for Medevac due to the severity of the injuries. More papers, more nods. O'Reilly arrived with the helicopter and took the injured to the hospital, along with Dr. Greene, and then some hours later your men showed up and escorted us here.

I leaned back in my chair and said, "That's what I know," which wasn't entirely true, but true enough for the moment.

CHAPTER TWENTY-SIX

"So, you know nothing of Senorita O'Reilly's run-in with the military or her theft of Senor Mendez's helicopter?"

I turned and looked at O'Reilly, trying hard not to smile and said in my sternest voice, "O'Reilly, you didn't."

As straight-faced as ever, she said, "Of course not, Boss you know I would never do anything like that. It's all a mistake."

I turned back to the chief and said, "There must be some misunderstanding."

He was shuffling through more papers and said, "We are still looking into the entire matter. These are just some of the accusations being made. We are trying to locate Senor Dobson, Senor Mendez's crew chief, who we know was also on this flight, we believe under duress. However, we have not been able to locate him since Senorita O'Reilly brought the helicopter back."

I put a thoughtful look on my face and said, "So, the helicopter that allegedly was stolen was returned to its original location, without the involvement of law enforcement until after the fact. Therefore, by definition, saying someone had stolen it would probably not hold up in a court of law, and since Mr.

Dobson cannot be found, there can be no verification of his being held under duress. There seems to be a lot of circumstantial and unsubstantiated accusations being introduced into this situation."

The chief was not rushing to judgement, which I thought was good. He said, "We are still investigating all aspects of this incident and, until we clear this up, I must ask Senorita O'Reilly not to leave the city until this is resolved. I am inclined to release her into your custody on the condition you make sure she adheres to my request."

"I agree to that completely and will help resolve this in any way I can," I said. "I'll give you our hotel contact information, and we are at your disposal."

"Thank you, Dr. Burnett." With that he and his crew stood and left the room. I looked around at the smiling faces and said, "I don't know about you guys, but I need a drink." We all stood and walked out just as Doc was coming into the building.

"What did I miss?" he asked.

I said, "Come on; we'll fill you in over margaritas."

An hour later, we finally pulled away from the police station, heading for Diego's Place. We were photographed, questioned, interviewed, and videoed by the local TV stations and local newspaper reporters, who were itching to get their story.

Dimitri was driving and said, "Well, so much for that low profile, Colt."

"No shit," I said. "Now, not only does everyone know our names and, what we look like, but they've found out we're here searching for the Golden Library." That we had saved someone of importance on the bus had made us local heroes. "Doc, who is the important person they were talking about? I never got a name or could make out what was being said, really."

"Well, Colt, it seems the pregnant lady, Senora Romero, was the sister of a priest who used to be in this area, a very well-liked priest, high visibility and all, not by his choice, of course.

Still not sure on all the details, but it seems like everyone in this city and region knew him or knew of him, and they all loved him."

"Great" I said.

"Hey, that's not all. The little girl with the head injury was the pregnant lady's oldest daughter."

"Are you kidding me?" I said.

"Nope," he went on, "I heard you being called a hero and, O'Reilly was Los Angel Rojo!"

"The Red Angel," Joe interjected.

O'Reilly grinned, "Must be my red hair, and I WAS flying, after all; sounds kind of angelic to me."

"Yeah? Ask Officer Rodriguez if he thinks you're angelic!" I retorted.

"Hey, I kissed and made up with him..."

"Yeah, right," I said just as we pulled up to Diego's and piled out of the vehicle. When we entered, we saw the place was full, much more so than usual. We headed for the back, toward one of the few empty tables in the place. As any good bar in the U.S. would have, Doug had about five flat screen TV's on the walls being fed by a satellite dish on the roof that also provided local channels. We were no sooner seated when, on two of them, from two different networks the coverage of us leaving the police station came on.

Dimitri said, "Hey, Colt, look; I'm on TV."

I said, "No shit, we're all on TV." There was an animated monologue being given by a reporter with a video of us trying to get into the Beast. Then there were video clips of the helicopter landing at the hospital, the injured being unloaded, and finally a shot of the helicopter hovering in front of a crowd at the airport and O'Reilly flipping the bird to someone.

I turned and said, "O'Reilly..."

"Hey, Boss, he deserved it!"

I put my head down on top of my hands on the table and

said, "Shit, shit, shit!" Doug had seen us come in and made his way to the table with a pitcher of beer and five mugs.

He raised the pitcher in a mock salute, "Hail the conquering heroes!" As he set the pitcher and mugs down, he said, "Boy, you guys really know how to make a news splash. I've had people coming by for the last hour looking for you guys. They found out somehow you all hang out here and, boom, the media types have been talking to everyone who might have met you."

I said, "Please, just keep them away."

"You may not want the publicity, but it's great for business; drinks are on me." Luckily, he was the only one who had noticed our entrance, and we were in a rather dark corner near the back, so that helped with our anonymity, at least for the time being. By the time the pitcher was gone, and that was pretty damn quick, two more appeared on the table. I poured myself another beer and asked Doc for an update on how the mother, daughter, and driver were doing.

"Well, mother and baby are good for now. I'm pretty sure she will deliver in the next 48 hours. She was almost due, and I think the crash will move things along pretty quickly. The daughter was still in surgery when they took me to the station. She had swelling, fluid building up in the cranial cavity, and it was dicey there for a while, but they were able to relieve the pressure, and her vital signs were good. The driver had broken ribs, a punctured lung, and a cracked sternum from hitting the steering wheel. He also had a head contusion from hitting the windshield, but I think he will be okay too. From what I saw, they have a very competent medical staff at the hospital. I talked to one of the emergency room doctors, who told me if we had been 15 minutes later, the young girl wouldn't have made it…"

We all looked at O'Reilly, who hadn't said a word, raised our glasses, and I said, "Nice flying, Red Angel."

"Hear, hear," the guys responded.

I think that may have been the first time I ever saw her blush. She raised her glass and said, "Thanks, guys."

Our fourth and fifth pitchers had arrived, and, as we filled glasses all around, I looked to the front door and saw a lanky guy in jeans, an Air Cavalry T-shirt, and a cowboy hat come in and scan the room.

"Hey, O'Reilly, isn't that your co-pilot?"

She looked toward the door and said, "Yep, sure is." As his gaze got to our end of the room, I stuck my hand in the air and motioned him over. He hurried our way, grabbed a chair, turned it backward, and sat down at the table.

"Jesus," he said, "I've been looking all over for you guys."

"Yeah, you and everybody else. We haven't been formally introduced," I said, "Colten Burnett," and shook his hand.

"James Dobson, but my friends call me Tex."

I introduced Dimitri and Joe and then said, "I believe you already know Doc and O'Reilly."

He smiled and said, "Yes, I do."

Then O'Reilly asked, "Where the hell did you go? I had no sooner landed and looked around, and you were gone!"

"I know; sorry about that, but I had to take care of something."

"Oh, really?" she said. "Like what?"

"Well, how about keeping you out of jail, for one thing."

"Well, you didn't do a very good job of it because that's where I wound up."

"No, I mean keeping you out of jail for a really long time for like stealing a helicopter…"

Another mug appeared at the table, and when Tex had a full glass, I said, "Okay, we all know what happened on the mountain, but after that, things get a little sketchy, so would you guys mind explaining?"

For the next 20 minutes, I got an update from Doc, O'Reilly, and Tex of their escapades with the military helicopters, the hospital stop and then the airfield incident.

After taking a large swallow of beer, I looked at O'Reilly and said, "No wonder you wound up in jail."

She laughed and said, "It could have been a lot worse."

Tex said, "I'm real sorry to have run off like that, but I wanted to try to talk with Senor Mendez before he saw everything on the news."

"And...?" O'Reilly queried.

"I got hold of him, and he was not happy! He was talking about pressing charges and having you thrown in prison; it was getting ugly."

"So," Dimitri said, "I guess we need to get you a really good lawyer."

"Unnecessary," Tex replied. "I talked him out of it."

Now it was Doc who said, "How the hell did you do that?"

"Well, I appealed to his humanitarian nature, which is a hard thing to do, and explained he could have you thrown in prison, but the woman you saved was Friar Gonzales's sister, Margarete Romero and the young girl was Lily, her daughter. I put a call into the hospital using Mendez's name before I talked with him. I wanted to know their condition before I called him, and they gave me the names."

"So, he knew this Friar Gonzales?" I asked.

"Oh, yeah, he was very well known and liked in these parts. He had been recognized by the government and the church for his work with the indigenous tribes in the mountains. He was quite a public figure before he moved to the coast to take over a small parish there... kind of like retirement. So, I told Mendez his helicopter was the only thing that had saved these people, and, of course Ms. O'Reilly's flying expertise."

"But what sealed the deal was when I told him that Captain Montego had refused to help. I guess he and the captain have some history and, from what I gather, it's all bad. I told him the press was all over the story and, if he said he had allowed us to use the helicopter instead of pressing charges, well, that would make him kind of a hero."

We all sat there stunned. Tex went on, "He liked that, so he will contact the police with his permission story, and we need to make sure we use his name and thank him for giving us permission to use his chopper in any statements we make."

I looked around the table and said, "That sounds good to me. Doc, O'Reilly?"

"No problem, Boss!" they chimed.

"Oh, one more thing, he said if there was any damage to the chopper, you guys would have to pay for it."

"O'Reilly," I said, "you didn't break his helicopter, did you?"

Finishing her beer, she said, "Naw, I just gave her a chance to run wild for a bit, but we will need to cover a full maintenance check and clean up, plus refueling, of course!"

I asked, "Tex can you see to that?"

"Yep, sure can."

"Then just send the bill to me at the hotel."

"Will do," he replied.

With that settled, we all seemed to relax a little more, and a pitcher of margaritas was ordered. That's when the reporter saw and recognized us. I saw Eduardo standing next to him, pointing in our direction. You little shit, I thought as I saw his ear-to-ear grin, so much for a relaxing evening as the guy headed in our direction.

The next morning, just after breakfast we got a call from the police requesting our return to the station as soon as possible. By the questions the media asked us on our way into the station, it was obvious they had interviewed some of the passengers, and more of the details of the events had been discovered in addition to some of Eduardo's stories. Once inside, we were escorted to another conference room, larger than the last one and it had a podium, a microphone, and a video camera set up. I looked at everybody. Tex was there standing next to a very distinguished looking dark-haired man about 5'7" and impeccably dressed in a white linen suit. The chief was there along with several other well-dressed dignitaries whom I found out were the mayor and a representative of the provincial governor. The chief came over and shook my hand, "Dr. Burnett, I believe we have finally sorted things out and hope you don't mind taking part in a small press conference to set the record straight. Senor Mendez has been gracious enough to fill us in on his part in the matter, so there will be no charges against your Senorita O'Reilly."

I said that was good news and thanked him.

He said, "Let me introduce you to Senor Mendez; he is eager to meet you." We walked over to where he and Tex were standing, and the chief made the introductions.

"Ah, Dr. Burnett," Mendez said putting out his hand. "It is indeed a pleasure to meet the American adventurer and hero."

I took his hand and returned his smile and said, loud enough for those around to hear, "I can't thank you enough for agreeing to allow us access to your helicopter in our time of need. You are truly a lifesaver and humanitarian."

His smile broadened as he shook my hand vigorously making sure to turn toward the cameras flashing away and saying that it was his pleasure to be of some small service in our harrowing rescue efforts. Smooth, I thought, this guy is really smooth and loves media attention.

"I also need to thank Mr. Dobson for his help in this endeavor, it was invaluable."

Senor Mendez acknowledged the comment as I shook Tex's hand with a pat on his back, saying that he is an excellent crew chief and a valuable employee. I nodded in agreement when

Mendez asked, "Could you introduce me to your pilot? I understand she did a magnificent job flying in perilous conditions and circumstances in order to affect the rescue." I saw him eyeing O'Reilly, who was looking lovely as always, even in her faded jeans, Pink Floyd *Dark Side of the Moon* T-shirt, flight jacket, aviator sunglasses perched on her forehead, and combat boots.

"I would be delighted to," and walked him over to her. He was in his late 50's, I guessed, and had an eye for the ladies. As we approached, and I made the introduction, she took his extended hand, and he immediately kissed it, almost salivating.

"It is a pleasure to meet you, Senorita; you are even more beautiful than Senor Dobson led me to believe."

I glanced at Tex, who was now blushing, and then at O'Reilly, and saw a slight blush come to her cheeks. Time to break this up, I thought, as I saw the chief walking towards the podium and said, "I think we are about to start."

"Ah, yes," Mendez said, still holding O'Reilly's hand "I hope we have a chance to talk more later. I would love to hear the details of your flight and the meeting with my good friend Captain Montego," he said with a sly grin and a wink.

Obviously, a disingenuous comment if ever I heard one. She said, "I look forward to it," and with that, he turned and approached the podium. Smooth, very, very smooth, I need to find out more about this guy I thought.

The conference lasted the better part of an hour. The captain spoke and then called Senor Mendez to the podium, where he gave an eloquent account of his involvement in the rescue and, of course, his permission to Tex to use his helicopter for such a harrowing emergency; he had to get a dig into the military and their inability to offer help. I got called to the podium, much to my chagrin, and as succinctly as possible recounted the story of the rescue and my team's part in it, being sure to mention young Eduardo's part and his heroic efforts. Then, before I could move away, the questions about our search for the lost Golden Library started coming fast and furious. Damn!

How long had we been looking? Were we going to follow leads that other explorers had used? Did we have new information? How long would we be in Ecuador? Those were just a few of the questions. I dodged and down-played as many as I could, trying hard to sound like a vacationer with a penchant for history, but had to answer some just to bring things to a close and turned the podium back over to the chief, who praised our heroism and daring in making the rescue.

As he finished, an aide handed him a gilded framed certificate of commendation signed by the regional governor, mayor, chief, and everybody that was anybody, which he then presented to me and my team. More group photos and questions for everyone... I made sure Eduardo was front and center. He was enjoying it much more than me; that's for sure. Once we extricated ourselves from the event and made it back to the Beast, we all breathed a huge sigh of relief. "You're right, Dimitri; so much for the low profile," I said as we drove away.

CHAPTER TWENTY-SEVEN

It had been a full week since the rescue, and the attention was dying down. We had gone to the hospital to check on the patients and found Senora Romero had given birth to a healthy baby boy. Doc had spoken with her and came out blushing. He reported that both were doing well. A top brain surgeon, paid for by Senor Mendez, was brought in from Quito and was treating her daughter. They had relieved the pressure and, from what they could tell, the swelling of the brain was going down. Her recovery would take a while, but they were optimistic that no permanent brain damage had occurred; time would tell.

Senora Romero had thanked Doc profusely for his help in saving her baby and daughter's life and vowed eternal gratitude to all of us for what we did. We found out that Fernando, the bus driver, was making a slow recovery and wouldn't be driving buses any-time soon, but his prognosis was good. Our spirits were much higher as we left the hospital. All's well that ends well, I thought as we drove away.

Leaving the hospital, our dogged reporter accosted us again. Now, most of his questions were about our hunt for the library, and most follow-up television coverage included information about previous expeditions and their lack of success. I tried to convey the fact that we were just amateurs in the information- gathering stages and had nothing new to add. After researching it, we weren't sure what was fact or fiction or where our investigations would take us. We were just adventure seekers on vacation! I was trying hard to divert attention away from our search.

It was about this time that I decided that a trip back to the States might be a good thing. It would let things continue to die down around here, plus we had been in country now for over four months, and I thought we could all use a break. I was eager to sit down with Nils, Lawrence, and Gus to get a full report on the status of our search for the galleon

I guess what sealed the deal on the trip home was Fitz's call when he asked, "So, that low-key visit to Ecuador, Colt, how's that working out for you?"

"Asshole," I said.

After a snort on the other end of the SAT phone, he said, "You guys have been splashed all over the media up here. American hero's in Ecuador and all that shit. You would never survive as a covert operative; hell, you've even turned O'Reilly into some kind of angel," he said and laughed out loud.

"Hey, it wasn't my fault. We were doing fine on the down-low, and then the fates intervened; what can I say?"

"Spoken like a true hero," he said.

"Well, we're coming home for a break; we need to regroup and review all the Intel we've gathered. We still don't have a good handle on a starting point, but I have some ideas."

He said, "Sounds good. I look forward to sitting down with you all and bringing you up to speed on our work here, although we haven't learned much more in your absence. Still more questions than answers, but damn interesting."

"Good," I said. "I'll let you know when we leave," and with that, broke the connection. Geez, media in the states too; must have been a slow news day. The power of modern communication technology!!! Over the next few days we put our things in order and made arrangements to leave the Beast at Sean's. He had a nice car-and-a-half locking interior garage at the back of his building where we could store the Beast and our gear. We gave Sean and Doug all our contact info stateside... phone and e-mail address, so they could contact us night or day.

We also included the special hotline international number and e-mail that Fitz had set up, which was manned 24/7; in case our personal contacts didn't work, they would still be able to contact us. The Hotel Condor had been more than happy to hold our three rooms for us for $300 U.S. dollars a week until we returned. We paid a month in advance, and everyone was happy.

Out of courtesy we notified Chief Gallegos that we were leaving but said we would return soon. He thanked us for the consideration and bid us safe travels, and so we found ourselves at Diego's for dinner the night before our morning departure. We were all a little subdued in our conversations, excited about going home, but somewhat sad at the prospect of leaving.

We were halfway through dinner when Tex came in, sauntered over to our table, and asked if he could join us. "Of course," we said, all thinking of him as part of our "new Ecuadorian" family.

"So, how long you all going to be gone?" he asked.

"Not sure," I responded, "a few weeks maybe a month." He knew about our other treasure hunting venture for the galleon and our need to check in on that.

"Well, it will be pretty dull around here with y'all gone," he said with a smile. I had noticed he had been staying in touch with O'Reilly since their historic flight together; she didn't look up from her plate, but I saw her smile.

Doc said, "Sometimes, a little dull is okay."

"Yeah, I guess so," Tex agreed, and then asked if there was a way he could stay in touch with us in the States, just in case, so we provided him with the contact info we had given Doug and Sean.

He then added, "Oh, Mr. Mendez was disappointed to hear you were leaving and asked me to convey an invitation to dinner at his place to you all when you get back to Ecuador."

I said, "Please thank him for us and let him know we accept and look forward to it."

He smiled, stood up, and said, "Will do. When you get back, just let me know, and I'll get word to him. Have a safe trip."

Before I could ask for his contact info, he said, "O'Reilly knows how to find me." With that, she looked up and gave him a mischievous grin.

"Great," I said, "we'll be in touch," and he turned and walked out. "I think someone is smitten," I said as I looked at O'Reilly; this time she did blush.

The next morning came early, and we took a puddle jumper flight from Cuenca to Guayaquil and got our non-stop flight there. Our flight back to the States was uneventful. I was getting real used to flying first class, I realized, and dozed off for most of the trip home. Fitz had a vehicle waiting to pick us up at the Orlando International Airport, and we went to his place before heading to the coast.

He brought us up to date on their progress, which as he indicated earlier, was not much further along than before we left. We were all bone-tired and glad to load up and head home. O'Reilly opted to stay at Fitz's for the time being, saying she would catch up with us in a few days. On our way, I sent Nils, Lawrence, Tony, and Gus a text letting them know we were back and would like to meet at the Lair as soon as they could arrange it. I wasn't sure what they were up to and said for them to let me know.

In the meantime, we would all be home resting and regrouping. It was about 6 p.m. when we hit the Cocoa area. We had all parked our vehicles in the Lair's parking lot, so Fitz's driver dropped us off there. We grabbed our gear, and all went our separate ways. I was looking forward to a night in my bed for a change.

The next morning, I slept in, and didn't get up till around ten, threw on my sweat pants and a T-shirt, made my coffee, and kicked back on my leather couch. I finished my first cup of coffee and headed back for my second cup when the computer jangled with its Skype ring and I walked over and saw it was Tony calling. I punched the accept key, and his smiling face appeared.

"Hey, Colt, welcome home."

"Thanks," I said, "good to be back." He said he had gotten the text and been in touch with the others. Gus was out at the search area but could be in tomorrow if that was good enough for a meeting. Everyone else was good to go then.

"Sure," I said, "let's shoot for one o'clock at the Lair." He said he would let everyone know and was eager to hear about the trip.

"Okay, see you then," I said and disconnected the call. Well, at least I had the rest of the day to relax a little and organize my thoughts, which meant taking another shower and hitting the bed again for another four hours. I woke up famished and, with nothing in the fridge, which I had cleaned out before I left, not wanting to come home to any science experiments gone bad, I figured I'd get dressed and find food.

The next day, we were all at the Lair by 1:00. We gathered in the conference room and, after welcome home by the galleon crew, we took seats at the table began our debrief, which turned out to be a cacophony of various questions, answers, and side discussions all going on at once. There were several... "Hero's, Holy Shits, You guys did what? O'Reilly didn't, did she? That can't be true, and do you guys know you have been on TV?"

I put my hand up and said "Okay, enough for now. Let's get down to business. You will hear all the gory details of our "adventure" soon enough, but for now, what's been going on here with the search?"

Nils said, "Well, we haven't found any trace of the ship yet, but we've eliminated a lot of the sections on our chart and now have a much smaller area to work, still using Tony's projections and computer model."

Gus chimed in, "The boys on the boat are doing a great job and have come together as a tight-knit team, and we've done a very thorough bottom search. I think we must be getting close; there's just not much real estate left out there to cover, so we'll either find it, or it's not in the area we think it is."

Tony jumped in and said, "It's there. My model says it has to be there. The sea just doesn't swallow up a ship that size and not leave a trace."

"Stranger things have happened," I said, "so, we'll just have to keep looking till we find her."

Nils had been out with Gus and spent several days working the site and said, "We'll keep running the side scan and using the Neptune data we got from Fitz. If it's out there, we'll find it."

Good old Lawrence had been balancing his schedule between his lady friends and the search and keeping track of the finances for the galleon team. We were still in good shape, he said, and his friends were happy, so life was good as far as he was concerned.

We all chuckled at that and Dimitri said, "No more California wine tasting excursions?"

"Hell, no," he replied, "I'm not leaving you yahoos like that again. I learned my lesson last time. I'll just have the wine sent here from now on!"

"All right," I said, "let's talk about Ecuador."

So, for the next hour, we covered the salient details of our trip and brought the guys up to speed on our contacts, the new vehicle, and our work to date. We hadn't made it to the village to try and find the Shuar elders, if they were still there, that was unfinished business, and we hadn't made many significant breakthroughs on where to start our search for the village in the journal, let alone the library. We felt like we needed more info than we had gathered. We recounted the stories of Father Crespi, his relics, and their disappearance after his death. There were numerous tales of expeditions finding caves, some with minor artifacts, but no library had been found.

All of us were surprised at how many expeditions had been mounted: German, French, Japanese, Scottish/U.S., and a number of smaller ones, mostly locals or amateurs with no real evidence of anyone finding anything. But there had been accidents and attacks by bandits or drug traffickers that had been reported, and expeditions ended because of them, so we knew we had to be cautious.

Lawrence piped up, "Hey, who was the kid in the picture with you guys?"

"Oh, I almost forgot about Eduardo." I filled everyone in on him and his contributions to our efforts.

"Wow," Tony said, "sounds like a resourceful little dude."

I said "Oh, yeah, sometimes too resourceful, but now one of the team!"

We spent the next few days acclimating ourselves to being stateside again and then took the *Lisa B* out to the search site. Gus had headed back out after our meeting, and we rendezvoused with him on a bright blue sunny morning offshore. It was good to be back on the water. I had almost forgotten the relaxation I felt being out there, and I could see it in the others.

Seas were calm as we rafted up with the *Falcon* and climbed aboard. Gus had two divers down, checking out some hits they had gotten on the side scan, but weren't turning up much. As we were looking at the print-outs on the chart table, copies of recent scans, and prints of the Neptune imagery, we saw the image of the shrimp boat we had seen before, a big blob on an otherwise flat undersea plain.

"I thought for sure we would turn up something by now," I said under my breath.

Doc was standing next to me and said, "Well she could be buried under who knows how many feet of sand by now."

"I know," I said "but we didn't even pick anything up with Neptune, and Fitz said it would go 10 to 15 feet below the sand bottom. I wonder if we screwed up and are looking in the wrong place?"

Doc rubbed his shaved head and said thoughtfully, "I don't think so, Colt, but…"

Yeah, I thought to myself, it's a big ocean!

Gus was standing there with us and said, "Well, we'll just keep looking till we find her. I've seen firsthand the luck you guys have, so I won't start doubting you now; that's for sure."

We both smiled at him. "Thanks for the vote of confidence, Gus."

He guffawed and said, "Hell, as much as you're paying me, I'm happy to stay out here searching till Hell freezes over," as he laughed and slapped me on the back. The thing was, I knew if I weren't paying him much of anything, he would still stay out here searching; he was just that kind of guy.

Another week passed with no new revelations and we were getting used to being stateside when I got a text from Fitz saying to get to the Lair; he had a message for me from Ecuador. I headed that way and contacted everyone from the road. I got there, and Joe and Dimitri were already there. They had been there working on our equipment, and Joe had been helping Fitz's guys with the noise issue he was having with the *Raven*. He said he thought they had come up with a solution and was looking forward to seeing or hearing how it turned out.

We all headed to the conference room and set up the link with Fitz; the others came in after we had Fitz on screen. Tony had a piece of paper in his hand and shoved it my way as he came in.

I looked at it as Fitz was saying, "We got an e-mail from one of your contacts, a Doug Robbins, who said this was urgent. That's what Tony just handed you. He sent it to both of the addresses you left him. Look at it, and we'll talk."

As I scanned the e-mail, I was surprised at its content. No niceties…he cut right to the chase and said, "Senora Romero has been in touch with me with a message from her brother for you. It is of the utmost urgency that you contact him as soon as you can," and finished with a telephone number in Ecuador. "Don't know what's up, but I suggest you do as the friar asks. Good luck, Doug."

"Got any idea what this is about?" Fitz asked.

"Not at all," I replied, "but I guess I better call him right away."

Fitz said, "You want us to place the call? It will go through our encrypted link, and we can all hear the conversation, but you do the talking?"

"That's fine," I said. Fitz looked over his shoulder said something, and I heard the call being placed. After a minute or so of international connections, I heard a phone ringing.

It was picked up on the third ring. "Si," a voice said.

I replied, "This is Colten Burnett calling for Father Eduardo González."

"Si, Si, Senor Burnett, this is he. Thank you for responding so quickly," he replied in English.

"What can I do for you?" I asked.

"Senor, you and your people have provided a miracle for our family. You saved my sister, her baby and her eldest daughters lives. We can never thank you enough and owe you a huge debt of gratitude."

I said that "I was glad to help, but he owed us nothing; I was just glad they were all right."

He said they were doing fine, and the daughter had regained consciousness and was recovering.

"Glad to hear," I restated.

"You are an honorable man, Senor Burnett, and I understand you are looking for the Golden Library."

I sat there with my mouth open. What the hell, I thought. "Yes, we are, Father," I got out.

"Well, I have something that may help in your search, but you must come pick it up right away; it is imperative you do so, as I fear it may be a matter of life and death."

With my mind racing, I said, "What is it?"

"Not over the phone," he said, "you must get here as soon as possible." He then gave an address in a small village on the west coast of Ecuador. "Please, Senor Burnett, I implore you to get here as soon as you can."

"All right, Father, I will leave right away. I can be there in…" I saw Fitz holding up eight fingers and said, "Eight hours, will that work?"

"Yes, yes, that would be fine."

"Good, I'll see you then."

Before I could sign off, he said, "And, Senor Burnett, be very, very careful; your life could be in danger." With that, a click, then a dial tone.

CHAPTER TWENTY-EIGHT

I sat there with my mouth open.

Fitz spoke, "What the hell was that all about?"

"I have no idea," I said as my mind tried to process what had just happened.

"No idea about this life and death thing?" he asked.

"None," I replied.

Doc said, "He sounded scared."

"Yeah, scared as hell," Dimitri added.

"Well, the only way we'll find out is to get back down to Ecuador," I said. "Fitz, you said we could make it in eight hours?"

"Give me a minute," he said as he turned away from the screen and spoke to someone. He came back on a couple of minutes later. Okay, you guys grab your shit. They're prepping *Tweety Bird* now and will have the *Raven* ready and loaded within an hour, so wheels up in ninety minutes!"

"So, sounds like you're going too?" I said.

"Oh, hell, yeah! If you're not sure what kind of life or death thing you may be walking into, I want to make sure you're not the only one having all the fun. Now, get your assess moving. O'Reilly will be there in 30 to pick you up. Oh, bring cash, a fair amount of cash!" With that, the screen went blank.

We grabbed our go bags we kept at the Lair; they had the bare essentials for a quick trip almost anywhere. We were traveling light this time and had set everything we needed to in motion. I stopped by the vault downstairs, pulled out one hundred fifty thousand dollars, stuffed it in a small duffle bag, and headed for the back door when we heard the chopper approaching. We loaded up and were headed back to Fitz's five minutes after the skids touched the ground. I climbed up front with O'Reilly and slipped on a headset.

"Life and death," I heard her say.

"Yeah," I replied, "sounds a little ominous."

"Ya think?" she replied. "Any ideas?" she asked.

"None," I said, "but we need to find out more about this friar as soon as we can."

"I've already got someone working on it," she replied. "We should have info for you before you get down there."

"You're not going?" I asked.

"Nope, with the colonel gone, I've got to keep an eye on the place, so you boys will be on your own." She turned and looked at me, "So, try to stay out of trouble," she laughingly quipped.

"Hey, with you not around stealing helicopters and punching police officers, that should be a piece of cake," I replied.

We touched down next to the hangar we had seen the big 130 in, and people were running around everywhere; we jumped out, and O'Reilly gave us thumbs up and lifted off to park on the other side of the ramp where they kept the Helos. As we entered the big hangar, we saw the *Raven* had been folded up and loaded into the belly of the highly modified C130-J and was being strapped down. We walked up the ramp as the last of the preparations were being taken care of, into a very noisy environment. It was a tight fit as we made our way past the helicopter toward the front of the plane.

It amazed me that they could get that thing to fit in here… ingenuity and engineering, what a wonderful combination. The 130 still had the jump seats that folded down on the fuselage walls that could carry about forty passengers or twenty-five or thirty fully-kitted airborne troops. There were eight more comfortable seats set up just behind the bulkhead separating the cockpit from the cargo area… ah, the first-class section I thought.

The loadmaster in a flight suit had a wired headset on and was directing the final loading/tie down process on the *Raven* and the loading and securing of some heavy-duty plastic military-type storage boxes. He saw us approaching and waved to us as he pulled back one of his earpieces and said, "Dr. Burnett, you and your team can stow your gear over there," pointing to an open hatch next to the seats. I nodded and motioned to the others. We stowed our gear, and he indicated we should be seated and put on the headsets at each seat. As I put mine on, he came over and showed me the switch wired in-line to the headset. He flipped it to the red-marked side, and I heard him say, "This is the command channel; it connects you with the cockpit." I heard Fitz's voice going over a pre-flight checklist and giving orders to the crew chief; the loadmaster flipped the switch to a blue marking, and having done the same to his, I heard him say, "This is a person-to-person channel. You will be able to talk to your people without interfering with the pilot's communications, and the yellow marking allows you to hear what's happening on the flight deck but not speak with the cockpit." I nodded, "Red communicate with cockpit; blue, my guy's cabin area; yellow, listen only flight deck." He gave me a thumbs up and, since I was on the yellow channel, heard him say as he flipped to the red, "Colonel, they're on board and strapped in."

"Roger that," came Fitz's voice. "Let's close her up and roll her out." I heard the loadmaster pass the command along and watched as people made final checks and left the plane. Moments later, the loadmaster closed the big ramp rear door, and interior lights came on, illuminating our space in an eerie yellow glow. I felt us begin moving backward out of the hangar and saw the loadmaster making final checks before taking a seat and strapping in. I felt us stop, and then the engines started up, one at a time.

As all four came online, it surprised me at how much quieter this bird was than other 130's I had flown in and jumped out of in my military days. The crew chief, sitting across from me, must have seen my expression of surprise when he held up his switch, and when I clicked over to the blue channel, he said "Must have flown on other 130's before."

I said, "Yeah, but they were much noisier than this."

"Yeah," he said, "the colonel has done a lot of work to this one, and it is almost comfortably quiet, not quite, but close." I agreed as I lifted my earpiece away for a minute to listen. The rest of the team had settled in and were getting ready for take-off when a red light came on overhead, and the crew chief held up his in-line switch, flipping it to red we all did the same.

Fitz's voice came over as the engines increased their rev's, "Gentlemen, this is your captain speaking Thank you for flying Non-Stop Trans Love airlines; please, make sure your seat belts are securely fastened, your trays are stowed, and seats are in their upright and locked position, and all electronic devices have been turned off... or we'll crash! Any loaded weapons or explosive devices should be safely stowed beneath your seat. Our flight time is about five and a half hours and we have 5 hours and 45 minutes of fuel on board. So, sit back, relax, and enjoy the flight!" We were hauling ass down the runway, and I felt the aircraft leave the ground. What the hell are we getting ourselves into now? I thought.

I keyed my mic and said, "Fitz you're freaking crazy."

I heard him laugh... "Only when I'm flying," he said, "only when I'm flying!"

About an hour and a half into our flight, the intercom crackled in my ear, "Colt, come to the cockpit. I've got something for you from O'Reilly." I made my way to Fitz, and he handed me a tablet and said, "O'Reilly said you wanted info on the friar and just sent us this. Take it with you and let me know what you find out."

I took the tablet and returned to my seat and started reading. It was a fairly thorough report on Father Gonzales, birthdate unknown, age unknown; he had been living in the Andes Mountains amongst the Shuar for over 50 years. No historical record of his training or where he had become ordained was found in the Catholic archives of Ecuador. He rarely came out of the mountains and then only at papal request. What? I thought. That's when I realized Doc was reading along over my shoulder.

When I looked at him, he said, "A request from the pope?" We read on: in 1985, when Pope John Paul II had visited Ecuador, he had arranged an envoy be dispatched ahead to have the friar available in Cuenca, where he had a private meeting with him for over an hour. Once the meeting was Complete, the friar immediately returned to the mountains. When Pope Francis visited in 2015, the same thing happened, an hour-long meeting, only this time the friar stayed in Cuenca. He made two trips back and forth to the mountains, and three months later, moved to a small village on the Pacific coast. There was no mention of mother or father, only of his sister, whom he visited both times he came for the papal meetings.

I looked at Doc and said, "Does this strike you as strange?"

He nodded slightly. "Usually, religious records are thorough, but there is nothing here, really."

As we read on, after each visit, the pope made a big deal about the work the friar was doing with the indigenous mountain tribes, primarily the Shuar, who, for centuries, had been bloodthirsty headhunters. Another strange thing was the pope would hold a small press conference after his meetings and then leave after having only short meetings with the cardinals and bishops of the area. It was almost as if his main reason for coming was to meet with this friar, but why?

That was the end of O'Reilly's report.

"Do you think the Vatican knows about this stuff? I mean the journal, library, and possible alien connection?" Doc asked.

"I don't know. If they do, the pope's visits make more sense, but why would this friar be contacting us?" That was a huge question that we didn't have the answer to. Not much else in her report to help us, I got Fitz on the Com and relayed our findings or lack thereof.

"That's rather strange," he said.

"Just what Doc and I were thinking," I replied. So, we were on our way to meet a mystery friar who had lived amongst the same tribe our 18th-century friar had, possibly in the same general locale, who said he had information that would help us with our search for the library. He also said it could be a matter of life or death... talk about letting it all hang out; that's exactly what we were doing. Guess that's why they call them leaps of faith!

We arrived at a small airport in Salinas about five hours later and unloaded the *Raven* for the final leg of my trip down the coast to meet the mysterious Father Gonzales. Later I found out the hard way that whole life in danger thing was real.

Chapter 1, Redux:

Three days later, after my meeting with the friar, and my recuperation in the hospital after having gotten shot, the hellish fire-fight on the dock, and my subsequent rescue by the guys in the *Raven*, we were high-tailing it out of the country under cover of darkness. I had hobbled aboard the *Tweety Bird* with Doc and Dimitri.

They guided me to my seat, and I buckled myself in and, as the engines exploded into life, I heard Fitz over the Com say, "All right, boys and girls, playtime is over, and it's time to adios on out of here," as he applied power and we rolled off the taxiway and surged down the runway. I guess it was the pain medication that kept me foggy, and I dozed on and off for the first couple of hours of the flight. Once my head cleared, I saw Joe sitting across from me with the metal briefcase on his lap.

He saw me looking at it and said, "Are you ready for this, Colt?"

"Yeah," I said, "I want to know if what's in there was worth getting shot for." He unstrapped and brought it to me. I stared at it for a minute and then popped the latches and lifted the lid. In it was a folded sheet of paper lying on a leather-wrapped package. I unfolded the paper and scrawled on it was La Confradia… what the hell? I laid it aside and slowly undid the leather wrappings on the package and found myself looking at another journal, much like the one we had found in the wreck. The leather was still somewhat supple and only slightly dried out.

I carefully opened it and saw some strange markings or writing on the first two pages and then recognized the unmistakable handwriting of our Jesuit friar from 1715. There were also pieces of knotted cord interspersed between pages in the latter part of the journal; they reminded me of bookmarkers I had seen for sale in the States, but those were more macramé kinds of things.

By now, the guys had gathered around, all peering into the case, "Another journal?" Dimitri asked.

"I think so," I said as I handed it to Doc and said, "Okay, Doc, tell us what we have."

He skimmed the pages quickly now being familiar with the friar's handwriting and syntax as I looked at the paper I had removed. What the hell is this about? I thought. Doc turned the pages faster, skipping some and examining the knotted cords as he came to them. He slowed and studied some of the pages more intently.

After several minutes, he looked up at our expectant faces and said, almost in disbelief, "I think what we have is the second journal our friar had promised to send to King Philip, which obviously never got sent. It's dated 1717." He had his Cheshire cat grin on again…

"And?" I asked.

"And I'm pretty sure it's information on how to find the library!"

THE END

ABOUT THE AUTHOR

A retired college administrator, Hep Aldridge is a certified scuba diver, cave diver and amateur archaeologist whose main area of interest is Pre-Columbian cultures of the Americas. He has led or been part of archaeological expeditions to Mexico and Honduras, making discoveries that have been reported in National Geographic Magazine.

Hep's related interest in space, and space exploration and "things unknown" was fueled by his father who worked for NASA. While living in New Mexico, he began to question the many strange and unexplained things he saw in the night sky in the mid 60's, and also developed an interest in lost treasure that has stayed with him his whole life.

The combination of these diverse interests led to the genesis of the Risky Business Chronicles, Book One, his first novel of a three part series.

Hep is an Air Force veteran and resides on Florida's Space Coast.

To be the first to hear about news, new book releases and

bargains from Hep Aldridge, sign up below to be on the VIP List. (I promise not to share your email with anyone else, and I won't clutter your inbox.)

- GO HERE TO SIGN UP TO BE ON THE VIP LIST :
https://mailchi.mp/b0c291dd854f/hep-aldridge

Learn more about Hep and his background on his webpage:
https://hepaldridge.com

You can write directly to Hep and connect with him online.

Email: cxburnett@gmail.com

facebook.com/hep.aldridge.7
twitter.com/AldridgeHep

Made in the USA
Columbia, SC
12 September 2019